CAFFEIN
PUBL

CW00493987

The Periwinkle Perspective
Volume Three
The Story Untold

Paul Eccentric

Fiction aimed at the heart
And the head…

Published by Caffeine Nights Publishing 2022

Published in Great Britain by
Caffeine Nights Publishing
Amity House
71 Buckthorne Road
Minster on Sea
Isle of Sheppey
ME12 3RD

caffeinenightsbooks.com

Also available as an eBook

British Library Cataloguing in Publication Data.
A CIP catalogue record for this book is available from the British Library
ISBN: 978-1-913200-25-1

Everything else by
Default, Luck and Accident

This book is dedicated to the lovely Carole Matthews, the lovely Kev and the lovely Nikki from Waterstones, Milton Keynes.

You're all LOVELY!!!!

The Story Continues…

Paul Eccentric, November 2022

Victoria is reaching for the stars;

She's going to send a rocket up to Mars.

Expanding her dominion,

in line with her opinion:

Victoria, Queen Empress of the stars…

The Periwinkle Perspective, volume three:
THE STORY UNTOLD

PROLOGUE...

LONDON, September 1898

"It is a curious thing, innovation; on the one hand, as predictable as the rising of the morning sun: ingenuity only ever a single step behind human desire, yet on the other, it is as unforeseeable as the weather that each new day brings with it..." (Octavian Periwinkle, British Prime Minister 1898–1899)

...Take the 'Ballentine Series IV Rebreather', for instance; an example of which, Virgil wore clamped firmly to the lower rim of his goggles whenever he ventured abroad these days. Whilst undeniably ingenious and lifesaving a device, it was, in the same moment, one so blindingly elementary that it was hard to believe why none had conceived of it sooner. There was, of course, a metaphysical answer to this poser, one that he, having been fortunate enough to have been imbued with the benefits of a classical education, could not easily discount. For had it not been Plato, some three and a half centuries prior to the birth of Christ, who had first declared that 'necessity be the mother of invention'?

However, as essential as Ballentine's contraption now was, for Virgil's money, it did have its negative points. If, as would have been the case until fairly recently, it had fallen upon Hamble Blaise to have lent her natural genius to such a collective conundrum, then he doubted not for a moment that the resultant device would have had a somewhat sleeker, more integral aesthetic to it, whereas Ballentine's effort was a much more cumbersome baggage, taking into account the auxiliary oxygen cylinder that the user was forced to carry (in most cases, slung over his or her shoulders) which connected, via a pair of corrugated brass pipes, to either side of the pump; itself sited behind a bulky, snout like grille, worn snugly over the user's mouth and nose. It had been said by the so often cynical gentlemen of the press that the Rebreather had 'a bearing as inelegant as that of those new-fangled, stacked tenements that were rapidly replacing the old shoe-box style terraces of the city's East End', and yet it was a contrivance that all bar the very poorest inhabitants of Victoria's Imperial Capital would scarcely dare step forth without.

The birthing of this simple, but ubiquitous, creation, had earned its father, Hugo Ballentine, the title of: 'Inventor Royal', and within fewer than eight months had seen him elevated from potless apprentice engineer to millionaire socialite in a single bound; such were the rewards for the pioneers of this strange new age. And to think that he had been accused of scaremongering at the unveiling of the initial model; conventional opinion back then, refusing to acknowledge that the alarming spate of sudden asphyxiations amongst those with a tendency to ply their trades out of doors, had anything to do with the near permanent smog that so enshrouded this great city.

But it had been with proof acquired through the deployment of another of Ballentine's artless, yet effective contraptions: the 'Atmospheric Sieve', that the inventor had been able to convince the Surgeon General that the levels of pollutants present in the city's air were above and beyond human tolerances, thus leading to the issue of the necessary royal endorsements that would ultimately attract a sponsor for the Rebreather's mass production.

It was not so many moons ago, Virgil reflected, as he posted his letter through the open slot of the red pillar box that bore the Empress' iron cast initials, since responsibility for such professional ratification would have been his to endow...

As much as he resented both his current personal predicament and; equally, the circumstances by which he now found himself forced to wear Ballentine's apocalyptic apparatus, there was at least an ironic upside to the latter concern: a fortuitous side effect of the omnipresence of the Rebreather, which was helping him to deal with the former problem. It seemed that public acceptance of the device had inadvertently brought about an era of anonymity. The fact that a man with as instantly recognisable a countenance as himself could perambulate unchallenged at any time of day or night among hoi polloi and urchin alike, had been the sole reason that he had been able to avoid arrest and incarceration for as long as he had. He considered this as he made his way confidently through the lesser tramped backstreets of Bloomsbury; merely a mould-beaten brass mask, powered by a remarkably small, steam-driven pump; fitted with a series of replaceable, muslin filters, between himself and those whom he passed on his way; each and every one of them, equally unaware of their fellow pedestrians' identities. It was a contrivance that had saved his life, not to mention the lives of countless others, and yet it would undoubtedly never have been considered had the alien interlopers that Victoria had so readily accepted into the bosom of her Empire, not come to share their advanced technologies with their more 'backward' celestial cousins. It was a device, without which, he would also have been unable to communicate with his dear Beatrice, even though, by dint of necessity, that communication was but a one-way street.

It had become his habit to walk the streets of London every few nights in search of a different pillar box within which to deposit his letters home. He longed to be more forthcoming with his wife; to be able to explain to her the truth of that which had befallen him, but he dare not, lest his missives be intercepted and a stray detail aid the authorities in finding his bolthole. He ached to do more than simply convey his love through parchment and ink; to tell her of what his old friend (and benefactor these past few months), Henry Jeckle had done for him; how, through Henry's associate, the mesmerist Ivan Stokes, he had been able to unlock certain memories concerning his recent past; memories that would explain the erratic behaviour which had led to his need to take his leave of her, taking up temporary residence with his old college cohort instead. Sadly, all that he had been able to tell her was that he was well and receiving treatment, and that he hoped soon to be in a position to reclaim his old life. Little did he know, at that point, that his fortunes were about to change...

Upon his return to Dr Jeckle's townhouse on the far side of Bedford Square, Virgil noticed two curious things simultaneously. There was a light on in the window, uppermost to the left of the building. It was a room that the doctor rarely used: a junk room, of sorts, where Henry kept several items of unfashionable furniture along with a large, iron cage that he had been reluctant to explain either the origin, or the use of. The room was generally kept locked and thus, a candle burning on the windowsill would be unusual enough to stand as a signal to Virgil not to re-enter the house until further notice. Of course, this did not necessarily imply that a problem was afoot; in fact, it was far more likely to have been used merely to warn Virgil that someone had come to call who it would be safer for him not to cross paths with. However, it was the second thing to have caught his attention that had led him to presume the worst.

It was a particularly foggy night, he having made his way home from gas lamp to gas lamp. From his position opposite, beside the gate which led into to the square's public garden, he could see two lights emanating from Henry's house: the afore mentioned 'warning' light and a narrow, vertical shaft at ground-floor level that told him that the front door was slightly ajar. Henry's butler, Taylor, was a cautious man. A stickler for household security, he was not prone to leaving doors nor indeed windows open in the normal course of events, and so something had, most assuredly, to be amiss.

Virgil had been considering his next move when he saw a third light; tiny, almost indistinguishable in the gloom. A pinprick of light, which flared momentarily, then disappeared, slightly to the right of the slim shaft spilling from the lobby beyond. It flared for a second time, then, a few seconds later, a third. With this, Virgil knew what he was witness to. There was a figure, only barely discernible, briefly with each tug that they made on their cigarette.

His instinct was to run: the thought of falling into the hands of the authorities so soon inspired panic in his heart, but instead he stalled. By the height of the shadowy figure on the doorstep (as ascertained by the distance between cigarette and step), Virgil realised that he knew exactly who he had espied and, therefore, who had come to call. The fact that the diminutive Egyptian; batman to his odious nemesis, had been ordered to the doorstep for a choke, gave him hope. It meant that Henry was likely, not only still alive, but was being treated with a modicum of respect; his opinion that the smoked leaf was potentially as bad for the lungs as the rising smog levels, obviously having been taken into account by his visitor.

Virgil could not say whether he was a brave man or not, as he could not recall a time when his mettle had been put to such test. He had done a lot of things in his life that few other men would have been prepared to emulate, but none that he would consider particularly courageous. He had taken life; an act that required nerves of steel and an action for which a soldier may have been commended; ranked heroic, even, though the lives that he had stolen had not been on any foreign battlefield. His victims had been sacrificed for the advancement of medical science: an act, by necessity, perpetrated in shadow and deceit, and although future generations would undoubtedly benefit from his surreptitious activities; would possibly even honour him; posthumously, once a significant amount of time had elapsed in order to satisfy the moral ambiguities; he doubted that his legacy would ever be regarded as a courage. Henry, however, was a brave man and had been a good friend to him.

He had clothed him and fed him in his hour of direst need; he had given him shelter when he had had nowhere else to go. He had provided him with a Rebreather and, most importantly of all, he had worked tirelessly to develop a serum that would stop him from reverting to wanton cannibalism whenever the urge overtook him.

Virgil owed it to Henry to make sure that the Secretary did not exact his anger on an innocent party, which left only a single course of action: an action which, coincidentally, was the very one that he least favoured…

"You see, Henry, I was right all along: the prodigal returns! That's twenty guineas you owe me; pay up, man."

Henry made no attempt to reply. His eyes closed, he appeared to Virgil to be sleeping quite soundly, slumped on his own silk-upholstered chez longue, his head, he noticed, resting against a blood sodden cushion; his evening attire, as tattered and torn as the soles of his inexplicably bare feet. The room itself was a shambles; furniture lay upended and broken: discarded as if thrown aside by a rampaging monster intent on clearing a path to its prey. The curtains in the bay window had been ripped from top to toe, by what would appear to have been a keen, extended claw, lashing out in order to bat away any obstruction to its murderous intent. It was as if a great bear had been let loose, only to have been recaptured and removed, all in the time that it had taken for him to walk to Bloomsbury to post a letter.

There was a small gash visible in the skin beneath his comatose friend's left eye and Virgil did not doubt that the wound would have corresponded precisely with one of the folding steel plates that served as armoured knuckles on the prosthetic hand that he had himself once fitted to the Egyptian.

The speaker turned his head away from the unresponsive man and smiled by way of welcome to the newcomer.

"We had a wager, y'see: Henry and I," he continued, as, stepping fully into the drawing room, Virgil unhooked his Rebreather and lifted his goggles. "Henry, here, was convinced you'd acknowledge his little warning and take t'yer heels. I, on the other hand, believed y'had a little more spunk than that."

His smile widened as he reached into the top pocket of his Westcott to produce a small, brown glass phial, "Oh, I do beg your pardon, Dr Periwinkle, but did I just confuse spine with self-preservation? I believe I did. You still lost though, Henry," he called over his shoulder. "It seems he came back for *this* rather than you."

Having turned himself in without ado to the agent on the threshold, Virgil had allowed himself to be escorted through to the drawing room, where he had been entirely unsurprised to find the Queen's Special Advisor lounging disrespectfully in his friend's fireside seat. As ever when he had encountered him before, he had the bearing of a spider at the centre of an enormous web.

Of Taylor, Henry's man, there had been no sign and, knowing their two uninvited guests of old, Virgil had doubted that this would turn out to be a good thing. He had, however, been pleased to note Henry's presence, though his friend appeared not to have noticed him.

"Henry?" Virgil enquired gently, ignoring his nemesis' bait. He made to move toward him, only to find himself rigidly restrained from behind by the Egyptian's steel hand.

"Henry is an innocent party," Virgil insisted provocatively, though fully realising the futility of any attempt to struggle against the agent's mechanical grip.

"Innocent?" the Secretary scoffed, feigning surprise that Virgil had dared even to suggest such a thing. "You would call the aiding and abetting of a wanted felon 'innocent'?" and he chuckled, as had always been his wont when he had the upper hand. "I feel sure that a court of law would likely decree otherwise. However, I am not an unreasonable man, Dr Periwinkle, and I may yet be able to persuade the Crown to overlook such an offence, if certain... *circumstances* could be met."

"You have what you came for," Virgil insisted, well aware that his own freedom was now forfeit, whichever way the next few moments played out, "I have offered no resistan—"

Ignoring him, the Secretary cut across his plea: "Of course, we would have looked you up sooner, but; dear Virgil, when you left, you omitted to leave us a forwarding address,"

Obviously relishing in the theatrics of the scene that he had set, he continued: "and then it came to me, in a trice! The only man in London, who could possibly have helped you, and a known acquaintance of yours, t'boot!"

"You *knew*?"

"Of *course* we knew!" the Secretary snapped. "Surely you didn't think you could elude me for long? Abdul, here, has been just beyond your shoulder for the past five years!"

As if on some prearranged cue, the Egyptian released his super-human hold on Virgil's shoulder and stepped around in front of him, smiling mockingly back. It was the first time that he had seen him in good light that evening and he was surprised to notice his ragged appearance. He was bleeding from a deep gash in his forehead: the result, apparently, of whatever had made ribbons of the curtains. His cheap suit was also torn, irreparably, and his left hand was wrapped in a makeshift tourniquet.

Virgil had first become acquainted with the Secretary's 'right-hand man' when Hamble, his extramarital love at the time, had caught the Egyptian attempting to burgle her workshop. The émigré snipe had lost his right hand in the process and the professor; ever a soft touch for a sob story from the downtrodden and the disenfranchised, had sent word for Virgil to attend her immediately, in order that he might help her to fit one of her early prosthetic replacements to the man's ragged stump. On hearing the scallywag's tale of woe, and as further recompense for the loss of his appendage, she had declared that from that moment forth, he would take on the role of her assistant. Little had either of them suspected at the time, that the burglary, and subsequent capture of the thief, had been an elaborately staged deception; courtesy of the Secretary, as a means to plant an agent on his tail…

"If that were true," Virgil ventured, turning back toward the head of the secret service, "then why did you not come for me sooner?"

"In order to lock you away?" his enemy scoffed, shifting forward in his seat, "Why, Dr Periwinkle, you had already saved me the bother by locking y'self in *here*."

"So why *now?*" Virgil asked, his eyes never leaving the phial in the man's hand.

"Because I now have need of your services once more."

Virgil felt a frown forming on his brow; an involuntary reaction to an unexpected line.

"Eighteen months ago; following your… murder of Lord Salisbury, your father assumed control of a caretaker government. This, of course, will hardly be news to you, neither will the fact that very few expected him to survive in the post, least of all myself, but he has surprised us all: not merely surviving, but positively *thriving*. Obviously, you will be aware that tomorrow this nation goes to the polls. Octavian Periwinkle is anticipated to win that election by a landslide—"

"And you need an advantage over him; would that be a fair assumption?"

The Secretary said nothing, smiling back through steepled fingers.

"Surely I would be nothing but an embarrassment to him: the *former* Surgeon General—"

"The post is still yours, Virgil: the current incumbent is not a patch on your good self."

"I imagine," Virgil responded, his confidence returning somewhat; outwardly displayed by the folding of his arms across his chest and the straightening of his spine, "that your alien 'allies' might have something to say about *both* those outcomes."

The Secretary chuckled again, though his eyes remained as unreadable as ever.

"You are quite correct, Dr Periwinkle. Our Martian 'allies', as you describe them, are still terribly keen to see your head severed from your person for the crimes you committed against their kin up on the Moonbase," and he frowned momentarily, before asking: "The estimable

Dr Stokes did manage to recover that particular memory for you, yes?"

"You know about Dr Stoke—"

"—however, I believe that their bloodlust could be… *satiated* by their holding of a card that could, if necessary, be used against your father."

It was Virgil's turn to scoff and he did so with relish, turning a full circle as he tittered and applauded the Secretary's audacity.

"Oh, Bravo," he said, "bravo! Do you really think me so vain, sir; so narcissistic, as to barter with my own family's trust, merely to assure my own rehabilitation?"

The Secretary's charmless smile was beginning to irk him now, as he held the glass phial at arm's length in front of him. Virgil half expected him to soliloquise, as if he imagined the little bottle were actually a bleached skull, previously the possession of a man named 'Yorick'.

"I thank you, Henry," he said instead, "for your part in all of this, but unfortunately your services are no longer required. Pay the man, will you, Abdul?"

There followed a single, muted gunshot, followed almost instantaneously by a spray of warm blood and brains, as the agent killed Virgil's only friend.

Very few would likely recognise the Secretary in the street; Rebreather or not, and yet this man's influence over the lives of each and every citizen of the Empire extended further than any one of them could readily guess. He was, Virgil understood, quite probably the most important figure on the planet and not a man to be trifled with.

Biting down hard on his tongue as he mopped blood from his cheek with a monogrammed silk handkerchief, Virgil refused to react to the atrocity that had just taken place.

"Don't worry, Virgil; I made sure to secure the formula upon our arrival, thus your conscience can be eased in the case of betraying your father's trust. You are doing this for 'The Greater Good'. For if you don't, then the public will never be safe from the monster within you…"

PART ONE

CHAPTER ONE:

THE GREAT ADVENTURER HIMSELF

Gordon had awoken in thrall to an absolute humdinger of a hangover. No stranger to the 'Tippler's Torment'; as it was known in London's more *serious* drinking circles, he had weathered enough of such stifling pre-breakfast effects over his lifetime to have become quite the expert on divining the difference between the self-castigating consequences of a night on the razzle and the chilling onset of a hitherto undocumented tropical lurgy. This, he therefore deduced, whilst struggling to focus on the alien surroundings in which he now found himself, was most definitely an example of the former!

He had a headache to rival that of every morning-after a post-expedition binge at The Adventurers' Club that he had ever foolhardily embarked upon, all bound up into one single, skull-shattering throb. It was as if the clapper inside of Big Ben had been removed, with his own head, knotted in its place, in some form of stylised, idiophonic torture, devised by any one of the vast number of aboriginal enemies that he had accrued during the course of his career as the Empire's pre-eminent adventurer.

And so he lay there for a moment; his eyes closed, concentrating on his breathing; hoping that if he did so, then the churning milk drum of his belly might eventually settle to a stagnant ache that he could contemplate living with for the remainder of the day.

Meditating, whilst making no effort to lift his head from whatever it was that he had commandeered to rest it upon in the closing, lucid moments of the previous evening, he attempted to gather together the various splinters of jumbled memory pertaining to the events that had led up to his current predicament. 'Who had been his companions at the bar on this spirituous sojourn, and quite where had they chosen for their final round?' As it was surely there that he had taken his final fall! Strangely, he could recall none of the usual ingredients that went into the fermentation of such an extreme after effect.

Straining the old, befuddled noddle that bit further, he eventually found himself unearthing a vague impression of an ambidextrous showgirl who, presumably merely for purposes of the stage, had adopted the name, 'Dolores', but the more he wrestled to bring her features back to the fore, the more he came to realise that; with the exception of her hands and her abnormally large breasts, she had no discernible features! It seemed far more likely, he therefore decided, that she had actually been no more than a fanciful denizen of the dream state that had followed it.

"Gordon!" he then heard; shouted, he fancied, though received as no more than a croaky whisper. 'Perhaps his head really *had* been used to strike that bell,' he considered, as he began to realise that his ears were in no better order than the rest of him.

"GORDON!" came the voice again, more urgently this time; a voice that he felt he recognised, though could not instantly place. Nevertheless, he did try to respond, but his throat was as dry as a sand sandwich and he found himself barely managing a toad's croak by way of reply. He tried once more to open his eyes and immediately, this time, discovered the source of the disembodied voice. There was a woman, hanging, tangled in a snake's nest of electrical cabling. She dangled a mere four foot above him like some kind of humanoid tarantula looming over her prey. Her face was lacerated, he noticed, with blood dripping from her forehead, cheek and jaw, to spatter against the cracked visor of the helmet that he had not, until then, remembered himself to be wearing. Her suit was grimy and torn, revealing further bloodied welts on the body beneath, and her large, round breasts were partially exposed. He presumed this to have been the catalyst for his not unpleasant, recent dream…

"GORDON," she pleaded with him, "you have to wake up. The hull was breached in the crash and I seem to have lost my helmet. Are you broken? Can you move at all?"

"Dolores?" Gordon queried, tentatively; those pesky details still fluttering around him like butterflies, yet evading all attempts at netting.

"No," the woman above him explained, patiently, "Alyce. You need to focus, Gordon. Our rocket has crashed. It is my belief that we were shot down… again. Can you move? I need your help."

"Alyce…?" he mumbled, "Alyce?" The name was ringing a distant bell, as was the extraordinary explanation for their current plight, "ALYCE!" he eventually spat; memories, like cogs in a machine, slotting into place, one to the next; one to the next… "ALYCE!" he repeated needlessly, as he pulled himself up from what he would later realise was in fact the side wall of the rocket; the floor, to his left, currently perpendicular to the pair of them. As he stood in the ridiculously light gravity, his helmet collided with an iron support beam and he fell straight back down again.

"Be careful, Gordon," Alyce warned, "on no account must you tear your suit! As with the gravity, the temperature here on Mars is much lower than you are used to."

'Mars,' he thought, 'yes! They had been travelling to the red planet: Alyce's home!' How the deuce could he have forgotten a thing like that?

"Gordon?"

"Yes," he said, "yes, of course! I was to be the first man on Mars! I thought you Martians were supposed to be a genial bunch; why the bally hell did they shoot us down?"

"Please, Gordon. If you can stand, then I need you to go to the hold and fetch me a replacement space suit and a new helmet. I may be a native of this world, but I have been away for some time and the cold is getting to me."

"Of course, old thing; lax of me... Remind me, though; seem to have lost me bearings, a tad, which way is the hold?"

"You'll need to climb down the ladder in the hatch in the floor—"

"Ah!" he cut in, suddenly realising what was wrong with the room, "The floor that is currently masquerading as a wall. Right ho. Don't go anywhere. Won't be a jiffy. By the way," he said, turning back to the friend that; until a few moments ago, he had entirely forgotten, "Probably best if you and I don't travel together again. One of us seems to be jinxing the other, what?"

His memory slowly returning, Gordon adjusted his previous self-diagnosis to one of light concussion: an affliction that, for the life of him, he could not recall the correct medical treatment for. Ought he lie down; put his head between his knees; raise his feet above his head or pour himself a stiff brandy? He could not decide. But whichever option was currently fashionable, time, he understood, was of the essence. Not only did Alyce need his help, but he had just remembered that there had also been a third member of their party; arguably, the most important of the three of them, though each had their part to play in the mission. Hamble Blaise, the ex-Inventor Royal, had been both their pilot and their engineer for the entirety of their eight month journey outbound from Earth; not to mention, the woman who had single-handedly jury-rigged the appropriated rocket in the first place, transforming it from the disassembled alien relic that had crashed on Earth over a century before, back into a ship-shape, inter-planetary craft, capable of traversing the two hundred and twenty-five million miles that she would need to travel in order to reach her target. She had done all of this without prior knowledge of either Martian engineering practices or the Martian language, in which the workshop manual had been written. She had had a little help with the latter, though, from Alyce, in the final stages of repair, but Gordon could still not help but be majorly impressed by his friend's unique genius in all matters technological; whether human or alien. Victoria's Empire had so much to thank her for; he reminded himself, though it was unlikely ever to do so again, if their visit to their closest celestial cousin was to be the success that their ragbag 'team' of dispossessed dissenters rather hoped that it would...

He had checked for Hamble as he had made his way through the wrecked, steam-filled rocket, calling out her name as he passed through each level. Eventually he found her in what remained of the hold. What remained was merely the hatch door, which instead of opening onto a roughly cylindrical, copper lined store room, containing what little was left of their canned and bottled consumable requirements, now opened onto a rock-strewn vista of autumnal reds and burnt copper hues for as far as the eye could see.

The hold had been the vehicle's penultimate level, beyond which had been the boiler room and the exhaust vents. Of these, nothing substantial was to be seen, merely fragments of ruptured copper plating and the odd spoilt food can.

Amidst it all stood Hamble: an angel in a goldfish bowl, gleaming in her Martian space suit. In her left hand, the steam pump rivet gun that she had built from scratch during the first four weeks of their journey and, in her right, what looked like a pile of flattened bean tins: her scratch emergency repair kit.

Growing up a son of wealth and privilege, Gordon could not say that he had even considered the idea of a thing, once discarded, having a secondary use. He doubted that it would ever have occurred to him to wash; cut and flatten out a tin can and then to use it to patch a hole in the hull of the groaning, creaking behemoth that had been their home this past half a year and more. That, he supposed, was the main difference between Hamble and himself: whereas he saw a pile of rubbish spread across the ochre plateaux, Hamble saw a cache of free, raw materials, not to mention, a perfect opportunity to recycle their waste.

Her arms full of gathered detritus, she was making her way over to what he now recognised as her mark two Range Roller: the steam propelled 'buggy' that she had found in pieces in the rocket's hold and, once she had built her steam pump riveter, had rebuilt to her own customised specification.

Suddenly she turned, having seen him loitering in the hatchway, and beckoned him over.

"Hold this," she said, once he was close enough for them to communicate with anything more sophisticated than a gloved hand signal.

Gordon placed his palm against the strip of tin that the inventor was holding against the door of the buggy, covering, for the most part, a deep diagonal gash in the vehicle's panelling.

"Hold it *still*," she asserted, as she positioned her riveter and depressed the trigger. Gordon felt the plate buck in his hand and pushed back harder, putting all his available strength behind the task.

"There, that should do it," Hamble concluded, returning the tool to its holster on her belt. "I take it you're in one piece, then?"

Gordon took a breath and opened his mouth with the intention of relaying the various trials that he had faced whilst navigating his way from one end of the rocket to the other, but Hamble bowled on regardless, "—though you're going to need a new helmet pretty sharpish. That'd be Alyce's blood on it, I take it? Where is she? Is she okay?"

"Well," he began, accepting the pile of hammered tin that she was holding toward him, "to answer that barrage in order: 'just about, yes; thank you for asking'; 'yes it is, though you'll notice it's not a healthy colour'; 'not looking too clever, I'm afraid; in need of a new spacesuit', and 'caught up in the wreckage, back in the cockpit'."

"Right, well get in, 'Captain'; I think I've got everything that's salvageable. Both the spare helmets are in the Roller, but sadly we lost the other suit. I'll see what I can cobble once we get there."

Gordon did as he was told. While technically the group's leader; owing to the fact that he was the Earth's only 'official' astronaut (and also by virtue of his status as the only *male* member of the party), he could not have been happier to defer to his pilot's authority. Not only was she not easily panicked in desperate and unparalleled situations such as this, but she seemed positively charged by the need to invent her way out of a problem. Not for the first time since he had made her acquaintance, Gordon considered whether the great patriarchal ideal into which he had been born and educated, was not merely a misogynistic anachronism ripe for the thwarting, as the likes of Nanny (who he now knew to have been Hamble's *mother*!) had always so heartily advocated. If, one day, it were to come down to a democratic vote, he decided then and there, that *his* cross would most definitely be in the women's box!

It was an ingenious design, The Range Roller Mark II. Four chairs slung independently from two horizontal crossbeams; two behind the other, themselves part of a cuboid cage made of welded steel poles. Riveted brass plating covered the framework of the box, which had a toughened glass, split-screen windshield at the front and a small steam boiler to the rear. Dwarfing the cramped cabin were its four huge wheels, a little like cartwheels, though of a heavier gauge, which extended equally above and below the cage, tilting slightly toward each other at the top. Mounted on its roof and between the wheels, was a pump cannon: yet another of Hamble's on-the-fly fabrications.

When he had first seen a horseless carriage, chuffing along The Strand in '84; its banksman a few fearful paces ahead, waving his pennant in order to alert other road users of the potential hazard crawling in his wake, he had not anticipated the idea catching on. It had seemed likely that it would prove to be simply another rich-man's fad, like the moving picture camera or the indoor latrine, but to see such an evolution as Hamble had concocted from spare parts and scrap metal, gave rise to both secondary and tertiary thoughts on the matter.

Gordon smiled and sighed heavily.

"You are, Hamble Blaise, without doubt, a veritable genius!" he blethered, as Hamble strapped herself in beside him and disengaged the brake. "Not to mention, a damned fine filly, t'boot! I must say I've become quite fond of you over the last couple of years," and he chuckled to himself. "If I were currently in a better position; vis-a-vie financial funds and official status, then I might well be of a mind to ask y'for y'hand."

Hamble's concentration appeared not to waver from the job at hand: pumping the button marked 'ignition' with her right thumb. Without looking up, she replied; quite soberly for Gordon's liking: "Then we must thank whatever deities watch over the people of this benighted planet that we are on a mission to rewrite everything that's happened in the past two years," and she turned toward him briefly, wearing what he considered a wry grin, moving the buggy forward as they began to follow the downed rocket toward its tip.

"That a yes or a no, old gal?"

"Don't push it," she answered, without taking her eyes from the view ahead.

"So," Gordon blundered forth, in an attempt to change the subject, "tiny little engine you've put in there; what's it run on?"

"Gin."

"*Gin*? But we only had the one case left!"

* * * * *

'To drink or not to drink?' As far as Iggi could see, these were the only two options open to them of an evening whilst they waited for Hamble and Gordon to reset the world.

Going out; or for that matter, going *home*, was, for the time being anyway, out of the question; what with the open bounty that the Secretary had placed on their heads. They therefore had no choice, but to stay put and to count their blessings; few that they may have been.

Lifting her tankard to her lips, Iggi considered their lot in light of all those who had not been lucky enough to have made it this far. Unlike poor Honoria Moneypenny, Katie Snodgrass, or the bulk of Europe's scientific elite, she and Tiny were at least still alive, and so if all they could do for now was to bide their time; to wait it out and hope that eventually they would all be free, then surely they were not in such a bad position after all?

There was also a war coming; a war that their countrymen were ill-equipped to win. Far better, she reasoned, to be here rather than there, if their friends were unable to avert the chain of events that had led the world to this irredeemable point.

And so, with their obligations fulfilled for the day; paying their way as part of the castle's retinue and thus ensuring their continued survival, the unlikely comrades had once again repaired to the mess hall for a little light libation, raising their glasses to their good health; to a hopeful future, and to absent friends…

"Sho, Iggi," Tiny slurred, wavering in the flickering candlelight afforded by the only wick left burning, "I've tolt yer orl abou' *me*; there ent nuffin' lef' t'say, bu' wha' abou' *you*, eh?"

"What *about* me?" Iggi asked, dryly; trying not to sound as obviously drunk as her companion.

"Well," he said, moving his tankard to one side and staring her straight in the eye; as best he could manage, anyway, "there'sh shumfin' I bin wan'in' t'ask ya' shince we firsh met, bu', quite frankly, y'shcare th'livin' *shit* outa' me when y'shober."

Iggi laughed; something that she was not known to do very often, but then, neither was drinking as much as she had done tonight!

'It had been a tough day,' she told herself: an excuse that she would be presenting as evidence in her defence, to her hangover-nursing self, first thing in the morning. Someone had taken a potshot at the Baron earlier in the day. Iggi had only just spotted the sniper in time; just as he had been about to shoot. She had taken him out, needless to say, but he had loosed his bullet anyway, which had clipped her upper arm; well, *Gerald's* upper arm, to be precise.

Ordinarily, a lead-in such as Tiny's would have caused her hackles to rise, but tonight… well, tonight was different. Tonight, it had been *she* who had sought out *his* afterhours companionship, rather than the other way around, and, with the assistance of a bottle and a half of the region's finest inside her, she found herself a little more disposed to respond.

"How did I lose my arm?" she asked, watching for his reaction.

"Eh?"

"That's what you want to know, isn't it?" she confirmed, as his eyes struggled to focus on her face.

'Sooner or later,' she knew, 'everybody did;' not that she had ever *told* anyone. For one thing, it was a matter of national security; not that that was a concern anymore, but just as importantly, she had made a point of never letting her guard down for long enough that anyone had ever felt it *safe* enough to ask.

"If I *tell* you," she said, with an attempt at menace, before breaking into another laugh that her friend matched, staccato for staccato, "then I'll have to *kill* you."

"I c'n live wiv tha'," he replied, slapping the table with the flat of his palm and guffawing loudly at his own gag.

"Alright," she said, pouring them both another drink, "why the hell not," and she stood up, tankard in hand, steadying herself against her chair back. "I'd been sent out to bring in the Dutchman," she began, "this was the Spring of '95; a couple of years before we two met."

"The Dutchman?"

"He was a cu… a cun… an occultisht," she slurred, "he had this idea that the Prussian royal family were vampires, 'cause apparently, some of 'em suffer from this rare, hereditary blood condition—"

"What *kind* of blood condish'n?" he interrupted, warily.

"Porphyria," she explained. "It makes the shuff… hic… shufferer extremely shensy… shenashit…

33

shenshative to light," and she paused to take a swig of her wine. "Apparently," she went on, after a belch that caused Tiny to once again dissolve into a fit of giggles, "it gets parshed on down through the generations. Anyway, the Dutchman, he found out that one of the Prinsheshes had the dish… ease, and nabbed her."

"Wash all thish got t'do wiv losin' yer arm?" asked Tiny, reasonably.

"I w's coming to that! Right, sho, this Princesh: Fu… Fu… Fedora, she's Queen Vic's great-granddaughter. Well, it was *my* job to get her back before he shtarted experimenting on her."

"An' you *made* it, right?"

"A *course* I bleedin' made it! Can you imagine the panic, both here *and* in England, if I *hadn't?*"

An' *was* she?"

"Was she *what?*"

"*Y'know… a vampire.*"

"I don't know! She sh… shertaintly wasn't very *nice*, but then, that's royalty for you. Anyway… Tiny? Tiny, are you listening?"

It was his snore that gave him away.

"*Tiny*! I was just getting to the *good* bit!"

* * * * *

"Here's the deal," she said, sounding for all the world as if she had spent the previous eight months trapped in close confinement between two Yankee cohorts, rather than a Martian linguist and the son of a British lord, "stop talking now and I'll put everything you've said since the crash down to a mild concussion, or, by all means, keep wittering, whilst I put a couple of rivets through your face plate and see how you take to the Martian atmosphere. Your choice, 'Captain'."

Hamble continued to hold her pump gun to the side of Gordon's helmet for the better part of thirty seconds after he had taken the wise decision to cease prattling; her eyes never leaving the road ahead, before finally lowering and re-holstering her tool, to continue the journey in silence.

It was an awkward silence; one that Gordon felt compelled to punctuate, but was saved by an even stronger mental desire to live to quip another day. And she was probably right, anyway, he realised; she usually was. It had been noted by a succession of trek-weary Sherpas that he was often afflicted by this overriding compulsion to talk gibberish, either at high altitudes or when he had spent too much time in the sun. He decided to add 'alien atmospheres' to his list of terrains to be avoided and duly kept schtum for the remainder of the drive.

Which, in actuality, was not all that long.

"There!" he suddenly blurted, as they rounded what they could discern of the rocket's nose cone. The force of their landing had caused it to embed itself in the russet-coloured shale and shingle that constituted what he could see of the planet's surface, "That looks like the bottom of the door."

Alighting the buggy, he and Hamble began frantically clawing at the rubble that was covering the door, clearing it enough so that they could locate the emergency release handle and force it open. They entered the cockpit to find Alyce still entangled in the electrical workings; the only difference being that she had lost consciousness in the interim.

"Not looking good," Hamble declared, "why didn't you get her down earlier?"

"I wasn't thinking straight," Gordon snapped, feeling a mite foolish and a tad more irresponsible, "I thought we'd established that."

"Well, help me now," and she pulled a pair of cable cutters from her wrap-around tool kit and lobbed them to him.

"Which—" he began, but she did not let him finish.

"*All* of them!" she berated, as she checked the patient for a pulse and lifted one of her eyelids, "it doesn't matter now; this old crate has made its last flight."

"Is she alright?"

"She's alive; no thanks to you, but she's not responding. Best we can do is to get her out of here and find some shelter before—"

Like an augur, it was an inventor's job to be able to envisage the future; for what use were they if they could not predict a forthcoming requirement and act upon it? Call it a sixth sense or a supernatural ability; Gordon could only marvel at Hamble's uncanny prescience; though not out loud, of course, as before she had even got the words out of her mouth, the rocket was rocked by what sounded suspiciously like a nearby explosion.

Gordon was thrown to the floor, but Hamble managed to hold her ground as yet more of the cramped cabin's inner workings became an outward tangle of excreted junk.

"Keep cutting!" she screamed. "We have to get away from here."

"What the bally hell was *that*?" Gordon snapped, retrieving the cable cutters that he had dropped in the fall; dragging himself back to his feet and dusting himself down.

Two more cut lines and their comatose friend began to slip a little, just as a second explosion moved the entire rocket a few feet to the left. Again, Gordon found himself in a heap, but this time with a freed Alyce atop him.

"Whoever shot us down," Hamble explained, as if, he felt, to an idiot, "is back to finish the job."

Hefting one side of Alyce onto her shoulder so that Gordon could slide out from underneath her, she instructed him; in no uncertain terms, to take her other arm and head for the Roller.

Once outside, the trio were showered in red dust and small pebbles: the result of a third explosion, unluckily quite close to the nose cone, but they made it through the hail unscathed to lay Alyce across the rear two seats and strap themselves back into the front. As Hamble pulled away, a direct hit on the cockpit that they had only just departed, sent a wave of debris into the buggy's path. Gordon felt the impact as pieces of rocket rained down on their tiny cabin from above.

"What in damnation is that?" Gordon demanded, spying the source of their immediate problem through the windshield, hovering in the air ahead of them. It reminded him of something, and not just the gigantic bird of prey that it had been designed to emulate. He had seen it before, somewhere, even though he knew enough basic physics to understand that its existence was as impossible as the rocket that they had just traversed the vacuum of space inside.

Beside him, Hamble smiled. She had seen it too, along with its friend; offset to the left.

"Good Lord!" she exclaimed, with a wide-eyed smile, as she navigated their way around the detritus-strewn flats, "I do believe they're Ornithopters!"

"Bomb laden Ornithopters!" Gordon corrected, "so what's an ornithopter when it's at home and why the deuce do I know that design?"

"You had a classical education, did you not? Don't you remember your Davinci?"

"*Leonardo* Davinci?" and then the penny dropped. Gordon made to slap his forehead, but slapped his hand against his visor instead, "Of course! Davinci's blueprints! But what the devil're they doing *here*?"

"Parallel evolution," Hamble explained, still smiling as she negotiated another hair-break turn around a boulder. "The Martians are really not that different to us."

Holding on for dear life as Hamble swung left, then right, then left again, in an attempt to rally their way to safety, Gordon considered what he knew about Davinci's proposals for flying engines. "But surely, Davinci's designs were flawed?" he eventually countered, "otherwise we'd have been flying since the fifteen hundreds."

"Alright: *almost* parallel," Hamble acquiesced, as she executed a perfect leap and landing over a narrow ravine, "Leonardo's ideas were pure genius," she lauded. "The Italian government of the time should have thrown money at him; assembled him a workforce; taken him seriously, at least, but no. The Catholic church had him arrested as a heretic and discredited his work. Don't you remember what Alyce was telling us a few months back about how religion never really caught on, on Mars?"

"I recall a debate on the subject which I *lost*."

"Well, unlike on Mars, it's been holding *us* back for centuries."

Another explosion directly to port, sent them hurtling uncontrollably toward a large hole in the ground. Yet another; right on their tail blew off their rear wheels, then, suddenly, everything went dark…

CHAPTER TWO:

FATHER AND SON REUNION

BAVARIA...

"The Baron... wants t'see us," Tiny announced, puffing and blowing as he stepped out onto the parapet, having hauled his ever-expanding bulk up the long, winding staircase to the castle's rooftop vantage point.

Iggi, perched on the highest point, still as a stone gargoyle, lowered her binoculars and turned to watch her friend, gingerly edging his way along the rooftop toward her. His back to the steeply angled tiles of the Great Hall beneath them, he moved obliquely like a cautious crab circumventing a seaside rock pool, and she smiled. He had made it quite clear to everybody in the garrison that he was not at all fond of heights, which was why she tended to come up here when she wanted a little space.

She liked Tiny, their friendship having grown over the past eight months or so that they had been stranded here; partly, she felt, due to the fact that, with the exception of the Baron and Mrs Blaise, whom they rarely saw in any kind of social capacity, they were the only two permanent castle residents who spoke any more than pidgin English. They had a shared history, of sorts, having bonded through a couple of life and death experiences over the past couple of years; in fact, it was probably fair to say that they had shared *more* together than either of them had done with anyone else before.A trust had begun to develop between them: a reliance that Iggi was finally learning to accept. They had both professed to having missed one another when they had been parted for that year, which gave her a warm feeling when she thought about it: a strange feeling, the like of which she had never known before, but sometimes… well, sometimes she just felt the need to give him the slip. His presence could be a little overpowering, as could his breath, ever since he had been introduced to Bratwurst and German beer, a habit that she had been attempting to get him to cut back on, not least for the sake of his heart, she felt, but also their continued safety. A bodyguard of his stature may well be useful for stopping a sniper's bullet, but only if he could respond quickly enough to throw himself unto the breach.

She cared for him; there was no point in her denying it; she loved him, in her own way: like an elder sister would a younger brother. And this was a good thing, she had decided: despite her Crown training; human beings were never designed to be solitary animals. Having him around had helped her to deal with the psychological problems that she had had in dealing with her transplanted arm, but try as she had, she could still not get used to spending so much of her time around him. She was a loner at heart; it went with her trade, and although she had exchanged the assassin's life for that of the VIP minder; which was very much a 'people' orientated career, she still felt the need to escape, periodically, if for no reason other than to 'get her head together'. For as much as she felt crowded, she was also bored. Being stuck in the castle for days on end, waiting for someone to take a sneaky potshot at her employer, was not the kind of role that she felt she could ever really embrace on a permanent basis. She longed for a bit of excitement; something more stimulating than simple babysitting duties, whether for the new leader of the fatherland or anybody else. She was grateful to the Baron, of course, for taking the pair of them in when they had had nowhere else to go, but she needed more than she had been offered. Perhaps, she wondered, as she looked across at Tiny, out of his comfort zone once again, perhaps this was what they both needed? The Baron had sent them on missions before; relying on their skills on the ground to contain elements disloyal to his leadership. They had proved themselves to be assets, despite their alien heritage; something that those closest to the new Chancellor had voiced their concerns over...

"Sounds ominous," she replied, as Tiny reached the midway point and paused, wheezing; his eyes closed as a light gust of wind whipped at the few strands of hair that still persisted to either side of his head, "any idea what he wants?"

"S-s-somefin' to do wiv a mission back t'Blighty. 'E nevva' said much, jus' asked me if'n I knew a few names."

Iggi moved toward him, stepping onto the crenelated battlements at the very edge of the parapet; a smile on her face and devilment in her eyes, as she had seen before how her apparent recklessness disturbed her friend.

Tiny closed the one eye that he had open whilst answering her question. "Don't do that!" he pleaded, "Me 'art can't take it!"

"Then lay off the sausages, fat boy!" she sniped, arriving at his other side and reaching for his arm, which was as rigid as the rest of him, "What names?"

"I d-d-unno," he stuttered, grabbing her wrist as he felt her nearness, "London types: lowlifes'n ruffians, 'e said."

Iggi led him back the six feet or so that he had managed to slope away from the door.

"Here," she said, transferring his hand to the rope rail on the stairs, "Can you remember any of them?"

"Not really. No one I'd 'eard of, anyways. Oh, 'e mentioned a 'Queenpins'; that one stuck. Sounded more like a chess move than a moniker. Mean anyfin' t'you?"

It should have done. Time was when she would have known every back-alley skiver'n conniver in the city, not to mention who they answered to and for whom they moonlighted, but she had been away from home for far too long, she realised; things had moved on. If an East End player had become known this far off their turf, then they were either a King or a Queenpin. It paid, in her profession, to know all the prime movers on her patch.

"Not ringing any bells," she admitted, following him through the door and into the stairwell beyond...

* * * * *

"Father..."

A single word, spoken to the back of his intended target's head, one word with which he hoped to convey so much.

He had not come here by choice, neither out of a sense of patriotic duty nor of family loyalty. He was here, he reminded himself, at the Secretary's petition.

Nevertheless, he had decided, if he *were* to be forced to reacquaint himself with the man standing before him; a man whom he had hoped never to cross swords with in his newly elevated capacity, then he was going to do it on his own terms.

He had rehearsed it over and over in the SteamSteed, all the way from Bloomsbury to Downing Street: that same word, delivered using every possible nuance and inflection, and yet still, he felt, he had managed to bungle his entrance, coming across as weak and tentative; subordinate, even, when addressing the one man whose opinion he found he curiously still cared most for.

A display of confidence had been his intent: a front-foot, territory-marking gambit that, if received in the spirit that it had been schemed, might have marked a positive step toward a new dawn for their somewhat non-functional familial relationship.

The execution, however, had gone awry; he had known it from the very moment the word had left his lips, though his father gave no indication that he had even heard his eldest son's introduction; keeping silent, his back to his guest, for longer than manners dictated appropriate.

Twelve gruelling seconds ticked by; dead time, during which Virgil removed both his hat and his Rebreather, his scarf and his overcoat, handing them all over silently to the valet, who, in his turn, had also been ignored in his own attempt to introduce the minister's three o'clock.

"Sit," Virgil eventually heard; a command, rather than a welcome, and one launched, he knew, though he could not see to confirm it, from behind that same tight-lipped snarl that had ever been his default.

And yet he found himself compelled to obey, and without hesitation, though he chastised himself inwardly as he did so for relinquishing what hand he felt he may have had.

The Prime Minister, however, continued to stare down into the street from his first-floor window, a plume of dull grey smoke engulfing his head as he chugged away at his pipe.

"I am led to believe," he eventually said, languidly from within his dissipating cloud, as if dictating a memo to an unseen typist, "that you have been... busy."

A statement and by no means a question that might require an answer, Virgil noted, judging by the smugly sceptical tone used to underline the last two syllables, "In fact," he went on; his voice now akin to that of a ventriloquist's: the pipe now held firmly between his teeth as he relit the bowl, "the Secretary informs me that you have been 'abroad'. A mission for the Empire no less?"

Removing his pipe, he waved it in Virgil's general direction, "Oh, don't concern yourself; I know better than to press an 'Agent of The Crown' for operational details. We call it 'plausible deniability' these days," and he laughed before taking another puff.

"Suffice it to say, Virgil, that I hope you make a better fist of 'diplomacy' than you did the medical sciences."

Saliva: bitter and metallic, welled beneath Virgil's tongue, but he fought the urge to spit. This was how it always began: the all too familiar stirrings of paraesthesia numbing the tips of his fingers and toes; his peripheral vision blurring and reddening from the outside in, like the dimming russet of a late summer's sunset. Instinctively he reached up to touch his breast pocket where he knew his daily ration of Henry's compound to be, and considered the genesis of his un-tempered affliction. It was the summer of '66: that fateful day that had shaped his father's view of him ever forth…

…They had brought her into the dining hall, bloody and screaming; father and uncle Boothby, between them. They had been shouting at him to do something, to save her; him, the student doctor, but he could do nothing without removing her under garments and investigating the damage caused by the accident: the two things that they had expressly forbade him do.

And so she had lain there; bleeding onto the table in front of them whilst the three men bickered; staining the white linen tablecloth beyond the housemaid's professional abilities to launder it; her cries turning to sobs, then to a single whimper and then… silence.

This 'Red Mist' with which he had ever since been plagued: anger mixed with impotence and guilt, manifesting itself as a full character metamorphosis: this was when he had first experienced it, in the hours following his mother's death; the indisposition that confounded his moral compass, stifling his ability to tell right from wrong…

…but this time he fought it, as he had been learning to do these past months. He closed his eyes, as his recently deceased friend Henry had shown him; drew the deepest of breaths, in through his nose, held it for a full twenty seconds, then released it, slowly through his mouth. He repeated the process one more time as his father proceeded to berate him for his most recent failure…

"…blah blah… I gave you a simple task and yet you let me down… Again!"

The reddening of his vision began to fade as he heard Dr Stokes' calming voice echoing around his skull and saw his gold watch swinging gently in front of his closed eyes. Slowly and calmly; his dander finally lowering, Virgil began to compose a reply, but, when the time came to verbalise it, found that his mouth was unwilling to co-operate…

"Well," his father continued, still refusing to turn and properly acknowledge him, "at least we can say that you're consistent."

Again, he laughed and again, as they ever had done, the throaty staccato beats of his father's tobacco-addled guffaw struck like bullets fired at his chest. He should not have been surprised; his father had always treated him in this way. Momentarily, he was jolted back in time to the hard wooden chair that still sat outside the old man's study. It was the final day of term and he was waiting to present his report, whilst mentally preparing himself for the thrashing that would inevitably follow whatever slight negative the old man might find therein.

Nothing had changed in all these years, yet he was a man of fifty-four now, and a father himself, twice over!

"I asked you to bring your brother home for a proper Christian burial; one year, four months and seven days ago. *Well*, boy? Explain yourself."

'Had it really been sixteen months?' Virgil asked himself, frowning; 'sixteen months since all this madness had begun?' He should have known that he would have wanted an answer; he should have been prepared, but he had been more worried about his presentation than he had his content: a line that had so often been used against him by headmasters of old. 'How could he explain that he had left the bodies of all three of his brothers on the Moon when he was not yet certain that their father even knew of Aubrey's demise and most certainly did not know of Gordon's?'

"Y'know, the Secretary speaks quite highly of you," his father cut in, unexpectedly, "seems to think you're more than the imbecile that you've proved yourself time and again to be. Says I ought t'cut you a little slack, don't y'know, on account you're the only one I have left t'hand."

Virgil's frown deepened as he considered all the various clauses of that sentence.

"As y'know," his father went on, tapping the bowl of his pipe against the painted wooden windowsill and discharging the still smouldering embers onto the corner of a rather opulent Turkish rug, before crushing it into the pile with the toe of his left brogue, "my hand has now been kissed and I hold the position of *'primus inter pares'*. You will, therefore, afford me due respect as such. Your brother Gordon has obviously surpassed you: first man to walk on the Moon; first human being to set foot on Mars; Earth ambassador to Mars: y'can't trump any of those achievements, of course, but y'can do your damndest not to embarrass me and to attend any state functions that I decree, with y'lawfuly wedded wife on your arm.

"Am I making myself clear boy!" he bellowed; a phlegmy gobbet of blood-tinged saliva spattering against the glass pane in front of him when his son dared to dally his response.

Virgil felt his cheeks flush red; a gradual return of the pins'needles that he had only just managed to suppress and the taste of blood on his own tongue. He wanted to defend himself; to explain to his father how Gordon's mission to the Moon had been a subterfuge on behalf of Victoria's private office; of how in truth, thanks to Dr Stokes techniques, he now knew that it had been *he* who had first stepped out onto the lunar surface, and that Gordon, far from residing on the Martian home world as advertised, now rotted with the corpses of his other two siblings in the Clavius crater, 239,000 miles above them, but he knew that such revelations would likely be received as mere poppycock and to attempt to prove them would bring hell and damnation down on his own head, just as much as it would ruin his father. He therefore opted to acquiesce with a simple 'sir', after dripping four spots of Henry's special tonic onto his extended tongue...

CHAPTER THREE:

HOMEWARD BOUND

"Oxygen!" said a voice quite close to his ear, and he opened his eyes to see a match flame lighting the lower half of a face: an otherworldly vision, hovering in the otherwise blackness that surrounded him. Gordon yelped instinctively, if not a tad effeminately, he considered, though recovered himself when he realised to whom the floating jaw belonged.

"I take it you've noticed we're breathing, despite the cracks in our helmets?" Hamble added to her previous observation.

If he were honest, it was a detail that had passed him by; the ability to breathe tending to be something that he generally took for granted. He had faced many a torturer's challenge in his time in the field: capture and incarceration rather going with the territory for an adventurer, but never had he faced suffocation as a means of punishment from a chieftain or a king whose deity he had angered in the process of liberating their treasures. Queen Wallazoo of Kathmandu, had once tried to drown him; in '88; if memory served, and her neighbouring warlord, King Bussto of the great tribe of Bussterds, had tried to desiccate him by locking him in a cave full of vampire bats for a week, though it had ultimately turned out to have been a tunnel, and he had escaped on the first night simply by following the bats. The only time that he had ever really considered that a lack of oxygen might be the cause of his ultimate demise had been back on the fake Moon, when he had been preparing to take off his helmet and—

"Gordon? Are you listening to me?"

"Oxygen," he repeated, dragging himself back to the present, "We've got some. Top hole! It's a little sour, though, wouldn't you say?"

"Musty," she said, moving away from him and waving her flame around as she reconnoitred the area, "nobody's been here for a while. A crypt, maybe, or an abandoned mine shaft? Definitely man made, or perhaps I should say 'Martian-made'—"

"It is a part of one of our old cities," said another voice, followed immediately by the sudden appearance before them of the ghoulishly-lit figure of the third member of their party. Bathed in an eerie, incandescent light that blanched her already pale complexion beyond that of a living organism, Alyce wavered before them like Dickens' Ghost of Christmas Future.

"Alyce?" queried Hamble, "are you… alright?"

Hamble had no need to spell out what Gordon was already thinking; their friend's post-life pallor and the dried blood tracts on her face and body told them both that she was, in fact, quite dead, yet mysteriously reanimated like the walking cadavers who had killed poor Sherpa Tilly in Haiti back in '96.

The illuminated zombie reached an arm toward Hamble.

"Careful!" Gordon warned, "I've seen this kind of thing before. One touch and—"

Alyce touched the panel on the side of Hamble's splintered helmet and suddenly she too was lit, though in a strobing fashion as if her connection with the afterlife was not yet complete.

"It is shorting," Alyce explained, turning toward Gordon, who took an involuntary step backwards and held his gloved index fingers ahead of him in the sign of a cross, "Try yours, Gordon."

"Don't come any clo—"

He felt rather than saw Hamble's hand connect roughly with what was left of his own helmet, and not a second later his own suit lit up akin to the girls'.

He screamed, to a chorus of giggles from both his companions.

"How *are* you?" Hamble asked of Alyce, ignoring the fact that Gordon was clearly hyperventilating beside her. "You looked dreadful when we picked you up."

"A few bumps and bruises," Alyce replied, "I have had worse. The cold was getting to me, though; however, I do not recall how we got down here."

"Range Roller over there," Hamble began to explain, illuminating the wrecked buggy with her flame before blowing it out, "we were trying to evade a flock of happy-zappy Ornithopters, when one blew a hole in the ground right in front of us and we lost our road."

"Happy-*ZAPPY*?" queried Alyce.

"Yes," said Gordon, "I don't think that's actually a word, m'dear."

"I'm an inventor," Hamble defended tightly, "I invent things. Get used to it."

"I think I understand," said Alyce, nodding, "they were firing at us in an indiscriminate manner, yes?"

"Like I said: happy-zappy."

"Were we heading anywhere in particular?" asked Alyce.

"Safety," Hamble replied. "Whichever way that was."

"Well, it'd seem you got it right," Gordon chipped in for good measure, just as the light emanating from the rim of his helmet fizzed and blinked out.

"The Planetary Defence Unit is not stupid," Alyce warned, "and they get so few alien incursions to deal with that they have the time and the will to be thorough. They will have identified the rocket by now and presumed it to have contained The Greckle. They will not rest until they find him."

"Well then, it'd seem we'd better get moving," Hamble insisted, "Any idea where we are?"

"Not as yet," Alyce told her, looking around the roughly hewn tunnel that had saved their lives, "We would appear to be in a service shaft, quite close to the surface. The floor has a slight gradient to it, getting higher on the other side of the buggy, so I would suggest that we head *this* way,"

"Downward?" questioned Gordon, removing his gloves and unfastening the buckles on the collar of his spacesuit. "I've fallen into a few ancient cities and forgotten necropolises in my time, and my first instinct has always been to find the quickest route *up*wards and *out*."

"It is probable that they will still be searching the surface around the point where they lost us," Alyce explained, taking a few steps down the passageway. "This; coupled with the fact that we do not have a working helmet between us, would suggest to me that we would be better heading further into the city."

"Down it is," agreed Hamble, turning to Gordon, "at some point we should find something that'll help Alyce to work out where we are and how we get from where that *is*, to where we're likely to find this Professor Boff. Coming?"

* * * * *

The Queen Empress Victoria was said to have been 'greatly saddened' by the tragic news concerning the death of her grandson, William II of Germany; according to the report that the Baron had translated for them, published in *The Berliner Morgenpost*, the following day. The British monarch had, however, refused to be drawn on the German paper's allegations that the Kaiser's 'assassination' had, in fact, been ordered by her own government, as her new Prime Minister's inaugural act of foreign policy. 'Their deaths would at least have been swift', the paper had gone on to confirm, 'as swift and as effective as the German government's response to this outrageous, unprovoked act of war…'

'Wilhelm II, his wife, his son and various other members of his extended family had all died instantly when the diplomatic Zeppelin in which they had been travelling had been struck, amidships, by an anti-airship missile, in the vicinity of Castle Greckle in Bavaria': so went the official line, which had been distributed via the international news agencies to newspapers and radio stations around the world within a few hours of the actual event. The Emperor had, apparently, been in the process of paying a surprise visit on the castle, in order to show his son the rocket with which he intended to conquer the Moon and thus prove Victoria's own claim to celestial domination, a sham.

Iggi Shikiwana, however, former British Crown assassin, now acting under the pseudonym, 'Inge Schwartz', bodyguard to the German Republic's First Chancellor: Baron Otto Von Greckle, was one of only four people in the entire world who knew the truth of the matter. The quartet knew because they had been the only eye witnesses not to have been killed along with the imperial entourage.

Wilhelm and his descendant's deaths; though ultimately rather convenient for the Baron, as they had inspired the German people to sue for a new system of government, replacing the old dictatorial model with a radical new democratic republic, had been purely accidental. His visit to Castle Greckle, that day, had not been advertised, (it would not have been a 'surprise inspection', of course, if it had have been!) and could not have come at a more awkward moment for the castle's owner, who had been in the process of defending his

Gothic stronghold from incursion by a ragtag assembly of British dissidents, intent on rescuing the kidnapped inventor, Professor Hamble Blaise; a party that had been led by 'Space Captain' Gordon Periwinkle and Iggi herself. The imperial airship 'CEZAR' had been attempting to dock at the castle's upper port, when the rocket in question, which was berthed within the White Tower, directly below the port, was suddenly launched. As well as the imperial transport, the resulting explosion had destroyed an entire wing of the castle, which had at the time been the base of operations for the German scientific elite, not to mention, levelling a substantial area of the forest surrounding it. The rocket, however, had survived the collision and had continued unhindered on its 'special mission' for the Baron, en route to Mars…

As the man responsible for designing and building the new weapons systems; currently being deployed in the war with the (no longer) United States of America, the Baron had been an easy choice to lead this new republic; as far as the voting public had been concerned, emerging early on in the debate as the single most likely contender for the role. His only serious opposition had been the retired former German Chancellor and Prussian Prime Minister, Otto Von Bismarck. In his day, Bismarck had been a popular and enigmatic leader: a favourite among the aristocracy as well as many ordinary Germans alike, but this was, most decidedly, not his day. Forced to resign the position of Chancellor earlier that year when he had fallen out with the Kaiser, he had, ever since, been said to have been in failing health. Luckily for Greckle, his opposite number had died of 'natural causes' a mere three weeks into his campaign; or so *The Berliner Morgenpost* had reported. In truth, Iggi, on a mission to prove where her loyalties had lain, had given him something of a helping hand.

"Why," Von Greckle had concluded, "leave a thing like democracy to chance?"

Rather than move to Berlin in order to be closer to the Reichstag, the Baron had insisted on staying on in Bavaria and commuting between the two, in the company of his two mysterious minders. An eccentric figurehead, little more was known about the new First Chancellor than his supposed appetite for war with the British Empire, which was how he intended for things to remain. The people seemed content enough knowing that their leader was responsible for shaping the way that the Kaiser had conducted the fighting on the North American front, along with his outspoken views on Martians.

Iggi could not help but raise a smile whenever she thought of this, bearing in mind information that only she, Tiny and Mrs Blaise were privy to, regarding their patron's true heritage...

"Iggi, Tiny, Good to see you. Come in; take a seat. Iggi: I presume you're going to tell me that it's too early in the day to share a glass of wine with me?"

Iggi smiled, something that she suddenly realised she had been doing rather a lot of lately. As if to bring herself to heel, she felt an involuntary twitch in her donor arm; a spasm, as its fingers clenched and unclenched at her side, reminding her not to get too comfortable. Beside her and, as ever, never a one for principled abstinence when it came to the fruits of their adopted nation, Tiny unhooked the pewter tankard that hung from his belt and held it out for their employer to fill.

As if on cue as they both took their seats, Mrs Blaise entered the Baron's office, but through the room's other door – the one that led directly to the sanctuary of his private tower. In her hands she carried a silver tray upon which was perched a matching teapot, milk jug and two bone china teacups with saucers, which she duly slammed down onto the Baron's desk whilst kicking the door closed behind her.

"'Ere y'go, Iggi luv. First fuckin' Chanc'la' an' 'e still ain't got the 'ang of 'ostin' a party."

"Methus— Misses Blaise!"

"Oh, come on, O'o; ligh'en up. You pays'em t'watch ya'. They'd be pretty shit minders if they 'adn't worked out th't you'n I w's sharin' a sack, now, wou'n't they?"

Iggi felt the smile creeping back onto her face, but stifled it, asserting control over her right arm by digging her nails into its palm.

"So, i's not a'nact?" asked Tiny, slower on the uptake than his position required.

"Star'ed out as'nact," said Methusela, pouring tea for herself and Iggi. "Leader'v th'second biggest Empire in th'world 'as to 'ave a consort, don't 'e? But 'e does like t'throw 'imself inta th'part, don't ya', ol' luv?"

"To business," the Baron reminded them seriously, taking his seat behind his ornately carved walnut desk and gesturing to his guests to take theirs in front of him. He took a swig of wine as they made themselves comfortable, then placed his goblet back on the table and took a deep breath as he readied himself to speak.

"As you are all aware," he began, gesticulating to encompass them all; his face adopting a dark, foreboding expression, as if he had been brooding on something overnight and had finally come to a decision that it pained him to deliver, "it has now been ten months since your friends left us, in the hope of finding a way of saving your race from the threat that my people's presence here poses. The journey to Mars should have taken them no longer than eight months..." and he left the statement hanging, momentarily.

Iggi had been well aware of the march of time, as, she suspected, had Mrs Blaise, and she was perfectly au fait with Tiny's views on the subject; barely a day going past when he did not ask her whether she thought anything had changed yet. The Baron's reminder had merely brought to the fore the shared fears that they all harboured over whether or not Hamble, Alyce and Captain Periwinkle would succeed in their goal or whether they would ultimately all have to learn to love the world in which they now resided.

"The entire plan," the Baron continued, "was, of course, something of a long shot. For a start, there was no way to know whether the rocket would even make the journey, and even if it *did*, whether or not it would be spotted by the defence grid and shot down before they even made planet fall." The Baron paused to massage the bridge of his nose. He had been so confident in the early weeks following the launch, Iggi remembered; she had never seen him this dejected. Even during the inquiry that the government had instigated over the death of the Kaiser; an ordeal that would have broken many a man of weaker character, his positivity had never been seen to waiver.

He had waited a long time to find someone as capable as Hamble who could repair his rocket and execute the plan that he had been working on since he had first become stranded here on Earth. It had been his unshakeable belief that there was a way to halt this inexorable tide of 'unnatural progress', as he had often described the technological leaps instigated by his people's interference; a way to reclaim the lives that they had all been intended to lead, that had kept the rest of them going, even when the plan had seemed so outlandish as to have been verging on speculative fiction.

The Baron sighed heavily and took another fortifying gulp of wine.

"We also had no way of knowing whether Professor Boff was still alive, not to mention how we might find her if she was, nor whether she would be prepared to hand over her life's work to a pair of aliens."

He was right, of course; she had probably always known it. The four of them had hung the highest of hopes upon an idea that, whilst it had seemed to make perfect sense at the time, away from the madness of the moment, now seemed too naive for words.

"I think," he continued, but Iggi's mind had raced ahead and beaten him to the denouement; reality dawning sharply for her, as if someone had just pulled a rug from under her feet. They had pinned everything upon a plan so unlikely and then had spent the better part of a year with their fingers crossed, trying not to scrutinise the details, and now, with a few, well-chosen words, their host was about to bring all of their dreams crashing down around their ankles.

"I think," he reiterated, a little more firmly this second time around, "that's it's about time we accepted the fact that we may never know whether they made it to Mars or not. I believe it's high time that we put those hopes aside and got on with plan B. I can't stall the consensus of a democratic nation for ever, you know."

"Woah, woah woah!" Mrs Blaise interjected, her grey eyes narrowing as she lowered the saucer that she had been supping from, "Are you *suggestin'*, sunshine, that we jus' f'get th'we sent my daugh'er out on a fool's errand t'die on'n alien world; draw a line unda' it an' move *on*? 'Cause if'n you *are*—"

The Baron turned to his consort in earnest, taking both of her hands in his own and kissing her wizened knuckles.

"Methusela, of course not! I was suggesting nothing of the sort. We must *never* forget the sacrifice that Hamble, Gordon and Alyce made for us and, indeed, for your whole race, but we are merely marking time here now, and for no good reason that I can see. I was a politician,

57

back on Mars, not a scientist. I knew Professor Boff and I knew of her work: she was a genius. She had petitioned me to champion her findings and to secure funding for her research. I understood the gist of her theory and it seemed sound enough to me, but I didn't necessarily understand the finer workings of it. It is possible that Hamble and Gordon have succeeded; that a new, alternate reality has already been splintered from the one that we are currently living; one where Hamble's own rocket never landed on the Moon. How would we tell?"

Frowning, Iggi interjected, "I thought you said that if that *happened* then *this* version would just 'blink' out of existence?" It was what she had told Tiny a thousand times already, "And that we would wake up in this *new* version presuming that we'd always been living that life."

"And you could be right!" the Baron conceded, turning back toward her, though not letting go of Mrs Blaise's hand, "I just don't know. Is that how it works? What if her machine merely causes a fork; the two realities running in tandem with one another?

"So, it might've already 'appened then?" Tiny said, entering the conversation with a quizzical frown of his own, chiselled into his shrunken face, "but... we'd never know f'sure?"

"Precisely!" agreed the Baron. "That was always a possibility. And that is why, all this time later, I think we should presume the *latter* and get on with causing as much trouble for the Martians on Earth as we possibly can."

"What are you suggesting?" asked Iggi, adding milk to her tea and sinking back into her chair, a hundred-fold happier now that she felt that she had a more positive role to play.

"The Senate; backed by the will of the people, is calling for us to take the war to England."

"And you've been stalling; yes, we know," she interrupted, keen for him to bother a point. "I may not have learned to speak German yet, but I'm becoming quite adept at understanding the repeated niggles we hear in the guard room."

The Baron's lips acknowledged a brief smile for the first time since their meeting had begun.

"Rumour is rife," he continued, "that the Martian refugees that your Queen has deigned to receive, have agreed to earn their keep by fighting against us alongside British forces in North America. Now, much as I know that this is *unlikely*; my people may be many things, but *soldiers* they are not, I am unable to convince the Senate otherwise without revealing my hand. I cannot yet, therefore, remove the troops that I would require for an all-out assault on London, from an already struggling front line."

"But you have another plan," Iggi presumed, finishing her tea and putting her cup back on the tray. 'Anything,' she thought, that might get them out of the castle before she went stir-crazy.

"You may recall that before you arrived here, I had gathered together a 'think-tank' of the finest minds in Europe."

Iggi winced inwardly at the thought of their bungled attempt to 'repatriate' the kidnapped scientists that they had discovered in the basement when she, Tiny and Gordon had first stormed the castle. Those who had not been picked off in their escape by sniper fire had died when the Kaiser's airship had exploded against the east wing.

"Their task," he droned on, "had been to help me to repair my rocket and the equipment that we brought here with us; all of which had been damaged in the crash. It was the Italian, Marconi, although at a loss to understand a Martian propulsion system, who not only managed to *repair* my communications system, but made quite significant modifications to it as he did so, which, since the arrival of my people here on Earth, has given me something of an unexpected advantage."

Iggi was aware of the Baron's technological advantage, but chose discretion rather than risk appearing overtly perfidious, in the same way that she had pretended not to notice his nocturnal liaisons with Hamble's mother. As an Agent of The Crown, she had found that it paid to be prepared, so she made it her business to know as much about the task in hand as it was possible to ascertain; one never knew when an apparently trivial piece of information might suddenly become a vital piece of intelligence.

"I have been able to tap into signals," he said, but again, she had already guessed where his explanation was headed, "signals that are being broadcast between the Martian settler ship in London and their base on your Moon, and I have picked up a few snippets of information that may prove to be useful."

"Concerning a certain 'Queenpins'?"

"The very same, yes. Are you by any chance familiar with that name?"

Iggi pursed her lips before replying, "Tiny mentioned her name earlier and I didn't think I was, but the more I think about it, the more it seems to be ringing a distant bell."

"Keep it ringing. It would seem that all is not well in paradise. There is an underground resistance to the Martian's presence, headed up, apparently, by this Queenpins character. It's a fairly ineffective movement at the moment; no more than an irritation, graffiti, 'No Aliens' signs in shop windows and hostelries; the odd thrown stone, but its influence is growing. Enough for it to have irked both the Secretary and the Martians. My opposite number suspects the hands of Bolsheviks and

Fenians behind some of their latest moves. I need you to infiltrate this group and to persuade them to carry out a particular act. It will be a signal for the beginning of the German invasion of Britain…"

* * * * *

On a fundamental level, a human being is like every other human being, regardless of where on Earth he or she may have been conceived. They have a shared genetic ancestry, and yet at the same time, every single one of them is unique; with variations in size, shape, skin and hair colouring abounding within the marque. Despite this, and whether they choose to or not, they are all able to recognise one another instantly as members of the same species. It would be unlikely, for instance, for a human being to be fooled by a member of a closely related species; such as a chimpanzee or a gorilla, masquerading as one of their own in petticoats or a top hat, and yet the Secretary, a member of an entirely *different* species; a native of an entirely different *planet*, had managed to infiltrate and live among them, in plain sight, for the better part of a century without any disguise whatsoever, and with none ever challenging him over the fact that he was, when all was said and done, something of an oddity amongst them.

For a start, he was taller than the average man; more often than not, the first thing that took people's notice; if only by a spare inch or two, and he had a chest that was broader than most, lending him the appearance of the type of man for whom contact sports were not something that one simply put aside on receipt of one's first weekly wage packet.

Both these traits taken together, coupled with the fact that he had managed to inveigle himself into a position of indisputable authority within a system where lack of deference or respect for one's betters was a punishable offence, meant that very few would dare to mention his other idiosyncrasies. His heavy-set brow, for instance, which was akin, though none dared say it aloud, more to the Neanderthal model than the Homo sapiens ideal. His facial features were sharper and more pronounced than might have been expected, set within a complexion that was exceptionally wan, at least in comparison to most other Englishman, if not, perhaps, to a native Scandinavian.

But the most alien thing about him, had anybody taken the time to check his credentials, was that he was considerably longer lived than had been believed to that point to be humanly possible.

Prior to the arrival in London in April 1898 of the first Martian 'refugee' ship, humanity had been hitherto unaware of its ever having encountered an intelligent being from a world outside of their own; rather presumptuously believing themselves to be the only sentient species at large in the entirety of the cosmos.

Upon learning that they were, in fact, not as peculiar as they had previously thought, many humans had turned to panic. Realising that the various religions and dogmas to which they had previously devoted their lives had been flawed, many had simply lost their minds; attempting to kill either themselves or those around them, as if that would have made the slightest difference to the truth that they had discovered! Of those who *were* able to accept the likelihood that they were perhaps only a small part of a much wider community of intelligent life forms, expectations of what a visitor from the stars might actually *look* like were multifarious. Curiously though, none seemed to anticipate the possibility that the Martians might appear 'human' like. Thus, what *looked* like a human and *acted* like a human, was, therefore, seen to *be* a human, and this was how it had been possible for the Secretary to continue; unchecked, nudging the human race toward greater integration, homogenising their differences in order to make them more compliant to the eventual Martian settlement plan that was now, finally, under way. He had done this by encouraging the leaders of the world's most prolific Empire of the time, Victoria's *British* Empire, to push its boundaries ever further; to absorb new peoples; new ideas and new ways of doing things and to utilise whatever help might be on offer...

But whilst rumours abounded in the popular press as to how many eyes and tentacles might adorn a green-skinned Martian's head, it seemed that their illustrators could imagine no other design for a craft capable of interplanetary travel, than something similar to the three phallic rivals that had entered Earth's 'Great Space Race' during the latter half of the 1890s (the polished steel pipe of the American 'US ENTERPRISE'; the Germans' burnished, ribbed iron, and slightly bulbous 'DEUTSCHLAND 1' and the contest's ultimate winner: the smaller, sleeker, Hamble Blaise designed, copper and brass-plated rocket ship 'VICTORIA'), thereby depicting the approaching Martian vessel in a similar, overtly penile design for the front pages of their first editions that day.

Commentators in attendance on Hampstead Heath on the night that the ship had arrived, had therefore been surprised, if not a little uneasy, to witness the gargantuan dimensions of the Martian saucer as it descended slowly through the clouds, extruding, then finally coming to rest upon what appeared to be a giant, metal cake stand.

The Secretary, however; from his position on the royal observation podium, offset to the left and behind both the Queen and the Prime Minister, had betrayed no outward emotion, supressing the smile that had threatened to overwhelm his face as he recognised the ship's design as one that had still been on the drawing board when he had last been on Mars. It would not have done to have blown his cover in the final moments of the mission, before he was able to leave this benighted world for good…

The Secretary had not enjoyed his time on Earth: the gravity was far denser than it was possible to acclimatise to and the climate much warmer than could ever be considered comfortable. The air, too, had been a little over oxygenated when he had first arrived, which had led to frequent headaches; not to mention, irreparable, long-term damage to his cardiovascular system. Thankfully, that problem at *least* had now been dealt with, since the levels of sulphur dioxide in the air had increased as part of the steam-powered revolution that he had been at pains to encourage.

He had collected not a single souvenir to take home with him and would miss none of the primitives whom he had been forced to spend his time with. He was tired and more than ready to take his leave of the place. He had been a child when he had volunteered for the mission, willingly having given up his family and friends for the chance to one day return home a hero. He had worked hard under exceptional conditions and for longer than most of his kind would ever have been expected to, and he had done so alone for the latter two thirds of the mission. This was to be the final scene of his final act as his people's agent on Earth…

'First Contact' had officially been made via wireless telegraph, through Admiral Harvey Haversack of Space Command, six weeks earlier; his was the name that would grace the history books ever after, but the first human to have 'officially' *met* with a Martian on Earth would be recorded as acting Prime Minister, Octavian Periwinkle; he and the Secretary having been on hand to greet the Martian ambassador when his ship had unexpectedly arrived in Parliament Square the previous March.

Arrangements had been made with the Admiral as to where the ship would land and how the initial meeting would be handled. It had been decided that the Queen; her Prime Minister; her Foreign Secretary, a Mr Cyril Pugh, along with the Secretary and Admiral Haversack himself, would meet with the Martians *inside* the Martian craft, however, not before a phalanx of the Crown's most high-ranking agents had entered and ensured the party's safety. A cordon was erected around the heath, with an ostentatious display of members of the household cavalry in full dress uniform, heading up the security: keeping the public and the press from crossing the barricades and any prospective enemy agents; Fenians, Bolsheviks, anarchists or general ne'r-do-wells, from gate crashing such a pivotal moment in the history of the planet.

In the event, the Secretary had entered the Martian saucer a few paces ahead of Queen Victoria and Lord Periwinkle, on receiving word from Abdul that the way ahead was safe. Just inside the door, they were met by a pair of space-suited Martians; 'females of the species', the Queen had noted, who had nodded curtly in formal Martian greeting before leading them onward toward their captain's office. The Secretary had felt himself relax at this point; it was good to be in the company of members of his own kind, again. He had often caught himself thinking in English these past few years and at times had worried whether he would even remember how to converse in his own language when the time came, but he resisted the urge that nagged within him, to tittle-tattle with the captain's guards.

The meeting went well. The council had chosen their representative wisely; both the Queen and Mr Pugh responding favourably to his charms.

"You remind me of someone," the Queen had told him, between sips of Martian tea and a slice of sponge, and for a moment, the Secretary thought that she was about to reveal him, but, after a brief pause, she had remembered where she had seen his like, declaring: "that new German Chancellor, fellow, the one who murdered my grandson! Yes, it's quite uncanny, is it not, gentlemen? They could almost be brothers!"

The meeting had lasted a few minutes shy of an hour and had been mostly productive; the only fly in the ointment having being Octavian Periwinkle, whose distrust of the visitors and their motives for coming to Earth could not have been more evident. Thankfully, for everybody's sake, Victoria's word was still law, at least from the perspective of social etiquette, and a few choice remarks from the country's longest-serving monarch to the man who, at that time, had merely been a 'caretaker' PM, had soon brought him to heel.

Her diplomatic duties discharged, the Queen and her party had then taken their leave of the captain, returning to the palace to discuss their initial impressions of the aliens with a select group of cabinet ministers; ranking members of the armed forces and senior members of the royal family. At her insistence, the Secretary had stayed behind; it would be *his* job, she had informed him, to iron out the details of the agreement; *his* responsibility to see that the Martian refugees understood their *debt* to Victoria and her Empire and the price that they would be expected to pay for their sanctuary here on Earth. The captain had already made it clear in his original transmissions that no matter what the provocation, his people could not be cajoled into bearing arms against her enemies. 'War', he had explained to the Admiral, was 'not the Martian way'. They *would*, however, be prepared to supply her with every technological advantage at their disposal in order to help her to expand her Empire to encompass the entire world, and it had been *this* offer that had piqued the Queen's interest and convinced her to let the Martians land and to meet with them in order to see exactly what advantages they might be able to confer.

The agreement to settle any subsequent petitioners would, she had declared through the Admiral, depend entirely upon the initial two thousand's willingness to submit to the contract that the Queen's party had put to them. She had left the meeting reasonably contented...

"Reefus Questergard," the captain said, switching from his stilted English to Martian, the moment the pair were alone, and indicating that the Secretary take the seat that the Queen had newly vacated, "it is an honour and a privilege to finally meet you," he told him; tells in his body language confirming his obvious excitement. "I doubt that you are aware of this," he gushed forth, "but my ship; the first of many bound for Earth, bears your very name!"

'Reefus Questergard', it was a name that he had all but forgotten; the one that, over his long life, he had used the least, but he was gladdened to hear that his people had *not* forgotten it, as it was the one that he aimed soon to reclaim. That they had named the first of their colony vessels after him told him that his sacrifices had not been in vain. He was remembered, his work revered, and he would be returning home the hero that he had always hoped he would be.

When he had first come to Earth he had adopted the human name 'Montgomery Plumb-Prendergast': a ludicrous, tongue twisting mouthful of a mantle, that he had stolen from the orphaned son of a British peer whose entire family had died in a recent, tragic fire. The son had also died, but not according to official records, and so Reefus had assumed the boy's identity until he had risen to replace his 'Uncle' as Permanent Secretary to the King…

"I have something for you, sir," the captain informed him, reaching urgently into a draw below his desk top and retrieving a small, wooden box, bearing the monogram of the Ruling Council, which he duly slid across the polished surface toward him.

Reefus accepted his gift with the traditional curt nod of the head, picking up the box and opening it to reveal a glistening ruby, inlaid into a golden broach inside.

"It is—"

"I *know* what it *is*, captain," he said, intrigued; removing the jewel from its box and holding it up to the light, "'Qweef's Medal Of Valour'," he acknowledged; the highest accolade that the council were disposed to award for actions above and beyond the call of duty. Frowning, he continued, "but I fail to understand why you are giving me this *now*. Unless things have changed drastically in my absence, protocol surely dictates that an honour such as this, can only be presented by a member of the council themselves. Why would they not simply wait until my return?"

It was the captain's turn to frown. Leaning back in his padded seat and steepling his fingers, he replied, "Because it is long overdue, and who can say when, or at this stage, even *if*, the council will visit their newest colony world to bestow this honour upon you in person?"

"I had *presumed*," the Martian who had briefly reattained the name Reefus Questergard began, "That I would be returning to Mars with *you*."

"It is hoped," the captain informed him, brightly, "that this ship will not *be* leaving 'New Mars'. We are here to *stay*, 'Mr Secretary'. The council honours you for your preliminary mission, but at the same time acknowledges that your *real* work here has only just begun. Your cover must be maintained if we are to successfully coexist here. 'New Mars' is not for *us*: those who will struggle to exist in such conditions; it is for our children and for *their* children: The 'New Martians' who will one day walk this world and breathe its air as if our race had always been here."

The Secretary had spent the greater part of his life on Earth. He was accepted as human. He spoke like a human and he thought like a human. He had recently found himself worrying that he was becoming *too* humanised in his responses, unflinching at the sight of death; glorifying in the removal of those who stood in his way. Martians were not murderers; it was not their way, yet he found himself wishing that his people could be more honest with themselves. A bloodless coup may have been more noble, but it was slow and its outcome less certain. Strength was what was needed, not diplomacy. They should have invaded a century ago; wiped out the indigenous population and terraformed their new territory as they had their own moons…

CHAPTER FOUR:

DOMESTIC SITUATIONS

That clock would have to go – damnable piece that it was. If his ability to recall could now be better relied upon, then he had a mind that the grandmother in question had been purchased by Bea; on both their behalves, as a gift for his brother and his brother's wife on the occasion of their wedding in '77. He would put it in the waiting room of his Harley Street practice, he mused, where it's overstated and unbalanced ticking might remind his new secretary to keep a more accurate eye on the amount of time that his patients ought to be billed for.

He had a view to replace the butler too, in due course. Radcliffe had also come with the house, having been in his late brother's service for the past twenty years. He was a perfectly adequate servant, of course: conscientious; consistent; a stickler for routine and convention, though a trifle priggish at times, for Virgil's liking. He had always thought so. Aubrey had seemed not to notice, even though it had been pointed out to him on more than the one occasion, but then Aubrey... well, Aubrey had always been a little bumptious for his own good; a pathological egomaniac, even as a child, who rarely took advice well, perhaps even *less* so during the latter days of his life...

"I said, I packed them off to Eton," his wife repeated, on noting the look of vacancy in her husband's eyes.

"Hmm? Oh, good, good," Virgil eventually responded, dragging himself back to the conversation in hand, "best place for 'em, what? The masters there won't have any truck with wimpishness. By the way, how is young Geoffrey's enuresis these days?"

"Virgil, if you mean 'does he still suffer from nocturnal incontinence,' then do please say so. That poor child was witness to things that *no* boy of his age should ever have to experience! However, in time, given a loving godparent's due care and attention, I dare say that he will make a full and boisterous recovery. In the meantime, dressing such a common and, quite obviously temporary symptom up to sound like a documentable indisposition, simply defers the blame for his 'occasional' bedwetting episodes, away from your family and onto the child himself. Not helpful, Virgil, not helpful at all."

Their much-anticipated marital reunion had not gone well, so far, though he was prepared to admit to partial fault on that front. Although he had kept his wife abreast of his mental recovery these past months; through the carefully worded letters that he had sent her, twice weekly during his extended absence, he had not offered her the chance to respond to his regular missives; instead merely imagining her sympathetic replies and taking into account nothing that may have been told to her by unscrupulous busybodies, whose wild revelations he had not been at liberty to disavow. He had expected her to have welcomed him home with an open heart; to have understood that he had had his reasons for leaving so suddenly after returning from his previous disappearance, and to have been happy simply to have picked up from where they had left off. But times, they were a changing; the Martians had seen to that. New ideas were circulating and being acted upon faster than at any time in their species' long history. The sexes were equals in Martian society: with male and female of the 'two thousand', happy to work alongside one another, regardless of the type of toil. Revolution was in the wind; he could feel it, and spreading with every gust. If they were not careful, then in short order, no human marriage would be safe…

"But we have another, more pressing concern than our *god*children," Bea told him, catching his eye for the first time since he had arrived in the entrance hall of number two, Alabaster Square, an hour ago.

Fervently he hoped that she was not about to reacquaint him with the anonymous letter that she claimed to have received some months ago, detailing his dalliances with the ex-inventor royal: the wild card that she had dealt him before his tea had even been drinkable. Yet at the same time he found himself worrying about what *else* she may have the audacity to lay at his door so soon after his humbled return…

"It concerns our daughter," she went on, as he supped nervously at his tea.

"Ethel or Tatiana?" he replied, although the question was hardly likely to have been a conundrum. Ethel, their youngest, had always been the model child: bright and cheerful and ever aware of her feminine function in society. She had married a naval officer from good stock; a man with a clearly defined future, and had so far bagged him both an heir and a spare. Tatiana, on the other hand…

His wife poured them both a second cup; pouting before responding: "Oh, the usual one," as if he really needed to have asked; as if his eldest were not attracted to trouble in the same suicidal way that a moth was to a flame.

Tatiana had never been his favourite, though he had taken great pains to appear to dote on each girl in equal measure; lest he repeat the mistakes that his *own* father had made and risk creating for himself a monster.

Tatiana had always been trouble: a tomboy and a knee scuffer from an early age, she had been the cause of an inordinate amount of stress for the family over the years. A spinster still at twenty-six, it was unlikely now that they would ever see her married off, particularly in light of the last episode, when she had fallen under the influence of a predatory deviant. It had only been through her mother's blue-blooded connections that she had avoided a spell in an asylum!

Instead they had packed her off to Scotland, to stay with his uncle Boothby, a Presbyterian minister on the west coast, where she had worked as his housemaid and secretary ever since. Virgil had only seen her once since then and had been gladdened, on that occasion, to note that her character had appeared transformed by her closer association with the church.

"What do you remember of the 'volunteer' whose legs you transplanted onto the Queen last year?" Bea enquired, changing her thrust and forcing him to recall the last time that he and his wife had been together.

Virgil frowned, unable to make the leap between the Queen's operation for gout and his eldest daughter.

"I thought as much," said Bea, folding her arms across her chest.

"I was not entirely—"

"Yourself, were you about to say?"

"I was under the impression," he responded, firmly; his patience finally beginning to wane, "that we had already established that point."

"That was your *excuse*, yes," she countered, continuing: "'a prostitute': that's what the Secretary told me; nobody of consequence. An inmate of Bedlam. A girl desperate enough to offer up her legs in exchange for her freedom."

"That was what I was told," Virgil agreed, "yes," as he wracked his befuddled mind to recall the details of the day in question, "and a fair exchange, under the circumstances."

It had been the day after his return from the Moon; not that he had known, at the time, that that was where he had in fact been. He had been under the influence of some serious medication; it had been as much as he had been able to do to focus on the job in hand, so he could be forgiven, surely, if he could not even recall the donor's *face*, let alone her name?

"Under the *circumstances*, perhaps. But *I* recognised her," Bea explained, "not immediately, of course; my focus had been on you, at the time, and that odious Secretary, but her face kept coming back to me. I knew I had seen it somewhere before."

Bea had been a guest of the Secretary, that day, and allowed to watch the operation from the viewing gallery. Strange as it may seem, Virgil considered, from above, she had probably had a better view of the patient than he had.

"And would you care to put me out of my misery?"

"Don't tempt me!" Bea snapped through clenched teeth. "It was the deviant who molested our daughter."

"Good God, woman, why did you not tell me sooner! We must get word to uncle Boothby right aw—"

"It's *far* too late for that," Bea croaked; tears beginning to well in the corners of her eyes, "She was here; a week ago, asking for money."

"The *deviant*?"

"No, our little girl! The Halfpenny woman had been in contact with her; heaven *only* knows how she found her! They intend to be together and 'bugger the law'; *her* words, obviously, not mine."

Virgil closed his eyes, lowered his face into his hands, exhaled slowly, then rubbed and lifted his face to look back across the occasional table that sat between them, meeting his now sobbing wife's gaze. Perhaps he had been naive, but he had had such high hopes for this afternoon. Following Henry's murder and his disastrous meeting with his father, just that morning, he had needed something a little positive to show him that his life was still worth living, but things seemed only to be getting worse for him.

"Prey, what are we to do?" he asked in desperation. "If word were to get out, and surely it must, then father would be ruined!"

Bea dried her eyes on her pinafore and glared at her husband.

"Your *father*?" she snapped, "that's the first thing that crosses your mind? Our daughter has taken to *lesbianism* and your only concern is how the news might affect your father's career?" And she stood up, placed her tea cup back on the tray and slunk toward the door, pausing and turning as she reached the threshold, "I've had Radcliffe put your things in the guest room. Dinner is at eight."

* * * * *

"You leave tonight," said the Baron, clapping them both on the shoulder in turn. Tiny winced, but Iggi held firm.

"You know what you have to do," he continued, nodding proudly at his favourite minders as he spoke, "my personal Zeppelin awaits. It will take you to Hamburg, where upon you will board one of our prototype submarines, under the command of—"

"'Old on a mo', y'baronship," Tiny interjected, holding up his hand like a schoolboy who has not quite understood the question put to him.

The Baron paused mid-sentence; his brows rising and his eyes widening.

"But did you jus' say '*submarine*'? As in 'boat wha' goes unda' th'water?"

"A U-Boat, yes, Tiny. We are building a fleet of them—"

"I thought it was *heights* you had a problem with," Iggi interrupted, frowning at her colleague; irritated, but at the same time fighting the urge to smirk, "ever since your ballooning experience?"

"Well, t'tell ya' th'truth," Tiny said through a grimace, "I'm not that keen on eeva." Wringing his hands nervously, he explained: "Not since me dear ol' muvva dropped me in th'sink when I w's bu' a nippa'."

The Baron scoffed.

"But Tiny," he insisted, "you entered my employ on the greatest of recommendations; from Space Captain Gordon Periwinkle himself, no less! You were his batman; his *Sherpa*, were you not? Surely you have conquered far more than a few *phobias* in your time?"

Tiny removed his bowler; bespoke and bijoux, and hung his head, revolving the miniature hat through his fingertips by its rim.

"Well…" he began, falteringly, "I bin in th'capt'in's employ for some time now; i's true, but circ'mstance 'as meant tha' I'm akchally yet t'start work f'r'im."

"You'll be alright," Iggi assured him, "just snaffle your sneeze weed and keep your eyes closed. It won't be for long and I won't let any of that nasty water get you," and she passed him the Luger that she had appropriated from the armoury for him.

"By the way," the Baron said, retrieving a sheet of paper from the file that he had been carrying. On its top left-hand corner had been clipped a small, monochrome photograph.

"Our agent in London supplied us with this, just this morning. *This*," he revealed, tapping at the picture, "is the mysterious 'Queenpins' whose trust you will need to win for this mission to be a success."

"I's a bit *dark*, ain't it?"

"The woman in question," the Baron went on, "is a *Negress*. This picture was taken for the records the day she was committed to Bedlam Asylum. She was released a few months ag—"

"'Ere, lemme see tha'," snapped Mrs Blaise, snatching the file from her lover's grasp. "Fuckin' 'ell; it *is*'n'all! Tha's Tuppence Ha'penny, tha' is! Cor blimey; y'don't wanna go messin' wit' *tha'*, ol' luv! She'd rip yer bleedin' 'ead off an' stuff it up yer arse'ole, wivart even takin' yer 'at off."

"Are you saying that you *know* her, Methusela?" asked the Baron, exasperated, "Why on *Earth*; woman, did you not say so before?"

"Why d'ya' *fink*, y'great 'airy twonk? You 'adn't shown me a pictcha' I could put a name t'before, 'ad ya?"

Mrs Blaise passed the file to Iggi; hoisted the hem of the ornate lace dress that she had taken to wearing when posing as the German Chancellor's consort, and perched her posterior on the corner of his desk.

"Met 'er in Bedlam, I did; quite a characta', tha' one. Arm wrestlin' champion've Elephant'n Castle afore they locked 'er up."

"What w's she in for?" asked Tiny, scrutinising the photograph with a deeply furrowed brow, as if he had never seen a woman of African descent in his life before.

"She 'as a penchant f'chuff," Mrs Blaise replied, causing Tiny to jump and drop the file as if it had been suddenly electrified.

"You ain't scared a'lezzers an'*all*, are y'boy?"

Before Tiny was able to verbalise the face that he was pulling, the Baron clapped his hands to bring them all to attention.

"Then there we have it!" he decided, with a smile. "Our way in, Iggi!"

"With *respect*, sir, cock off!" Iggi replied in the negative.

"But it's perfect!"

"For *whom*?" Iggi snapped, a little too close to his face, she judged, for his comfort.

"But I... we... I thought..."

"Oh, *did* you now!"

"Y'gotta' admit, gel," Mrs Blaise said, coming to the Baron's defence, "th' signs're all there."

"The short hair," said the Baron, seriously.

"All girl school," said Mrs Blaise, her former teacher.

"An' the men's cloves," added Tiny, sheepishly.

"You *too*?" Iggi spat, disgusted with the people who she had been on the verge of considering her friends.

"Well, you were *wrong*, alright! *All* of you!"

"Ah," corralled Mrs Blaise, tapping the side of her Romanesque nose, "but *she* don't know that, does she."

"*No!*"

"Then we shall find another way," affirmed the Baron, "my apologies, Iggi—"

"Fing is," Mrs Blaise countered, "there prob'ly *ain't* anuvva way t'do this. Tuppence'd sniff you two out in seconds, an' you need 'er t'trust 'em. *I'll* 'ave t'go. She *knows* me. We 'ad an undastandin', me an' Tuppence,"

"It's too dangerous—" the Baron began to protest, but Mrs Blaise deftly cut him down.

"Lissen, sausage breath, I jus' dun fifteen years in the 'ardest 'ell 'ole on Earth, so don' y'be talkin' t'me abart dangerous, less'en you're finkin' of playin' snakes'n bleedin' ladders wiv th'man what ate is grandma fer a two-bob bet."

* * * * *

"...And I say, they need to prove their loyalties, like every other citizen of this glorious Empire!"

The Prime Minister rose from his seat, leaning forward across the table; his weight borne by the knuckles of his balled fists. He loomed over the handpicked members of his war council, catching each man's eyes in turn as his own roved the room. "We are at *war*, Mr Secretary, at war," he said; slowly and deliberately and without any hint of emotion, finally coming to linger on one of only two of the room's occupants not to be a serving cabinet minister. "It will be the war to end all wars," he proclaimed, "a war that will eventually see every nation on this planet united under a single sovereign."

Pausing to relight his pipe, Octavian Periwinkle failed to notice the anxious and furtive looks being exchanged between his cohorts at the war room's round table, but the Secretary did not.

"According to the very latest reports from the front," he continued, chugging on his pipe, "we are currently taking heavy losses in North America. We need to replenish this deficit in short order if we are to continue to help the Yanks to *hold* that line, let alone *advance* and retake the stolen states.

"Furthermore, the war office has it on good authority that the Hun are preparing to make good on their threat to bring the battle to our *own* shores. With two thirds of our armed forces already committed overseas, we are in dire need of fodder."

Clamping his pipe between his teeth, he began to stroll around the table; a cloud of smoke following him like a steam train pulling out of a station, "So gentlemen, you will understand the grave dilemma which we currently face and, therefore, my reasons for proposing such an... extraordinary bill at this time."

"But, Prime Minister," blustered Pugh, the Foreign Secretary, who, The *Permanent* Secretary noted, seemed to be having something of a problem with an errant fountain pen, judging by the inky mess of his fingers and the blotted blotter before him, "what you are suggesting, well... it's unconstitutional, at the very *least*; it has no legal precedent! There *have* to be exceptions to such a ruling. For instance, when you say *all* men over sixteen, surely you don't mean to include the sons of *good* families;

of the titled and the land owning; the families of generals and clergymen? There would be *outrage*, sir; the Lords would never agree to such a thing."

Stopping directly opposite him, Octavian paused, took a puff, then withdrew his pipe.

"Well, *obviously*, there would have to be *some* concessions, point well made, Mr Pugh, if the bill were to make it all the way to the statute books. For a start, certain professional occupations would have to be exempted, unless we intend to leave the *women* in charge of everything from medicine to politics?"

He paused again, this time to ride the collective guffaws that his out-dated, chauvinistic comment had incited, "but; by and large, yes: three years compulsory military service for *all* men, living within the bounds of Victoria's Empire, up to the age of… ooh, shall we say… thirty-five? Penalty for noncompliance: military firing squad. If it's good enough for the Hun, then it's good enough for us!"

"Preposterous!" said the mutton-chopped minister for justice, Mr Arthur Balfour. "Doesn't stand a hope! Besides which, this is the *British* Empire. How many *foreigners* have we taken civilisation to: built roads for, and railways, come to that; installed systems of law and order; erected churches and staffed schools for, and precisely *what* have these primitives done for us in return? I move to amend your draft, *sir*; *exempting* those men born in Blighty herself."

"Here, here!"

"Here, here!"

The Prime Minister smiled.

"You propose that we give arms to the natives of countries that we have already *defeated*, sir? Are you *mad*? Precisely *how* would you ensure that they not then turn those weapons on their own governors?"

"Gentlemen, gentlemen," said the new home secretary; a Mr Winston Churchill, in his first contribution to the debate that had been raging this past hour and more, "If I may?"

"The floor is yours, Winnie, old chap; fire away."

"Quite. With respect, I believe that we are missing a trick, here. You see, our workhouses are bulging with the feckless and the down at heel; our prisons stacked with petty criminals whose crimes were often committed against a backdrop of poverty and ignorance, and whom we are feeding and sheltering for currently no positive return. Surely it would make even *more* sense to give *these* idle souls the chance to fill our battle fields; if nothing else but to earn their redemption from society?"

Octavian's smile widened. He had a soft spot for the new boy, the Secretary had noticed. All of the best advice had been to give the post to someone with a proven track record, but Octavian had been insistent on Churchill's appointment.

"You may recall," he responded, more gently than he had done to Pugh, "that Lord Salisbury; my immediate predecessor, had a mind to educate those very same wastrels and loafers, in the hope of breaking them of their inherent torpor. He was defeated by the chamber for the very same reason that *your* amendment would see *this* bill scuppered. It is all very well that these 'n'er-do-wells' *die* a patriotic death for us, but what if they were to *live* to return home? What then, Winnie, old fruit? To train a man to fight and kill and then to let him loose in society when our need for his services has expired, is no different to educating a commoner above his station, as our previous Prime Ministerhad regularly advocated. We would be creating a rod for our own backs, gentlemen; so, no. Keep the prisoners in the prisons; the madmen in the asylums, and let the ordinary man step forward and serve his country. The new law will be called 'National

Conscription' and yes, Mr *Secretary,* I will be expecting those members of the 'Two Thousand' who chose to take lodgings here in England, to play their part. As her illustrious majesty's *liaison* with the Martians, I will leave it with you to work out how best to handle the details.

"Now; if everybody has said their piece on the matter, I would quite like to move on t—"

"I would remind you, *Prime Minister,* that the five hundred Martians who elected to stay in England, are here at Her Majesty's *behest,* working tirelessly to update our factories with superior technologies and to educate our home-grown industrialists in the workings of such machines, in order that we might make this country the very *hub* of mechanised industry for the coming of the new century—"

"Technologies, *sir,*" Octavian insisted, pointing a finger to the ceiling, "that have so far blackened our skies and clogged our air, to the point that no man dare venture abroad without a mask behind which to hide his face! You have your instruction, Mr Secretary: act upon it.

"Now, if we are we all finished?"

He did not wait for a reply and none present responded to his obvious feint of a challenge, "Then I would like to move on to the *second* item on the agenda."

The Secretary smiled, sat back in his chair and folded his arms across his chest. He had not anticipated Octavian's strength of character in the post, having previously dismissed him; regarding him a mere bench-warming, 'Port and cigar' politician, than the unctuous autocrat that he saw emerging before him. Perhaps old Spatchcock had been right about the man, after all? He would have to watch him more closely as he tightened the screws…

"Although it has been eighteen months since the Ripper last struck," Octavian went on, despite the fact that his audience was getting restless. In the same way that a yawn can become contagious, each and every one of them had checked his pocket watch during the past five minutes and raised his eyebrows before closing and replacing it.

"*The Times* would have us believe that the streets of this great city are considered among the most dangerous in the civilised world. With its unnatural plethora of pickpockets, cutthroats and con artists, not to mention, a Fenian and a Bolshevik around every dark corner, these days: is it any wonder that we are so ridiculed in the European papers?

"However, an even greater threat to our national security has begun to emerge in recent months: a home-grown rebellion that could well divide our nation, at the very point when we need to unify it.

"Mr Secretary," he said, moving two cabinet ministers to stir, only to realise that it was toward neither of them that he was staring, "I have asked that the Martian settlers be included in my proposed National Conscription. This is *not*, as you may be thinking, simply because I do not trust their stated motives for coming here; moreover, it is because they are the *focus* of the civil unrest that I fear may well undermine us. Everywhere I go I see hand scrawled signs in the windows of our shops; our public hostelries; our bordellos and our boarding houses, insisting 'NO ALIENS' be admitted. I have seen barges on the Thames float by with the legend: 'ALIENS, GO HOME!' painted onto their tarps. And only yesterday, a gutter snipe was arrested in his attempt to paint the slogan: 'ALIENS OUT!' onto the very door of Number Ten itself!

"The Met have him in custody as we speak: swarthy chap, by all accounts; not even an Englishman! I suggest,

Mr Secretary, that you send a couple of your 'special agents' to retrieve him before the boys in blue render him incapable of revealing any useful intelligence—"

"The matter is already in hand, sir," the Secretary assured him; grinding his teeth as he did so, "rest assured, the Crown Agency already *has* a man on the inside. The Anti-Alien League has been under investigation for some time and shall be brought to heel well before the majority of the public even note their existence."

"Then, gentlemen, that concludes today's 'special session'. Admiral Haversack, a private word before you depart, please…"

* * * * *

"Goodnight, Winnie; my regards to Lady Jennie."

Churchill doffed his Homburg; nodded and smiled politely at the Prime Minister as he passed, before following his fellow ministers out into the corridor that would lead them back toward the Home Office.

"Lady *Jennie*?" enquired the Admiral, as the PM pulled the door of the war room to. It had sounded suspiciously like a code phrase to him; one that he was hitherto unfamiliar with, and as the highest-ranking serviceman on the special advisory council during a time of war, he felt it his business to know as much about *any* given situation as the PM was prepared to impart.

"His *mother*," the Prime Minister replied, dryly, "spectacular woman. Shame old Randolph got to her first."

The Admiral gave a short cough to clear his throat and to announce his intent to shift the conversational emphasis back onto a more professional footing.

"You wanted to speak with me, sir?" he reminded him.

"Take a seat, Harvey."

The Admiral retook the seat that he had only recently vacated; folding his hands on the table in front of him. He watched as the PM lingered in front of the drink's cabinet; his back to the room, finally choosing a bottle of his favourite Irish whiskey, from which he poured two generous measures...

The son of a distinguished Admiral, Harvey Haversack's meteoric rise through the ranks had been noted by the new Prime Minister, whom he had first met at a party, held by the then new Prime Minister, Lord Rosebery, in the March of 1894.

He had begun his career as a soldier, rather than a naval man, as had been the family custom up until that point, with a posting in 1872 to Asante, West Africa, under the command of Sir Garnet Wolseley, where he had been commended for both his bravery and his ingenuity in the field. Upon close of play, had had received his first promotion to lance corporal, with his advance to sergeant coming under the command of Lord Chelmsford, two years later, when he had miraculously survived with only relatively minor injuries in the battle to retake Zululand. In the September of '82; back under the command of Wolseley, he had been promoted once again, to captain, as his unit was honoured for defeating Arabi Pasha's army and helping to reinstate the pro-British ruler, Tewfik, in Egypt.

A spell in military intelligence had followed this, during which, one particular secret mission had seen him loaned to the Americans where, in order to help demoralise the trade union movement, he had bombed a labour rally.

However, despite his exemplary record; in private he was a less confident individual than those around him might have realised; one who often felt that he had thrived, merely due to his having an uncanny knack for being in the right place at the right time. In situations where he found himself called upon to offer strategic, military advice to civil servants, for instance; men, often many years his senior, who had them*selves* seen active service in either India or the Crimea. He often found that such pressure gave rise to an internal quandary, regarding his right to the position that he held at such a young age, though outwardly he made sure to keep his feelings of inadequacy firmly in check.

His unusual elevation had, in part, been due to his being promoted to the then recently fledged space programme; his immediate predecessor's untimely death in the role, and, of course, the man in front of him now; his 'unofficial' sponsor: his wife's grandfather, Octavian Periwinkle…

"Your thoughts, Harvey, a penny for them," urged the Prime Minister, placing a glass on the table in front of him, "strictly off the record, of course. I need to know where you stand on the alien question."

"The 'alien question'?" the Admiral queried.

"Precisely," the PM affirmed, "I don't like 'em. I don't like 'em at *all*, Harvey, and I don't trust 'em; any more than I either like or *trust* that damned Permanent Secretary. But most of all, they're a bloody inconvenience."

The Admiral raised his eyebrows. Over the eighteen months or so that he had been posted in London, he had been yet to speak to *anyone* who either liked or trusted Montgomery Plumb-Prendergast, but none would have dared voice such an opinion, lest the 'Ripper of Whitehall' turn his attentions on them.

"If I didn't know better," the PM went on, "I'd say the bounder was in *league* with them."

"That is… quite a claim, sir."

"Well? Permission to speak freely, Admiral. What's y'take?"

"On the Secretary or the aliens, sir?"

"The aliens, a'course! No one likes the Secretary."

Harvey thought hard before responding. Although he was aware that in some circles, such thoughts might have been considered treasonous; truth be known, he neither liked nor trusted Octavian Periwinkle, nor many of the *other* Periwinkles that he had so far met.

"They are a distraction," he eventually admitted, "a potentially dangerous distraction, that we could well do without at this time." He paused to sip his whisky before continuing, "I don't trust them, but then it is my *job* not to trust *any* foreign national. They are technologically superior to the human race and, although they have so far professed to be a peaceable species, we cannot yet rule out the fact that this may not *always* be the case. I would *strongly* advise not picking a fight with a force whose strengths and weaknesses yet remain a mystery to us. We should be cautious, as I suggested when first contact was made, and vigilant. I understand that the Secretary has sent agents to monitor those aliens who opted to live and work in the continental colonies?"

"You are correct," said the PM, "and I heartily agree that we dare not move against them at this time. However," said before throwing back the remainder of his own drink, "I believe that this would be an expedient time to... shall we say *provoke* them; to poke a stick into their nest and see how they respond?"

"Sir?" the Admiral enquired, having felt sure that he had just explicitly advised *against* such an action.

The Prime Minister smiled, obviously sensing his reticence to condone whatever his superior might be of a mind to suggest.

"You were seconded to military intelligence for a while, Harvey, were you not?"

"You know I was, sir; that was, after all, how I came to meet Ethel and yourself."

"So it was. And in 'military intelligence' you were often *used*; as I believe the American *government* used you in Chicago in '86, to carry out 'deniable' acts, both at home and abroad?"

He would not have been worthy of his rank if he had not been able to see quite where their 'off the record' conversation was headed.

"Yes, sir."

"Then you will understand *fully*, I am sure, that which I am about to ask of you…"

* * * * *

In 1829; during the second of his two tenures as Home Secretary, future Prime Minister Robert Peel had lain down the cornerstone of what would eventually become 'The Metropolitan Police Force'. It was an idea that he had lifted from the Secretary's predecessor; the Martian infiltration agent (code named 'Uncle'), who had created 'the Crown Agency': a force of highly trained, thoroughly dependable and utterly incorruptible specialist law enforcers answerable only to Victoria herself, during the second year of her long reign.

The Secretary had little time for what 'the peelers' had become over recent years; considering them no lesser thugs and footpads than the bottom feeding miscreants who they spent their days in pursuit of.

To his mind, there was but one exception to this rule: Chief Inspector Frederick George Abberline; the detective who he had been moved to take to task over his investigation of the Ripper murders, a decade ago. Abberline, he had quickly discovered, had been in possession of a dose more 'nouse' than the average street-walking bobby was likely to have been gifted, and his investigations into the Whitechapel murders had been straying a little too close to the truth for the

Crown's comfort. The Secretary's long-term plans would not have withstood the killer's identity being made public at that time, and, as he could not trust his pawn not to aid the police in their unravelling of the wider conspiracy, should he have found himself apprehended; he had been forced to intervene in person. The Chief Inspector had not taken kindly to the Secretary pulling rank on him, though as a patriotic man; one who clearly respected the chain of command that he had chosen to work within, he had done what had been required of him without due debate and had, to that day, kept his findings to his chest...

"I will take it from here, sergeant."

"Oh, *will* ya' now? An' 'oo mights *you* be, then, eh?"

The visitor sighed audibly as he removed his gloves; relieving each finger in turn, slowly, from left to right.

"If you would be so good as to inform Inspector Abberline that the *Secretary* is on the premises and does not wish to be disturbed for the next half an hour—"

"'Oose secret'ry'd *that* be then, eh? Nah, come on; gertcha: out y'g—"

Rarely had the Secretary found the need to visit Scotland Yard in person in the intervening years, and so, unlike his standing within the Gothic corridors of Westminster or the hallowed halls of the royal palaces, his face here amongst the 'boys in blue' was not a passport to instantaneous servility.

Releasing his hold on the sergeant's windpipe, he reiterated his introduction with emphasis on the definitive article: "*The* Secretary," he explained, unambiguously, gently allowing the man's feet to kiss the floor, then, once more bear the full weight of his overindulged belly.

"You are relieved, sergeant," said an unseen voice from outside the cell: a speech pattern that the Secretary recognised instantly, even though its bearer could be seen only in silhouette, backlit, through the crack in the door, "our 'visitor' has twenty minutes. If he is still here after that, then you and your boys have my permission to *explain* to him the *proper* procedures in an investigation of this kind."

"Right y'are, guv," said the sergeant, rubbing his throat as he closed the door behind him...

"Abdul," said the Secretary, unusually addressing his prime agent by his given name; the name that he had been arrested under, "I received your message, though next time perhaps you could choose a slightly less 'anarchic' target? Our new Prime Minister is not as easily assuaged as his predecessors, and the League's activities are beginning to worry him. I don't need him believing that matters are getting so out of hand that he feels the need to go behind my back."

"Yes, boss. Sorry, boss."

"Now, you have information for me: a command structure at the very *least*; names, *Some*thing I can *work* with?"

The agent smiled: a broad, toothy grin that told his master that his past six weeks in deep cover, infiltrating and gaining the trust of the leaders of the Anti-Alien League, had not been in vain.

"Their leader, you *know*, though it will be surprise, I think."

The Secretary sat back in his chair and folded his arms, raising his left eyebrow.

"Well?"

"The one known as 'Queenpins' – *real* name: Tuppence Halfpenny."

The Secretary frowned. Of all the known anarchists and agitators currently at large, *this* was not a name that he had expected to hear.

"It's pronounced 'Ha'penny'," he advised, "and you're *sure* about this, yes? She's not just a lieutenant or a contact?"

"She is big boss," Abdul confirmed, "and little boss is called 'Charna'."

"Charna? Not a name that we know. Male or female?"

Abdul's smile widened ever further as he removed his tattered fez and retrieved a several times folded piece of paper that had been pinned inside.

"All here," he said, passing the note to his employer.

Abdul had been correct: The Ha'penny woman *was* known to them, but merely as a treasonable malcontent, and one who had already been 'dealt with'. This new schismatic persona warranted further, immediate investigation...

Tuppence Halfpenny was a deviant; at least, by the sexual standards that these people had set for themselves at this stage in their evolution, and one who had made no attempt to hide her proclivities by marrying herself a 'beard', as society lesbians had been doing since time immemorial. As the daughter of a former slave and her somewhat 'cosmopolitan' master, her uncommon pigmentation had ensured that the only work available to her be either deep below stairs, or deep beneath the sweaty mass of a cabinet minister with a penchant for the exotic, and thus, he had always presumed, her 'beard' acquiring fortunes severely limited.

It was quite probable that, due to the regular services that she provided for the 'members', she would have been allowed to have continued with her distasteful lifestyle, underided, but she had made one rather unfortunate tactical error. She had fallen in love with the daughter of the Surgeon General; his wife a minor member of the royal line. To this end, she had been committed to Bedlam for life, only recently being released, when she had been offered a macabre trade in exchange for her freedom…

"You have done well," the Secretary admitted, tucking the note into his top pocket, "Is your hand still loaded?"

"One shot left,"

The Secretary dug into his breast pocket and pulled out six bullets, which he rolled across the table toward him.

Abdul retrieved them, putting two into his own pocket and slotting the others directly into a slot on the wrist of his artificial hand.

"Stay here for one hour," the Secretary informed him, and then shoot your way out. I know it's tempting, but *do* try *not* to kill a police officer. You know how to contact me when you have more information."

The Secretary left the station; relinquishing control of the prisoner to the duty sergeant, and hailed himself a SteamSteed on the kerb outside.

Abdul had done well; the information that he had relayed, being of greater value than anything that the regular security service had managed to attain in twice the time frame. He had many such deep-cover agents in play around the world at any given time, gathering and coding information for him and sending it back via the repurposed Martian transmitter that he kept hidden in the basement of the Palace of Westminster. Initially, this task had fallen under the remit of The Cell's technical support team: the technicians that had been stationed on the Moonbase; those same technicians that Virgil Periwinkle had recently both killed and eaten. However, this more 'hands-on' approach to intelligence collation had been instigated long before the Surgeon General's cannibalistic faux pas, having been necessitated by the humans' discovery of radio waves back in '86, and it had since proved to be a perfectly adequate substitute; under the circumstances, for the accumulation of time-sensitive data.

The majority of his agents were like Abdul: trained in the arts of deceit, disguise and espionage, but there were others: ordinary people who he had abducted and 'altered', before sending back into the field as 'sleepers'; unaware of their status until such time as they could be of use to him. They could then be activated through the 'Pilot Discs' that he had placed inside their skulls, and operated remotely through manipulation of the device that he always kept on the end of a chain in his Westcott pocket.

Closing the cab's door behind him, the Secretary sank down into the seat therein and removed the device from his pocket. He smiled to himself: the smile of a man who knows exactly where in the pack the ace of spades is hiding. He had chosen well with this particular sleeper, having had no idea quite how conveniently she might later have become placed. Tapping the roof of the cab with the heel of his cane, he eased back into his seat and pressed the activation button...

CHAPTER FIVE:

NO SUCH THING AS COINCIDENCE

"Anything?"

"Nothing. It is as The Greckle suggested: she appears, simply, to have disappeared."

Whilst Alyce had been accessing the records: a series of transparent celluloid slides that had to be enlarged under a microscope before they could be read, Gordon had been perusing the drawers, the shelves and the many ransacked cupboards that ranged the walls of the abandoned communications tower, in search of something distinctly Martian that he might 'borrow' in order to display in the trophy room of The Adventurers', back home. He had heard Alyce describe the records system to Hamble as 'Micro fish'; which had seemed to him, an unlikely way to store information, and after that, as would often happen when people began to talk of technical things in his presence, his mind had begun to wander.

"It is most strange," said Alyce, as he sifted through a pile of papers, inked in a script that, to him, could have been Cyrillic or Greek or even Chinese, "but there *should* be mention of her *here* at least. I have accessed the scientifica's data base, but can find no record of a Professor Boff ever having existed. Oh…"

"'Oh' *what?*" asked an intrigued Hamble, as Gordon alighted upon an instrument that looked like a wireless, but which would have been far too small for purpose, "What in the *world* is a 'database'?" He asked, but Alyce ignored him.

"Tell me what you remember of The Greckle's explanation of the professor's discovery," she asked instead.

Hamble's pause concerned Gordon, as he had been wracking his own mind just as Alyce had questioned his friend, but had so far also drawn a blank. This had not unduly surprised him, but *Hamble's* reaction had.

"I can't... I don't seem to be able to... It's *there*; I can see it, but it's *slippery*, and I can't *focus* on it! It's as if someone were trying to steal the very thoughts from my head!"

Alyce was smiling now, just as the furrow on his own brow was deepening.

"Do you not *see*?" she insisted, "She *is* here; she is *alive*, and we now have the answer to how her technology works!"

"We *do*?" a thoroughly confused Gordon queried, idly fiddling with the buttons on the device's frontage.

"Oh, yes!" exclaimed Hamble. "She's used the machine recently, hasn't she? Reality has shifted and we're caught in the eddy as reality resets itself!"

"We would probably not have been aware had we not have been in the process of researching her at the time!" said Alyce, whilst scribbling frantically onto a piece of paper that Gordon could have *sworn* had not been blank a moment ago.

"I think I'm getting this," he said, edging his way into the girls' conversation, "the last time I was in London, the talk of the scientific set was of 'MCUs'. Now, let me see—"

"Multiple Concurrent Universes," Hamble translated for him, as if the fashionable theory had also been at the forefront of her own thoughts.

"That's the fellow!" acknowledged Gordon, "Well, the idea went—"

"—that every major event sparks a split in causality, giving birth to a parallel universe where everything hinges on a different outcome to said event?" offered Hamble.

"Yes," Gordon agreed, slightly deflated, "*that*. Well, that's what *we* thought the professor was *doing*, wasn't it?"

"Creating alternative versions of the here and now," concluded Alyce. "Yes, but we were wrong. It *is* a time machine after all; she is using it to rewrite *history*!"

"Damn shame," Gordon replied, "I won't pretend to understand the ins'n outs of the whole thing, but I must say, I was quite sold on the notion that there might be other '*me's*, out there; maybe some who've made one or two better choices than the original; perhaps even one who managed to get it on with me sister-in-law, Ah...said that out loud, didn't I?"

Without even the slightest warning, the device in Gordon's hand suddenly burst into life; a gruff, male voice blaring from the grill on its back. In his shock, Gordon lobbed the box into the air, only for Hamble to catch it, a gnat's whisker before it hit the floor.

"What're they saying?" snapped Hamble, passing it to Alyce.

"They know where we are and their orders are to 'shoot to—'"

"Over here!" called Gordon, beckoning the girls towards a cupboard that he had investigated earlier on the far side of the room.

"I think we're *past* 'hide'n seek'!" snapped Hamble, flapping her arms like a penguin hoping to kick evolution into reverse, "I can hear them on the stairs!"

"No, he is right!" said Alyce, gathering up her notes and hooking Hamble's arm as she passed; leading her towards Gordon, "Look! It is an elevator!"

Alyce pushed Hamble inside and closed the door behind them. There was a cage door on the inside that had to be closed before the manual ratchet handle on the side wall could be operated, in a similar fashion to the paternoster lifts of home. Once secured, Gordon began turning for all that he was worth; the descending cage clearing the bottom of the wooden door above, scant seconds before several bullets blew through it to impact on the back wall.

"*Faster!*" screamed Hamble, bracing herself against the sides.

"I'm going as fa—"

"Let *go!*" shouted Alyce.

"*Really?*"

"YES! Both of you, climb up the sides of the cage!"

As they did so, the speed of their fall increased.

"BRACE FOR IMPACT!" Alyce shouted, above the furious ticking of the released ratchet, "…Aaaand JUMP!"

All three of the elevator's occupants jumped; half a second before the cage connected with the ground, to land in a heap on the floor, though slightly less jarred than they would otherwise have been.

Alyce held the transmitter to her chest, protecting it from the impact. A voice crackled from its speaker; distant and less distinct than it had been before.

"They don't know which level we're on, but they're hoping it's not the lowest, as nobody wants to risk coming this far down. They *will*, though; once they've checked all the others, so we'd better get moving."

* * * * *

"Where are we?" asked Tiny, shakily, from his cramped corner in the dingy confines of the stern; a position that he had held, without moving for anything more than to scratch his arse or to shiver in the cold with the rest of them, for the entire thirty-two hour journey across the

North Sea: bent double against the curve of the iron rib, looking for all the world like a giant prawn in a bowler hat.

They had spent the majority of the trip skimming the waves, as the miniature submersible was able to move faster when surfaced than it could whilst submerged, which had been something of a disappointment to Iggi as she had never ridden a submarine before and, unlike Tiny, she had been quite looking forward to savouring a new experience. They had finally dipped to 'covert mode' with the lights of Southend in sight, entering the Thames estuary; she had noted, at a reduced speed of seven point three knots for the final leg of their journey up river.

"S'nt Katharine Dock, by the looks of it," she replied, squinting into the periscope that bobbed and dipped, just above the waterline. She felt a wave of something comforting engulf her; a peculiar, happy feeling that she could not quite put her finger on, as she surveyed the view of London, as ordinarily only seen by the floating gulls that had strayed upstream in search of an easy meal.

She was home. She had not previously appreciated the hold that this ancient Roman city had over her. She could not even recall particularly *liking* the place before leaving it, but it had been where she had first been found, swaddled in a blanket; wrapped in her dead mother's arms, on the grimy stone steps of 'St Barrabus Academy for Stray Girls'; not so very far from where they were now, and therefore an affinity that she had previously been unaware of must obviously have developed.

Suddenly, the lens went black, as something bulky drifted across in front of it. Squinting further in order to focus on the obstruction, she jumped as; just for a moment, she saw an eye staring back at her; a cold, dead, unblinking eye, which she realised was attached to the head and thus the body of a bloated; partially eaten 'floater'.

"Yep," she confirmed; looking back over her shoulder at her two companions, "definitely London."

Mrs Blaise was again perched over the porcelain chamber pot, in the narrow and worryingly damp footwell between opposing bench seats; an unhealthy-looking strain on her face as if she were studying a detail on the wall ahead, in the dim, emerald glow of the dashboard lights.

"Fuckin' alien shite 'as give' me the *clap*," she answered, though Iggi had been sensitive enough not to have asked the question.

The captain, who had uttered not a single word since they had left the port of Hamburg, and, now that she thought about it, had even received the unlikely trio in silence on the dockside before that, merely saluting as they descended into the tub, pulled the creaking sub into a roughly forty-five degree turn to starboard, bumping against the bloater, which snagged against the stalk of the periscope. Thus, it accompanied them in to a covered boat shed, whereby they broke the surface as the captain steered them toward the pier.

"Sheisse!" said the captain, breaking his unwritten vow as he struggled to unwind the hatch in the roof.

Her eye back against the periscope, Iggi was quick to spot the problem.

"There's a sodden body straddling that hatch, heavy with the weight of London's sewage," she explained, turning to the captain, "er... Tauchen?" she said, attempting to recall what little guardroom German she had managed to absorb over the past few months and hoping that she had just told him to submerge rather than to swan dive, "untertauchen?" she attempted to clarify, but the captain seemed to have understood her meaning and nodded his affirmation. But just as he reached his control board, they felt as well as heard a heavy 'clunk' from above, as if something solid had just landed atop them. The wheel of the hatch that had previously been stuck fast then suddenly began to spin free, opening them up to the rank London air.

The captain was the first to poke his head up through the aperture, releasing as he did so, the collective stink of more than a day's worth of circulating sweat; urine and flatulence as he ascended the ladder, though it was rapidly replaced with the stench of rotting fish and... something sharp; tangy and acidic that Iggi could not easily identify.

The three 'agents' followed him up and out onto the quayside, where, in what light in the gloom was afforded by a handheld gas lamp, Iggi was just about able to make out three spectral figures; each in a dark, floor-length cloak and what appeared to her to be 'plague masks', as remembered from her lessons of the city's past.

"Here," said the closest of the figures, his accent betraying his Germanic heritage. He passed them each a similar face covering to those of their own and demonstrated their use, "You vill need to vear zeze. Za city iz not az you might remember it; a lot haz changed zince za arrival of za... außerirdischer. I am Herr Ludwig, head of zecurity at za embazzy. I vill be your contact here in London; anysink you need, I vill endeavour to supply for you, but I vould ask you not to vizit za embassy unlez in abzolute emergenzy."

As he spoke, the other two members of his party were helping Tiny and Mrs Blaise into their masks. She heard an: "Oi, 'ooknose, wha' the fuc—" from her former teacher, with whatever else she may have had to say on the subject, thankfully muffled by the mask.

It seemed that the masks were of a 'one-size-fits-all' design, which saw the aide assigned to Tiny having to whittle a few extra holes into the leather straps of his, owing to her friend's particularly small head.

"You vill need to change za filterz daily," Ludwig informed them, "or elz za pollution vill kill you. Night-time iz za vurst time, but I vould advize you to vear it venever you are abroad. Zare are spare filterz in za bag; a zmall purz of coin for za purchase off ezzential comeztablez; a British made veapon und ze timer devizefor ze explozivz zat you vill deliver to za anarchien."

Iggi nodded; awkward in what he explained was a 'Rebreazer'.

"Ve are alvays being vatched, agent," he said, passing her a note, "hence za body in za vater. Captain Himmler vill now take you furzer up river. Good luck, agent Schwartz. Heil Greckle!"

The next time the sub surfaced it was against a short wooden pier in the shadow of Blackfriars Bridge. Iggi unfolded the note that Ludwig had given her and read: 'YE OLDE CHESHIRE CHEESE'.

She knew the pub well, but few Londoners would not at least have heard its name, since Dickens had immortalised it in his *Tale of Two Cities*. As well as Dickens, it was and always had been, the haunt of many a celebrated wordsmith, along with its fair proportion of scum and villainy; not that the two professions were mutually exclusive! Known as a place 'to be seen', it was, therefore, equally a place to disappear, as who would notice that bolting cutpurse amongst such infamous regular patrons as Arthur Conan Doyle and Alfred Tennyson?

It was only a short walk from the pier: up to Fleet Street and then to the second of its four courts, but it was made much harder going by the decreased visibility.

"Where did all this fog come fr'm?" asked Tiny, from close to Iggi's left ear, though she could barely make him out walking beside her.

"If you believe the Germans, it has something to do with the Martians," she replied, considering herself nasal, speaking from behind her mask, "You still behind us, Mrs Blaise?"

"Nah; few steps in front," confirmed the old woman, adding: "Now, when we gets in there, best you leave the intra ductions t'me. Tupps 'as a mean temper on 'er, on accounts of 'er 'avin' a 'uge chip on 'er shoulda'."

Iggi chose not to argue with her. It was, after all, the reason that she had come with them, though she felt it highly probable that she could have held her own quite adequately against the undisciplined fruitcake that she imagined their contact to be...

The ceilings of Ye Olde Cheshire Cheese were low, which meant that the level of ambient tobacco smoke hung lower than in the pubs and hostelries that had been built after the 1600s, when the average punter was generally of taller stock.

They unclipped the front pieces of their masks, but kept their hats on as they made their way through the bar. Apparently, today was their lucky day. To their right, occupying an un-curtained booth with two other distinguished looking gents and a pair of ladies of dubious comportment attracting a fair amount of attention from the bar's other customers, sat the American scribbler, Samuel Clemens; better known to his readers as Mark Twain. He was holding court, as was his wont whenever he was in town, she knew, and so, whilst Tiny found them a table with an unobstructed view of both the front door and the door to the next room, Iggi ordered up the first round, unremarked upon by those who may ordinarily have slipped surreptitiously from the room at having clocked her mug.

"Did they say she comes 'ere ev'ry night, then?" Tiny enquired, as Iggi returned with their drinks, "only we could be a long time waitin' if it's jus' somewhere she's been seen."

Iggi took a long gulp of her beer, smiling to herself. German beer just was not the same!

"She'll be 'ere," Mrs Blaise confirmed, returning from her sweep of the establishment's other nooks and crannies, "Found this in th'gents khazi,"

"Mef, y'can't go snoopin' in the *gents*; 't 'aint right!"

"Well, they ain't *got* one f'rus an' I needed a waz!"

Mrs Blaise passed the hand bill to Iggi whose smile grew wider.

"Local league *arm* wrestling?" she said, frowning, "tonight."

"I 'ad a discreet word round," Mrs Blaise continued, gingerly taking a seat and draining her glass in one, jaw-dislocating gulp, "Tupps is the local champ, so if'n she don't show, she forfeits 'er claim an' 'as t'star' over ag'in."

As if following a prearranged cue, the door then swung open and in walked a tall, lithe looking woman in a floor-length duster and a brown bowler hat perched atop a mass of unruly blonde curls and adorned with the distinctive fawn and white wing of a barn owl. Her skin betrayed a heritage halfway between Angola and Iggi's own country of origin; glowing golden in the light from the fireplace and marking her out as an exotic element amongst the other drinkers. Yet the most fascinating detail of all was not the fact that, like Iggi herself, she wore the type of clothes more commonly suited to a man of that era than a woman, but, moreover, her legs. But for the whirring cogs and gears that ran down the outside of her brass-plated shins like an insectoid exoskeleton, forming ever cycling spurs where her natural ankle joints should have been, one may have presumed that she wore the most elaborately over decorated boots to be found in all of London, but Iggi knew better; recognising the handy work of Hamble Blaise the instant that she saw it. Her left hand touched her own right, remembering when she too had possessed such an exquisite artificial appendage.

Two cohorts accompanied the woman: one male, she decided, the other not so; the features of both still hidden by their masks.

"Lady'n gen'leman," Mrs Blaise announced to the table, drumming her fingers against its top, "I gives ya', Tuppence 'A'pe'ney…"

* * * * *

If he had not just survived a nerve jangling, two hundred or so foot plummet, down a shaft that had been hollowed through solid rock; inside a cage that had promptly collapsed the moment he had stepped from it, then Gordon would have found it hard to believe that what he was looking at now was indeed an underground city at all.

Subterranean metropoli abounded in the lesser exploited corners of the Earth, but rarely were they more elaborate than a few chiselled porticos and hand chipped burrows, built as either tombs or shelters or places to store unwanted statues and boxes of treasure. Quite frankly, he mused, once you had explored one necropolis, you had pretty much explored them all. This, however, was a world away from the barrows and mausoleums that he had previously discovered; quite literally…

If Gordon had idly expected an abandoned Martian city to have resembled the plans that he had seen for London's new underground railway network, then he would quite rightly have deserved the kick in the teeth that he felt that he had just had. The lift had deposited them inside what at first sight had appeared to be a large, glasshouse; indicative of something that he might have expected to have found at Kew, stuffed full of butterflies and exotic plants from around the world, like they had been when he had visited with his father, an age ago. However, of plants and insects, *this* glasshouse was bereft; exotic or otherwise. On closer inspection it seemed to be merely a continuation of the room at the other end of the shaft; similar looking 'futuristic' machines adorning the desks, and an abundance of abandoned paperwork littering the floor. Through the tall glass panels he could see down onto the world below; surveying it like a god from his spectacularly appointed position. He could have been standing on the roof of The Café Royal, looking out and down over Piccadilly Circus and all the great Georgian buildings that made that particular junction of roads, famous the world over, for this was no mere underground tunnel system, like he had witnessed on the upper levels; it was a proper bricks and mortar modern city, on a par with London, but one that had been built beneath a huge, stone umbrella! It had been planned too, and then added to organically, over time; judging by the variations in design and materials used–

"GORDON!" he heard Alyce call, insistently, from somewhere behind him, hauling him from his reverie, "We need you!"

They all did eventually, he mused; turning back toward the lift from which he had been thrown; amazingly intact.

"Quickly!" Alyce urged, beckoning him toward a prostrate Hamble who had clearly not had the same lucky landing that he had.

"Corks!" he exclaimed. "Is she alright?"

"No," Alyce replied, "she is not. I believe her left leg to be broken, possibly also her hip. Here, hold this; I am attempting to stem the bleeding—"

"You're bleeding yourself!"

"I am aware, thank you. My earlier wound has reopened and I believe I have broken this arm as I am struggling to move it. Also, I do not seem to be able to stand on this foot."

It was not unusual for Gordon to walk away from a near disaster unharmed; it happened all the time. He had always put it down to the Sherpa's Code, which explicitly stated that a Sherpa should endeavour wherever possible, to throw himself into the path of trouble; taking the bullet meant for his master, every time. He had lost a lot of Sherpas in the field over the years in this way, but had never forgotten their sacrifice and had always made sure to do the decent thing by their families. Barring the bullet that Abdul had put clean through his shoulder, back on the Moon, the year before, and which was still surprisingly tender to the touch, he, however, had barely even faced a scratch in all these years; luck seeming to favour him like the man who has learned to cultivate the four leafed clover.

"This is the surveillance hub," Alyce explained, I used to work in one similar to this before I was posted to your Moon. There should be an emergency kit on the wall by the door. Can you fetch it?"

Carefully extracting his hands from beneath Hamble's head, Gordon headed toward the door, which, he noted subconsciously, was ajar.

"Found it," he called back, as he wrestled in his panic to extract the box from the catches that held it in place.

Without warning, a hand suddenly shot through the gap in the door, clamping down firmly over his own. Instinctively, Gordon tried to pull away, but his attacker's grip was firm and he found himself forced backwards into the room by a short, wizened Martian, who held the index finger of their free hand to their pursed lips.

"Time is short," the interloper said. "Please forgive the impropriety, but if I release your hand, you will hear me speaking to you in Martian rather than human."

"Professor Boff?" presumed Alyce.

"At your service," said the Martian, "I would have come to your aid sooner, but it took time to extricate your exact position from the records and I had to complete my work on this translator device first. I apologise, Gordon, but it only works whilst we are touching palm to palm."

"You *know* me?" was all that he could think of to reply. "Has my fame spread so far?"

"I know *all* of you," the professor replied, dragging Gordon with her as she knelt by Hamble and Alyce. "I know who sent you; why you came here and *what* will happen to you if you don't come with me now."

"I am not sure that we should move her," said Alyce.

"We have to," said Boff. "She dies here from her wounds in thirty cycle's time; we need to break that event. You, Alyce will be shot dead by the planetary defence team shortly afterward, whilst trying to protect Gordon, and Gordon later cracks under torture."

Neither Gordon nor Alyce had an answer.

"Gordon!" Boff snapped, "wake up. Fetch the stretcher that I left in the corridor. We only have a few cycles."

Something solid clanged against the roof of the lift cage.

"Smoke grenade," said Boff, "now move!"

* * * * *

"Was it someth'n' Ah said?" asked Mr Twain of his fawning companions, as his audience's interest in his story was abruptly stolen by the Cheapside arm wrestling champion's arrival; breezing past his booth like a disconnected minor royal at the opening of a new workhouse. The writer laughed off his obvious embarrassment, loudly ordering another round of drinks whilst the stragglers tagged onto the conga line that followed in Halfpenny's wake; Iggi, Tiny and Mrs Blaise adding to their number as the throng passed their table...

The back room was dark and already crammed with more punters than Iggi would have believed possible by the time the trio stepped through the door. At its centre sat a small, square, table-for-two; the room's only light source: a dim electric bulb, dangling by its cord above it, wearing a broad rimmed cardboard shade.

The table was ringed by two rows of stools; mainly catering for fans who might have been of the 'fairer' sex, behind which stood two rows of standing punters and behind *them*, raised on a wooden platform in order to slightly elevate their eye line, were three further, shoulder-to-shoulder lines of docker types, each one holding a brimming tankard and their preferred choice of smoke.

Their target was already in position on the far side of the table; a table, she noticed, set for a championship-level match. Iggi knew the rules well enough: the ability to be able to arm wrestle being a required discipline for agents of the Crown. She had been good at it too, but sadly, when she had been fitted with her prosthetic arm, she had been instantly disqualified from participating; contenders being barred from wearing affectations or adornments of any kind below the elbow during a match.

Two chalk elbow rings had been drawn around a bottle to the right of each position with a line drawn horizontally across the centre of the table, effectively cutting the field of play in half; knuckles 'pinned' to either side of this line, denoting a win.

"Good evening, ells'n gees," said a squat, stout man in a tattered topper and a garish, multi-coloured Westcott which strained at its three remaining buttons and whose mug was definitely familiar to Iggi from back in her agency days, though his name and list of crimes currently defied her powers of recall. "Welcome to the all London League Arm Wrestlin' Championships, 1898," which elicited a roar of excitement from all those gathered, "you all know the rules," he continued, strutting around the table like a complacent cockerel in a coop full of broody hens, "no spittin'; no bitin' an' no throwin' stuff at the comba'ants. Queenpins is in the chair an' she *stays* there 'til ev'ryone 'oo *wants* a go, 'as 'ad a go. Are we ready t'fight?"

Another roar of approval preceded the arrival of the first contender; a mountain of a man with a gorse like beard, so obfuscating of his facial features that he would probably not have needed to wear a Rebreather outside in the smog.

"Arry Arbuthnott'; as the compere introduced him, took his place opposite the reigning champion; raised both his hands above his hairless head and wiggled his woolly fingers to show the crowd that he had nothing to hide. He then proceeded to crack each of his knuckles in turn in a vain attempt, Iggi presumed, to intimidate his opponent.

"'Arry is the reigning champion of 'Ackney Marshes," the compare revealed, "a docker by trade, 'e enjoys dog racin'; bare knuckle fightin' an' crochet. Are we ready?"

Another roar went up and Iggi saw Tiny remove his hat and drain a line of ale from its brim, courtesy of one of the over excited revellers who had followed in behind them.

"Both feet on the floor,
thumb knuckles to the fore.
Shoulders square;
le's keep this fight fair... READY?"

Elbows within their respective chalk marks; hands clenched over the centre line, the battle for the title commenced; the crowd shouting their near deafening support for whomever they were the most afraid of.

The two hands held firm: locked together like the two plates of a steam press, shaking slightly, but neither side showing signs of ever breaking that deadlock.

Fifty seconds in and a bead of sweat suddenly appeared on Arbuthnott's bald head, springing from just above his wiry eyebrows to drip in a continuous line, down over his face, only to be lost in the thicket of his curly black beard. Another drop followed suit, this from a little farther back on his pate; another and another, yet still their grip barely wavered.

Opposite him and showing no sign of being 'fairer', Halfpenny began to smile. She reached out with her free hand; lifted her tankard and took a swig. Arbuthnott frowned and it was this momentary dip in concentration that lost him the round.

"FOUL!" he argued.

"Bollocks, was it!" spat the compere, "round two. Ready?"

Their elbows back on their marks, the second round began, but Iggi could see that the challenger had lost his confidence, and it only took the champion half the time that it had taken in the first to defeat the East End pretender, hands down.

It was a 'best of three' score and so Arbuthnott graciously conceded; shook the winner's hand; grabbed his coat and stalked through the assembled, last seen heading for the bar.

"Next up," announced the compere, pulling a list from his back pocket, "is Dilbert Davenport: three times champion of The Isle Of Dogs; chief enforcer for Mungo Jones, the infamous Docklands Drowner; his interests include, knocking up concrete; tying knots and sewing sackcloth.

Both feet on the floor,
thumb knuckles to the fore.
Shoulders square,
le's keep this fight fair... READY?"

Davenport also lost in the second round, distracted by the coyest of winks; not from Halfpenny herself this time, but from one of her two cronies, who by this point in the proceedings had removed their masks to reveal two striking *female* faces: one, for the unmissable; near perfectly horizontal scar that slashed her features from ear to ear, and the other; the distractor, for the confidence and nobility of her set; something that Iggi was well aware, was evident *only* in those of high breeding.

The compere introduced three more contenders: representing the constituencies of Tobacco Dock Fitzrovia and Somers Town; the first and third of which, following the exact same pattern as before, but the second; Fitzrovia's challenger, one Orville Fortescue, smashing out in the first round with a badly broken wrist.

"Before'n I reconfer the title," the compare announced, giving the reigning champion the chance to down a fresh pint, "it is tradishnal on these occasions t'open th'floor ta' any uvva comers. Do I 'ear a challinge fr'm the room?"

Iggi presumed it to have been simply the excitement of the moment, as she could think of no other rational reason why Tiny would have contemplated raising his arm to volunteer, but raise it he did. Luckily, she was on hand to be able to intercept him before the compere's roving eye spotted him waving his hat, but not before Mrs Blaise had managed to grab Iggi's *other* arm and raise it for her.

"Over 'ere, stumpy," she called out, "my girl'll 'ave ya'!"

"An' we 'ave a contenda f'th'throne, ells'n gees!" sang the compere, "Wha'da'we calls ya', luv'?"

"Well, if you call me *luv'* again, I'll break your face."

"Ivy Smiff," said Mrs Blaise, from beside her, "Bes' arm restla' in the 'ole've… 'Arra on the 'Ill."

"Mrs Bl—"

"'Er int'rests includes, sedition; revolution, an' kickin' arse," the old woman adlibbed, before catching the champion's eye across the floor and adding: "Alright, Tupp? Long time, no see, eh?"

Urged on by Mrs Blaise's bony left elbow in the small of her back, Iggi made her way to the table; cheered and jeered in equal measure by the crowd. She had no clue as to what game Mrs Blaise thought she was playing, but it was a dangerous one and one that she would be made to pay for later. Iggi's face may not have been seen on these streets for some time, but the downtrodden had long memories and were unlikely to believe that she had long since 'retired' from the agency. At any minute she was likely to feel the chill of cold steel against her skin, once word got around of who she really was.

It was, however, too late to do anything about it now, without compromising their chance to make contact with the woman on the other side of the table, so she removed her duster and her hat and rolled up her sleeve to show that she wore no affectations. Which was, when she remembered, what Mrs Blaise seemed to have forgotten: her right arm.

Tuppence Halfpenny frowned, staring at Iggi's transplanted limb. Then she looked at her face, squinting, as if trying to stare through her.

"Well, now," she began, "tha's certainly an *arm* I know, even if I don't know th'face. How d'you come to 'ave it up *your* sleeve then, *Ivy*?"

"It was left to me by a friend," Iggi lied. "He died and found he didn't have much use for it after that."

"I've fought tha' arm afore," Tuppence went on; assuming the position, "the ink's th'giveaway, y'know."

There was indeed a tattoo, halfway up the forearm: a crucifix with a serpent winding its way around its cross beam. It was only a small mark, but it served to remind her that she had killed a man out of fury rather than duty.

"Gerry Periwinkle, the Bishop of Clerkenwell. Well, well," mused Tuppence, "who does that make *you*, I wonder?"

The two women clasped hands over the chalk line, thumb knuckles raised and ready to fight. The compere stepped in front of the table and raised his arms to the mob.

"Fa' th'title," he announced, turning back to the competitors,

"Both feet on the floor,

thumb knuckles to the fore.

Shoulders square;

le's keep this fight fair... READY?"

And the fight began. Traditionally, this fight was the hardest of the evening for the defending champion, who had already played nine rounds to the contender's none, but Tuppence's grip was still every bit as vice-like as she suspected it had been from the off. Iggi had never felt particularly at one with Gerald's arm. She had coped with losing her original, although it had been a wrench at the time, and had grown perfectly attuned with her prosthetic replacement, other than for the constant pain that it had given her, but her donor arm had always felt as if it were trying to assert its own will over the rest of her body. She was aware how ridiculous that idea sounded. She had voiced it only the once, one drunken evening in the castle, back in the early days, when the four of them had been getting to know one another, and she had regretted it ever since. A month or so later; as a favour, whilst on a trip to Vienna, the Baron had insisted on treating her to a session with Dr Freud, who had merely confirmed the diagnosis that she had always suspected: that her problems with the 'donated' limb were most likely of a psychological nature, rather than, as she had considered in some of her more paranoid moments, that it was in fact, haunted. However, this knowledge was of scant comfort to her when she found herself unable to rely upon its co-operation when she needed it the most. It had a tendency to do what *it* wanted, rather than what *she* wanted it to do, and although the nerves had been fused with *her* nerves; their actions now determined by the will of *her* mind rather than *Gerald's*; the veins carrying *her* blood through them, with no longer any vestige of its previous owner's, she could still not guarantee that it would not let her down at the most inopportune of moments.

However, its grip on Halfpenny's own hand was firm and steady and without the slightest of wavers. She felt the muscles of Gerald's sausage-like digits tightening; crushing her opponents rather more feminine fingers between them. At the same time she felt the tendons and the ligaments in her hairy forearm; along with those around her bicep, flex in preparation for a surge of strength which, when it came, slammed her opponent's knuckles to the table with such a ferocity that it surprised even her.

"PIN!" shouted the compere, above a screaming crowd that consisted of just Tiny and Mrs Blaise. From all others present, rose merely a collective gasp followed by silence.

Halfpenny's face betrayed her shock, even though she had as good as acknowledged facing off against that same arm before. Perhaps Gerald had not been as good when the arm had been his?

"Positions… Round two… READY!" said the compere, whose name had just come to her. 'Max the Tax': so known for his propensity for taking large percentages for arranging anything from cockfights to assassinations.

The second round was a much easier win for Halfpenny, presumably due to the fact that she had been *expecting* the prettier of her two aides to drop a bottle beside the table, thus distracting Iggi; just momentarily, but enough for her to lose her concentration.

Iggi knew that she could have quite easily have won the third. Halfpenny was flagging, though none bar herself were likely to have noticed. Up until that point she had played reasonably fairly, but a kick under the table from one of her opponent's artificial feet; a kick that she could feel to have drawn blood, even through her leather boots, told Iggi that her point had been made and that there was nothing to gain from further humiliating the woman…

* * * * *

Although their individual words had been as gibberish to him: as nonsensical, he supposed, as the communications between a pod of humpback whales, the overall thread of what had been said around him had been much easier to absorb. He had sensed the note of dread, concern, present in the voices of both his alien allies as easily as if he had been able to participate in their fraught conversation himself; as he and the professor had hauled his immobile friend's stretcher along a series of dark corridors, down a short flight of steps and into what was obviously a laboratory of some kind.

Once inside, they had hefted Hamble onto a table that Boff had prepared accordingly; only then did he turn to help the wounded Alyce, whom he had been supporting against his shoulder for the duration. He eased her down into a comfortable armchair, where she slumped; her pained expression easing as she was able to relieve her damaged foot.

Their burdens thus relieved, Gordon then reached out and grabbed the ancient Martian's hand, feeling the by now familiar tingle as he did so, of the metal translation disc that she had affixed to her palm as it connected with the skin of his own.

"Bit of a big coincidence, what?" he posed, still wary of their apparent saviour's somewhat sudden and, none could deny it, *contrived* appearance in the surveillance hub. If Hamble had been conscious, then she would no doubt have derided him for being slow on the uptake; an habitual affectation of hers that he had always resented, but with both his travelling companions out for the count, Gordon felt the need to assert some form of control over a situation that was rapidly overtaking his capacity to keep pace with. "We arrived here," he said, awkwardly, as yet still uncomfortable with the need to hold the old woman's hand in order to make himself understood, "in the vague hope of finding exactly you; though we had no idea of where on the entire red planet you might have been, nor even *if* you were still alive, and then, fully five minutes later, you find *us*, and it turns out that your laboratory has not only been prepped for our imminent meeting but, in fact, only feet away from our exact position?"

Boff turned toward him, her expression dark and unreadable.

"There is no precedent in nature for coincidence, Gordon," she told him, squeezing his hand as she spoke, as if chastising him in the manner that Nanny had often employed when he had strayed too close to the duck pond. "If you think that you have experienced one, then you have likely fallen victim to the tinkerings of a time traveller. I am not the only one out there, you know. It's really quite simple," she explained, in that same tone that the peculiarly bright often chose for speaking down to him, "I have lived past this moment and have travelled back in order to rescue you. Why?" she asked, but without leaving him space to rally a reply, "because I happen to disagree strongly with what has been done to your planet by my own people and wish to do my part to help you to restore your original timeline. I moved my laboratory here once I knew the best place to intercept you. Now," she said, checking her pocket watch, "we may have saved Alyce's life, but Hamble has only eighteen cycles left to live. I have some important things both to say and do, in that time, *if* we're to avert that event, so please don't interrupt me again."

With those words, she pulled away from him, breaking the translation link.

Gordon merely watched, redundant: unable to think of anything more useful to do, as she reached out and drew toward her, what to him, with his limited frame of reference for Martian 'doodads', appeared to be a Davenport writing desk on metal castors, that had been fused with a piece of the dashboard from their broken rocket.

The desk was adorned with a randomised pattern of buttons; dials; levers and sockets: some of which had cables dangling from them. Taking the ends of two such cables, Boff attached them to Hamble's temples by means of two rubberised suction pads. She produced a small, steel syringe from the top pocket of her lab coat which she then screwed a needle to; released a brief fountain of whatever opaque blue liquid was circling inside it, and proceeded to inject the remainder into the top of Hamble's arm. She beckoned to Gordon to take both *her* hand and Hamble's in his own.

"Can you hear me, Hamble?" he heard. Boff's lips were close to his friend's left ear, but he could see that they were moving in such a way that they did not match the words that she was saying. "No, don't try to move," she said, putting a hand on Hamble's chest to restrain her as she stirred, "stay quite still and just listen to what I have to say to you. You are going to be alright, Hamble. In a few cycles, what has befallen you will never have happened, though, I hope for all of our sakes, you will still retain the memory of it. I am going to send you both back along your own timelines. Do you understand me?" Hamble nodded weakly, confirming; Gordon felt, both her understanding of the process and her consent to proceed, and so, mutely, he followed suit, "I call this process 'The Rewind'," Boff continued. I can take you back to any point in your lives, in the hope that you might find a way to avert our agent's interference and restore your planet's future. Unfortunately, I cannot take you back to when he first arrived on your world, as, as Alyce informed me on our way down here, neither of you were born at that time—"

"Why would that matter?" Gordon interrupted, not quite grasping the meaning of the term 'Rewind'. "We're happy to go as far back as required."

He had presumed that a 'time machine' would have been housed inside some kind of a large chair apparatus, akin to the fictional imaginings of HG Wells and his contemporaries, and he told her so, "You know," he went on, blithely, as she raised her eyebrows and tilted her head, "one simply dials up the year that one wishes to visit; back or forward, then pulls a large, red lever and 'Bob's your uncle', as a cockney might say."

"Then these 'cockneys', that you speak of, obviously have no greater grasp of time travel theory than *you* do!"

Boff chided. "Now, pay attention!" she snapped, as she replaced the needle on her syringe and removed the air from it with a short blast, "the past has happened: we can remember it, therefore it is a fact. We can pinpoint a moment that we have lived and return to it in order to 'edit' it, like one would a reel of film. By this *same* token, the future is thus yet to happen; its outcome, by no means a certainty, therefore it *cannot* be visited."

Frowning, Gordon could not help himself from asking the most obvious of questions at this point: "Then how do we get back? To our own time, I mean. Once we've done the deed; changed whatever needs changing. How do we shift *forward* to see if it worked?"

"You don't," she replied, turning to make some alterations to the equipment that Hamble was wired to, "not in the way that you are imagining, anyway. You will have to do that in *real* time. I wish we had the time that I could explain to you the workings of my discovery, but we don't. Hamble has to go now. I think it best that I send you both back to a time shortly before you were chosen for the Moon mission. You'll have to work it out for yourselves from there, but think very carefully before you make any changes. Fore knowledge is a dangerous commodity. Although you will be living your lives a second time, you should still remember the future that will no longer be. Don't forget: even the smallest changes have consequences."

Gordon felt a prick as she injected him with the blue liquid, through the canvas sleeve of his space suit.

"Sit," she ordered, and so he did, which was lucky as his head had begun to swim; memories of recent events spinning as they surfaced: the underground city, their fall down the lift shaft, running through the tunnels, their escape from the Ornithopters. He saw the red planet's surface, as viewed through the rocket's windscreen, seconds before the explosion; the blackness of space, the explosion as they had collided with the Zeppelin, Nanny, Tiny, the Moonbase, Virgil...

As she had done with Hamble, Boff hastily attached two suckers to his own temples. "Find each other quickly," she said; "it will make more sense if you work together. Besides, I'm willing to lay odds on Hamble having understood more of this than you."

"But what about Alyce?" he asked, looking across the room at his Martian friend; memories now flooding his mind, each one dredged and flung carelessly into the whirling vortex.

"Alyce will be fine; I will take care of her," she promised. "She's where she needs to be. Now, good luck. We won't meet again."

The next thing Gordon knew...

CHAPTER SIX:

THE ANTI-ALIEN LEAGUE

There were a great many differences between life in London and that which he had been used to back in Kali: The Martian capital, from whence he hailed. The first of such to have come to his notice had been the issue of unchecked vagrancy, which was rife to near epidemic proportions in the poorest quarters of Victoria's Imperial city. The problem had no such modern equivalent on the planet that he had left behind, which, he had presumed, had been the reason why the oddness of its flagrancy had struck him as hard as it had. Everywhere he walked he had found himself accosted by beggars of one sort or another. Whilst some brazenly petitioned for alms, without a care for how they might be perceived by those whose charity they sought, others offered themselves up for the most undignified of personal services, and still others felt it necessary to present entertainments, of a kind, in exchange for people's pity. Initially, it had fascinated him: the very lengths that the downtrodden and the destitute had needed to stoop to here, merely to be able to feed and to clothe themselves in times of hardship. On his home world, a far more advanced and civilised society had long ago initiated a simple, yet effective system of social care, which saw every citizen taxed in order that every citizen be eligible for fair and dignified aid in times of crisis. It had been more than a century since anyone had had need; either to prostrate or to publicly humiliate themselves, simply in order that they might survive another day!

But his concerns for the native vagabond's welfare had soon turned from novelty to annoyance, the more that he found them impeding his progress; clogging the streets and thoroughfares with their props and their gatherers and causing a public nuisance, as they peddled their dubious 'talents' in order that they might appear worthy of public sympathy.

Worst of all of them, however, to his mind, at least, was the 'busker': a subset of the common or garden mendicant; he, or indeed she, who felt the need to disguise their poverty behind a scurrilous desire to live life as a peripatetic 'turn' or troubadour, as he had heard tell was their designation of preference. They were 'an irritant, a hazard and a sign,' his younger self had remarked to the two senior members of the infiltration team, of just 'how far the human race had yet to evolve in order to be ready to accept the Martian colonisation programme.'

It had been the now deceased third member of the team: 'Auntie'; the strategist amongst them, who had taken him aside that day and taught him a most valuable lesson that he had never forgotten…

"Look again at your struggling paupers," she had told him, "and tell me what you see."

After a moment's thought, he had explained: "I see those whom the people of this world would rather *not* see, battling to *be* seen, lest they die due to their fellow's disinterest."

"Good," she had replied, "you are learning, but there are two other stories playing out, here too. The best way to come to understand a species is to corner it," she continued, "then step back and watch how it reacts. Does it cower; roll over and show you its belly in supplication, or does it turn, with unexpected ferocity and take the fight to its oppressor? Watch, Reefus," she had pressed, highlighting a single act playing out in

Covent Garden as they passed by, "watch, and learn. Do you see the juggler?" She had asked him, "he who concentrates so hard to keep the balls turning in the air, like the elements of a great plan kept spinning until they are needed? Now watch as his assistant lays a series of obstacles in his path and he attempts to cross from one side of the piazza to the other, without ever losing control of the balls. First, he blindfolds the juggler, then he scatters a pile of bricks ahead of him. These are superseded by a slalom of bottles and next, a slanted plank, leading up to the apex of a barrel. There is another barrel, a short distance away; the two joined by a taught line between them. The juggler has constantly to alter his route; feeling his way by instinct, but he does so without ever losing sight of the original plan, to keep all the balls in the air in synchronised motion."

Reefus had smiled and nodded as the analogy had sunk in. "Now," she had said, a smile on her own face, "there is an even *more* important lesson to learn from all of this. Check your pockets."

He had done so, only to discover that whilst his attention had been held, his pockets had been picked…

* * * * *

"Am I to surmise," the Secretary began, folding closed his newspaper and removing his ocular aide, "to judge purely by the supercilious halo that you seem to be wearing; that your impracticable bill has been ratified by the Lords?"

"Unanimously," the Prime Minister replied, in such a tone as to suggest that no other outcome had ever seriously been considered on his part. He tugged at his lapels as he spoke in order to straighten his jacket from where it had ridden up over his bulk during his long walk back from the chamber to his office at Number Ten, and he turned to smile at his uninvited guest. If he had been surprised to find that his advisor had let himself in to his private sanctum and made himself comfortable in his absence, then he gave no indication of it; bowling ahead with his dispatch regardless, gratified, apparently, to have had such an opponent on hand to gloat to. He removed his hat and hooked it onto the wooden stand by the door, adding: "With immediate effect. Give us six months," he proffered, "merely to arm 'em and train the buggers up, and our boys'll be singing carols on Von Greckle's very doorstep in time for Christmas! What d'you think about *that*, Mr Secretary?" and pushing the flaps of his jacket through the gap in the back of his chair, like a concert pianist readying himself to begin a recital, he sat down behind his desk.

The Secretary unfolded his legs; stood up and strode toward the window.

"You *know* what I think, Octavian," he said, darkly; his back to the Prime Minister, "as I know that you are *also* well aware of Her Majesty's views on the subject. And as for the *public*—"

"I don't give a *fig* for the views of an ailing monarch that *you* have kept in place, these past years by hook and by crook; this is a democracy, damn you; a bally democracy! I'm *here* by the very will of the public, and I think you'll find that they're four square behind me. You tend to forget my 'unprecedented majority'," he added, spittle welling at the corners of his lips. "You've read t'day's *Times*; I see, so you will no doubt have noted that I am being hailed 'The Father of The Modern Age'. Four sons," he drawled on, as he no doubt had been doing all afternoon in the house, "all of 'em at the top of their individual fields; there's even a statue of me youngest, in Trafalgar Square! *That's* what the public sees, don't y'know, and that's what they want from their leader: a father figure. Someone, to whom they can look up to, someone who has their best interests at heart. A man; Mr Secretary, who is not afraid to stand up to those who seek to put them down! Someone who believes in them; someone who knows how to get the best out of those in his charge—"

"This has got to stop, Octavian," the Secretary said, turning to stare the minister down. It was a threat, but one delivered softly and without recourse to a verbal outburst; knowing, as he did, that to lose his equanimity with such as Octavian Periwinkle was to instantly lose the advantage. "As the leader of the largest conglomeration of states on the planet," he explained, as if this was news to the man behind the desk, "you hold the fates of millions in your hands. You have seen what the Germans have been able to achieve in America. An advance at this juncture would be folly."

The Prime Minister remained silent for a moment, almost as if he were contemplating his advisor's advice, but then quietly asked:

"For whom, Mr Secretary?" splaying his hands to emphasise the point being made, "For me? I think not. 'War maketh the man'," he quoted, "especially if that man is a Prime Minister in the early days of his tenure. For the Queen, then?" he went on, shaking his head, "No; I hardly think so. Once we own the land of her fathers; having executed the very man who murdered her grandson, she will be as putty in my hands. For *you*, then?" he posed, pushing back in his chair and steepling his fingers across his chest. "Yes," he nodded, "instability is your greatest fear, is it not? It's the thing that you've striven your whole career to avoid. And why *is* that, hmm? You see, I've been looking into you, 'Mr Secretary'; you and your little 'agency'."

The Secretary folded his arms; crossed his left foot over his right and leant back against the windowsill, humouring the Empire's current political string puller.

"I don't trust you, Mr Secretary, but unlike my predecessors; none of whom trusted you *either*, by the way, I am not *afraid* of you. I *know* that there is a connection between yourself and these bally aliens; you're too damn close to them! You speak of them as if they are in some way *above* the trivialities of mankind; oh, yes: it's been noted. One might even conclude that you are in *league* with the devils. That you have, perhaps, been *compromised*, sir! You underestimate me at your peril—"

Smiling broadly, the Secretary pushed forward into the room, clapping his hands slowly as he moved.

"Bravo," he said, patronisingly, "bravo. I had wondered how long it would take you to succumb to such paranoias."

"How *dare* you, sir! I think it's time—"

"Time," the Secretary repeated, dropping back down into the chair in which he had been lounging when the Prime Minister had returned. "Yes. You know, I think you're probably right. It *is* time: time that I made a few things clear to you before you make the biggest mistake of your misbegotten career."

Octavian rose from his seat, his right arm pointing toward the door.

"Sit down and *listen*," the Secretary insisted, calmly, but firmly; channelling the juggler that he had observed all those years ago; along with the street mesmerist and the ragamuffin, employing the faintly hypnotic note to his vocal delivery that he had used to such great effect on the four separate prime ministers with whom he had worked over the past three decades, on the occasions when they *too* had tried to assert their will against his.

Octavian Periwinkle was a man who liked to spar. He was a bully whose leading tactic was to goad and whittle until his opponents lost their equanimity; digging deep beneath his enemy's skin in order to bait his temper, thus undermining any argument that they may have had with him. He was not used to those who refused to rise to his call and so; seemingly startled by the Secretary's effrontery, he did as he had been told, though with no uncertain amount of blusterment in the process.

"Yes," the Secretary gently pushed, "I *would* like to see our visitors thrive here on Earth. I believe it is in *both* species best interests to have them do so. The Martians possess knowledge and technologies *far* in advance of Earth science at this time. They have access to medicines that could eradicate many of the ailments that are currently killing the human race, almost as quickly as it has the capacity to replace itself. But," he said, pausing momentarily whilst he leant forward for emphasis, "while an apparently peaceful race, it is worth noting that they do have access to chemicals and mechanicals that, should they ultimately feel threatened, could wipe out all life on Earth in the blink of an eye. Think about *that* before you rattle your sabre too loudly; you need to tread carefully, Mr Prime Minister. Our alliance with these people is but a fragile one, and one currently held in balance by my wits alone. Your task," he said, with a wry smile, "your *remit*, if you will, is to represent the will of your people. In order to do that effectively you have to be prepared to *listen* to them. *I'm* listening to them. I hear them calling for female suffrage; I hear them calling for higher standards of public health and sanitation and I hear their call for the implementation of a social welfare system. But what I *don't* hear; Mr Prime Minister, is their clamour for war."

The Prime Minister, who had remained silent throughout his advisor's speech, smiled tightly and drained his second glass.

"You're a strange one, Plumb-Prendergast, and that's a fact," he said, standing to pace the floor between his desk and his visitor, "whilst on the one hand you are in possession of a keen intellect and a unique instinct for how best to play an opponent; y'might have made a fine politician, if you'd had a mind to, on the other hand, you are something of a dinosaur; an anachronism: a holdover from an era long past, and, damn yer eyes; for all your cross-party clarity of vision, y'don't seem t'be able t'see it! Your opinions, *sir*, for what they are worth, have been noted. Now get out of my office and, next time you wish to speak with me, kindly be good enough to make an appointment with my secretary."

* * * * *

"'Ello Mef," Iggi heard; a muffled introduction intended for Mrs Blaise, though said close enough and clear enough to wake her from her enforced slumber.

Iggi opened her eyes to darkness, but it did not take a highly trained agent like herself more than a separated second to put two and two together and work out that her aching and ringing head was, in fact, inside of a sack. Without moving sharply, so as not to alert their captors to the fact that she had awoken, Iggi squinted through the rough weave, scanning the dingy room. She could make out two people other than the speaker: two guards, either side of their leader.

"I's good t'sees ya'," their erstwhile kidnapper continued, unaware that Iggi was earwigging, "fought you w's dead, I did; mourned ya', I did; shed a likkle tear, I did, when they tolt me you'd gone," and she paused as if replaying the scene in her head. "See, no one gits aht'a Bedl'm, duz they? Not lessen i's in a box. So, when they said you w's gone, well; wha' w's I t'think?"

"*You* did," Mrs Blaise replied, provocatively, Iggi felt, from a couple of feet to her right, "If *you* go' aht, why cout'n' I?"

Pins and needles in her extremities told Iggi that she was bound to her chair; she had to presume that her former teacher was also restrained in such a manner, though minus the hood, and, judging by the snoring coming from her left, she realised that Tiny was probably in a similar position, though that he must have been administered a stronger dose of whatever those noxious rags had been laced with. At least, she thought, they were all three accounted for.

"Well, see, I 'ad somefink they needed," explained the voice, which Iggi now guessed to belong to their target: Tuppence Halfpenny, as the double amputee rapped her knuckles against her prosthetic legs in answer to Mrs Blaise's unvoiced query. It was a sound that Iggi would have known anywhere: that dull, metallic clunk; hollow, but hardly empty, and she realised that, if she strained, she could just about make out the mechanical whirring of the pistons and the gears within them as she paced up and down in front of her prisoners.

"Swapped 'em, I did," she said, as if proud of such a ghoulish exchange, "f'me freedom. Bu' tha' don' explain you, Mef, now duz it."

"Me daugh'a," replied Mrs Blaise, "she's a famous scien'ist, y'know; jus' like 'er ol' man afore 'er. Good girl, she w's, an' loaded, t'boot. Bought me freedom, she did."

"An' where's she now; this famous daugh'a a'yours, then, eh?"

"Brown bread," the old lady mugged, thankfully, for once, sticking to the agreed script. It was not the truth; not as far as they knew, anyway, but it was near enough, and it would not be too difficult a job to corroborate, "Discredi'ed 'er, they did an' made 'er aht t'look like a defecta'. Bast'ds, all of 'em! An' all a'cause she w's a wom'n doin' a man's work! 'Ow'd y'like that, eh, Tupp?"

The revolutionary did not reply.

"Look, Tupp," Mrs Blaise went on, "i's me, Mef: yer ol' mucka'. Why'ad I tell ya'porkies, eh? I come t'you 'cause I fought we could *'elp* each uvva. This country's goin' t'th'dogs, righ'? Well, I 'eard you w's plannin' a revaloosh'n. Iggi, 'ere; she's an assassin, an' Tiny, there… Well, e's gotta be useful f'summit; 'e's a qualified Sherpa! An' if y'looks in me indispensable 'ere—"

"We already did," Halfpenny told her. "Where d'ya' get th'bomb, Mef?"

"Like Ah said," Mrs Blaise lied on, "me daugh'a w's a scient'st, weren't she? An' there're plen'y more where that come fr'm."

They had been later leaving the pub than they would have liked; losing sight of their target in the process, on account of two unhelpful things: Mrs Blaise's urinary condition and the fact that Iggi had been clocked by the compere, Max The Tax, whilst she and Tiny had been waiting outside the conveniences. He had accosted them in the alleyway, threatening to inform those punters still yet to disperse that she was, in fact, a Crown agent; this, if she would not guarantee his immunity from whatever sting or other it was that she was working. A quick glance back over her shoulder and into the bar had informed Iggi that, between the three of them, it was probable that they could take on the entire bar in relatively short shrift; sobriety being on their side, if not numbers. However, they were supposed to have been keeping a low profile; not drawing unwanted attention to themselves, although Mrs Blaise's little improvisation during the arm-wrestling affair had fair scuppered the chances of that!

"C'mon, Iggi… Whaddaya' say, eh?" Max had pleaded, his croaky, over-used ringmaster's voice raised an octave by the filter in his top-of-the-range Rebreather, making him sound rather like a crow warning a magpie not to stray too close to its nest.

"I's tha' or a lynchin," he had insisted. "You ain't none too pop'lar 'round 'ere—," but any further argument was abruptly curtailed by the clobbering that the grasping MC had duly received, courtesy of Mrs Blaise's trusty 'indispensable'; the heavy bag that never left her side.

"Fuckin' chancer," had been his epitaph, conferred by the aforementioned redundant elocution mistress, who had then bent down and unstrapped the stunned fellow's face mask, adding: "bes' way t'deal wit' th'likes of 'im, Ah reckons," exposing his already overworked lungs to the noxious night air...

They had left Wine Office Court and stepped back out onto Fleet Street, a little over eight minutes behind Halfpenny and her cohorts. It would have been difficult enough to have ascertained the direction that their target had taken in the dim gaslight afforded, without having to strain to see through glass lenses and then smog that was thicker than a fisherman's winter long John's; but the problem had resolved itself in short order, when an explosion nearby had blown the three of them from their feet, depositing them onto the shit-strewn cobbles in a tangle of arms and legs; not all of which had been their own.

The light afforded by the ensuing fire, emanating from a large building not far away, highlighted a number of people in close proximity, whom they otherwise would not have known to have been there; some of them stirring from whence they too had been thrown by the blast, whilst some lay as still as the bricks and the rubble that had accompanied their flights. A wooden sign board lay smouldering in the gutter nearby, reading 'Lockharts Dining Roo'. The name rang a distant bell for Iggi; she had been there at some point in the not too distant past. 'But why,' she wondered, 'would anyone bomb a restaurant? There had been a newspaper office above it, if, in her addled state, she was remembering correctly; 'the more likely target?' she pondered briefly, before her

Rebreather was suddenly torn from her face to be replaced by a damp rag that smelt of...

Chloroform...

Her hands were still bound together; a sensible precaution on Halfpenny's part, she conceded, but Iggi was no longer itching beneath a rough hessian hood. They were all three conscious now and revealed; though she could not be certain that Tiny was not suffering a mild concussion, judging by the somewhat vague expression carved into his already crumpled face. They were seated along one side of a long, expensive looking table, in a room that had once had a much grander purpose than that which it currently enjoyed; simply to go by the peeling wallpaper and the cobweb festooned, though decorous, moulded plaster ceiling. Ragged and part rotted curtains hung to either side of a line of mismatched slats of recycled timber, which had been nailed to the outside of the now glassless window frames. The table itself: walnut, if she was not mistaken; similar to the one that adorned the Baron's great hall, had sadly probably passed the point where a decent French polisher might have been able to save it; etched as it was with all manner of initials and slogans that, if ever the place were to be raided by the bluebottles, ought to help form a fair forensic case against the League's membership.

Opposite the drowsy trio sat Tuppence Halfpenny, her eyes wide and her hair even wider; her ever present stooges: the pretty girl and the scar faced one, sat to either side of her. In the centre of the table; where a silver, tri-pronged candelabra should have graced, sat the Baron's bomb, its clockwork timer still, as yet inert. Quite how it was still intact and had not blown them all to Deptford by this point, was anybody's guess; it having not had the safest of journeys, thrust inside Mrs Blaise's trusty indispensable all the way from Bavaria. Iggi had initially put the Fleet Street blast down to a snatcher, having made off with the old woman's bag, only to set it off accidentally, but then on second thoughts, had attributed it to the League themselves. However, judging by the direction that the current conversation was headed, there was obviously another hand at play here.

"I take it," said Halfpenny to Mrs Blaise; still labouring under the misapprehension that she was the group's leader, "tha' lars' night's explosion was your doin'?"

Before Iggi could frame a reply, she felt the heel of Mrs Blaise's boot digging into her ankle. Iggi faltered, catching the wide grin that the old woman was using by way of a non-committal answer to the question posed.

"Jus' 'oo *are* you people?" Halfpenny asked, intrigued, Iggi judged, but not apparently angered that another group may have been working her patch.

"IRA," said Mrs Blaise; apparently their new mouthpiece. "'Iggi's Revalooshon'ry Avengas', at y'service."

They had had a script; it had all been worked through in the Baron's office before they had left Germany. They had all agreed that, once in London, she, Iggi, would take the lead, as she knew both the city and its lowlife inhabitants better than either of her two companions. It had been a good plan and she felt sure that it had had legs, but for Mrs Blaise and her constant extemporisation!

Of course, an agent in the field had to be ready to alter her plans on the fly, and Iggi had been ready for just such a situation, with a plan B and a plan C already simmering on the backburner of her mind. The old lady, however, was undermining her at every turn. She made a note to rein her in, just as soon as the three of them were next alone; if ever that time came.

Tuppence Halfpenny smiled, revealing a set of teeth as blackened and ravaged as the old woman who she was sat opposite. Iggi could guess the type of diet applied to the poor souls that inhabited the asylum where these two had met and wondered that they had survived their sentences at all; their minds and bodies apparently no more addled than the girls who worked in the Lucifer factories. She beckoned her disfigured friend closer with a pull of her pinky, then whispered into the girl's ear. Scarface then made her silent exit.

"We migh'," Tuppence went on to suggest, "pool our resources, as i' were. Wha's y'take on these alien coves?"

Iggi closed her eyes, praying that Mrs Blaise stay on track.

The old woman took a sharp intake; pouted and winced, before replying: "One 'ad 'is way w'me, a while back," she said, and Iggi held her breath, "'e give me a righ' dose, so 'e did! Me chuff's bin aligh' fer an 'ole mumf!"

Halfpenny set her jaw, whilst 'the pretty one' winced; the first expression that Iggi had seen her pull.

"Victoria's world ain't dun me no favours," the revolutionary said, her eyes betraying her deeply held resentment toward the system which she obviously fully intended to subvert. "In America; where me ol' man cum fr'm, they'd call me 'mula'o',"

Iggi had heard the word, on her travels, but usually pronounced with a double 'T' preceding the 'O'. It was a derogatory term, used to describe a child of mixed heritage. She too had been described as such, though admittedly, not since entering the service.

Iggi had no memory of her parents, but had been reliably informed that her mother had been of 'Christian' stock, though the note that had been found among her deceased parent's effects had listed her married name as

'Shikiwana'. No clue had ever been found as to her father's origins…

"'Arf-breed, is wha' Ah usu'lly ge's, though; *'arf-* breed! An' Ah w's *born* 'ere! Yet them aliens; they cums 'ere from Mars an' gets trea'ed wiv more respec' than I'll *evva* get! Y'know, me paren's call't meTupp'nce Ha'p'ney, 'cause they reckoned i' w's all they w's likely t'get f'me. 'Ows abou' tha', then, eh Iggi?"

Iggi was startled to find herself suddenly pulled into the conversation.

"Wha'did they call you, eh?"

After a moment's scarred deliberation, Iggi replied firmly: "Mestiza."

Father McNulty; the priest who had taken her in, had preferred this equally distasteful, Spanish equivalent of the term, believing that; owing to her more 'olive' toning, as he described it, that her father had been of Mexican blood.

"'A's a new'n on me," admitted Tuppence, "cracka'; coolie; creole; caramel: Ah fough' Ah'd 'eard 'em all. Good shot, are ya'?"

"The best."

"Nice. So wha's wrong wif th'muscle 'ere's 'ead?"

"It was shrunk by Jivaroan headshrinkers in Peru."

"Ah fough' they cut 'em off first?"

"They tried. He's tougher than he looks."

"Where are we?" Tiny suddenly asked; the first words that he had spoken since the blast. "Where's th'capt'in?"

Iggi kicked him under the table as Tuppence's eyes began to narrow, but Scarface also suddenly returned, bending to whisper into her leader's ear. Tuppence smiled and clapped her hands together.

"Looks like you w's tellin' the tiles, Mef, mate. Welc'm t'th'fam'ly," and she struck out her own hand to shake those of the assembled 'IRA', introducing her two friends as: Tyana and Slash…

"Jus' one fing, though…"

Iggi held her breath as Tuppence affected a deep, suspicious frown. She leant back in her chair, staring intently at Mrs Blaise.

"Wha's 'appened t'y'voice; y'used t'be all lardy da, back in the 'ospital?"

CHAPTER SEVEN:

THE BRASS FIST

"Telegram f'Doctor Periwinkle! Telegram f'Doctor Periwinkle!"

Ada smiled at the boy in the hat, two sizes too large for him, in that way that maiden aunts were wont to do when greeting nephews whose cheeks they had not pinched since the previous Christmas. She stood, her slender-wristed hand angled toward him; waiting to relieve him of his duty, just as Virgil, having heard the boy's exhortation, entered the lobby from his surgery beyond.

Snatching the missive from the boy's grip, he delved absently into the left-hand pocket of his Westcott as he read, whereupon his fingers alighted upon a loan brass farthing which he duly flipped behind him toward the telegraphist's runner.

"A fadge?" the boy remarked, expertly catching the coin, like a stray dog might a strip of discarded rind thrown from a butcher's back door.

Virgil, his hand on the brass handle of his surgery door by now, pulled himself up sharply, turning back towards the ungrateful urchin; his cheeks flushed to scarlet.

"What did you say?" he blustered.

"S-sorry, guv'," the youth stuttered.

"You're paid for your day's work; are you not, boy?"

"Yes, guv'," said with eyes now lowered in deference, "s-sorry, guv—"

"Then be grateful that you are offered a gratuity at all!"

"I's jus' tha'," the boy continued, sheepishly; fiddling with his lowered face mask as he fumbled for the words.

Despite himself, Virgil raised his eyebrow, allowing the boy to speak.

"Wha' wiv me ol' man an' both me elder bruvvas receivin' their call up papers this week, *my* earnin's is all we got now; wha' wiv eight moufs still t'feed, an'all."

"It's hardly my fault that your father couldn't find a hobby!" Virgil spat, but the boy was ready with a quip of his own:

"Beggin' ya'pardon an'all, sir, but i's *your* father's fault tha' I'm now th'family breadwinn—"

"Insolent whelp!" Virgil replied, clipping him around the ear so sharply that his hat flew from its unsteady perch to disappear down the stairs toward the street door; its current owner beating a hasty retreat in its pursuit. "How dare you talk back to your betters!" Virgil called after him, feeling the heat rising within him, "I will be speaking with your master; don't think for a moment that I won't!"

He heard the street door slam below them and turned back to his secretary; the telegram screwed tightly in his fist, "What is this country coming to, Ada, I ask you! Our streets full of all manner of anarchist, alien and deviant alike and a place t'boot, where even the common guttersnipe presumes the right to an opinion."

He paused while he fished frantically in the pockets of his jacket, searching for the little brown phial that contained his pills; panic rising by crescendo until finally he located them: tucked beneath his handkerchief in his uppermost pocket. Removing one, he placed it under his tongue, consigning the rest to his pocket. He took a deep breath in through his nose, then slowly released it orally, as Dr Stokes had advised he do in times of undue stress.

He had found himself requiring of Henry's unique restoratives ever more frequently, these past weeks; whenever, in fact, he found himself suffering from either anxiety or general perturbation; the two states often even

138

occurring concurrently whenever he thought about his eldest daughter and the promise that he had made to Beatrice to extricate her from the clutches of the pervert under whose spell she had fallen.

He took another breath and turned back toward his secretary.

"It would seem," he continued, unscrewing the note and rereading its content, "that there was another explosion last evening; the third in as many nights. Mark my words, Ada: the streets of this fair city are no longer safe for the likes of you and I. We must be extra vigilant."

Donning his hat; his goggles and his Rebreather, he reached for his overcoat, turning back to his secretary only once he had toggled the final button.

"Ada, would you be so good as to cancel the rest of my morning's appointments? It would appear that I am required; with some urgency, over at St Bart's."

* * * * *

"Doctor Periwinkle… sir," said the Admiral, turning away from the nurse with whom he had previously been consulting. He removed his gloves and held a rather unconvincing hand forward in greeting, "it was good of you to come," he said, though his eyes betrayed their owner's true feelings toward him.

"Admiral Haversack; Harvey," Virgil responded, as keenly as he could; meeting the man's offer and raising it with a firm, paternal grip. "I take it I am not here at the behest of the Secretary?"

"That is correct, sir," the Admiral replied, a little uncomfortably; furtively, even, Virgil decided. "Please; if you would be so good as to step inside?"

It had been a while since these two men had spoken. It had; perhaps, been inevitable, then, that such a reunion; when and wherever it was enacted, would be a somewhat awkward affair...

When they had first met, Harvey Haversack had been the much-decorated intelligence officer with the distinguished military service record behind him, to whom Virgil had harboured not the slightest objection to granting the man's request for the hand of his favourite daughter. He and Ethel had been married later that same year and their union had so far provided Virgil with two delightful grandsons, for which he was immensely grateful, as he sincerely doubted that his other daughter would be following suit in the near to middling future.

It had been during the second year of Harvey and Ethel's marriage that his son-in-law had accepted a 'sideways promotion', joining the newly fledged 'Imperial Space Agency', under the command of Admiral Archibald Spatchcock, where; if all had gone to plan, Harvey would have become the Empire's second only astronaut, following in the giant footsteps laid down by Virgil's own brother, Gordon. However, the Mars Mission had been postponed at the very last moment; much to Harvey's deep regret, and he had instead found himself relegated to a post in Mission Control; where he had been that fateful day when the Martians had made first contact.

Following the death of Admiral Spatchcock, Harvey had once again been offered promotion; this time to the post of Admiral, in command of The Imperial Space Agency. It had been in this capacity that he had been on hand to receive the man known to have murdered and eaten the entire crew of the Martian Moonbase: his wife's father and the man whom he had been pointedly trying to avoid ever since...

"You'll remember my brother, Reginald," said Harvey," a statement delivered with confidence, when it should, perhaps, have been posed as a question. It was the first time that morning that his son-in-law had said anything with an appreciable measure of conviction.

He was led into a small, side ward, intended for those patients whose status within society afforded them the right to a little privacy whilst they were recovering.

Virgil recalled meeting the man in question briefly on two previous occasions, though neither time engaging in any more than polite introductory banter. The first had been at his daughter's wedding, where he had acted as his elder brother's best man, and had taken an unrequited shine to his spinster daughter, Tatiana. The second had been at the christening service held for one of the grandchildren, but he was jiggered if he could remember which one.

He had been a rather handsome young man, Virgil considered; if memory served, though from the look of the poor fellow now: propped up in bed, with his head; his chest and his arms entirely swaddled in white crepe bandages, that was no longer likely to have been the case.

"Good God, man!" Virgil exclaimed, "However did he get into such a state?"

The Admiral moved to join Virgil at his younger brother's bedside.

"I take it that you have heard about the bombing spate?" he enquired.

"Blasted Anti-Alien League? I'd have had to have been on the bally Moon not to have done!"

"Quite," said the Admiral tightly and quietly, though not so quietly that Virgil did not detect a note in his voice.

"This latest one was in a ladies' outfitters on The Strand, was it not?" Virgil ventured, "What the deuce was y'brother doing there?"

Somewhere in the back of his mind, Virgil recalled seeing the patient in uniform and realised that he must have been on hand in some kind of an official capacity. "Had you been given a warning?" he asked, "Was he trying to defuse the bally thing?"

There was a short, pregnant pause before a reply was proffered:

"Something along those lines."

The Admiral then took a different tack: a more familiar entreaty than the one of professional detachment that he had previously sought to maintain.

"He's my brother, sir; the only one I have. The doctors say that he will likely regain his hearing, in time and that it is possible that his sight loss may also only be temporary, however, his right hand…"

"Will obviously not be growing back of its own accord," Virgil finished for him.

"He is to marry in June," Harvey continued, as if further personal detail might convince him to help.

Virgil removed his hat and lifted the patient's note board that hung over the brass railing at the bottom of his bed.

"Replacement appendages do not come cheap," Virgil explained, "and, since Professor Blaise's unfortunate defection, such mechanical prosthetics as would be required have become increasingly hard to source. Added to which," he went on; an idea taking shape within his muffled grey cells, "I imagine you would like to see your brother aided… *surreptitiously*; would I be right?"

Harvey nodded emphatically, like a child offered a sugar mouse on a day that was not her birthday.

Something about this whole sorry story had unsettled the man; he could read as much from his demeanour. It would have been so much easier for him to have gone through the proper channels; to have alerted the Secretary to his dilemma, unless…

"It will not be easy Admi… Harvey," Virgil told him, "such devices are a finite resource, but… I believe I could locate one; yes, I'm almost certain I can."

"Then consider me forever in your debt, sir."

Virgil smiled broadly, clasping the Admiral's shoulders, "Harvey," he said, elongating his name, "think nothing of it! I myself am one of four brothers and let me tell you, there is nothing that I would not do for any one of them. It's what families do, is it not? And you are a Periwinkle now."

Pulling a calling card from his wallet, and a pencil from an inside pocket, he began to scribble a note, leaning heavily on the patients' note board.

"Have him brought to this address at ten o'clock tonight, and I will do what I can for him. Oh, and Harvey?" said whilst easing past him on his way to the door, "there is but one small thing that you might do for me in return…"

* * * * *

It is said that in times of sudden mortal fear: at that pivotal moment of panic, when a person believes that their bus has come early and that their number is most likely up, an edited montage of their life's most fundamental highs and lows will rush before their peepers, as if in preparation for scrutinisation by Saint Peter; the celestial accountant, outside the Pearly Gates of Heaven.

Gordon was no credulous newcomer to such apocryphal axioms, having stared down the twin barrels of impending doom on any number of occasions over the course of his danger-baiting career. There were, in fact, few ways that had not been attempted; as far as his potential expungement from the universe was concerned, though on each and every occasion, he had indeed been rescued; at the penultimate moment, most often, by one doughty Sherpa or another, and so his life in film; played now in flashback before his very eyes, was an experience that he was better acquainted with than most.

However, the hallucinogenic flickers of a life well lived, that were currently showing to this vulnerable audience of one, seemed different, somehow, to those that he had experienced before: far more distinct, he fancied, and too chromatic to be mere illusions of the psyche. Far from the series of strobing impressions that he had previously borne witness to, the acts playing out before him now seemed somehow real; tangible, as if he could reach in and touch them; interact with them, even, but no… There was something wrong with the picture. It was going too fast and yet faster still, the further he travelled back along his own time line. It was as if the cables had been cut on Scarborough's funicular railway, whilst the car in which he had been travelling had been stalled at the top of the cliff; picking up speed as it dropped toward its ultimate destination on the promenade below.

But that was not *all* that was wrong with his all too comprehensive trip down memory lane. Worst of all, he now realised: everything was going backwards!

* * * * *

Strolling along the Victoria Embankment, the Secretary took a deep and fulsome lungful of the now all-pervasive sulphur dioxide gas that hung like a noxious shroud over the city that had claimed his soul; courtesy of the many factories in the metropolis that his kinsmen had helped to adapt under the auspices of improved industrial efficiency. He savoured the bitter taste on his tongue and luxuriated momentarily, in the euphoric sensations that it evoked throughout his Martian born body. Such 'pollution', as the broadsheets had condemned it, reminded him of his home, where an atmosphere such as this was as natural to the life that had emerged there as the oxygen-rich mix of Earth was to its own native population.

Home, he pondered, and not for the first time that evening, aware that he was going to have to find a way to quell these all too recurrent reflections, upon which, he had noted, he was allowing himself to become distracted.

He had been resident here for far too long; had seen far more of the city's gradual evolution than many of the shorter-lived natives around him. Unlike the majority of the wraithlike entities now passing him, silently in the smog; their humanity hidden behind brass-rimmed engineering goggles and oxygen-fed filtration masks, *he* could remember a time before Bazelgette had reclaimed this slice of land, building the brick promontory along which the wealthier classes now chose to promenade of an evening. How many of their faceless number, he wondered, would recall the time when the 'embankment' had been but a 'bank'; a treacherous mud flap of marshland, with the great river below him much wider and shallower at this point, causing many a scow to beach its load in the dark; to the delight of the early morning mudlark? As he walked he considered George Vulliamy's misnamed 'Dolphin Lamps' that spotted the paved walkway at intervals, and he harked back to the brief attempt to electrify the line, before their ultimate return to gaslight, and the primitive world that these people were so reluctant to leave behind them. A short blast on a ship's horn jolted him from his reverie, penetrating, as it did, the murk-muffled quiet, and followed, almost instantaneously, by the shrill of a pair of Peeler's whistles;

one within yards of his position, the other a short distance behind.

The Secretary removed his watch and noted how perfect the timing, as the sound of several sets of running feet pounding on the flagstones, reached his ears.

Their lungs were not the only part of a Martian's body more readily adaptable to an alien environment than their human equivalents, as both his hearing and his eyesight too had become that much keener, making it easier for him to see into the gloom and to calculate the size and weight of the approaching bodies. As the first set of footsteps drew close, he lunged into the fog; reaching for the leading figure, whom he dragged from his course to hold behind the Egyptian obelisk, known colloquially as Cleopatra's Needle. Clamping his hand over the diminutive runner's mask, he held him still as the peelers hurried past, continuing to blast their whistles in order to keep track of one another in such hazardous and visually challenging conditions.

Once he felt sure that the man's pursuers had made sufficient progress in the direction of Westminster, he released his prisoner.

"What news, agent?" he enquired quickly of the target of the officers' ire, knowing that at any moment they might lurch once again from the haze.

The agent bent forward, his hands against his knees, and retched while he fought to regain a regulated breathing pattern. Hugo Ballentine, the Inventor Royal; in the instruction manual to accompany his patented Rebreather apparatus, had advised against exertion of any kind whilst encumbered by his equipment. There had been a number of deaths attributed to hyperoxia, during the device's early developmental stages, when test subjects had begun to hyperventilate due to an acute claustrophobic reaction to being trapped behind it. A surfeit of oxygen, he had warned, being almost as dangerous as a total absence of such.

The Secretary reached behind his agent to adjust the intake valve; a safety feature that had been added to later models, and within a few moments he was once more breathing freely.

"Bombs," he began, pulling himself back up straight. "Not work of League. Happ'ny think it work of new recruits."

"New recruits?"

"Yes. Call themselves 'IRA'. However, recruits deny involvement."

"Hmmm," the Secretary mused, "descent within the ranks, eh?"

According to the dailies, the public's mood; vis-a-vie the recent spate of bombings that had been attributed to the nihilistic band of agitators and reactionaries that Agent A had successfully managed to infiltrate, was one of collective terror. Letters had been published in *The Times* calling for: 'The regular beat bobby to be armed with rifle and bayonet,' and for: 'an expansion in the ranks of the military forces in order that these revolutionaries be curtailed before they can undermine the stability of the nation; which, if left unchecked, would inevitably lead to invasion by a foreign power.'

But who was it that was so terrorising the capital if not the Anti-Alien-League, he wondered?

"What do we know of this 'IRA' faction?" the spymaster asked; this new appellation being entirely unknown to him.

"The Happ'ny woman does not entirely trust them," the agent replied. "They have yet to be introduced to wider membership, but big meeting tomorrow night," he revealed, as the Secretary stroked his chin. "New plan to be announced; new members will be there."

An idea had struck him: a radical notion; one unprecedented in all his years in the post, but it was an idea that fitted the few facts available to him and an idea that suited the personality of the most probable perpetrator of such an audacious deception. Could it be; he considered, that this so called 'IRA' were also a plant, but as part of an operation run by the British Intelligence Service rather than through his own Crown Agency? Was it possible, he then extrapolated, that the Prime Minister himself may have been using the League to bolster support for his own bill?

"I need to know everything about these newcomers as soon as possible," he said. "She would have checked them out in the same way that she did you. Find out who did their checks; find out *what* they know and get me detailed descriptions of them. I will need to see you again as soon as you know their next target."

FEBRUARY, 1895

The first thing that Hamble noticed when she awoke was that she was no longer in pain, though her head was spinning like a veritable dervish, as if to suggest that she had spent the previous evening over the road in The Imperial Arms, attempting to top her own, unrivalled in-house record for competitive gin drinking. Her mind was a jumble of blurred images and half-remembered dreams, as a night of drunken games in the company of the Chelsea Irregulars might have attested to. She should still have been able to recall something of the evening with a degree of clarity; though, whereas, as things stood, she could not even summon up her movements for the previous week! In fact, if anybody were to have asked her now quite what she was doing lying in a crumpled heap on the dusty, oil-stained floor, she was likely to have told them that she had tripped and fallen down a ludicrously large rabbit hole somewhere along The Kings Road, only to have awoken sometime later, to find herself a character inside a children's picture book.

Opening her eyes, she was relieved to find that she was not in an anthropomorphised animals' wonderland at all, but at home in the Old Fire Station, Chelsea; though how she had ended up there, she had not the vaguest notion. In assessing the facts, as her father had always taught her to do, it appeared that she had fainted, which was not like her at all.

She sat up, rubbed the dust from her eyes and licked her teeth, then cupped her hand over her mouth and sniffed her breath to test for alcoholic residue, but found nothing to suggest a night of debauchery on 'mother's ruin' with a squad of part-time hose monkeys. It was then that she realised that she was stone cold sober. What had she been doing, she wondered; unable either to coax her memories or to grasp the slippery threads of the dream from which she had just been torn.

She had expected to have felt pain when she had awoken; that, she remembered, but why was that? Had she been having a nightmare; one in which she had experienced a near-death scenario? Damn it, but it was at the very edge of her perception simply refusing to be called to account! However, she *did* remember falling; falling and landing, painfully, though not down a giant rabbit hole! The hole had been squarer and wider than a bunny's burrow, and tooled; more like a mine shaft than a hole. And there was a name too... Alyce? No, that was stupid; Alyce was the girl in the book!

"Abdul?" she enquired, noting the state of disarray surrounding her. Had she been robbed; was that what had happened? Had she been attacked in her own home, knocked to the flags and then left for dead? And where was that blasted factotum of hers? What in blue blazes was she paying him for if she still had to do everything herself? "Abdul?" she tried again, louder this time, just in case he was actually doing something useful like washing the Range Roller out in the yard, "tea, Abdul; now!"

But... wait a minute... 'Who the bloody hell was *Abdul?*' She *had* no factotum; she had never been able to afford one, yet she could see his face, as clear as day in her mind's eye; his untamed monobrow, bristling like a paintbrush moustache, hovering above his hooded eyes as if he were standing on his head. Or was this something else? Was she, in fact, remembering the face of the man who had robbed her?

"Hamble?" she heard: a voice that she recognised, but most certainly had not expected to hear. "Hamble?" it repeated, "I know y're out there, girl; I can hear y'talking. I need a hand, here. I'm running out a'steam."

Hamble turned toward the source of the voice: her late father's den; previously the Fire Chief's office, on the far side of the workshop. But had she and Abdul not dismantled the little lean-to sanctuary late last summer in order to make room for the mark 111 rocket?

And then he appeared, like Jacob Marley's ghost, exactly as she had last seen him, settled in the wooden wheel chair that she had designed for him, complete with its refillable oxygen tanks and breathing apparatus; front mounted steering wheel, handbrake and gas lantern, and the big brass winding wheel on the back, for its inbuilt clockwork engine.

"Don't just sit there, girl," he snapped; disdain in his tone, "I'm in need've a wind."

DECEMBER, 1898

Virgil had never forgotten the incident that had inspired him to devote his life to healing. He had been six years old. Father had called him to his study, early one Saturday morning to give him the news that his grandfather had 'passed'.

Used in a context other than simply to describe the movement from one place to another, the phrase had been new to him and so he had ventured to ask what may have been meant by it.

"He's dead!" his father had elaborated, irritated at having had to elucidate further, "he has expired."

Yet Virgil's expression must have betrayed his failure to fully comprehend an idea that he had no real frame of reference for, bar the stories that his mother would tell him of Jesus; who had 'died and then risen again'.

Spying this, his father had tried once more. "He has gorn," he had said; enunciating each word clearly and precisely through gritted teeth, "to meet… his… maker."

"Oh," Virgil had then replied, still not having quite grasped the finality of the concept, "and when will he be back?"

"He won't!" his father had spat, "Good God, boy; what does that bally Nanny teach you?"

And so he had taken the subject up with his dear M'ma.

His mother, however; to his thinking; then as still now, had been yet more obtuse. Having been both the daughter and latterly to become the *sister* of Presbyterian Ministers, *her* take on the matter had naturally been biased toward the indoctrination that she had received from an age not dissimilar to his own.

"Your Grandfather resides with Jesus, now," she had attempted to explain, "he has come home."

"Does Jesus live in Cardiff, too?"

He would always remember asking this question; something that his father had never let him forget.

But his mother had merely smiled at his naivety and stroked his hair, replying: "No, child; Jesus died long ago but then he rose, and now he resides within the hearts and minds of every one of us."

Nanny Ermintrude's counsel had been far more pragmatic.

"Tuberculosis," she had said, matter-of-factly. "It's an illness. People catch it and then they die."

"Like a cold?" he had asked.

"Yes," she had said. "But Tuberculosis is an illness for which there is no medicine, and so; unlike the colds that Gerald and yourself caught last winter, the people who catch *this* illness do not get better."

"But *why* is there not a medicine for Tooberkalosis?" he had asked, reasonably, he had thought at the time.

"Oh, I'm sure there will be; one day," she had said. "The doctors of the future are sure to find one eventually…"

His heart had skipped a beat the moment the SteamSteed had turned into Millman Street and Virgil had seen the old fire station; planks hammered into place over its entrance doors, as well as the windows and the winch door on the first floor. As they had drawn closer, he had also noticed a sign that had been nailed to one of the boards, warning: 'DANGER! KEEP OUT, BY ORDER OF THE CROWN'. Strangely, it had not occurred to him that; as a defector and traitor to the British Empire, Hamble's assets would naturally have been seized forthwith.

He had paid the cabbie, and then dallied a moment on the cobbles, until both he and his clamorous contraption had clattered from sight. He had then ducked, judiciously into the alleyway that led to the stables at the building's rear; he hoisted himself up onto the back wall, and dropped down into the courtyard beyond, where upon he was successful in jemmying the locks and gaining an inconspicuous entrance to the building. His heart had, however, sunk once inside, faced with the devastation that had been wrought upon his former lover's home. Hamble had never been what one might describe as 'particular' in the way in which she kept house, but even *she* would have been appalled by the chaos that the Crown's agents had left behind them. And that had been the moment that panic had set in. If the Secretary's agents had done this much damage in their search to prove Hamble's guilt, then they would probably already have found that which he *himself* had come here to find, and Captain Haversack would have a wasted journey.

However, the agents' search had not been as thorough as their paymaster might have expected of them, completely overlooking the building's cellar, the entrance to which, to be fair, was well hidden, under the heavy wooden workbench in the centre of the workshop.

On a chain hung from the rafters over one end of the bench, dangled a large iron hook. Once winched down, the nib of the hook could then be passed through a steel ring that was affixed to that end of the bench, which, once winched back *up*, would lift the bench; which was hinged against the floor at the other end, to reveal a spiral staircase leading down into the building's bowels. It had, so Hamble had once explained to him, been her bolthole throughout her youth and had ever since remained her private sanctum.

And that was where he had found it; along with her many plans and blueprints of inventions; some already made reality, but many, curiosities yet to come. 'The Brass Fist': the prototype; the world's very *first* brain powered, artificial body part, had been put to secondary use as a paperweight. It had been the first, most definitely; and now, without Hamble's unique expertise in the field quite so readily to hand, sadly, it would also probably be the last that might be available to him to fit…

The operation had gone to plan; it had been the sixth such replacement that he had fitted and so he could not say that he had not had enough practice at fusing bone to brass and connecting ligaments to copper wiring. It had taken him the better part of three hours to complete, on Hamble's workbench, with the patient's own brother acting as his nurse. On completion, he had received his fee: an envelope containing a single slip of paper, bearing a single line of hand-written information: intelligence that confirmed his earlier theory, that the Intelligence Service knew perfectly well the location of the so-called League's base of operations, but had done nothing to curtail their machinations.

Packing the brothers into a hansom; all the better for a slightly smoother ride back to St Bart's, Virgil donned his coat; pocketed the note and reached for the phial in his top pocket, only to discover an indelicate tear in the cloth of the garment: a rive that had almost completely removed the pocket and everything therein. It must have happened whilst he had been clambering over the wall into the back yard. Hastily attaching his Rebreather, he hurried outside to search the cobbled compound, frantically attempting to strike a Lucifer to light his way, but to no avail in the sulphur-dioxide-heavy atmosphere. The smog was such that he could barely see three inches past his nose; a near impossible ask, then, to expect to find something so small in such poor visibility. But find it he did, after several frantic minutes scrabbling in the dark, though his relief was to be temporary, as the bottle was broken; its contents no doubt dissolved into the puddle in which he had discovered it...

CHAPTER EIGHT:

ANARCHISTS AND INFILTRATORS

Castle Greckle, Bavaria, 1898

It had been three days since his team had departed for London. The Baron had expected to have heard at least something from them by now; even if only to confirm their having successfully located the target. Yet they had remained steadfastly incommunicado with his people at the embassy.

According to the regular reports that he received from his ambassador, the Anti-Alien League had recently stepped up their campaign of civil disobedience in the capital; somewhat exponentially; if he was also to believe the British media, having somehow acquired both the ordnance and the manpower to detonate several bombs in strategic sites scattered around the city. As yet, his spies had been unable to explain the group's sudden elevation from minor public irritation to full blown national inflammation in so brief a time period, unless his agents had decided to go 'off-piste'.

However, it seemed to him unlikely that this was their doing. He had sent them, armed with a rather powerful explosive of their own: something with which the Baron had expected to pique the reportedly unarmed League's interest; something that his network had assured him was outside of this crude clique's ability to source for themselves. His plan had been twofold: to give this ragbag conglomeration of malcontents access to a weapon with which to make a proper stand and; in the process, to rile 'the two thousand' into believing that their sanctuary was in jeopardy, thus shocking the British government into believing that they were fighting a stronger force than they had previously believed and distracting them whilst he readied his forces for a full-scale assault. But somebody had beaten him to it.

Observing as from a distance, Greckle felt that the most likely scenario was that a secondary force was in play: one with access to military-grade armaments and experience, but who were at once content to allow the League to take the credit for their work. In the eyes of *this* impartial viewer, there was only one viable suspect, and judging by this suspect's *Times*-reported reaction to the League as a 'real and present threat', he did somewhat condemn himself.

The Baron realised that he had underestimated the new Prime Minister and put the lives of his friends in grave danger in the process. It would seem, then, that Mr Periwinkle hankered for war after all; just as much, perhaps, as did the German Senate, and that he was *also* as prepared as they were to use his own people's fears as a basis to mobilise support for domestic militarisation. Oh, how he must be mourning the loss of Lord Salisbury, Greckle chuckled to himself!

"Oberst," he asked, turning towards the officer currently in charge of the war room; the newly built, multi-level operational headquarters, stowed within the White Tower: a space which had only recently become available following the hopeful return to Mars of his rocket, "how many Zeppelins do we currently have stationed in North America?"

The Oberst pulled a grey, cardboard file from a stack of such, opened it and read out the answer:

"Eighty-six, sir," he replied, sombrely. "I regret to report that we lost the Bismarck only yesterday."

The Baron pouted, stroking his grey flecked beard.

"Order the twenty furthest from the front line to disengage," he said. "Order them to gather as many troops as their captains will allow and to bring them home, but *without* overflying the battle zone. Is that clear, Oberst?"

"Sir!"

There was one thing that he particularly liked about commanding Germans, he decided; returning to his spot before the window, overlooking the forest below, and that was that when one gave them an order, they obeyed it; immediately and without question, unlike his English agents, who always seemed to believe that they knew best…

* * * * *

"Can't say as I cares much, f'bein' this end a'town," said Mrs Blaise. "'Stoo close t'the asylum, f'my tastes—"

"Shitsticks!" said Iggi, pulling up sharply and ducking into the doorway of Alfonso's barbershop, on the corner of Petticoat Lane.

"Whassa' matta'?" asked Mrs Blaise, quickly following suit and ushering Tiny in behind her.

"Over there," Iggi began to explain, pointing toward a figure on the other side of the road whose silhouette the fog was rapidly claiming, "bloke in the red fez—"

"Looks like Abdul," said Mrs Blaise.

"You know him?"

"Course I do!" the old woman replied, lifting two fingers to her mouth; presumably, Iggi thought, with the intension of whistling him, but realising as her digits arrived, that her mouth was covered by the grill of her Rebreather.

Iggi smiled behind her own mask.

"How do you know Abdul?" she asked, watching as the figure dissolved into the fog, just slightly ahead of them.

"'E w's the Pr'fessa's 'ouse boy," Tiny answered for her, "dit'n't much like 'im, meself; shifty little sod, 'e w's. An' 'e can't make tea f'shit."

"Of course he was!" Iggi remembered, recalling how she and Tiny had first come across the recalcitrant Egyptian on the road to Cefn Garw the previous summer. He had been Hamble's driver!

At the time, Iggi had been unaware of his true nature as an Agent of The Crown. She had always known that the Secretary kept agents whose identities even their fellow agents were not privy to: his 'elites', he called them: agents who he used for deep-cover operations. However, she had never met one; not that she was aware of, anyway. Abdul had been the agent sent to retrieve her, before she had had the time to enact her retirement plans. It had been *he* who had beaten her to Father McNulty, denying her the chance to exact hers, and her old friend Katie's, vengeance against the perverted old priest. Until now she had not put the pieces together; though to be fair to herself, she had been out of her tree on morphine at the time!

She had seen him after that, though; during her reprogramming sessions, but again, her mind had not been entirely her own, as they had kept her dosed whilst the Secretary's prime agent had tortured her in order to 'aid' her reinstatement to active service.

"He's also a Crown agent!" she told them now, "the Secretary's right-hand man, in fact. I didn't know at the time, but *he* was the bastard he sent to bring me back in! If he's here now," she considered aloud, her hand moving to cover the hilt of her pistol, holstered at her side, "then that can mean one of only two things. Either Ha'ppeny has a *spy* in her camp, drip feeding information back to the Secretary, or he's part of a Crown operation to close the League down tonight. We have to warn them."

* * * * *

It was a relatively obscure address, but then; Virgil supposed, what self-respecting anarchist was going to site their secret hideout in the middle of The Strand, or anywhere else; for that matter, where they might easily be detected by those against whom they wished to rail. It was, however, an area that was far from unknown to him. He had taken lodgings here in Whitechapel during his training at the Royal London; only a few streets, in fact, from where he now stood, staring at The Frying Pan: the public house that had been his local during his heady student days. He had returned to the area some years later in order to pursue his 'further education'; a place where the passages and alleyways were as familiar to him as were the bone saws and the scalpels of his doctor's bag. He was not proud of the man who he had been back then; indeed, the memory of those... extracurricular activities haunted him still; the blood curdling details revisiting him frequently, whenever he utilised the knowledge that he had so crudely acquired.

It felt to him curiously brazen, disrespectful, even, to be returning to this locale again now, after all this time away. He had been shocked to have read the address that his son-in-law had handed him; never having expected that he might find himself here once more. The longer he had maintained a distance from the scene of his 'fact finding forays', the easier he had found it to contextualise his actions and to forgive himself for that which the Secretary had bade him do, a decade past.

But now he was back; purely out of necessity, he told himself; revisiting in order that he might rescue a girl from no less a predicament and from no less of a monster than he had himself been; the irony of the situation at hand being far from lost to him...

His hands were a sweat inside his leather gloves, as was his brow; trapped behind Henry's mask, and his heart raced like that of a fox, run to ground by the Boxing Day hunt.

Harvey had shown his appreciation by furnishing him with certain information, procured through his contacts within the service: information that Virgil would not otherwise have been in a position to source. Ethel, his other daughter and Harvey's own wife, had already attempted to whittle the same from him on her parent's behalf, he had told him, and even Beatrice had entreated him over tea and crumpets at The Ritz, but the conscientious Admiral had steadfastly refused to be moved to betray his oath; until, that was, he had found himself in need of Virgil's unique services.

An address was all that the family had been pleading for; a location for the Halfpenny woman, as they had all been of the opinion that 'free' or otherwise, the service would have been worth nought if it did not keep a wary eye on former criminals such as she.

Ultimately, Harvey had come up trumps; not only supplying an address for their relative's kidnapper, but also joining a few dots for the Periwinkle clan and informing him of a time and a date when both his daughter and her kidnapper would most likely be on the premises: further proof, if any had been needed, that the Intelligence Services were one step ahead of such dissidents, but for reasons best known to themselves, were happy for them to continue to undermine civilised society; for the time being, at least. It was to be his best hope of finding Tatiana and returning her to the bosom of her family, though sadly for *him* it was quite probably the *worst* timing to be making such a move. The Secretary had been restricting his access to the drug that had been keeping his mind within the bounds of sanity, in order that he might keep him tethered until such time as the rogue had need of him as leverage against his father. Having lost his last two doses, he was now completely at the mercy of the caged beast within; quite uncertain of just how long he might be able to keep such an abomination at bay…

A huge faux frying pan hung over the doorway of an ironmonger at the Sandy's Row end of the street. Rising from the fog, it creaked on its rusted chains as he passed. It was the marker that he had been looking for. Beside the shop's entrance was a smaller door, one set back into the adjacent brickwork; a door split horizontally in the stable fashion. A sign at eye level, nailed to the wood declared: 'SOUP SUNDAYS', alluding to the premises' part-time function as an alms dispensary to the poor.

Virgil checked the pistol that he had tucked into his belt; pushed at the door and stepped through…

* * * * *

"Excuse me, but do you have such a thing as a 'skillet'?"

His interest piqued immediately, the ironmonger excused himself from his previous customer; leaving her to peruse the shop's rather impressive assortment of Babushka-like stewing pots alone, then turned to the three newcomers at his counter and ushered them through a beaded curtain and into a back room, replying; somewhat theatrically: "Why, yes of course, sir– madam; we have quite the extensive range, if you would care to step this way?"

As secret passwords went, it was a queer one. Iggi was not even sure that she would have known a 'skillet' if someone were to have crept up behind her and landed her over the head with one, and Tiny had been convinced that it was a type of freshwater fish. Of the unholy trio, only Mrs Blaise had ever been married, and was therefore the only one amongst them with first-hand knowledge of wedding gifts: "the only time y'r ever likely t'see one," she had assured them…

The inventor, Hugo Ballentine, could quite easily have retired following his patenting of his ubiquitous Rebreather masks. However, game changing as his creations had been for Londoners of the century's final two years; in that they allowed people to perambulate abroad in the now choked metropolitan air without risk of instant asphyxiation, it had come to his attention that not all internal environments could be said to be entirely airtight, nor could be adequately made to be so, thus; in many cases, necessitating the wearing of the cumbersome devices on the inside as well as the out.

To this end, Ballentine had ensured that yet unborn generations of his line reach retirement without ever the need to do a day's work, by unveiling the 'Domestic Rebreather': a bulky, tallboy sized, steam-driven pump that chugged away in the corner of any room that one cared to place it, dredging any poisonous fumes that may have seeped in through an ill-fitting window frame, or during a person's entry or egress; passing such gasses through an internal filtration system, and releasing a soothing lavender infused scent in their stead.

By late 1899, these devices could be found in the corners of most middle- to upper-class homes, offices, large shops and eating establishments. Luckily for Iggi and her Revolutionary Avengers, small shops such as the ironmonger in Frying Pan Alley, did not own a Domestic Rebreather, and so; when met at the entrance to the shop's back room by the League's doorman: a short chap with a fez atop his anonymising face mask, they were able to enter and to take their seats without being discovered...

* * * * *

He recognised her now; of course he did, in fact he could scant believe his failure to have done so on the day that he had removed her legs. A striking character; despite her deplorable personal proclivities and her nefarious past, Virgil had to admit that she did cut quite the dash as she slunk onto the stage, perfectly well attuned with the only pair of mechanical legs in existence.

They had been designed and built by Hamble to be worn by the Queen herself, when it had proved essential to remove the monarch from below the knees in order to save her life, but Victoria had rejected her bespoke brass prostheses, preferring instead to step out on a pair of purloined human legs.

Virgil wondered; not for the first time since Bea had made him aware of just whose legs he had appropriated, whether the Secretary's choice of donor had not been quite as random as he had admitted. Certainly, he would have had no reason to suspect that Virgil would have later given the girl the unused prosthetics, merely in order to provide himself with something positive with which to engage his mind in the hours directly following the operation, and thus keeping himself from succumbing to the symptoms of his malady. Had the Secretary a sense of humour after all, he wondered, or; more likely, had he chosen the Ha'penny girl simply to spite him, fully cognisant of their previous connection?

Fervently he wished now that he had known on whom he had been working, and had feasted upon the girl's guts when he had had the chance. Many lives would not since have been lost if he had eaten her then; the former Prime Minister's, for one…

Along a narrow corridor, through a long-abandoned kitchen, Virgil had come upon a chair facing an apparently bare wall. Only once he had taken his seat did he spy the two small holes that had been drilled into the partition at around the average human-head height. The primary function of the room next door seemed to be a meeting hall, though he could see that it also doubled as a store room for the ironmonger that fronted it. There was a small stage at the far end, though it was really no more than a series of wooden planks resting atop four old tea chests, with benches made from the same materials arrayed in rows in front; each one bowing at its middle as it strained to bear the weight of a line of disaffected lowlifes, incognito behind their Rebreathers. Nowhere could he see Tatiana, which by no means meant that she was not present.

Tuppence Halfpenny shushed the assembled, who had been applauding her entrance, and took her place at the lectern at the front of the stage. It was at this moment that he caught sight of a figure to the right of the stage that he recognised; a figure whom, although hidden behind a mask along with everybody else, Virgil knew instantly could not have been anybody other than Hamble's Egyptian factotum, Abdul. There were two obvious tells: his stunted stature and the fact that he still had on that ridiculous red fez!

'So,' he thought to himself, reaching for the gun that he had taken from Hamble's den, 'the Secretary had a man on the scene, did he? He must, therefore have known that Tatiana was a part of this 'League' and had omitted to tell him.' Virgil smiled behind his own sweat drenched mask. It would be his lucky day: two birds with one stone…

* * * * *

According to the intelligence gatherers at the German embassy; on the basis of whose shadow skulking, Iggi and her comrades were currently working, the Anti-Alien League were nought but a ragtag, tin-pot organisation, barely ranking as a prickle in the British government's 'thorn in side' stakes. The very fact that they were so significantly insignificant was supposed to have made their infiltration a simple matter, with string-pulling once inside the organisation, a complete doddle. The recent bombing campaign, however; not their own work, but attributed, none-the-less, seemed to have brought every rabble rousing revolutionary and long-suffering libertarian scurrying from beneath their moss-encrusted stones, all keen to throw their own two penny worth into the new reformation mix.

As things stood, this was not necessarily a bad thing. The Baron's plan had been for them to sow descent: to focus Periwinkle's government inward, whilst his own machine readied itself for the invasion, thus catching Octavian with his britches down. However, this sudden expansion in the League's ranks had obviously come to the attention of the Secretary, and he had sent his best agent to infiltrate the group, presumably to ascertain their strengths and weaknesses and to determine whether or not they were receiving foreign aid. Luckily for them, his agent was not what one would call a master of disguise, so with the element of surprise on her side, this time, it ought to be a simple matter, both to pay him back for what he had done to her when they had first met, and to nullify the risk of their being discovered before they had had the chance to fulfil their mission…

Iggi's eyes had not left the back of Abdul's head since they had entered the room. She had barely heard a word that Tuppence had said since instigating the meeting, whilst she had tried to work out how best to nobble her opponent before the League's leader did something regrettable, like mention them by name.

The room was packed. Of the three of them, only Mrs Blaise had taken a seat, with Tiny and herself, along with a further twenty or so late comers, left to idle by the room's only entrance. Abdul was only a few people from her. If she could just inch forward by degree, then she could slip a knife between his ribs; pierce an organ and step back before anybody noticed…But something or someone had distracted him; his face turning quickly towards the back of the room. She watched as he flipped secondary and tertiary lenses down over the goggles above his Rebreather, adjusting them by means of a cog and wheel arrangement on the side of his mask. And then he was gone. If Iggi had not been watching him specifically at that moment, then she would not have seen him move. He had been trained to be able to steal away unnoticed; skulking like a cat in a mouse's wake; even amidst a crowd such as this, but then, so had she. And so she followed him back into the shop, though staying behind the beaded curtain until she had seen him pass through the street door. No sooner had it closed behind him, than her hand was on the knob, turning it quietly before following him out into the smog. She could not allow him to gain any distance as visibility was poor to completely shit, but then neither could she move too quickly and risk losing her advantage. Stepping cautiously out, she feared for a second that she had already lost him as all was silent and as still as an abattoir after hours.

A near-distance tinkling sound; like steel cutlery being dropped onto a stone floor caught her ear and focussed her mind. Turning sharply to her right, she noticed that the door to the adjacent premises was ajar; a door that had been closed when they had passed it a short while ago.

Iggi may have left the service behind her, but she would never be able to stop herself from thinking like a Crown agent. These buildings were cheap; the dividing walls between them, often merely plaster, wood and lathe. What if Abdul; in his guise as Ha'penny's own security, had not been distracted by something *inside* the room at all, but by something beyond it instead; hence his heading next door in order to counter the threat rather than moving toward the back of the room? It crossed her paranoid assassin's mind that they could all have just walked into a trap. The mysterious bombers; whoever they were, could be about to strike again, and if they were who she had her suspicions that they *might* be; namely British military intelligence, whipping up a lather in order to discredit the League; something that she had not only seen done before, but had herself been a part of, then what better time to strike than whilst the bulk of London's anarchist community were gathered together in the same venue and at the same time…

* * * * *

'What did she think she was doing, dancing around the stage like a thing possessed? Why couldn't she just stand still so he could shoot her?'

The muzzle of his pistol rattled against the sides of the eye hole in the wall that he had poked it through.

"Come back, damn you!" Virgil snapped, lifting his goggles, as he could no longer see through the condensation that had formed over his lenses. His eyes stung, but whether from the sweat that poured down from his forehead or from the noxious chemicals at large in the air, he could not say. In fact, there was currently a lot that he could not say: the infection within him; if that was indeed what it was, now raging through his system like influenza through an East End rookery.

"Virgil Periwinkle," said a deep, heavily accented voice, close to his right ear.

He turned from his peephole in time to see a plague doctor in a fez raise a brass fist and punch him in the face. The impact cracked the Bakelite surround of the detachable filter that covered his mouth and nose. A second blow shattered the pump housing and cracked the air intake pipe; cutting off his oxygen supply from the tank on his back.

Inside the maelstrom of his fevered mind, the final connection to Virgil's human nature was severed by a third, catastrophic blow, which broke open the remains of his Rebreather, finally freeing the monster within him, and it reared up from the depths, claiming final dominion over his soul.

He had fought it for so long. Ever since he had stalked these streets in search of unholy knowledge, this brute had dwelt within him, itching to claw its way to the surface. He had suppressed it then; battling its inhuman desire to possess him. And on the Moon, such evil had been allowed to assert control; up there amongst the aliens, whose internal workings had made no sense to him. But there would be no going back this time. There was blood in his mouth; he could taste it against his tongue, and although on some level, the beast that had once been the highest-ranking medical practitioner in the Empire knew that it was his own, its tang still drove him wild with the anticipation of the kill.

Reaching forward with almost supernatural strength and speed, he took hold of the sides of his attacker's head and pulled him in, whereby he opened his jaw and bit off the man's nose.

His right cheek was to follow: a carnivorous kiss, whilst his hands pressed in like a vice, forcing the bones in his skull to shatter and the brain within to pulp, forcing it upward to fill the fez that had, miraculously, still been perched atop.

Dropping the no longer advancing carcass, the monster became aware that there was another stood before him: a female, this time; his heightened olfactory senses informed him. In her right hand she held a pistol, but her hand was shaking; almost as if it were fighting her for control of the weapon. She had removed her goggles as she attempted to take aim and he could see the fear in her eyes as she fought the will of her rogue limb. It excited him, but only for a split second; his very last split second before she divested him of his misery once and for all...

CHAPTER NINE:

THE SLEEPER AGENT

"Bugger," said Iggi, turning the body of the rabid animal that she had just put down, with the toe of her boot. Now that it had stopped slavering, she realised that she recognised the face. She had just killed another sodding Periwinkle! It was no great wonder, then, she considered, as she re-holstered her gun, that Gerald's arm had fought so valiantly against her discharging of the weapon.

'How was she going to explain this to Gordon?' she wondered. She was not convinced that he had entirely forgiven her for the last one yet. That was, she reminded herself, if he was still alive himself, which was still by no means a certainty!

"Iggi?"

It was Tiny's voice, muffled through his Rebreather, but close behind her.

Then Tuppence; from somewhere behind Tiny, asked:
"Wha's goin' on? Who fired tha' shot? Is tha'—?"

"Abdul, yes," Iggi replied, "or what's left of him, anyway. Killed by *this… thing,* which I just put down."

"Wha' is it?" Tuppence again.

"It was—" Iggi began, but again she was interrupted, though this time by a voice she did not recognise.

"My father."

The prettier of Tuppence's two minders had stepped forward, passing Iggi on her left, to kneel beside the more complete of the two corpses in front of her.

"Y'killtanuvva of th'Peri—"

"Stow it, Tiny," snapped Iggi, stepping forward and dropping to a squat beside her victim's daughter. "I had no choice," she said; it was me or him. You can see what he did to—"

"There was no love lost between my father and I," she said, in the most refined of upper-class accents. "Quite frankly, I believe you have done me a service. What I *don't* understand, however," she continued, pulling herself back up to her full height, "is why he killed poor Abdul."

'Poor Abdul?' Iggi mused, but she remained silent; listening intently to a distant ticking sound. As she began to push herself up, she caught sight of something underneath a chair that sat a little way beyond both the bodies. It would not have been possible to have seen it from any other angle, she realised, not in the dimly lit back room of the soup kitchen.

"Tuppence?" she said, slowly and coldly. "You need to get your people to evacuate right now."

"They evacuated 'emselves, th'moment they 'eard you fire tha' gun," Tuppence replied, stepping forward, "Wha—?"

"Good," said Iggi, standing up slowly; turning and gesturing that everyone move back, "'cause there's a bomb underneath that chair and its ticking has just got louder. Everybody, RUN!"

She felt the blast lift her from her feet and propel her in the direction that she had been running. She felt herself rammed against something hard and solid and then...

FEBRUARY, 1895

Jutting his jaw and pursing his lips so as to ensure a smoother, tauter, surface: a path of least resistance for the newly sharpened blade, he drew the cutthroat slowly across his stubble-addled chin, slicing against the grain for a closer, longer lasting finish. Wiping the razor against the dampened flannel that he had slung over his left wrist for the purpose, he then angled his cheek in profile and prepared for a second strafing run…

Gordon had awoken that morning mired by the oddest of preternatural feelings. A most decidedly queer sensation, by any accounts. It was as if he had suddenly forgotten something of absolutely vital import that he had been about to do that day. And this niggled him, as he had always prided himself on his singular ability to be able to recall even the finest of details pertaining to adventures long since passed, for the cobbling together of hair raising, on-the-fly anecdotes at society luncheons and the like.

It quite disconcerted him; he was loathed to accept, awakening to find his mind so preoccupied by a problem so inconveniently anti-productive. He had things to do, today: important things; things that required his full and undivided attention. He had not the time to waste dredging for a morsel of missing information, denied to him as with a fading dream; which, with the opening of the eyes, leaves nought but a vague vestigial of the night's mental meanderings.

He swiped again at his bristled face: a sharp upward motion, this time, but endowed with perhaps a mote too much pressure, for he felt a sharp nick; which upon inspection in the bathroom mirror, revealed a pinprick swell of blood, scarlet against the white suds surrounding it. In short order, it became a rivulet that dripped from the square of his chin, to mix with the soapy water of the bowl beneath.

He cursed aloud at his most pubescent of errors, dabbing at the bloody spot with the tip of his flannel. He was to host a dinner in a jot under two hours' time, followed by a lengthy disquisition on his recent adventures in The Congo, where he had come face to face with indigenes of the most sanguinary nature, yet had returned; reportedly, without a scratch. The last thing his reputation as a staunch and virtuous orator needed now was a persistent shaving cut, smudging his starched collar and dripping into his minestrone. Reputation was all, in this game, he knew, if his funding line was to remain free flowing.

Having doused his face in both warm and then ice-cold water; all the better to close the pores, Gordon placed a small tear of tissue over the wound. He then reached for his scissors and began a systematic topiarisation of his moustache.

Yet still he found that he could not dismiss from his mind, that which had so discombobulated him since first he had rubbed the dust from his eyes. Perhaps, he thought, it was because it was a feeling that he recognised; having indulged its like before, though for the life of him he found himself at a loss to recall the when. He had consulted his diary before beginning his ablutions, but had found nothing scribbled on the day; bar the prearranged 'dinner and discourse' at The Adventurers', to suggest a second, forgotten appointment. He had searched his wallet for anomalous calling cards; acquired since arriving home on Tuesday, in the hope that one might spark a memory of a promise made, but never committed to paper, but had yet drawn a blank there too. And then, as he was checking the balance of the two drooping handlebars of his pride and joy, a name came to mind in a flash. Three names, to be precise, occurring in quick succession: 'Alyce; Boff and Hamble', though he could think of no one who he knew by any of those most unlikely of monikers…

DECEMBER, 1898

After decades of unbounded autonomy in the field, the Secretary found himself; not unreasonably, aggrieved at his suddenly being called to report to a 'superior'. He was aware that his resentment toward such an unanticipated turn was likely affecting his judgement and stifling his ability to do the job to the extent of his abilities, and this he found intolerable.

The human Queen had always had quite the penchant for 'summoning' him to her side; as had her numerous transient prime ministers down the years, but that was all a part of the broader game, as far as he had been concerned; a game that he had himself set in motion, and so he would answer their entreaties simply because it was in his interests to do so. But things were different now, for the most important individual in Victoria's Empire; the arrival of the 'two thousand' had changed everything.

He was reminded of this fact as his SteamSteed drew up outside the recently installed, ornate iron gates of the 'Martian Embassy to Earth' for his monthly briefing. For the first time since Uncle's death; upon which he had assumed command of the mission at hand, he now found himself no longer the architect of his own destiny…

The ambassador; the man previously in command of the ship that had brought the first wave of settlers to Earth; itself now ring fenced and repurposed as his permanent 'embassy', was the man to whom the Secretary reported. He was young; far *too* young, in the Secretary's opinion, to have been handed such a huge responsibility. He suspected nepotism; that was how such appointments were usually decided on Mars; unless, of course, things had altered drastically in his extended absence; the ruling clans having somehow lost their suzerainty.

When first they had met, he had found the man respectful, almost to the point of reverence, but his humility had begun to wane all too quickly once he had begun to settle into his new post as mission controller. The Secretary now found himself likening the man to one of those newly wealthy, bourgeois industrialists with such a desperate desire to impress; who rode those damnable penny farthing contraptions across the junction at Oxford Circus with no real purpose nor appreciation for the positions of anybody else around them. Sacrifices had been made by the original infiltration team; forfeitures toward which he was singularly unprepared to make concession, not to mention show the slightest sign of respect for during these regular rebukes, and so the Secretary had quickly grown to abhor these audiences with the man who would one day oversee this planet on behalf of the council; a man who had so far made little effort to get to know its people nor to understand their ways. In fact, as far as he had been able to ascertain, in all the months that he had been stationed here on Earth, the ambassador had yet to set foot outside the confines of his ship!

"Reefus Questergard!" he announced, as if it had been some considerable time since the pair had convened, rather than the twenty-eight local days that it had actually been. He beamed as his agent on the ground was escorted into his inner sanctum by two burly guards. "It is good to see you again," he said, in perfect, if not a little stilted English, rather than the Martian that he would ordinarily have reserved for such meetings. He rose from behind his desk, smiling unnaturally, dismissed his guards with a blink, then thrust forward a rigid hand in greeting; but the Secretary merely frowned in response. When it became apparent to the ambassador that his guest had no intention of accepting his proffered hand, he instead, somewhat stiffly, used it to indicate the chair in front of him. "Please," he said, diffidently; if the

Secretary was not mistaken: the wind blown from his sails, "take a seat."

The Secretary had meant no particular offence by his refusal to make physical contact with his superior. Martians were not a naturally tactile race, preferring instead to greet each other with a more civilised contortion of their brow muscles; by which method they had learned that it was possible to convey the requisite level of either deference, decorum or dominion, that each party felt the need to commune to the other at the outset of a conversation; as, he felt sure, would the members of *any* race who valued their health over their need to be 'familiar'!

It had been a part of the Secretary's own remit as an infiltration agent to absorb and adopt such human conventions as 'the hand shake', in order that he might better 'blend with the wildlife', as it were; in the same way that it had been essential for the two thousand colonists to assimilate such primitive idiosyncrasies, quickly, in order that they might be more readily accepted into human society. As to why the ambassador suddenly felt the need to debase himself in such a manner, when the nearest he had come to meeting a human since his initial royal reception had been his calls for the Secretary to attend him, was entirely beyond his ability to reason.

"As this is an *official* meeting," the Secretary said, pointedly and in Martian, finally deigning to accept the offered seat, "I would prefer it, ambassador, if you were to use my official title."

"So noted," said the ambassador, his forced smile; yet another native observance, dissolving as he interpreted the exaggerated facial contortion that his underling was projecting. "To business, then, *Mister Secretary*."

He took a breath before continuing: "When first you broke radio silence to contact the council," he began, his tone now altered and more professional sounding in their native tongue, "you led us to believe that your mission objectives had been achieved; that the human race was as close to becoming a single, homogenised genus as was necessary for our requirements. It would appear, however, that your judgement was in error."

The Secretary's frown deepened as he considered where the ambassador's line may have been heading. Surely he was not still alluding to the Moonbase massacre? He had already been hauled over the coals for this particular oversight: punished by the council with their refusal to allow him to return home. It had been a single tactical miscalculation in a career that had spanned more than the average lifetime of any single life form on this planet. Any negative ramifications for the overall plan had been dealt with expediently and forthwith. He had underestimated some of the pawns on his game board: that had been his mistake; one that he would not be making again. He had misjudged the ingenuity of Hamble Blaise; the extent to which Virgil Periwinkle's mind had been damaged, and the sheer, blind tenacity of the man's younger brother, Gordon. But those problems had been rectified. He was a strategist; he did not leave things to chance. There were many ways to achieve the same ends, he knew, and only a fool would put all of his eggs in the same basket. His wits were far sharper than many of those on the Ruling Council and his ability to out-manoeuvre an opponent, rated second to none. By the standards set down for him, he believed that he had acquitted himself admirably and had nothing more on this subject about which to feel contrite.

"Were you aware," the ambassador went on, "that a Martian rocket left Castle Greckle in Germany, ten local months ago?"

"But of course," the Secretary replied, glad that today's admonishment would be taking a new direction, "my agent on the ground informed me that The Greckle fired it at the German Kaiser's airship in order to kill him, thus instigating a chain of events that enabled him to take his place as the country's leader."

"Did this agent *also* inform you that the rocket was not destroyed, but instead travelled on to *Mars*, where it crash landed just south of Kali?"

The Secretary's slight hesitation at this sudden and totally unforeseen revelation negated his need to answer the question asked of him.

"Was it manned?" he posed instead.

"It was. The planetary defence unit tracked three occupants leaving the rocket and entering the abandoned city of Kalora: two humans and a Martian. The Martian we were able to identify as a junior obs' technician; thought to have been killed in the Moonbase massacre. I have pictures of the two humans. Do these faces mean anything to you?"

The ambassador slid two grainy, monochrome photographs across his desktop toward him, both seemingly having been taken from the air. The first was quite obviously Hamble Blaise and the second, after some deliberation, would seem to have been the late Gordon Periwinkle.

The Secretary shook his head.

"Agents of The Greckle?" he suggested, frowning deeply. "But what is their objective?"

"We won't know *that*," the ambassador replied, "until we have them in custody, but suffice to say, these humans of yours seem somewhat less malleable than you had assured us that they would be.

"While at first your report of your work here appeared accurate," the ambassador continued, gathering back the pictures and slotting them into a file. "Victoria's Empire does; after all, encompass the majority of the civilised quarters of this world, it has since come to our attention that this apparent unity is a far more fragile state than you may have intimated. Are you also aware," he asked him, leaning forward slightly, in a move that reminded the Secretary of the current Prime Minister, "that Greckle controlled 'Germany' is preparing to invade the very seat of your Empire's power?"

The Secretary winced inwardly as he listened to this second assertation. He had spies inside Germany; deep-cover agents, whom he trusted implicitly, yet he had heard nothing to suggest that The Greckle was in such a position. True, since losing Von Bismarck, his main asset, intelligence had been patchy, but he refused to believe that agent F had been either lost or compromised.

"And what would give you that impression?" he asked, pointedly refusing to appear unseated.

'Had the Prime Minister's sabre rattling provoked its intended response?' he wondered, 'a response so recent that his agent had yet to get word to him?'

"Our observers on the Moon have identified twenty airborne dirigibles, retreating from the continent that I believe you know as 'North America' and heading for this particular island on a variety of different vectors."

"No airship has yet been able to breach this country's anti-airship batteries," the Secretary replied, discretely removing the miniaturised transmitter, disguised as a fob, from his Westcott pocket and calmly pressing the activation button on its top once more, as if merely checking the time. "Not without first having been dismantled and brought here by boat," he added, feigning confidence while he currently felt no such thing.

"We believe," the ambassador went on, "that the recent spate of bombings in the capital are possibly part of a German campaign to 'draw your fire', as it were; to keep you occupied and looking inward whilst—" but he paused mid-sentence as an alarm klaxon began to sound throughout the ship. "Perimeter alert," he said, toggling a switch on a raised wooden mount on his desk. Inset was a speaker grille and from the box's top protruded an adjustable brass arm, bearing a microphone. The ambassador pulled the microphone toward him, shouting: "Report!"

A few beats later, a tinny voice could be heard breaking through the grille, "Nothing to worry about, sir; it's probably just another badg—"

FEBRUARY, 1895

Gordon had closed his talk as he had closed each and every one of his nine post-adventure seminars to date, in the time-honoured fashion; laid down by the 'Ancient Order of Adventurers' as far back as 1715, with an ovation for the Sherpa whom he had lost during the expedition's final leg. As per tradition, a collection had been taken by Rumpole, the club's secretary; to be donated to Shadwrack's dependants, and a round of ale purchased from club funds, to be distributed between the man's colleagues, who had been mourning his loss in the basement tap room whilst Gordon had been delivering his epitaph in the members' dining room above.

But that was not how things were done over at the recently inaugurated 'National Geographical Society', a fact that was diligently pointed out to him afterwards at the bar, by none other than Israel C Russell, the man who had headed up the Society's first sponsored expedition, to Alaska, back in '90; to great public acclaim.

"We do things a tad more *progressively* over there," Gordon was informed, by the only man not yet to have laid his hat firmly in one camp or the other. 'Apparently,' he had gone on to explain, it was 'Society policy' only ever to engage Sherpas *local* to the area that one intended to discover. Caddies with *local* knowledge and *local* contacts being both cheaper and; to the Society's mind, anyway, 'superior'.

"One is less likely to *lose* one's help if one employs from *local* stock," his contemporary had rattled on, quite regardless of the many pouts, moustache twitches and raised eyebrows that his oration was eliciting among his peers. "D'you see?" and with this he added his tankard to the line on the counter awaiting a refill, courtesy of Gordon's tab. "Thus avoiding," he went on; to the indignance of all those present, "the need to ask one's fellows to dip into their wallets in order to recompense grieving families at the close of every bally adventure."

He had always been a tightwad, had old Israel, not to mention something of a braggart, and Gordon found himself willing away the time until his rival's resignation in '97, when they would finally be shot of the old windba— but hold on a moment! How did he *know* that he would go on to *do* that; two unlived years from that point? Yet absurd as the notion clearly was, he remembered it, none-the-less; as clearly as he could recall the wording of the letter itself, which had been pinned to the cork board in the lobby by Rumpole, for all to sneer and jeer at.

'The National Geographical Society represents the future of academic expeditioning', Russell had written; a copy of which he had also lodged with *The Times*: 'Whilst The adventurers are nought but a band of over privileged kleptomaniacs, with little or no interest in discovery, other than that which they can stuff and mount or purloin for the trophy room of their tawdry clubhouse.'

The date atop Russell's pen and ink tirade had been the first of March, 1897, but how could Gordon possibly have *known* that when that date was still yet to occur? He was pondering such a convoluted conundrum when his mind was once again assaulted with recollections that had no cause to exist...

...He is down in the tap room, this time, attempting to engage the services of a new Sherpa. He is standing on a stool in front of the bar, when suddenly, all hell breaks loose! An assassin has entered the club, all guns a'blazing; *his* name etched into every bullet...

...Gordon staggered, spilling his porter down his shirt front in the process; much to the amusement of his fellow members and thus exacted with a roar of inebriated approval. The unwarranted image had begun to fade, but his head still span faster than a child's wooden top. In the vague distance he could still hear old Russell, droning on; as was his way, about some such or other, but he struggled to focus, as yet another gratuitous scene unveiled itself...

...There is a name on the tip of his tongue, this time: a name that he knows means nothing to his conscious mind, but he can see her there, prostrate before him; battered and broken and about to breathe her last: *Hamble*!

They are not alone; there is another with them... a 'doctor' of some kind. He... no *she*, is connecting wires to Hamble's temples. She is talking to him, but her words make little sense: "I have lived *past* this moment and have travelled back," she says, which he presumes he has misheard... "I call this process 'The Rewind'," and again his cognitive processors are foxed. 'Rewind?' He thinks; as in 'reverse; back up; back track; unravel'...? "You must find each other quickly..."

...And then the floor hit him squarely in the jaw. Came at him; he would later forswear, with all the prejudice of a pugilist's dominant fist.

"By jove, are you alright, sir?"...

He eventually came to, to find himself in Rumpole's private office; the mounted head of a Tasmanian Devil staring down on him in an accusatory fashion as he lay on a chaise longue with a tartan blanket thrown across his chest.

"Y'seem to've taken a turn," the club secretary explained, passing him a tot of French cognac.

"Hamble," was all Gordon had to say by way of a reply, to which Rumpole merely frowned.

"Beg pardon, sir?"

"*Fez*!" was the next random word to cross his lips, followed by: "*Abdul!*"

"No, *Rumpole*," said Rumpole. "The fez?" he then enquired, doffing the culturally misappropriated affectation that he had lately taken to wearing, "me uncle brought it back from Egypt for me. Sir; ought I to call you a doctor?"

"*Virgil!*"

"Y'brother? Yes, of course! I'll send for him right away."

DECEMBER, 1898

Her ears were still ringing, even though it had been the better part of two hours since the bomb had gone off, making whispering; for Methusela, a practical impossibility.

"This iss s...s...supposed to be a c...covert operation," croaked Iggi, from somewhere close by, who as far as *she* was concerned, should really have been in a hospital receiving professional care for the wounds that she had sustained back in Frying Pan Alley, rather than hiding in the bushes on Hampstead Heath, attempting to co-ordinate an assassination. She was a tough'en, that one, and no mistake; she always had been, even as a kid, but judging by the extent of her *external* injuries, she would not be for very much longer if she did not get medical help. She had lost an arm; though oddly that seemed to be more of a relief to her than a concern, and she had broken her leg when she had been thrown past the rest of them to impact against a wall on the other side of the street. She had suffered burns to her head and had lost most of her hair, and her face was as lacerated as a fish filleter's fingers after a night on the sauce. At first sight they had presumed her dead, just like Tupp's scarfaced minder, who; although she had been a step ahead of Iggi in the race to outrun the blast, had somehow ended up on top of her; her neck broken and her bottom half missing in action. But Tiny had found a pulse in Iggi's neck; weak, but none-the-less present, and he had carried her back up to Petticoat Lane. The rest of them had staggered behind like a line of blind orphans on a rope, as not a one of them had a single disc of glass left to their goggles. Remarkably, apart from Iggi's, everybody else's Rebreathers had still been in a workable condition and only Slash's oxygen tank had added to the fireworks, and so Tupp had managed to cobble up a replacement for Iggi from her late friend's mask. The fact that all bar one of them had survived the explosion at all and; excepting Iggi, with no more than surface abrasions and hearing loss to report, had been nothing short of a miracle; not that Methusela believed in such things. She would not like to have taken even a stab at the odds of the bomb inside her indispensable still being inert, yet inert it was, and ready for the task that it had been brought all this way to perform...

They knew that they had to move fast. It had been Iggi's guess that the soup-kitchen bomber had been a member of the security services. This she had presumed because, of all of the city's other likely suspects, none would have had access to that kind of ordnance, nor the ability to pull off such a co-ordinated campaign. It made sense. Tonight's League meeting had attracted revolutionaries and dissidents from far and wide; all willing to throw in their lot with an expanding League. If Iggi had not shot Virgil when she had, then the throng would not have been spooked and that wily old bastard, Octavian Periwinkle would have been free of the lot of them in a single strike. And if that were indeed *true* and it did seem the most likely scenario; according to Iggi, then a clean-up squad would not be far behind them; the type of clean-up squad that left no survivors.

And so it was now or never, Tupp had decided, bundling them into a pair of passing Hansoms and heading north toward their target...

"Lissen," was what she had been attempting to whisper, before Iggi had croaked her reprimand, "we gotta' lil' problem wiv th'bomb. I's broke. Th'timer's knack'ed. I can't reconnect th'bloody thing. It'll still go boom when we need it to, bu' is' gunna 'ave t'be se' off by 'and."

"I...I'll d-do it," said Iggi, her voice only mildly quieter than her own.

"Nah, y'won't," Methusela told her, resolutely.

"I...I'm d-dying," Iggi persisted, "n-no point in us b-both—"

"Y'll never make it over th'fence. Tiny?" called Methusela, "Now, I don' wan' no argumen', boy; jus' sling 'er over y'shoulda' an' git 'er t'th' embassy. *Now*! Tupp?"

"Over 'ere, Mef, luv."

"Right. Tupp, you an' whasser name—"

"Tyana—"

"Yeah, that. You two go *wiv* 'em. Once the 'Un find out she's Octavian's gran'daugh'a, y'll be well safe. Wiv 'er as an 'ostage, we migh' even save a few lives."

"But Mef," Tiny protested. "You *can't*."

"I '*ave* to," she told him, striking a Lucifer so that she could better see the bomb in the gloom. "I's wha' we came 'ere t'do, wa'nit? We star' a war; we convince th'Martians that we ain't worth invadin'; they fuck off back 'ome, an' th'survivors build a *new* world wha's alien an' Empire free."

'Hmm,' she , 'that plan had made a lot more sense when Greckle had explained it to them, back in the castle.'

"*Tha's* yer plan?" asked Tuppence. Nobody else had said a word.

"Yep. I's all we got. Now fuck off, th'lot a'yer. Bit a luck, me daugh'a 'll still come frew, an' nun a' this'll even've 'appened."

'Mad ol' Mef': that was how they saw her. That was how *everybody* who had seen her since her release from Bedlam, saw her; with the exception of Greckle. He had spotted something else from the moment he had clapped eyes on her. "Something," he had told her; much later, when they had been alone together, "distinctly Martian…"

Shortly before Hamble had bought her mother's freedom; whilst the paperwork had still been going through, Methusela had been visited in the asylum by a creepy government official who had introduced himself simply as 'the Secretary'. He had stood by as they had strapped her to a gurney and wheeled her down to the infirmary, where she had been met by a masked surgeon whom she could have sworn she recognised. The surgeon had told her to bite down hard on a leather-bound stick that he had duly placed between her teeth, before proceeding to operate on her skull. She had not been told what the surgery had been for, but she had been a changed woman ever after it; losing her upper-middle, home-counties accent; her sense of smell and most of her teeth to whatever had been done to her, and it had not been long before she had become aware of an occasional spectral voice, whispering instructions inside her head; impelling her to do things that she would not otherwise have done.

Her daughter had been content to put the changes in her mother's character down to her years spent incarcerated with the insane, but Greckle had seen it immediately for what it was.

"I believe it would be known in your language as a 'Pilot Disc'," he had told her.

"A Pilot disc?" she had queried. "Wha' the fuck's one a' them when i's at 'ome?"

"It is an obscene relic of an abandoned technology that was outlawed by the Martian council decades ago," he had explained. "A small, round receiver is attached to the inside of the subject's skull; no larger than a penny piece. For the most part, the wearer is entirely unaware of the device's presence; save for the odd inexplicable headache and a vague feeling of being watched, but should the bearer attempt to step out of line, then they could be coerced, with a little gentle persuasion, into doing their controller's bidding instead. In effect," he had revealed, "he has turned you into a sleeper agent; presumably so that you could keep him abreast of your daughter's movements. When my agents brought her to Germany, I imagine he simply impelled you to follow her."

"So 'ow d'we get th'fuckin' thing out?" she had asked; reasonably, she had felt.

"We don't," he had said. "We *leave* it there, for the time being, and we use it to feed him disinformation. How often do you hear his voice?"

"Not much b'fore, but since 'e tolt me t'come 'ere, i's bin all th'bleedin' time! I's as much as I c'n do t'block th'barst'd out!"

"Then I shall show you to my transmitter room," he had said. "Stay close by my side at all times, Mrs Blaise, and tell no one of this; *you* will be my secret weapon..."

What Methusela would not have been prepared to do in order to help wipe the smug smile off of her former employer's face, could have been written onto the back of a penny black. She could think of nobody worse for the role that he was currently mangling, than Octavian bloody Periwinkle; an office that as far as *he* was concerned, he had been born to hold. It was funny, she thought, as she dug frantically at a fox hole with a stick, trying to expand it enough so that she could wriggle her scrawny old body beneath the fence; in the tragic sense of the word 'funny', obviously, how authoritarian positions were so often filled by the persons least suited for the job. The only role that Octavian Periwinkle was a *worse* fit for than his being Prime Minister; thought the woman whom he had once hired to bring up his children, was fatherhood. Sadly, however, the nearest she was going to get to repaying him for the things that he had both said and done to her *and* to his four sons; whilst the younger two had been in her care, was delivering the bomb that would kick-start the war that he would go on to lose. Sadly, she mused, as she dragged the lower half of her body through, he would never know that it had been her who had done it.

She had struggled for the past few weeks to resist the broadcast voice of the Secretary, as he had attempted to impel her to report on Greckle's readiness for war, but ultimately, she had succeeded in defying the machine inside her head, as she had been defying the influence of male domination her entire life. If he had thought that a mad old bint from Bedlam would have been an easy touch, then he had been very much mistaken. She had been a domesticised daughter and a pilloried wife. She was a suffragette: a nineteenth-century woman with a mind of her own. Fighting back was something that she had spent her whole life doing!

She was beneath the ship now, having inched herself along on her belly. The saucer bowed at its centre point, not quite touching the turf of the heath. This, she deduced, would be the best place to detonate the device for maximum effect. The timer mechanism discarded, she held in opposing hands, the two bare wires that its removal had revealed. It was at this moment that a deep, resonant drone chose to begin pulsing inside her head.

She could not have explained quite how she had known, but she felt certain that it was an instruction from the Secretary to contact him immediately. It hurt with the ferocity that she would have expected if someone had warmed a poker in a watchman's brazier and then poked it into her ear. With all her might she resisted the strangely compulsive urge to back out from beneath the ship and to head to the nearest telegraph office. And then, just as suddenly, an alarm klaxon began to sound, adding to the cacophony inside her head. Tears streaming from her already stinging eyes; blood dribbling, now, from both her nostrils, Methusela Blaise forced her hands toward one another until the bare copper wires touched. There was one word on her mind as the resulting explosion tore her and the Martian Embassy apart: a name. Hamble…

CHAPTER TEN:

THE END OF THE WORLD

FEBRUARY, 1895

"'Amble? 'Amble, girl! Get that skinny arse a'yours up 'ere now; I needs ya!"

It was the oddest thing, but every time she heard her father's voice it made her shiver, involuntarily; as if someone had just walked over her grave. And when she saw him, the feeling was twofold; as if she were looking directly at a ghost. 'But why should that be?' she wondered, questioning her own sanity, and not for the first time over the past two days. Her father was not dead, he was very much alive, though she had the weirdest feeling that he *should* have been; as the fractured, shifting memory of his funeral and of the eulogy that she had delivered to their friends and family, felt as real to her as the taste of cold tea against her tongue did now.

Unable to sleep, Hamble had spent the night pouring over her notes for the Brass Fist, an invention of her father's; but, as usual, a working prototype that *she* had actually put together. It was something that they had been working on for some time, and by royal appointment, no less: a prosthetic replacement hand for high-born amputees; stronger and more durable than its flesh-and-blood equivalent and with various built-in upgrades, such as a wrist mounted watch; a skeleton-key finger attachment and a pop-up palm compact for the ladies. Actually, realising the model had not been the problem. She had put it together in a little under a fortnight, utilising scraps of copper and brass plating left over from the white elephant that had been his Moon rocket: the rocket that now took up a large amount of their available working space, not to mention their most valuable resources. She had based the Fist's design on a plated steel gauntlet that she had 'borrowed' from a suit of medieval armour that stood in the vestibule of the British Museum. The only problem with it had been the power source. Her initial plan had been to use a 'sun catcher'; another of her father's ideas that she had brought to fruition. She had installed the original on the roof of the workshop to focus the sun's rays through a giant magnifying glass, positioned above a tank of water, but although the idea had been sound enough in theory, a rooftop in 1890s' London had probably not been the best place to have tested it. A steam pump had been her second thought, but she had quickly dismissed this, too, as just as unworkable.

And then it had hit her, just as she had been dozing: a flash of inspiration from wherever it was that such things came! She had dispatched a telegram to the palace immediately; to the shifty mandarin who had charged her father with the project in the first place, requesting an audience with the Surgeon General. She had spent the rest of the night checking; rechecking and refining her idea of fusing bone with metal, muscle with rubber and nerve to wire.

The idea had come to her fully formed, much like the 'memory' of her father's send off. She had seen the operation being done: experienced it in the strangest of waking dreams. It was almost as if she had actually been there and was in fact remembering rather than merely imagining!

"They're sending a cab!" her father went on. "We'll be meetin' with the Surgeon Gen'ral. Best frock, 'Amble, my luv; I don't want you showin' me up. Oh, an' brush yer 'air! Y'can explain t'me 'ow it works on the way over."

"Ah, Harold, old man; good t'see you. It's been too long! Harold, would you allow me to introduce the Surgeon General, Dr Virgil Periwinkle? Dr Periwinkle: Harold Blaise, the Inventor Royal."

"Very pleased t'meet you, sir," said her father, offering his hand to the Queen's physician, who bent to take it in both of his, shaking until the point that she quite expected him to need the device that they had travelled there in order to demonstrate.

"Hamble," said Hamble, offering her own hand to the doctor, as it was clear that her father was not going to make an introduction on her behalf.

"Charmed," said the doctor, taking her satin gloved fingers in his and raising them to his lips. "You must be the professor's daught—"

"His *assistant*," Hamble interrupted, firmly, but with a sardonic twinge that caused him to both smile and, in the same moment, to raise a questioning eyebrow.

Dismissing her entirely for the second time of meeting, the apparently nameless 'Secretary' rolled her father to one side.

"Would you care f'r a mid-morning snifter, old man?" she heard him ask. "Before we get down to business?"

"Don't mind if I do, sah," her father replied. "Hamble? You're alright explaining m'workin's to the doctor, aren't you? Don't need me for half an hour or so?"

"I think I can manage," she said, resignedly; hefting the case that he had had her carry from the cab, up onto the doctor's workbench.

It was strange, but she could have sworn that she had seen this Doctor Periwinkle somewhere before, but for the life of her, she could not recall the where. She checked herself as she felt a tingle of instantaneous attraction toward him, but also something else; something that she could not quite put her finger on. Was it *fear*?

She judged him to have been in his late forties; his slicked, dark hair which had begun to grey at the temples being the giveaway of middle age, as; other than that, he had the bearing of a man a good few years younger than he no doubt was. He was bright, ebullient, even, though he had about him an almost tangible air of sadness. Nothing instantly definable, but it was as if he carried within him a heavy mental burden of some kind. The ring finger of his left hand told her that he was spoken for; though he had been fiddling with it incessantly since she had entered the room, as if it irritated him so; and the photograph on the wall above his desk confirmed the presence, not only of a rather regal looking wife, but also of two pretty young daughters, although judging by his own likeness in the family portrait, the grouping had been captured quite some time ago.

She was going to enjoy working with him; she knew this immediately, and her father would hate that, which was all the more reason to…

…she staggered; her head suddenly pounding and as heavy as an anvil, as if it were being used to house a raging lunatic, like those with which her mother was currently being forced to billet. She reached for a chair to support her as the maelstrom whirled within her skull, threatening to overwhelm and to over balance her. She saw a bill, posted to the brickwork of a dark, foreboding alleyway; beyond it, nothing but a swirl of dark grey fog, picked out in the fading flicker of a gas lamp. The words 'WANTED' and 'REWARD' were picked out in jet black ink; topping and tailing the bill, around the picture of the man into whose arms she had just fallen…

"I say," said the doctor; his arms around her as if they were concluding a dance. He lowered her into the chair that she had grabbed at for support and produced a phial of smelling salts from his Westcott pocket.

"I'm so sorry," she said; inhaling sharply of his offering. "I don't know what came over me."

"May I get you a glass of water?" he enquired, "and then, perhaps, I should recall your father?"

"No," she replied emphatically. "I'll be right as rain in a moment, and besides, I need to show you how the Fist works…"

DECEMBER, 1898

Kalora City, Mars…

(Translated from Martian)

"You appear troubled, child," prompted Boff, looking up from her work and lifting her goggles away from her eyes to rest them against her forehead. "It's that sigh that gives you away, dear."

Putting down her soldering iron, the professor swivelled her chair to face Alyce, who was sat, a little way away from her, hunched over the makeshift communications board and the notebooks that she had been studying for the past two hours. Alyce, in turn, removed her headset, put down her pen and rubbed at her weary eyes.

"Just… frustrated," she explained, angling to face the professor. "It has been three cycles now," she reminded her, "and yet nothing appears to change, neither here nor on Earth. You said that we would not be aware when the shift occurs; that the new reality will seamlessly replace the old, and that our memory of events from *this* reality will disappear with it, but… explain to me again, please;

because I do not think that I have understood correctly: How, then do we know that it has not already happened?"

"Because you still know to expect it," Boff said, brightly and with a kindly smile that reminded Alyce of someone else; though she could not recall quite who: the creases around her sunken eyes deepening and the wrinkles at the sides of her mouth spreading ever outward across her time ravaged cheeks, like ripples responding to a pebble dropped into a subterranean reservoir.

"It would be my guess," the professor continued, unperturbed at having to repeat herself, "that they are yet to have made a significant enough change to affect the wider universe." And she leant forward to rest her hands against her knees, "the larger the adjustment; the greater the effect on the fabric of the cosmos. Smaller changes do not always make a difference to the overall plot. Tea?"

Alyce smiled and nodded her approval at the suggestion. She had grown quite fond of the tea-obsessed old professor over the cycles that they had spent together; hunkered down in the rubble-strewn mid-levels of long abandoned Kalora.

When they had first come to Mars in search of her help, Alyce, Hamble and Gordon had not had the first idea of what to expect of her. It was likely; they had decided, that if she did actually exist and that they were able to make contact with her, then she would not have been instantly sympathetic to their cause; after all, to ask for her help would be to expect her to betray her entire race for the benefit of three complete strangers. It was quite possible, they had all three agreed, that she would have instead betrayed *them* to the Martian authorities. It had, of course, to use Gordon's parlance, been more than probable anyway, that they had embarked upon an 'interstellar wild goose chase', as they could not even be sure that they would find her; let alone be certain that she had ever really existed at all! The Greckle's memories of her had been hazy at best: almost as if she really had been nought but the bedtime story that Alyce had been taught as a child. The professor had since explained that this was because she had spent numerous rewinds attempting to remove herself from the planet's historical record.

Alyce would have expected such a person to have been bitter and paranoid, rather than the philanthropic Samaritan that they had ultimately encountered; having spent so long running and hiding; trying to protect her great discovery from being taken from her and misused by the council. However, she could not have been more wrong...

The kettle whistled and Boff proceeded to brew them a fresh pot of tea. Resting against the worktop in the galley as she waited, she indulged Alyce with another, slightly more detailed explanation:

"On each of the occasions that I have used the process myself," she began, "I have known the exact moment that I would need to rewind *to*, and precisely what events I would need to edit in order to rewrite the outcome to my advantage. In some cases, this has meant simply not doing something that I had previously done. For example, the second time around, I did not attend the council audience that The Greckle had organised on my behalf, whereby we were to have presented my discovery in the hope of receiving a development grant for The Rewind project. In the original version, both Greckle and I were arrested and charged with crimes against our people, but on my edit; with the benefit of a little hindsight on our side, we were both able to avoid the meeting and thus evade imprisonment. I took my discovery and went into hiding, after helping The Greckle to flee to Earth; not that he will remember it quite like that, of course! On other occasions, I have had to make more significant alterations to established events in order to stop other people from doing things, or even to coerce them into doing things that they had not previously done. Each time I knew exactly what I was doing. However, Gordon and Hamble had no such luxury. I chose their edit point for them based on information that I had been able to glean from Gordon on a previous attempt to rescue you."

"A previous attempt?" asked Alyce, bemused; having not considered the possibility that Boff's rescue had been anything but fortuitous timing.

"Oh, yes," Boff admitted, turning to stir the tea in the pot, "In the original version, none of you survived long enough to reach the edge of Kalora! You were destroyed by a missile fired from an ornithopter. But I rewound and scuppered that particular ornithopter before it left its bunker.

"On the second attempt you were all killed in the tunnels; the third: captured and tortured after your fall down the lift shaft."

"So, this was your *fourth* attempt to save us?" Alyce asked, astonished to realise quite how lucky she was to be alive.

"Fifth," Boff corrected her, "I couldn't rewind them without at least an idea of how far they needed to go back. I gained that information on my fourth attempt, but Hamble died before I was able to programme the machine. Fifth time lucky."

The concept of travelling backwards along one's own timeline still baffled her and so she pushed again, leading with what she had understood: "And whilst everybody else's memories of their previous lives disappear," she said, hoping that she had finally managed to get her mind to hold onto the basic mechanics of the operation, "yours are retained because you are the only one to have lived that alternative?"

"Precisely," Boff replied, pouring two cups and passing one to Alyce. "Eye of the storm, my dear. I remember because it was I who made the edits. As fa's as everybody else is concerned, they are living those moments as they happen. I am the only one to have moved, therefore only I have lived past that moment in order to have a memory of things any other way. Simple! Your friends Gordon and Hamble will also retain their memories of their former lives lived, but we will not. In this instance it is only they that have moved. Well," she said, a new crease folding into the collection on her brow as she paused, "I hope they do, anyway."

"You *hope* they do? Is that not the whole point of sending them back?"

"You forget, child; this technology was developed with Martian biology as its template; mine, in fact. Until now, I was the only one to have traversed time in this way. Although the human physiognomy is very similar to our own, it is by no means the same. Given time, and a human specimen to work with, I'm sure I could refine the process to account for any genetic variables but, as you will recall, we were somewhat pressed for time—"

"So, they might *not* remember?" Alyce asked, for the first time realising that the life that she was currently living might not have been as temporary as she had presumed. "And what happens if they do not?"

Again, Boff smiled widely, and this time Alyce remembered on whom she had seen it before: her grandfather, just before he had breathed his last in the euthenasium.

"There are always other options," Boff said, supping at her tea, "when you are in possession of a machine such as this."

Alyce took a thoughtful sip of her own. There was still one thing that eluded her about The Rewind process; something that the professor had said to Gordon just before she had sent him back.

"You have explained how it is not possible to rewind a subject any further than their own years," she said, "I understand that, but would it not have been easier for *you* to have rewound along your *own* timeline; back to a point before the original infiltration team were sent to Earth? Could you not then have rigged their rocket to fail, as you say that you did with the ornithopter that would have killed us?"

Boff laughed, as if the answer to such a question were almost too obvious to warrant a reply.

She finished her tea, retaking her seat at her desk as she did so.

"There is," she said, ominously, "a side effect to The Rewind process." Her smile receding as she spoke. "It took me a while to notice it," and she paused, as if in thought.

Alyce raised her eyebrows in the hope of encouraging her to continue.

"I am not as old as I look," she eventually revealed. "If I had never used the machine, then I would currently be a mere fifty-two orbits old; far too young to be able to rewind to such a target! However, each time I *do* rewind, I seem to age by that same amount again. I have, therefore; all told, lived my life three times over, giving me the rather haggard look of a woman of a hundred and fifty-eight! That is the refinement that I am currently working to adjust, as I now have a somewhat limited number of rewinds left to me."

"I am sorry," Alyce squirmed, "I did not know—"

"Don't be, child. How could you have known? This is why I did not expunge the memory of my life entirely. I needed The Greckle still to be able to remember me;

along with some semblance of the plan that we had concocted together, so that he would send you to me. However, I could not risk the council unravelling our plan and so I travelled back and took myself from them. Gordon and Hamble; though I fear it will mostly be on poor Hamble, are our last and best hope to save the people of Earth—"

A light had begun to flash on Alyce's lashed-together console, instantly distracting them both.

Alyce hurriedly pulled her headset back into place and scanned the paper readout as it ticked slowly from the machine.

"I was able to intercept the signal being transmitted from our base on the Earth's Moon," she said, as the paper revealed the latest news of events on the Earth's surface. "It would appear that a bomb, with explosive capabilities in advance of anything that our intelligence believed the humans capable of creating, has exploded in the imperial capital. Its epicentre seems to have been the Martian settlement ship—"

"Could it have been an accident? Could the ship's engines have overloaded?"

"Doubtful. They were apparently powered down at the time. Ah…"

"There's more?"

"Several armoured airships have been sighted approaching the same city, dropping bombs of their own. It would seem that the humans are at war…"

FEBRUARY, 1895

"So, this is where you spend your days when you're not bothering tigers and baiting cannibals, what?"

Enter Virgil Periwinkle, the elder of the Periwinkle quartet: the most accomplished; the most respected and the most advantageously paired of the four brothers; let no one forget it.

It had been a little over a year since the two brothers had last met; it having been the occasion of Ethel; Virgil's youngest daughter's, wedding, in the private chapel on the family estate in Sussex. Incidentally, Gordon recalled, it had also been the last time that he had seen anybody that he was related to, though he had an inexplicable headful of memories concerning adventures with so many of them, that he found himself currently unable to account for.

"It is agreeable to see you too, brother," Gordon said, shifting into a sitting position on Rumpole's chez longue and draining his medicinal cognac.

"I'm the bally Surgeon General, y'know," Virgil reminded him, pulling up a chair and sitting himself down beside his patient, "not some peripatetic country quack making house calls on a boneshaker!"

"And yet still you come. Thank you, Virgil; your loyalty to your kin is to be lauded."

There was little love lost between these two sibling parentheses. Virgil had made it known from the outset that he wholeheartedly disapproved of Gordon's chosen profession, citing it as 'merely an excuse to drink gin on foreign verandas at another fellow's expense'; a belittlement that Gordon had taken quite the exception to at the time.

He wondered now as he had often done before, what the estimable Mr Freud might have made of his opposite number? On the one hand Virgil did like to make a public display of the burden that his younger, less auspicious brothers presented him, but on the other, Gordon knew; having gossiped endlessly on the subject with the man's dear wife, the ever-delectable Beatrice, he did like to castigate himself to the point of unreason for his failure to save their mother; hence his presence at Gordon's side now.

"What seems to be the problem?" Virgil asked, as if Gordon had been quite any patient wealthy enough to seek out his expertise in the opulent surgeries of Harley Street, "some bizarre tropical malaise, I shouldn't wonder, or, by chance, a simple case of *'coup de soleil'*?"

"Very droll," replied Gordon, presuming the second of his brother's sarcastic diagnoses to have alluded to the tan that he had acquired since last they had met, "but not very professional,"

"Look toward the light, would you? There's a good chap. Hmm…"

"Hmm?" Gordon repeated, perturbed by Virgil's pause.

"Y'pupils seem exceptionally dilated," Virgil noted, "have you taken a blow to the head recently?"

"I fainted," Gordon recounted, "in the club; at the bar. Bashed the ol' noggin as I went down."

"*You fainted?*"

"Clean away."

"*In company?*"

"In front of the whole bally membership!"

"Good God, man!"

"Why? What d'you think's wrong with me?"

"Father was right! You're a bally molly, man!"

"A mol— how dare you, sir! I know which side my butter's toasted; from which side me shirt buttons, don't y'kn—"

But he was interrupted by the thrusting of a wooden stick into his mouth.

"Say 'aah',"

"Aaaah,"

"Good. Now, can you stand?"

"I think so, yes," said whilst whipping the tartan blanket from his knees and swinging his feet to the floor.

"Then I'd like t'see you walk over to the window; turn around and head ba—"

But Gordon did not hear any more of his brother's instructions. Once again, the floor had risen up to greet him; his chin taking the brunt of the action this time around…

…he was in what appeared to be a charnel house; bodies strewn around the walls in great piles. He was there with two fellows that he could not name, though one had the distinctive bearing of a Sherpa. His other brothers were also present: Aubrey and Gerald, though neither was conscious nor in particularly rude health. Virgil was there too; though in a state of dishevelment that belied his character, and beset by a frenzy that knew no name…

…"Gordon? GORDON!"

A sudden slap to both cheeks brought him bolting back into the here and now.

"Ow!" he exclaimed, opening his eyes to see a much cleaner cut Virgil, looming over him like a vulture contemplating carrion on the Savannah plains, "Is that how you'd treat the Duke of Argyle?"

"Thought I'd lost you, old man. Do you feel any pain anywhere; ears ringing, numbness of the extremities?"

"Only around the chops, thank you!"

"Here," Virgil said, refilling Gordon's glass from the crystal decanter on Rumpole's desk, "drink this."

Gordon did not wait to be encouraged further.

"You were convulsing," Virgil informed him, "thrashing about like a man possessed. Has this sort of thing happened to you before?"

"How the bally hell should I know!" Gordon snapped; aware that he had begun to shake, and so pulling the blanket from the chez to wrap around his shoulders. "Me mind was elsewhere."

"Where, exactly? Could you describe it? An ethereal dreamscape, no doubt: no up nor down; floating in a miasma of coloured swirls—"

"If you're about to suggest a dalliance with the poppy, then I should ask you to take your leave," Gordon replied, pointedly; suddenly cold, even though a fire smouldered in the grate in front of him.

"Then where were you?" Virgil enquired. "It might help my diagnosis if I were to know some details."

"In the future," Gordon said, though wished immediately that he had not, as the look on his brother's face, though initially quite priceless, quickly took on the countenance of a High Court judge in a black cap, about to pass sentence.

"The future?" Virgil asked, as if the concept of such a thing even existing was an utterly preposterous suggestion. He pulled a note book from his Gladstone and began scribbling furiously.

"The future," Gordon reiterated firmly, "as in, scenarios that have not yet occurred, but which I am remembering in detail as I would recollect a night at the New Regency theatre."

Virgil stood up; tore the note that he had written from his book and tapped twice at the oak panelled door. It was opened immediately, with Rumpole's great beak of a proboscis clearly visible through the crack, as Virgil passed him the slip of paper before returning to his brother's side.

"Tell me more," he said, pouring a cognac for himself and setting himself back down in Rumpole's seat.

The shivers had passed and his temperature was returning to normal, though Gordon was aware of a slight tingle persisting in his fingers and toes.

"It is as if I have already experienced events that are still yet to pass," he said, qualifying his observation: "quite ridiculous, I know, but there you have it."

"Are you alone in these… dreams?"

"Not alone, no, though my companions are not always currently known to me."

"And in these dreams, are you aware that you are, in fact, dreaming?"

"They are not dreams, Virgil; lucid or otherwise. They are far too detailed; the plots are linear, and although fantastical, there is a definite logic to them."

"Do you 'recall' any names?" Virgil pushed, "names of individuals that you 'don't yet know'?"

"Several," Gordon confirmed, "though one in particular does come to mind: a name that is repeated, over and over. A woman's name; I am sure, though one that I am certain I have heard nowhere before."

"And that is?"

"Hamble."

"Hamble?"

"Have you ever heard of that name used before now?"

Virgil paused, frowning.

"You *have*; haven't you!"

"Only once," Virgil admitted, "and recently too, though I grant you; it is an unusual name, but it is by no means unique."

"Where?" Gordon demanded, "Where did you hear it? I must know! It is imperative that I find the girl with this name!"

"I say, calm down, old man; you're getting hysterical—"

A knock at the door interrupted Virgil's verdict and he moved quickly to answer the summons, as if, Gordon worried, it had been expected.

Two men entered the room: two burly gorillas of men, both dressed in long white coats; one bearing a large and lethal looking syringe, whilst the other held out a strapped jacket with arms designed for an orangutan.

"No," Gordon said, the penny dropping; dragging himself along the wooden boards on his posterior in the direction of the window, "How could you? I'm your brother; your bally brother!"

DECEMBER, 1898

'Guilt', apparently, was one of the tenets of self-consciousness: 'evidence, therefore'; Tiny had been led to understand, 'of a highly evolved intelligence'. He had read this in an article on the differences between 'sapience' and 'sentience', in a back issue of *The Modern Heretic*: a science and philosophy-themed periodical that he had found lurking in The Adventurers' library the previous year, whilst he had been waiting for Captain Periwinkle to conclude an interview with a journalist from the self-same publication.

According to the author of the article, that if he recalled correctly, had been titled: 'That Which Sets Mankind Above Beast', the ability to experience such an emotion; or indeed its equally elusive bedfellows: shame, pride and hubris, was exclusively attributable to your Homo sapiens.

He had wondered then as he wondered now, quite how such an all pervasive and burdensome feeling could be considered a positive trait in the human being; as to his mind it fair fogged the workings, often to the detriment of his capacity for reasoned and rational thought.

He was reminded of the way that he had felt during his trial, following the death (whilst in his care), of his former employer: the redoubtable Major Henry Fanshaw, OBE; the much-decorated old war horse; society raconteur, and latterly 'Gentleman Adventurer' (with tendencies toward the suicidal), whose nieces had tried to sue him for his failure to keep their uncle alive. Although he had gone on to be exonerated of any and all blame for Fanshaw's tragic demise, Tiny could still not help but feel a twinge of guilt; even all this time later, whenever the memory of that unfortunate episode resurfaced…

The guilt that he felt now, however, was no mere twinge. It transcended, even, the metaphorical birch with which he beat his back whenever he allowed himself to remember how he had let Iggi down the last time, by getting himself shot and thus not being conscious when Agent X had ripped off her arm.

This new guilt, though, was total: it was all consuming and life altering. He should never have let her investigate the soup kitchen alone; he should have gone with her! If he had have done, then perhaps she would not now be in the state that she was: battered, bruised and still bleeding from injuries sustained by her having been too close to the bomb when it had detonated.

Since arriving at the Hun embassy, Iggi had received only the best of medical assistance; courtesy of the Baron's personal physician, who had been flown to England as soon as the German leader had become aware of his agent's mortal plight; it having been considered unlikely that she would have survived the return journey herself.

"W-we d-did it," Iggi mumbled, much as she had been doing since he had first brought her to the embassy. He had added his own affirmations the first few times that she had said it, but he had soon come to doubt that she could hear or even understand him, so instead, he had simply kept a vigil; sitting alongside her bed and stroking what parts of her head were visible beneath the crepe, and had not been burnt away by the searing heat of the explosion.

Yes, they had done it, but quite what had they done? The plan had seemed quite obvious when the Baron had explained it to them, back in Bavaria, all those weeks ago. They were to make contact with the League and to give them the wherewithal to destroy the alien ship. This act, coupled with a subsequent attack at the heart of the British Empire by their sponsor's army, was to have destroyed the Martian's faith in their Earth agent, causing them to rethink their colonisation plans and return to Mars.

But what he, Iggi and Methusela had not devoted enough consideration to, had been the loss of life: the lives of their selves and their own countrymen that was to have been the direct consequence of their unpatriotic actions. He had family out there amidst the ruins of London: a father, a mother and three older brothers, even if the other two did not. Had they fallen victim to the Hun bombs that were, even now, peppering the city of his birth? Yes, they had done it; they had brought about the circumstances that, in the long run, may yet prove to save the human race from alien domination, but at what personal cost had they done it? Methusela was dead and Iggi would be following her quite soon. His only hope now was that Tyana and Tuppence would reach the safety of Castle Greckle, and that the Baron might find a way of using the former as leverage in order to bring about a swift end, both to the invasion and to the stranglehold that the British Empire had over the wider world.

In the meantime, all he could do was wait; wait and wallow in the guilt that threatened to consume him…

MARCH, 1895

A walk, she had always insisted, cleared the head and sharpened the senses; it aroused her with all the tingling intensity of a backhanded slap to the face, whilst flushing out any stagnant thoughts and lingering paranoias, of the kind that tended to fester during times of prolonged incarceration in her den. A walk, that was, in the countryside, or at the very least, around one of the royal parks: clean, *fresh* air being the key; air of the quality that the human body required to reoxygenate the blood and allow the lungs to properly filter the impurities that plagued the smog-addled air of the city.

Among the many and varied benefits currently being associated with regular perambulatory exercise, weight loss and posture realignment seemed the most regularly noted by her peers. However, Hamble was not and never *had* been prone to the vanities of the average woman; she was therefore much more interested in the fact that it was now believed that such a daily routine actually stimulated the blood flow to the brain, thus improving the faculties and decreasing the likelihood of developing ailments commonly associated with stress and nervous disorders; in short order, helping to stave off lunacy!

In fact, walking, it seemed, was quickly becoming the great panacea of the age, endorsed by doctors, debutantes and politicians alike. Quite why its undisputed benefits had taken this long to become so roundly recognised, God only knew, as Hippocrates had lauded it: 'mans' best medicine' some two thousand years before the Sunday afternoon promenade had become *de rigueur* for the Chelsea set!

Hamble's mind: the very workshop of her soul; ordinarily so ordered and precise a place, had lately become as cluttered and chaotic as a totter's yard on collection day, and she desperately needed to find a way to purge it. Mad she most definitely was not: not yet, anyway. No more, she was keen to aver, than was her dear mother; though the poor soul languished still; and for nought but a crime of passion, in that godforsaken hellhole that they had the nerve to call a 'hospital'.

This she could be certain of because, despite her recent confusion, her ability to make rational, sober decisions had remained singularly unimpaired. She merely needed the chance to order the jumble of contradictory thoughts, currently assaulting her senses and thus stifling her ability to work.

To this end, she had taken herself off up to Kensington Gardens in the hope that the exercise might help to exorcise her problem. It felt as if there were two people sharing the same brain, each jostling for control: two distinct versions of herself, though one: the interloper, bearing recollections of times yet to pass. The sheer ridiculousness of such a thought was far from lost on her, but there was no other explanation for what she had been experiencing of late. She had solved the brass fist's irritating power problem; not because she had been blessed with a sudden flash of divine inspiration, but because she had *remembered* having done so before! She had *known* it to have been a memory; she had *felt* it to have been a memory, but a memory that belonged inside somebody else's head. An *older* version of her own, perhaps? The same could also be said of her meeting with the doctor. It had been nothing more than an impression at first; a flash of familiarity that could easily have been born of her having read and absorbed the papers that he had published on human anatomy. His observations, which had been seen as somewhat radical; controversial, even, for the time, Hamble had researched in order to better understand the workings of the human body so that she might build the perfect prosthetic replacements. But it had been more than that, she had soon realised, as she had begun to 'remember' a more personal relationship with the man in question: an adulterous liaison, by all accounts, which, as she had followed it through, had eventually led to her remembering quite *how* he had made his unique anatomical discoveries and how that had made her feel about the man and the work that they were to embark upon together.

This in its turn had led her to recover yet *more* memories, all of which, she was certain, were of events yet to unfold...

She had begun to write them down in a journal, if for no other reason than to convince herself that there was a sense to them: a linear progression; as they had arrived in such a jumble and in no discernible sequence, laying atop one another like displaced leaves in an autumnal gust.

Planting herself on a bench beside the lake, she took out her book and began to read what she had written. She could not be certain that she had recorded every snippet in precisely the correct order, but a story was starting to unfold: the tale of her life between *now* and, as far as she could tell, two years hence. She was hoping that the farther she pushed, the better chance she had of uncovering the how and the why of her peculiar situation.

The memories were flowing much more freely now, as if she had unblocked a swirling sink full of ideas and could now see them more clearly as they flashed before her eyes...

...she was inside a rocket; a far more advanced version of that which she had been building for her father these past months. She was attempting to fathom its workings with the intention of helping its owner to... to repair it? And there was something odd about its owner; something 'alien', for want of a better term. He needed her expertise: her unique insight, much as her father always had. He needed to fly his rocket to Mars, in order that he might—

"Hamble, isn't it?"

Hamble looked up, torn suddenly from her reverie; angry and unable to hide the fact as she took in the figure before her from which the squeaky voice had emanated. He was tall and slim; wiry, she would have said if she had been describing him to a bluebottle, and dressed in an immaculately tailored, tweed three piece. His face was not unpleasant, though she did not find herself attracted to him. Somewhere at the back of her mind his countenance stirred another memory…

"Your father thed I might find you here. The name'th Ballentine, *Hugo* Ballentine," the stranger continued, "I'm to be your father'th new apprentithe. He gave me *thith* to path to you, if I were to come acroth you."

Too stunned to respond to his outrageous statement, Hamble found herself reaching to accept the proffered note in silence. It was a list of general comestibles; for the immediate procurement of.

Hugo Ballentine removed his topper and planted himself down on the bench beside her in a single, balletic twist to the side, that Hamble found herself registering as a tad on the effete side. He removed the right hand of his two black leather gloves and offered her his limp, desk-bound hand, which again she took, automatically; her mind too fogged to resist.

"Delighted to meet you," he went on, perched in such a position as to suggest that he was most probably a eunuch, "your father askth that you explain to me the working printhipleth of hith portable 'Iron lung' devithe, tho that I may improve upon ith dethign for him—"

"The 'Rebreather'," she corrected, "the system by which I have kept him *alive* these past five years."

"The very thame!" he replied, "marvelouth contraption!"

It was only then that Hamble noticed his rather debilitating lisp and realised that she really ought to help him to correct it. Rolling back her sleeve, she balled her dominant hand into a fist and swung at the man's face, dislodging the cartilage in his nose and splitting his lip in a single punch…

"'Amble? 'Amble, is that you?" she heard, as she let herself back into the Fire Station via the yard door, "did y'get me suppositories? Me arse is on fire!"

Professor Harold Blaise, sitting in the clockwork chair that Hamble had designed, built, and spent a good deal of her time winding up for him, was at his bench pouring over her plans for the 'VICTORIA' when his daughter strode into the workshop behind him.

She slammed a brown paper parcel down onto the table, but the old man merely smiled rather than flinching; continuing to stare down through his looking glass.

"I see you've *met* Hugo, then," he said with a chuckle.

"Oh, you think my reaction's *funny*, do you?" Hamble snapped, circling the heavy wooden bench so that she was facing him. She bent down; her hands splayed, palms flat against the table, like a cat who had finally cornered a rat and was now preparing to pounce.

"Not s'much *funny*," he responded, removing his pencil from behind his ear and using it to draw a line beneath her drawing, "but predictable. I 'ope you 'aven't 'urt 'im too badly?"

"He'll live," she assured him, "though I might have introduced a new nasal quality to that girly voice of his."

"Ooh, nasty," her father chuckled, looking up at her for the first time since the conversation had begun, "still, it's 'is 'ands an' 'is mind I'm int'rested in, not 'is conversation."

"How *dare* you!" she blustered, "after all I've done for you! You'd have been bed-bound half a decade ago and *dead* before your fifty-eighth birthday, if not for me—"

"For which I'm grateful," he said, swapping pencil for pen and signing his name at the bottom of his daughter's plan. "*Truly* grateful. But I 'aven't got long f'this world, an' I need someone t'take over me mantle—"

"And I've *proved* myself time and again to be perfectly able—"

"You're a *woman*!" he interrupted. "Doesn't matter 'ow *good* y'are; no one's ever going t'take ya' seriously as an inventor. I needed a *son*, not a daugh'er—"

"Ballentine is not your son!"

"An' you're not me bleedin' daugh'er, either!"

Hamble frowned; for the second time that afternoon, unable to find the words.

"Yer mother 'ad a fancy fella'," he went on, "got 'er up the stuff, didn't 'e. Y'never wondered why I never fought 'er corner when they said they were going t'put 'er in the 'ole? Y'didn't wonder why I never visited 'er in there? She was an *embarrassment*, my girl! I 'ad a reputation to up'old; I 'ad a royal *warrant*! I let yer stay; *both* of yer—" and he paused to pull his breathing mask up and over the lower half of his face. He took three deep in-breaths and then continued to speak, his voice now tinny and distorted through the Rebreather's grille. "Even raised you as me own. I gave you everything I 'ad," he insisted, "I didn't 'ave ta'. Could'a put yer out on the street when they took 'er away—"

"So why didn't you, eh? Why didn't you, *dad*?"

Harold took two further wheezing breaths, but did not reply.

"Because you *needed* me, didn't you?" She told him, "Not just to skivvy for you, but to continue your work. You were a great man, once; I looked up to you. My father: the greatest inventor of our age! I should have let you go after your stroke; after that great mind lost its thread, but I didn't, did I? I made you this chair and that bloody mask; I kept your reputation going by doing all your work *for* you."

Hamble straightened up and walked around the bench to stand behind the man whom she had always thought of as her father. Slowly, deliberately, she turned the valve on his oxygen bottle to the off position.

Harold gasped, fighting for air.

"Want me to turn it back on again?" she asked, caustically, and he nodded vociferously back, "then pick up that pen and start writing. There: just above where you've signed my plan. 'In the event of my death, I Harold Gervaise Blaise, of sound mind and... *body*, hereby bequeath all my worldly goods, along with my patents and my intellectual properties, to my only daughter: Hamble Veracity Blaise, dated the fourth day of March, 1895'. There. That wasn't too difficult, was it?"

"T-t-t-"

"What's that you're saying? T-t-t-turn it back on again? Do you know what? I don't think I will..."

A walk, Hamble found, particularly around one of the royal parks, was a good way of clearing one's head. Strolling along the edge of the Serpentine for the second time that day, she reviewed her actions of the past few hours, to the incessant beating of her own racing heart. Her decision not to switch her 'father's' air supply back on until *after* he had wheezed his final, had not been premeditated. Murder had never been something that she had contemplated before that day, or so she had thought, but then it had come to her: like a moment of déjà vu, and she had realised that she *had* done it before! She remembered it happening in exactly the same way; could see herself making that self-same snap decision the first time around and knew that she would probably do so again.

Had her future self travelled back in order to *stop* herself from killing him? If so, then she had failed. She was still missing those last few memories: the ones that told her why and how she had come back, and then; suddenly, she remembered...

JANUARY, 1899

"Bally Hun have brought down Nelson!" bellowed Balfour, as he stomped into the bunker, his moustache bristling; his cheeks as ruddied as a freshly painted pillar box. Behind him, his aide struggled along the corridor in his wake, bearing three leather cases and a pile of overstuffed files that almost completely obscured his view of the way ahead. "Bally bad show, what?" the Justice Secretary remarked to the room in general, planting himself down in his customary position, to the right of the Prime Minister. "Took his head clean orf, they did, with one of those damned Zep'lins a'theirs, then turned around; bold as a punch-drunk prozzy in Pimlico, and rammed his column like a child might topple a tower of bricks! Saw it with me own eyes; would've scant believed it otherwise. No sense of propriety, y'Hun: savages in spiked hel— Not *there*, Phipps; *there*, damn you!" he bawled at his teetering minion, who was attempting to lower his burden onto the table without dislodging anything important, "and hurry up and find me the passage that lists war crimes from A to Z."

"Arthur," said Octavian, quietly and without ceremony; peering up over his spectacles to acknowledge the latest arrival, whilst simultaneously continuing his task of countersigning the stack of papers that his own hovering aide was waiting to deliver.

From somewhere close by, a muffled explosion was felt rather than heard, rocking the foundations within which they cowered. Gently, almost imperceptibly, like the first tentative flakes of snow on a winter's morn, a mixture of dry plaster and dust began to flutter down from the low ceiling, to settle on the round table of the war room.

"St Stephen's Tower's gorn too," said Pugh: the Foreign Secretary, planted to the left of the PM, who, as the bomb had detonated, had dropped his biscuit into his tea. "They found Big Ben in the ruins," he said, "cracked completely in two!"

"Bastards!" pronounced Balfour, wiping a line of righteous spittle from his chin, "absolute bally bastards; every man jack of 'em!" and he slammed his fist into the table, causing his panicking aide to react quickly in order to avoid a paper landslide. "St Paul's'll be next, you mark my words—"

"Mister Balfour," said Imelda, Pugh's niece and somewhat over assuming private secretary, tartly, as she attempted to fish the remains of a digestive from her uncle's cup with a teaspoon, "the latest figures suggest that we may have lost as many as a *million* civilians in the past week in the capital *alone*; possibly *twice* that number *again* in the country as a whole, and yet *you* seem more outraged at the idea of a broken bell? Shame on you, sir; shame on you!"

Beside her, Pugh closed his eyes resignedly. His inability to keep his presumptuous relative in check had made him the subject of no uncertain amount of ridicule in cabinet circles, as she baited her betters with unreasonable regularity; in the hope of changing the world into which she had been born.

"Imelda," he said, weakly, though his faltering rebuke was as moot as ever, falling on ears quite deaf to nineteenth-century etiquette...

'Bloody Balfour', as the object of the insubordinate secretary's wrath was commonly known among his detractors, was not a man to be interrupted mid-rant. The nephew of the country's previous Prime Minister, he had been considered by many to have been his uncle's natural successor. His indignation at the fact that the party had chosen Octavian Periwinkle in his stead, had ensured that his own easy ire was never that far from the surface. A wealthy aristocrat: a viscount and an Earl, Balfour had never attempted to feign an interest in the lives of the ordinary man, but as those around the table that day knew; by apparently insinuating that a prized national monument was of greater intrinsic value than the people whom they were pledged to defend, he was merely attempting to deflect his impotent anger at the situation in which they currently found themselves: a coping strategy, some may have said: bluff'n bluster for the sake of preserving his sanity, as, like all of them present, he was so far out of his depth as to appear to be drowning in his own disproportionate patriotism. These were trying times, they were all well aware, but order still had to be maintained, as the 'Tiger of the Whitehall typing pool' was about to discover…

"Miss Rutherford, did I *solicit* your opinion?" spat Balfour, turning sharply toward the impudent underling. "No," he answered for himself, "I don't believe that I did. When I *want* a woman's opinion, I will be sure to *ask* for it, though I fear that by the time such occasion arises, I'll likely be six feet under! Now, hush, girl; *men* are talking. Why not do something useful and make us all some tea."

"Has anybody seen Winston?" asked a concerned Octavian Periwinkle, signing his last signature; choosing to ignore the Foreign Secretary's relative's impropriety along with her subsequent dressing down. He replaced the cap on his fountain pen and dismissed his own aide with a flick of his hand,

"Ah," said Balfour, turning toward the Prime Minister and removing his rather battered topper, flicking dust from it with the back of his hand, "knew there was something else I had to relay. Poor chap's bought the farm, I'm afraid; went up with the Home Office. Incendiary device, by the look of it; damnable mess."

"Pity," admitted the Prime Minister, though his face betrayed no sign of emotion, "boy had a bright future ahead of him."

"Well he had quite the bright *end*, by all accounts!" quipped Balfour, to silence from those gathered; though the look on Imelda Rutherford's face was loud enough to speak for all of them.

"Then consider yourself Home Secretary from this point forward," Octavian announced. Another explosion; even closer than the last, caused the sequence of bare bulbs that hung in a long line from the Whitehall bunker's entrance to the centre of the war room itself, to flicker, and a small crack in the mortar between two lines of bricks at the top of the east wall to advance a little further downward.

"To business then, gentlemen," he said, seriously, "I call this extraordinary session of the war council of Great Britain and her territories to order at..." and he paused to check his watch, "8.15 on the first of January 1899.

"Now, you don't need me to tell you that the situation that we face is grave..."

At forty-two, Harvey Haversack had been unusually young to have been awarded the rank of 'Admiral'. It had, however, been something of a two-edged sword for the eldest son of Britain's former ambassador to America; as, whilst the course of his career could certainly be said to have been exceptional enough to have warranted such an expedient fast tracking, it had escaped the notice of none among his peer group, quite how often he had found himself in 'the right place at the right time'. Of course, it was not impossible for serendipity to have favoured him in such a way; coincidences happened all the time, after all, and how often was it said that some people were just 'born lucky'? But when viewed in combination with his atypical personal connections, this latest act of happenstance would have been of no particular wonder to any of the few that he numbered friends among his service contemporaries. He was, however, willing to lay odds that none of them would have envied him now, if they had been alive to witness his latest unexpected promotion…

"With the Palace of Westminster, now reduced to rubble, and the pillars of our great society felled and thus entombed within it ruins," Octavian continued, aiming, Harvey presumed, for poetry, but instead; to his mind at least, merely exposing his congenital lack of basic human empathy, "it would seem that, all bar a handful of provincial members and minor civil service functionaries, we four are all that remains of Her Majesty's democratic government… for the time being, anyway. To that end, you will note that I have proposed the promotion of our de facto military advisor; Admiral Haversack, here, to the role of 'Acting Minister for War', pending; of course, Her Majesty's ultimate approval, which of course goes for you too, Arthur. Harvey will; in due course also need to be made a life peer; but in the meantime, do either of you honourable gentlemen have any objections to his appointment?"

None were tabled, but Harvey was left to wonder whether this was due to the fact that there *were* no other likely contenders for the post, or simply that they were all entering the first stages of shock as the reality of their catastrophic situation began to sink in.

"Good. Over to you then, Harvey; if you would like to bring us all up to speed on the latest word from military intelligence?"

Harvey took a breath as he prepared to make his maiden statement as a member of Her Majesty's government. All eyes were upon him, he felt; all eyes expectant.

"The train carrying Her Majesty; the Queen Empress," he found himself explaining extraneously, "The Prince of Wales; the rest of the royal family, along with the wives and families of the four of *us*: you will all be relieved to learn, has arrived safely at Brunel's Box Hill bunker in Corsham."

"Well, thank the Lord for small mercies," said Balfour. "Well done, son."

"I was not aware that the facility had yet been completed," said Pugh, dabbing at his forehead with his handkerchief. "Are we fully staffed?"

"One hundred and fifty handpicked experts," said Harvey, "everything from parlour maids to engineers; governesses to marksmen. The base is fully equipped and stocked with enough non-perishable supplies to last the entire community for two years. It is utterly impregnable: bomb proof, flood proof and poison gas proof—"

"Excellent news!" said Pugh. "When do we leave?"

"We don't," said Octavian, grimly, "that is rather the point, Cyril. With our assets secured, it is the task of those of us remaining on the *out*side to fight on to the last, safe in the knowledge that we can never be blackmailed into handing over the keys."

Turning back to face Harvey, he asked: "Is there any further news of the whereabouts of that damned *Permanent* Secretary?"

"No, sir. We are still unable to trace him. As you will recall, he was last seen by a porter at around nine fifteen on the evening of the 24th, engaging a SteamSteed outside the Palace of Westminster. The company who *own* the SteamSteed in question have since reported that they have seen neither *it* nor its driver since that very evening. We therefore have to conclude the likelihood that the Secretary may have been travelling within the radius of the blast zone when the embassy bomb was detonated."

Harvey paused for a measured beat to allow his speculation to penetrate, before continuing, "and if that were indeed the case, then it is probable that we will never know his fate for sure. As you have seen for yourself, sir, everything within half a mile of ground zero was completely flattened."

"Not so permanent now, eh?" quipped Balfour, "Good riddance to bad rubbish, I say; never trusted the cove, meself, Oh, and *on* that subject, *Minister*," he added, with an inflection on that last word that Harvey was not at all certain how best to interpret, "have the Martians made any comment vis-a-vie our request for military assistance?"

"None, sir—"

"'Arthur'… please. We are 'colleagues' now, after all."

"No, *Arthur*," Harvey corrected himself, awkwardly, "they are yet to respond to our calls, I'm afraid. In fact, we've heard nothing from them since before the bombing, though we have tried repeatedly to contact their base on the Moon. We must, therefore, accept the possibility that, either they wish to remain neutral in human conflicts, or that they may *also* have been approached by Von Greckle."

"So, what *is* our current military position?" asked Pugh, noisily wrestling with a new packet of biscuits, a second ahead of Imelda Rutherford's delivery of a fresh cup of tea all round. "Tell me that we at least have the Hun on the run?"

Harvey paused once again, attempting, for the first time, to think like the politician that he was now expected to be; trying to frame a response that might show their position in a slightly less negative light, however, at the last moment, chose the path of honesty instead. His family were safe and well inside the Box Hill bunker; *all* their families were. In the grand scheme of things, was that not the best that any of them could hope for now? If those assembled had to go down with the ship, then so be it, but if they did, he decided, then they at least deserved to know the truth.

"Quite frankly… gentlemen," he admitted with a sigh, "we haven't a hope. Our forces are depleted and our towns are overrun, and the reinforcements that we were relying on via our recall from the American front were taken out of play whilst attempting to cross the Atlantic."

"So we are dying on our arses," said Balfour, wide eyed and dreamlike, accepting his tea without a word of thanks to the 'waitress'.

Octavian rose from his seat and hammered his fist into the table.

"Enough!" he spat, surprising everyone, but causing only the Home Secretary to spill tea all down his front, "I won't hear defeatist talk around my table, d'you understand? We fight on, I tell you; to the last man standing if necessary! We're British. We wouldn't have conquered the bally world if we had given in every time some painted jungle-bunny threw a pointed stick our way! We have an Empire that straddles the globe, damn you! This is a setback, granted, but there is nothing the enemy can offer that would lead me to consider capitulation!"

The awkward silence that followed his outburst was broken by the sound of approaching footsteps in the corridor beyond; leather on concrete and in something of a hurry too. They were eventually revealed to belong to Peabody; the Prime Minister's personal aide, who skidded to a halt in the open doorway, panting furiously.

"Prime Minister," he said, pausing to catch his breath, "urgent telegram for you, sir!"

In all the years that he had been associated with the Periwinkle family, Harvey had only once seen the head of the clan express an emotion that could have passed for a normal human response, and that had been on his and the old man's granddaughter's wedding day, and even *that* had been as fleeting as a pang of conscience to the pilot of Zeppelin.

However, the storm that had raged behind his eyes until only a moment ago was to be quelled in an instant by whatever news had arrived, courtesy of the telegram that was gently shaking in his hand. Instead, what he saw there now was the weight of age and responsibility that one would have expected to have seen etched into the features of a man in his position facing a predicament such as they were; something that had certainly *not* been there when he had ordered the assassination of his eldest son, a week earlier, merely to stop him from scuppering the plan that he had put in motion.

"Sir?" Harvey felt himself enquiring, where Balfour and Pugh obviously knew better.

"It's over," the Prime Minister announced, calmly and resignedly, "Von Greckle is demanding our immediate, unconditional surrender," he told them. "He has my granddaughter: he has Tatiana. And he's threatening to torture her if we so much as hesitate…"

PART TWO

CHAPTER ELEVEN: BUTTERFLY WINGS

MARCH, 1895

He had done it, apparently, for his own good. Virgil had been quite insistent upon the matter, going so far as to repeat the phrase several times whilst his youngest brother had been being bundled unceremoniously into the horse-drawn cage. It had been as if he had been attempting to instil a mantra, Gordon had felt, one ultimately intended to convince him of his need to accept the doctor's considered, professional opinion; gladly and without ado, whilst in the same moment, exonerating himself of any blame for the rather uncomfortable situation in which they found themselves.

'For his own good.'

At the time, Gordon had been loath to consider such a thing of his brother, as, in his wider experience, the Periwinkles rarely did anything without an ulterior motive of some kind; this particular generation of the family being something of an egocentric breed at best. As the youngest of them, Gordon knew to his cost just how selfish and indeed mercenary they could be; with none feeling it beneath them to take whatever chance came to hand, if it meant minimising the number of shares to be paid out in the event of the patriarch's death. Ordinarily, he would not have trusted a single one of them, but he found himself wondering now if perhaps he may have been a little hasty in his trite condemnations of his siblings, as all the available evidence seemed to point toward the fact that Virgil may well have been acting with altruistic intent after all! For how could he deny that, in his hour of direst need, they had all given of their time so generously to pay him a visit? Gerald; Aubrey; Aubrey's obnoxious wife, Gertrude; even their father had left a cigar smouldering in an ashtray in Piccadilly and crossed town for a quick gawp at his wayward son; each, though, leaving within ten minutes, declaring their unequivocal endorsement of Virgil's original diagnosis.

Aubrey, it would seem, had come merely to gloat, though Gordon had found himself unable to hold this entirely against him, by simple virtue of the fact that the poor sod had recently discovered himself impotent, somewhat dashing his self-confidence. He was after all, the father of twins!

Gerald, on the other hand, had at least shown a glimmer of sympathy for his brother's plight; though he had been equally as keen, it had transpired, to secure the exclusive use of Gordon's Shoreditch, post-adventure bolthole as a quiet little spot where he might 'audition' new members for the cathedral choir.

Their father, however, had been as paternal as ever, enquiring of the director as to the possibility of his son's permanent sedation. He had even offered to pay for a full lobotomy; going so far as to offer up his eldest son as the best man for the job, fearful, as ever he was, of having the family name dishonoured, thus adversely affecting his chances of his ascending to the post of Prime Minister at some future date.

Beatrice, he had been gladdened to note, had declined the opportunity to add her countenance to the rabble's number, and for this he was truly grateful. His mind, he felt, was unlikely ever to recover from having her see him like this: buckled into a straitjacket and chained to a wall in the cell reserved for lunatics of breeding...

'For his own good.'

Who was he to argue with the majority view? When he added the facility director's own professional opinion to the first-hand witness reports supplied by his nearest'n dearest, the case against him seemed undeniable. Who was he indeed, but a sorry little man in chains with a head full of thoughts that had no business bothering him? This 'Gordon Periwinkle' chap, he decided, as the last of his kin, had turned their backs and headed off; his name to remove from each of their final testaments, was obviously as cracked as charged!

"It is the patient's belief," he heard the director explaining, to the white-coated doctor who loomed above him; in whose lair he had awoken to find himself, "that he has walked upon the surface of the Moon. He would have us believe," he continued, from outside of Gordon's tightly restricted eye line; as if such extraordinary proclamations were an everyday occurrence, "that our government is being manipulated by Martian infiltrators for their own nefarious ends. He also claims," he droned on, as the doctor whose table Gordon found himself strapped to, forced a leather-bound, wooden bit between his teeth, "to be able to see into the future."

If Gordon had been in any doubt as to his fractured sanity, then hearing his own insane assertations repeated back to him should have been confirmation enough that he was currently in the best place for him. For there was more; so much more, in fact, attestations even wilder than those presented; memories of a life lived outside of the bounds of time: faces, names, places...

...An electronic buzzing sound brought him back to the moment, the result of the doctor firing up whatever up-to-the-minute medical contraption he was about to use in order to cure him of his mental malady. Gordon tensed as two rubber suckers were spittle dampened and affixed to his temples. He frowned, remembering something similar happening to him before; quite recently, in fact, if he recalled correctly. Perhaps he had always been mad, he wondered; the adventurous tales that he laid claim to, nought but figments of an over active imagination and with treatment of this kind a daily routine for him?

No! He remembered now! He had been on Mars, with Hamble; with Alyce and… Boff—

Gordon's back arched involuntarily; his extremities straining against the leather bonds that held him in check, as the doctor threw the switch that sent a spike of electricity coursing through his system. Nerve endings from top to toe flared in response—

"What did he just say?" he heard the doctor ask, as the pain receded and Gordon felt himself slump back down onto the bed.

"'Hamble', I believe," replied the director. "It's a river in Hampshire, if I'm not mistaken."

"Why would he shout the name of a river at a time like this? Most people call out the names of a loved one, or just go 'aaargh!'"

"Perhaps we misheard him? He may have been a gambler?"

"Or a rambler? Turn up the voltage, if you will; I will try again."

Again, Gordon felt his body arch as the pain ripped through him, like a wildfire tearing across moorland; through gorse and bracken, dried and brittle after a long, hot summer.

"Well that was definitely a 'Hamble'," said the director, through the screaming and the bubbling in Gordon's ears.

"I have a mind that it's also a name, you know," the doctor said, "a girl's name, though one of the less common ones."

"You're right, of course," replied the director, "one of our most frequent visitors is a Miss Hamble Blaise. The daughter, incidentally, of Professor Harold Blaise: the man who designed and built the machine that you are currently working with."

"Is that so?"

"Indubitably. We have his wife here, you know. Mad as a hatter."

A third jolt, this one with the intensity of the previous two put together, finally withdrew the burden of consciousness from him; enveloping him in the darkness of the hereafter...

When he awoke; some indeterminable time later, Gordon initially mistook his sackcloth-padded cell to be the reception hall of the afterlife, having quite expected that final shock to have extinguished his spark once and for all, blowing his soul clean through the veil of oblivion. It did not, however, take him long to realise his mistake, though it was the straight jacket and the wooden bit between his teeth rather than the lack of a heavenly host or a bevy of gossamer winged virgins, that gave it away.

The skin around his temples was burnt and blistered and his head ached as if he had been caught in the firing line of a herd of stampeding elephants. 'Why was there never a Sherpa around when you needed one, these days?' He pondered; images of all those times when his trusty factotums had bravely stepped ahead of him to claim in his stead whatever bullet, spear or arrow had been sent his way, flashing before his straining peepers. One day, he decided, there and then; in a rare moment of philanthropic, shock-therapy-induced clarity, he would sit down and list them all by brave mortal deed, engraving each and every one of their names upon a polished brass plaque, to be affixed to the podium beneath his own statue in the lobby of The Adventurers': there for all to see, the great debt that he owed to them all. If, that was, he were ever to survive his current ordeal and live the future that he now saw so clearly in his mind's eye.

Gordon tried to stand, but found that whilst he had been sleeping, some bounder had nipped in and removed all the bones from the lower half of his body, replacing them with custard or some other such dairy-based delight, which; whilst quite welcome at that moment from a sustenance point of view, had no real buttressing qualities and was therefore of no practical use in a skeletal capacity.

But whilst his body may have been banjaxed, inside his noggin the lamp burnt ever brightly. It was as though the treatment that had been so designed to disabuse him of the fantastical imaginings that had seen him incarcerated here, had actually done him a service after all! He could see clearly now: all of the details of that which had befallen him over the past couple of years. He remembered the Moon and Hamble and Alyce, and he remembered their mission and the journey to Mars. He remembered Naraminda Boff and her weird 'Rewind' doodad. He also recalled having read 'The Time Machine', on route to The Congo in '96, and he wondered now why the Martian professor could not simply have used Wells' idea as her template for a time travelling device, as it may have saved them a lot of buggering about in the long run!

"Gordon?"

Gordon did not need to look up, as he recognised the voice as instantly as he would have that of his childhood nanny, whose presence somewhere nearby had just given him an idea.

"Beathrippp?" he mumbled, his heart sinking at the thought of her seeing him this way.

"So they were right," his sister-in-law replied, her two hands gripping the bars of his cell from the outside; a single tear dripping from her left eye, "You are as Virgil described," and she dropped to a somewhat unladylike squat in front of him, her fingers still tightly clutching the rusted iron bars. "I had hoped that they were mistaken; that this was just another of their cruel attempts to see you disinherited, but alas…"

Gordon slithered toward her as best he could, dragging legs that still adamantly refused to be coaxed back into the fold. With an insufferable six or so inches to go, the chain that was attached to the leather belt around his waist, suddenly snagged, jarring him to a whiplashing halt. He saw her flinch, uncertain; he imagined, of just how dangerously unhinged he might have become.

'Help me!' he attempted to say, but his efforts were as unintelligible to him as they must also have been to her; the bit between his teeth and the foaming spittle that it induced, muffling any attempt on his part to appear even vaguely sane.

She was sobbing now. Far from the 'pre-emptory trickle', she had entered the 'full on deluge' stage; a mere notch, he knew, drawing on his vast experience of the fairer sex, from 'hysterical collapse', yet she made no attempt at this juncture to wipe her eyes; eyes that were reddening by the second.

"Oh, Gordon," she blubbed, the kohl that had lined her lids now running south to form muddy rivulets against her flawless alabaster cheeks, "it is more than I can bear to see you in this state," she confessed. "You have been my friend; my confidante; my brother; my… If only…"

'Her "if only"?' he thought, squinting perplexedly; a squint being the only expression that he currently found himself capable of formulating, 'what in the world was an "if only"?'

"For years," she went on, wetly; snuffling back on a throat full of phlegm, which weirdly he found more erotic than he realised he should have done, "for so many years, I have harboured thoughts: wicked, unholy, perfidious thoughts; thoughts that I knew could never be requited, and for a man far nobler than my husband could ever be. I have allowed myself to indulge these fantasies; yearnings, that, were I not from the lineage that I am; if revealed, could well have seen me committed here in your place."

She paused, momentarily to pull a monogrammed silk handkerchief from her reticule; blowing her regal button of a nose before continuing, "I entertained these notions as a form of release: an escape from the torpid reality of my existence whenever my husband," and she hesitated as if considering her words, "your brother, was away. It was silly of me, I know, and reckless, not to mention traitorous and adulterous; if only theoretically, but these thoughts have helped me to navigate the turbulence of a cold, loveless marriage—"

'Was this the afterlife after all?' Gordon pondered. If there really was such a thing, then this was how he imagined it might be! All that he wanted, right here in front of him: the woman whom he had privately lusted over these past decades, finally declaiming lustful desires of her own, but with an iron cage; a wooden bit and a straightjacket between himself and consecration. In a moment she would no doubt begin to remove her clothes; possibly even to douse herself in clotted Devonshire cream, as he had oft imagined. This was his punishment; this was the debt that had to be paid for all those lonely nights when he had…. and then it came to him! As Beatrice continued with the unburdening of her deepest and darkest, (and in ever more explicit detail, too!) Gordon rolled onto his back and began rubbing the back of his head against the padded floor. It did not take him very long to move the strap that was buckled behind him and that held the bit in place between his teeth; just enough so that he could spit it free and sit himself back upright.

"Beatrice!" he exclaimed, as soon as he had cleared his palate of foam, "I am not a madman! You must help me!"

He could not decide whether the expression on her face was one of relief; surprise or pure embarrassment...

* * * * *

A small, red bulb winked twice at the edge of his periphery; blinking in tandem with a strangled, electronic 'buzzing' sound, that called to mind the remonstrations of an angry wasp, trapped inside an upturned glass by a cruel, quite probably spoilt, schoolboy. The Admiral jumped. It had been the better part of a year since the bunker had been 'wired', yet still he found himself startled by these invasive mechanical contraptions, to the point where he regularly choked on his mid-morning tot; lost his thread mid-chastisement, or simply awoke; startled, from what had been a perfectly serviceable dream about life on the ocean wave.

Together, these untimely irritations amounted to a signal, sent by his secretary; seated just outside his office door, who issued them as a modern-day replacement for the gentle rapping of knuckle against wood, that had served so well for all these years, as a way of informing him that his attention was required.

"The Secretary is here to see you, sir," said Moneypenny, thinly, through the wire grille set to the right of the bulb.

"One moment," the Admiral replied, remembering, for once, to flick the associated switch to the 'speak' position before responding.

Returning it to 'receive', he turned his attention back to his current visitor. "Well, Colonel," he said, as he lifted himself out of his seat, "all that remains is for me to bid you welcome to the fold and hope that you will be happy with us here at 'Command And Control'."

Taking his superior's lead, the Colonel rose from his seat opposite, holding out his hand to be received and shaken by his new employer.

"Take the morning t'familiarise y'self with the layout of our installation," he told him, "any queries, I'm sure y'll find me secretary, Moneypenny, more than accommodating. Ah!" he then announced, acknowledging his 'twelve o'clock', who had opened the door to let himself into his office, "Mister Secretary."

"Spatchcock," replied the visitor, curtly, with a nod; eyeing the Colonel like a new world colonist of old might have viewed a line of subdued natives on market day.

"Allow me to introduce Colonel Haversack," the Admiral said, as Haversack himself faltered in the doorway, apparently uncertain as to whether he ought to salute or offer his right hand to the newcomer, whose reputation was surely to have preceded him. "The Colonel is t'be our new Chief Of Staff, down here," the Admiral explained, "seconded from security, don't y'know. Came highly recommended."

The Secretary paused, turning slightly to take in the bunker's new coordinator. He smiled, almost menacingly at the man, then, as something of an afterthought, offered his own hand; breaking the awkward impasse.

"Pleased to meet you, Colonel," he said, "I am, of course, aware of your record. Recently married; are you not?"

"I am, sir," replied the Colonel.

"Hence the transfer to a more… *convivial* home-based role?"

"…Yes, sir." Haversack replied, with the slightest of hesitation.

"Very wise," the Secretary confirmed. "I am sure we will meet again, Colonel," and with this, he dismissed the younger man and turned back toward the Admiral, planting himself in the seat recently vacated by the Colonel…

The Admiral waited until the door had closed completely before transferring his full attention to his guest.

"So," he asked, retaking his seat behind his deliberately imposing desk, "to what do I owe the pleasure?" He was, however, as wary as ever not to put too strained an emphasis on the word 'pleasure', in the hope that he would not be construed as sarcastic or insincere, though both parties knew full well that; whilst he may have been duty bound to take orders from this high ranking civil servant, and to present himself in such a way as the man might deem 'deferential', he none-the-less regarded *any* so called 'superior'; who had risen to such heights without first having served at least a minimum term in one or other of the imperial services, to be quite beneath his contempt.

The Secretary smiled once again, though this time in such a way as to subtlety inform his subordinate that he was by no means ignorant to the degree of unvoiced animosity felt toward him.

"I thought you might like to hear," he began, wearing the expression that he regularly employed when patronising someone of the Admiral's rank and standing, "of our illustrious Majesty's latest wheeze."

The Admiral braced himself, placing a stubby forefinger on the intercom switch that would relay his voice to the similar apparatus on his secretary's desk outside.

"Moneypenny?" he barked, his voice carrying easily through the wooden door, "two large Napoleon's, if you'd be so kind."

Admiral Spatchcock had been in this identical position many times before, and he steeled his resolve in order that he might not appear disrespectfully unenthusiastic in light of whatever overreaching acquisition his patron now considered essential to the imperial cause. Wherever in the world it might be that Victoria now wished to claim, it would be from *his* office that the ensuing campaign would be managed and *his* business to ensure that the Queen's wishes were fulfilled to her satisfaction.

"She is keen to expand her Empire yet further," the Secretary revealed, rather unsurprisingly. "Though *up*wards," he said, pointing a finger toward the low, concrete ceiling, "rather than *out*wards, this time."

"*Upwards?*" the Admiral queried, affecting a look of bewildered incomprehension, just as his secretary stepped into the room bearing a silver tray on which their drinks were balanced.

"The Moon, old boy," his guest translated, as if such a ludicrous suggestion should have been immediately obvious to all, "she means to conquer the Moon!"

The Admiral tapped his pipe on the edge of his desk, dislodging any spent tobacco, then proceeded to refill the bowl from a pewter box that he produced from an inside pocket.

"Thank you, Moneypenny; that'll be all for now," he said, reaching into his jacket's breast pocket and producing a box of Lucifer's. "And how the *deuce* does she expect to do *that?*"

The Secretary reached for the glass closest to him, lifted it; instinctively chinking it against the other.

"Professor Blaise has built her a rocket," he explained, "untested as yet, but the theory appears sound enough."

The Admiral lit his pipe, chuffing at it a couple of times until he was sure that the flame had taken, and then removed it from his mouth to allow him clearance to knock back his brandy. The furrow on his brow deepened to a trench as he considered the Secretary's unlikely explanation.

"In an afternoon, I suppose?" he asked, foregoing his intention to appear unsarcastic and therefore unpatriotic. He paused to cough, then, puffing once again on his pipe, proclaimed: "The Yanks and the Hun have been at that game for bally years, battling to be the first to get a man on the Moon. They've put thousands of dollars and just as many marks into building and testing the most advanced machines this planet has ever seen, and all without an ounce of success. Yet ol' Harry Blaise believes he can knock one up out of old tin cans and biscuit lids and have us on the Moon by teatime, I suppose? Poppycock, I say; it can't be done, old man! Come back to me once we've built a flying machine capable of traversing the channel without drowning its pilot and I might begin to take you seriously!"

Again the Secretary smiled. It was an affectation that the Admiral had grown to resent.

"Think it through," the Secretary said, sipping at his drink, "I shouldn't need to spell it out to a man of your experience, but whichever nation is able to lay claim to the satellite first, becomes; from that point forward, the most important power on the planet. Unsurpassable. Invincible! Victoria *must* go to the Moon," he insisted, "Victoria *will* go to the Moon! The *how* we will trust to Blaise; I have spoken with him recently and he is confident that the task is achievable, but in the *mean*time, it will be *your* task to convert this bunker into a 'Space Command Centre' and to recruit the man who will become the most famous human being ever to have lived…"

* * * * *

Chan Chan, Peru; just north of the capital, Lima, 1893; on the trail of the lost treasures of the Inca…

They had camped for the night beside a fresh water pool; inland a couple of miles from their destination. Hot, sweat-soaked and tired; the pair had stripped to their undercrackers and waded straight in, too hungry to contemplate any possible rum consequences for their rash actions. Bellamy, ever the hunter gatherer, had entered slightly ahead of Gordon, armed with a long, thin branch, at the end of which he had tied his gutting knife.

"Any idea what kind of fish we're likely to find, old man?" Gordon had only just asked, when his senses were suddenly assaulted by the scream to top all screams, followed, almost immediately, by his Sherpa's sudden disappearance: dragged beneath the surface of the otherwise placid waters, leaving nought but a small cluster of dissipating bubbles in his wake.

By the time he had reappeared; apparently lifeless, to float in water thick with his own blood, Gordon was bankside, back in his shorts and brandishing his revolver, having shot an entire round into the pool in the hope of convincing whatever monster of the deep it had been that had attacked his aide, to release its prey before the poor bugger drowned.

On spying the body, he had naturally thrown down his gun, and used his Sherpa's own makeshift fishing pole to hook and haul the man to the bank, whereby, for the next gruesome half an hour or so, his resolve as both an adventurer and a gentleman had been tested to its limit.

When recounting the tale over dinner at The Adventurers', some months further down the line, he had chosen to gloss over the bit about his having spent more time mouth-to-mouth with his Sherpa than he had with any of the society heiresses whom he had courted over the past five years. He had also omitted to relate the part about his having become more familiar with another man's todger that day, than he had probably ever been with the contents of a lady's 'private' garden, as he had attempted to sew up the wound that had been left where Bellamy's tallywags had formerly swung.

He had always known that he would recognise that particular scream again, if ever he were unfortunate enough to hear it; a fact that had been confirmed just a moment ago, when he had heard it repeated from somewhere close by, and with pinpoint accuracy...

"Nanny!" he exclaimed, as his former governess appeared at the bars in front of him, puffing, as if she had been running.

"Gordie!" she replied, pausing to catch her breath, "after all these years! How the devil are you?"

Gordon had been on the verge of responding that actually, it had not been all that long really, when it suddenly dawned on him that he had recently travelled in time, so for him it may not have been quite as long as it would have been for her. The fact that she seemed to have lost her curiously acquired Whitechapel back-alley accent, also seemed worthy of note; along with the loss of her hair, but in the end, he chose merely to reply, "Mustn't grumble." It seemed as appropriate a thing to say as anything.

"It's good to see you again," Nanny said, whilst hurriedly thumbing her way through a large brass ring of keys; as normally worn on the belts of the hospital warders. She was searching, apparently, for the key that might fit his cage door.

"Shame it couldn't have been under better circumstances," she said, as a second character stole into view: a large; obviously female figure, of African-British heritage, if he was not too mistaken. The new arrival spat as she stepped up to the bars, and what appeared to be a bloodied conker landed between his feet. Its twin she held in the palm of her hand, until she flicked it all the way to the back wall of his cell.

'Well,' he thought to himself, 'that does at least explain how Nanny had come by the keys, along with the scream that had preceded the two ladies' appearance!'

"Allow me to introduce Tuppence Ha'penny," said Nanny, to which her aforementioned associate bowed; either theatrically or sarcastically, he was unsure which.

Both women wore regulation 'white' cotton, hospital smocks; open at the back in line with the crack of each patient's arse. It was only upon noticing this that he realised that he too was bare from the waist down; unless one were to count the leather strap that attached both front and back panels of his straight jacket, via the obstructed gap between his legs. He was reminded of a dream that he had once had; well, more than once, actually. When he thought about it, finding himself thus exposed in an awkward or serious situation, tended to be a common theme of his nocturnal musings. He had always put it down to the somewhat repressed nature of his upbringing: never having seen a filly with her drawers down until he had been hovering on the precipice of his thirties.

"My, how you've grown," said Nanny, finally locating the key and stepping in to greet him with a hug.

"I can only apologise for my current attire," he said, unable to reciprocate the greeting due to the copious amount of straps and buckles that held his arms fixed firmly against his body.

"Oh, tush!" Nanny clipped, "I've seen it all before. Now, which of these damned keys unlocks your chain, I wonder?"

"'Urry it up, Mef," urged Tuppence; one eye on the fob that she had presumably stolen from the now anorchous warder, who was currently bleeding out in the corridor beyond, "y've go' free minitts lef'!"

"I take it you got my message, then?" Gordon asked, attempting to shift the subject; aware that his rescuer's friend was currently eyeing his own unmasked truncheon, like a hungry blackbird might an ingenuous earthworm.

"Your friend, Lady Beatrice paid me a visit and explained your predicament," Nanny reported, "didn't understand a word she said; poor girl, but I passed it on to my girl when she came to visit, and bingo: she came up with a plan to get us *both* out of this cess pit!"

"One minni'," said Tuppence.

"I'm going as fast as I can!"

"I'm jus' *sayin*'"

"There!" exclaimed Nanny, turning the key and releasing Gordon from his bond, "Now quickly! Get the other side of the bars and brace yoursel—"

Her timing could have been marginally better, thought Gordon, who had barely made it out of his cell before it had become nothing but a pile of dust and broken bricks: the bars that had once separated it from the viewing gallery; behind which the three of them had retreated, now the only barrier between themselves and freedom.

Straddling the rubble was a true sight for sore eyes: Hamble's Range Roller, although with what appeared to be the wrought iron 'Victoria Gate': the entrance to

Kew's famous botanical gardens, welded to its rear end and recently used as a battering ram.

"Quickly! Get in!" shouted Hamble, appearing in silhouette through the swirling dust motes, like one of the ghosts of Sherpas past, who danced in the smoke cast by late-night campfires on silent plains in countries as yet unspoilt.

She had on an old, brass Merryweather-style fire helmet; her welding goggles clamped across its vent, beneath a wind-up, broad-beam lantern that she had bolted to the front; straight through the 'Kensington and Chelsea Fire Brigade' crest. Like the proud Bloomerist that she claimed to be, Hamble wore a pair of oversized, brown twill dungarees, gathered at the waist with a wide, leather belt, under a floor-length, storm-proofed duster that would not have looked out of place on a seventeenth-century pirate. Dainty, brocaded ankle boots made an incongruous addition to the ensemble; an outfit that his mind would duly store, so that on lonely nights in single berth cabins; crossing angry seas, on route to uncharted territories, he could transpose the faces of whomsoever he wished, thus helping to relieve himself of the boredom of the outbound journey...

They scrabbled over the fallen bricks, Hamble falling back to help Tuppence with her mother.

"Nice look, Gordon," he heard from behind him. Hamble was, of course, referring to his lack of trousers and the fact that; with his arms still strapped in the poise of a sleeping saint, he could do nothing to shield his trailing dingle-dangles from her opportunistic eye line. "It's a little risqué," she continued to mock, "but with your reputation; who knows: it just might catch on."

Gordon's pithy retort was to be lost to posterity, however, over ruled by the crashing sound of bells ringing and whistles shrilling.

"Everybody in!" Hamble hollered over the din, ushering the escapees into the vehicle ahead of a line of hospital warders who had appeared from the other side of the courtyard.

Gordon had never ridden in the Roller before. He had first seen it, briefly, back at the quarry in South Wales, what seemed like a millennia ago, now. Hamble had used it to rescue all those who had not had to travel back to London in the rocket!

He had seen it properly the following Spring, during one of his friend's dinner parties, back at the Old Fire Station, when he and Tiny had been given the grand tour of her workshop. That had been when he had first realised what it was.

It had once been a horse-drawn fire cart that had been left behind when the fire brigade had relocated to larger premises, but Hamble had stripped it down; reinforced it with steel plating and steel axles, and added a steam-powered, chain-driven beam engine; a scaled down version of Watt's original model, though improved upon by her own fair hand. She had added a cab to the front end; a trebuchet to the rear, and lastly, painted the whole marvellous machine black. Back in '97; or was that forward? (this whole issue of time travel was frankly confusing him), the Range Roller had spawned a whole new generation of steam-driven Hackney carriages (the infamous SteamSteeds); but as yet, in 1895, there was nothing on the roads of London to match the Roller for either speed or manoeuvrability…

* * * * *

The world turned on what to some, often appeared to be the most insignificant of pivots. Iggi was probably more acutely aware of this fact than most, given that it was her job to create such nexus points; sculpting the world in the image that her imperial paymasters chose to promote. For the most part, her particular line of work involved the putting down of seditious criminals, who, if left to flourish and to disseminate their vile, anarchic ideas amongst the general populace, posed a significant threat to the stability of the Empire, but occasionally, as per the mission that she was currently embarked upon, she might find herself called upon to save the lives of individuals deemed essential to that same plot. Few knew how often the fate of civilised society in the late nineteenth century had relied upon Iggi Shikiwana's ability to be able to shoot straight. For she was good at her job. At that moment in time, she was quite probably the best assassin that the Crown had in its employ. She did as she was bidden: she killed whom she was tasked to kill; she rescued those in need of retrieval; and, most importantly, she asked no questions. After all, she was a Crown agent: hers was not to doubt the establishment's judgements as to whose opinions were right and whose wrong. She simply took the shot and collected her wage...

'Butterfly Wings': that was the term that people used to explain how the smallest of movements eventually begat much larger, earth-shattering phenomena.

She was facing just such a phenomenon now, as she lay face down in the middle of Commercial Street; exquisite pain coursing through her body; her right arm bent at an impossible angle behind her. To either side of her, horse-drawn traffic; barrow pushers and bicycles pulling large, laden trailers, continued about their business, ferrying their wares to one or other of the nearby markets, their attention drawn; not to the figure lying broken and bleeding on the ground, but to the steam-driven monstrosity that had just knocked her down, as it swerved this way and that in the direction of the river.

She tried to move; to extricate herself from further danger, but every time she attempted it, her brain insisted that horizontal was the new vertical and the fashionable way to proceed from this point forward.

"Gawd, luva' duck!" She heard, in a perfect tenor, cutting through the gabble and hue all around her. "Out th'way! C'mon, now; can't y'see there's a man down?"

Obscenities rained down on her as drivers and hauliers reacted to this giant of a man, who had taken it upon himself to stand in their way, diverting them around her prone body.

"Where's it 'urt, mate?" he asked, having been confused; as men so often were, by her androgynous styling.

"Everywhere," she croaked, as a passing horse evacuated its steaming load onto the cobbles, mere inches from her face.

'Of all the places to find herself momentarily distracted,' she thought, 'it would have to have been whilst crossing one of the busiest thoroughfares in the city!' She felt almost as embarrassed as she did sick and twisted. 'How many times had she dodged a bullet with her name clearly carved along its shank? How often had she survived supposed suicide missions: target acquired, and barely a scratch to her body to suggest that the operation had been something of a tricky one?'

And yet she had somehow managed to get herself run over whilst crossing the bloody road! It was humiliating!

Iggi tensed as her Samaritan gingerly took hold of her burning right arm and, ever so carefully, replaced it by her side.

"That 'urt ya' mate?" he asked, as if he genuinely cared.

"Do it again and I'll kil—" she started to whisper, but before she could complete her threat, she found her conscious mind making a rapid, tactical retreat…

She stirred to the sound of a large, heavy man, pacing the boards of what, by the hollowness of the echo, she took to be an upstairs room. On seeing her eyes open, the giant who had saved her, she presumed, earlier that day, dropped to his knees beside the bed that she had been laid upon and began to plead.

"Beggin' y'pardon, miss," he begged, "but I 'ad no idea; 'onest, I di'n't. Fought you w's a bloke, so I did; fair'n square! You 'ad britches on an' ev'ryfin'. Give a bloke a chance, eh? Y'could'a died art there!"

"Woah, woah, woah!" she said, her head still a spin and pounding from where it had connected with the cobbles earlier. She lifted her left hand to shield her eyes from where far too bright a light was seeping in through a gap in the ragged curtains, and focussed for the first time on the hulk before her.

"Where am I?" she asked, as menacingly as she could manage, "what time is it; hell, what *day* is it, even?"

"My 'umble abode, Miss; lunchtime, an' tomorra'; fr'm your p'spective, anyways. Well," he babbled on, having told her precisely nothing of any use so far, "i's akshally t'day, but i's not th'same t'day as it w's when you got run over."

"So you're telling me it's Tuesday; anything between midday and half past one, and that you brought me home rather than taking me to a doctor?"

"I ain't got th'coin f'quacks, miss," he told her, "all I got is wha' y'c'n see 'ere."

Iggi scanned the cell as far as she could without moving her head. The room was tiny; smaller even than her own vardo, out on the marshes. She tried to move: to shift herself into a less painful position; if indeed there

249

was one to find, but failed, miserably. She winced, though caught herself from crying out. She knew nothing yet of her supposed 'saviour' and so could not afford to let him know just how incapacitated she was. For all she knew, he could have been in league with the maniac in the motorised carriage; he could even have been an acolyte of the Dutchman, sent to delay her and keep her from carrying out her mission.

'Damn, but he had already done that!' she thought. She had been on her way to Mermaid Quay; she had had a boat to catch! After weeks of skulking in shadows; intimidating contacts and greasing palms, she had unearthed a single scrap of information: a window of opportunity; a single twenty-four-hour period when she knew *exactly* where Van Helsing was going to be. It was her one chance to take out that lunatic vampire hunter and return the princess to the bosom of her family!

She tried again to move, but the giant stopped her.

"Who are you and who do you work for?" she demanded, with as much posture as she could muster whilst lying flat on her back; unarmed and with no idea what he might have done with her clothes. "What did you do to me?"

"Y've bust yer arm, miss," he said, gently; offering her a mug of hot tea, "badly. Don't worry, though: I've reset it an' splin'ed it. Y'dislaca'ed y'shoulder, an'all. I put tha' back in too. Oh, an' yer ankle's badly sprained an'all. Y'll live, though. I'll get yer s'm soup."

As he turned away from her, Iggi allowed herself to relax. He seemed harmless enough; if not a little 'touched', and he *had* saved her life. She was weak. She had been out for the better part of a day. She needed to refuel before she did anything else.

"Th'name's Tiny, by th'way," he said, his back to her whilst he ladled what smelt like 'meat' stew from a pot on the stove and into a tin bowl. "An' as fa' 'oo I works fa': the answer's no one, righ' now."

Tiny turned and placed the bowl on a wooden stool beside the bed. Carefully, he then hoisted her into a sitting position, before furnishing her with a spoon and passing her the bowl; appropriating the stool for himself whilst she ate.

"I w's on me way to a new job; me first since qualifyin'," he explained, "I'm a Sherpa, y'see," he said proudly, "or at leas' I *was* t've bin. Still, I 'ad th'choice, di'n't I?" He went on, as Iggi sipped at her spoon, "I could've lef' y'be; pretended like I 'adn't sin yer: like ev'rybudy else dun. I coulda' still made me boat, but see: I ent like tha'."

"Your boat?" she asked, between lifesaving mouthfuls of hot, chewy… something or other.

"I should'a bin meetin' th'Major at St Kaffrin dock," he said, "E'd've 'ad me struck orf th'regista by now, though."

"I… I'm sorry," she said, gagging as she swallowed. "If it's any consolation," she coughed, "I've probably lost my job as well; I had a boat to catch, myself."

"A wom'n workin' on a boat? Tha' why y're decked out like a bloke?"

She thought about explaining herself. It was obvious now that he was no enemy agent: he had neither the wit nor the mendacious nature required for that kind of work, but then *she* had neither the strength nor the inclination for convoluted explanations, so she simply answered: "Something like that, yes."

"Funny, in'it," he said, smiling, and revealing what were quite probably the scariest set of gnashers that she had ever seen on a human being.

"What is?"

"Well, 'ow th'world works, an'all. This time yestad'y, I 'ad me 'ole future mapped out. I w's g'na be the bes' Sherpa Major 'Enry Fanshawe'd ever 'ad."

'Yes,' Iggi thought to herself, 'and I would have had a Prussian princess under my arm and been on my way home, looking at a hefty early-bird bonus!'

"An' now look at me," he went on.

"You do realise," Iggi cut in, "that the average life expectancy for a Sherpa is 'one adventure'; two if you're lucky enough to outlive your adventurer?"

"Ah, b't wha' a way t'go!" he said.

'Quite, quite mad,' she thought to herself, as she shovelled in the final spoonful. The only trade that she could think of with as unlikely a survival rate as a Sherpa, was that of the assassin. In common with the Adventurer's caddy, a Crown agent never lived to see their retirement, either finding themselves shot down in the line of duty or hunted down if they went astray, for fear that the information that they had been privy to would be all too useful to the opposition.

This, she knew, would be the fate awaiting her now. Having failed to intercept Van Helsing whilst she had had the chance, it was unlikely that the Queen's great-granddaughter would survive her ordeal at his hands, and if that were to be the case, then a sacrifice would likely be demanded. The agency did not accept failure; not at this level of the game. It was all very well having a flawless reputation, but as soon as an agent dipped below their anticipated standards, they were likely to find their selves 'pensioned off' with extreme prejudice.

And this had been no ordinary mission, either: the fate of the entire world had been in the balance! There was only one way that she could think of where she might possibly redeem herself and that was if she were able to get word to the Secretary; to at least let him know that she was out of the game and to give him the chance to send someone else in her stead. It was a risk: one that the more she thought about, the less she rated her odds. She was safe for the moment. X was unlikely to be able to find her here. She would stay put until she had recovered enough to move: it would give her time to consider her options. If she played her cards right, then she might be able to get Tiny to help her. She had money stashed away; money meant for her 'retirement'. She had always intended to be the one to beat the system; to have scraped enough together to have eventually been able to fake her own death and to have bought herself passage to the Caribbean. Perhaps this was a sign? Perhaps this was one of those pivotal points on which the world was said to turn…?

CHAPTER TWELVE:

JUST THE CHAP

Gordon was not a happy flyer, much preferring to travel by boat or even by train, than by airship, balloon or rocket: all of which he had had the misfortune of having had to utilise over the past few years. Travels by air had never gone well for him, and so he had formed the opinion, based upon recent, hard-won experience, that flight ought to be left to those creatures to whom God had gifted wings, such as birds and insects and, at a push, bats. Gordon was not at all fond of bats; his chiroptophobia having been brought about by his having been incarcerated in a cave full of the flappy, leather-winged blighters some years ago, or was that an adventure still to come for him? He hoped to God that he was not going to have to live through *that* little episode again! However, if anything deserved to have its wings *clipped*, then it was not the *bat*, but that scourge of the foreign sojourn: the not so humble, mosquito. 'If there really *was* a God up there,' he told himself; sitting on his cloud, making whimsical decisions as to *which* animal had the power to inflict misery over which *other*, then to grant such specialist abilities as flight to those with the nastiest of bites, merely proved how much the old man preferred Martians to human beings!

Gordon's *second* least favourite mode of transport; he had just decided, was the Range Roller: a truly abominable way of getting from A to B, if anyone were to ask him! The streets of London were simply not designed with such careening behemoths in mind. The damned thing had a top speed; so its designer had rather zealously pointed out, of fifteen miles per hour! Well, if today's journey typified his friend's driving style, then he was here to say that it must also have been its vehicle's *bottom* speed, as she had not noticeably dipped below that line at any point between the asylum break and Chelsea! He was reminded of their jaunt across the burnished surface of Mars in this vehicle's ad-hoc successor, and of exactly how *that* journey had gone for them!

'She'll apply the brakes in a moment,' he had thought to himself, as they had thundered across the alien terrain.

'She'll apply the brakes in a moment,' he mentally willed her *now*, as they belted along the King's Road, in much the same way as he imagined Charles II doing (the road's instigator) on his regular excursions from St James' Palace to Kew, all those years ago; back when there had no doubt been considerably *fewer* road users at large to impede his progress!

'She'll at *least* apply the brakes before she hits those gates,' he hoped, as the entrance to the yard behind the Old Fire Station hove into view, but still she kept her foot on the accelerator pedal.

But with feet and inches measured in single digits before they ploughed straight into solid wood, the gates suddenly swung open of their own accord, clattering closed behind them, as Hamble finally pulled up the brake and they came to a dead stop, rather conveniently, right outside her back door.

"Spring loaded kerb stone," she said, before anyone was able to catch their breath and voice the question on all of their lips, "and a series of weighted cables attached to the inside of the gate. Soon as I hit it, a catch releases—"

"Well, please don't do it again!" said Gordon, nasally, who, still ratcheted into his straight jacket, had therefore been unable to put his hands out in order to brace for the impact.

"Your gratitude is duly noted," said Hamble, offering him a rag to mop his bloody nose…

"How much do you remember?" Hamble asked, putting two steaming mugs down on the workbench in front of him and planting herself down opposite. He had tasted her tea before and frankly did not rate it, but he accepted it readily, this time; never having been more grateful for something hot, wet and sweet, than he had been at that moment; bitterly over brewed and tart on the tongue or otherwise.

"Everything," he said, confidently, "it all came back to me with a jolt. At least, I *think* it did," and he frowned, as a thought suddenly occurred to him. 'How would I tell if I'd forgotten anything?'

"Do you remember Mars?" she asked, adding: "Professor Boff and her 'Rewind' device?"

"Absolutely," he affirmed, "I remember Alyce; eight months going stir-crazy inside a tin can, and I remember the reason that we went there in the first place."

"Then we're on the same page," she said, sipping at her tea and smiling at him; something, he noted, that she had not done for some considerable time. Had she at last found it within herself to forgive him for his spur-of-the-moment transgression of a few months back? Were they once again to be friends? It would be of help if they *were* to be able to put such mistakes behind them; if only in the short term, in order that they be able to work closely together to see through the plan that they had hatched whilst on route to the red planet.

Having freed him from his restraints she had lent him a pair of dungarees to hide his indignity; which was a good start: a pair almost identical to her own. It would seem that she had a reasonably inexhaustible supply of said outfits at her disposal as she had offered two further pairs; one each, to both her mother and to the Tuppence woman, whose turn it currently was in the tin bath. She had also swapped his straight jacket for a cleanly pressed shirt. It was hardly a J Arthur Turnbull, the likes of which ranged the rails of his own wardrobe over in Shoreditch; but there were times in one's life, he had begrudgingly come to accept, when beggars could hardly be said to be choosers.

"There are boots a plenty in that locker over there," she had said to the three of them as one, as she had brought in the first bucket of water for the bath, and Gordon had completed his civvy attire, thusly.

"It's good t'see you in one piece," he told her; recalling the mortal state that she had been in when they had last been together, "thought y'might not've made it there, for a minute."

"Why, thank you," she said pouting coquettishly. It had been a *very* long time since he had seen her do *that,* in fact, he had made a conscious effort to forget that she even *did* that...

...There had been an evening; somewhere towards the back end of their long, drawn out voyage to Mars, when their regular game of 'I spy' had become rather tired and decidedly gin soaked, and he had drunkenly managed to convince the girls to 'beef it up' a little, by adding in a round of 'strip I spy'. Quite frankly, he had not expected either one of them to have gone for it, but eight and a half months on tinned rations and with nothing but stars to count for variation, must have become as boring to *them* as it had been to *him.* Alyce had passed out, halfway through 'something beginning with N': gin and the Martian constitution not being a wonderful mix, and Hamble, he recalled, had gone on to lose the match. One thing had led to another (briefly, no tongues) and the next thing he had known, she had been treating him as if he had just suggested asking Alyce to join them for an interspecies three-way! She had continued to cold-shoulder him in this fashion for the remainder of the trip; until, in fact, she had fallen down the lift shaft, and so it was nice to see a return to her previous form…

"I… Imust apologise," he said, staring at his tea. Much as his adventures away from the class-conscious insularity of the Periwinkle clan had instilled in him the requirement for such basic human traits as contrition and humility, he could still hear his father insisting that 'to err was to defer'.

"For *what*, exactly?" she asked, frowning; as if his list of recent iniquities read like Buck House's weekly shopping list.

"For snapping at you earlier," he clarified, "it was… unforgivable of me."

"Then I shan't bother to waste my time forgiving you," she replied, pursing her lips into another coy pout that was to stir his nethers, regardless of how hard he tried to focus his mind on such past experiences as field medicine for injured Sherpas.

"You could so easily have left me there to rot," he reminded her, "my family were certainly of that mind."

Hamble smiled inscrutably from across the bench.

"Well," she said, supping her tea; her smile becoming a broad grin, "I won't say as I didn't consider it, but there *are* times, Gordon Periwinkle, when even *you* can be of use."

"So, what's the plan?" he asked, flatly; choosing simply to ignore her jibe. He had long ago conceded that, not only was her mind more attuned than his own to envisaging that which needed to be done, but that his wits were no match for hers if she chose to instigate a battle of such.

"Well," she began, taking a breath, "I've had a few weeks to consider it; to make a few adjustments and to manoeuvre the odd pawn, but I think our original plan pretty much still stands."

This surprised Gordon, as one part of that plan in particular: *his* main contribution had been somewhat scoffed at, at the time.

"Even—"

"Yes," she interrupted, "even *that* part. I'd say it's fairly *crucial*, actually; having had time to consider our options, and I apologise to *you* for having poo-pooed the idea out of hand."

"Apology accepted," he said, the arch of his spine flattening by a degree or so.

"It'll be *your* job," Hamble continued, "to work out how best to *achieve* that particular end, whilst I put *my* talents to use on the technical front. You're going to need help, though, and I need my mother and Tuppence with me."

Gordon smiled as a particular face crossed his mind, "I know just the chap for the job…"

* * * * *

"Ah!" the Secretary declared, "Agent A. And about time too." As the most trusted member of his private army let himself in to his chambers on the uppermost floor of the Palace of Westminster. "Any word yet on agent Z's position?"

Responsibility for the Crown Agency and any operation carried out in its name, fell, as it had since its inception, under the personal purview of the Permanent Secretary. At any one moment, it was possible for him to have as many assignments in play as he had agents with which to appoint; each clandestine mission being as vital as the next to both the security and the furtherment of the British Empire that he had sworn to serve. It was impossible for him to know the exact location of every agent at any given time. He had, therefore, to trust in their individual abilities to be able to complete the tasks to which they had been assigned. His agents were second to none: handpicked for their particular and often unique skills. He therefore encouraged a certain degree of autonomy where the actual execution of their duties was concerned.

He had, however, to admit, if only to his inner monologue, to having become a trifle obsessed with the details pertaining to this particular operation. The ramifications for the world order as it currently stood; should his agent fail to deliver 'the goods', were extreme indeed; not only where the ensured stability of the Empire was concerned, but also to the success of his own mission here on Earth. Equally as crucial was the neutralisation of the Dutchman himself: an unusually delicate exercise, involving the co-operation of a hostile power with a vested mutual interest in the mission's positive outcome. It was an operation that, if handled inexactly, could have far reaching, long-term consequences for both the British royal family and that of their Prussian/German counterparts.

To this end, the Secretary had sent Iggi Shikiwana: the Crown's foremost assassin, and the agent with the highest success rate in the field of abductee retrieval. However, nothing had been heard from agent Z; Shikiwana's field designation, since she had sent word that she had tracked her quarry to a location just south of Paris. It had been more than a week since she had made that report; time enough for her to have both located and executed her target and returned home triumphant. He had therefore appointed A to investigate...

Abraham Van Helsing; the Dutchman in question, had been a celebrated professor of haematology at the

University of Amsterdam. Recognised as the foremost luminary in his field, he had ultimately fallen from grace when, in 1888, the Dutch authorities had been shown evidence of certain 'diabolical experiments'; undertaken at the university and in the name of 'scientific research', which had resulted in the mutilation and subsequent deaths of various student 'volunteers'. After a short show trial, the Dutch medical council had declared him insane, interring him at Het Dolhuys: Holland's most notorious insane asylum.

The Secretary was aware that he should probably have acted sooner and taken him out of the frame when he had first been made aware of his inexplicable release, and he would have done; had he have thought for one single moment that the German government would be so lax in their own security arrangements as to allow a maladjust such as Van Helsing to get close enough to kidnap a member of their own royal line! Nobody, it seemed, had taken the man's phantasmagorical threats seriously; neither the royal families themselves, nor the German or British governments, though each had had as much to lose as the other if the honour and repute of their respective monarchies were to be brought into question.

If they had expected Van Helsing to have learned his lesson: to have simply disappeared; never to accuse one of noble blood of the curse of vampirism again, then they had been sorely mistaken; as mistaken as they had been when they had previously presumed that no sane citizen would likely lend credence to his hysterical absurdities. They had been wrong then and they would be proved wrong again, if that lunatic were not caught and expunged as quickly as was humanly possible…

"I check among her usual contacts," A reported, pulling the stub of a cigarillo from beneath his fez and lighting it. He inhaled sharply and shook out the match before replying, "no one see her for week,"

"Have you spoken with Captain Rackham?" the Secretary asked, referring to the commander of the department's submarine; berthed at Mermaid Quay and utilised whenever an agent needed to travel to the continent incognito.

"No show," he replied, which the Secretary took to mean that Z had missed her prearranged rendezvous with the captain, and was, therefore, presumably still in London.

Panic began to set in as his mind began to riff on the consequences of her failure to complete the mission. If Van Helsing were able to prove his assertion that certain members of the royal line had the hereditary blood disease, porphyria: a condition commonly, though wrongly, considered to be akin to 'vampirism', then they would likely revolt; both here and in Germany, calling for the dissolution, no doubt, of both country's monarchies. Without Victoria on the British throne, the Empire would quickly wane, and his lifelong sacrifice would have been for nothing.

"I ask around," A continued, his cigarillo never leaving his lip; entirely indifferent to his employer's rising consternation. "I offer description. Two men recall seeing man similar to Z, knocked down in street, near market, then taken away by giant."

"A giant?"

"Yes, giant."

"Then find the bally giant!" the Secretary snapped, "it can't be too difficult, surely! No, scratch that," he said suddenly, his brow furrowing, "send X. If Z's been compromised, she's to kill her on sight. If not, I want her back here to explain herself. I need you to take over from Z. I want the princess alive, Abdul, if at all possible, but Van Helsing has to die. Is that clear?"

"Yes, boss."

It had been in the March of 1895, as he recalled, that Tiny had graduated from the Royal College of Sherpas. Gordon had imbibed this information, along with the name of his first employer; the names, trades and medical peculiarities of various members of his extended family, and a whole host of other riveting personal details concerning the pre-employment years of his favourite batman, during the year that they had spent together, touting his book around the libraries and concert halls of Great Britain. Traditionally, the bartering of such tawdry tosh and trivia would have taken place during the long, dark nights spent under foreign skies; gas lit beneath canvas, whilst trying to ignore the nocturnal rustles and hoots of the local fauna; the exercise thus being passed off as a bonding ritual between two unlikely companions sharing an extraordinary experience. However, circumstances having conspired as they had, the pair had been yet to share a real adventure as master and Sherpa, and so Tiny had contented himself with relaying his oral memoirs whilst propping up the bar of whichever hotel they had found themselves in on any given night of the tour.

At the time, Gordon had foreseen no such likely occasion when banal arcana of this description could possibly have been of use to him, and he remembered explaining this to his friend in the hope that he might just shut up and carry the bags. It had proved a wasted exercise, though, as Tiny had seemed quite determined to fill him in on every lost second from the day of his birth to the day that they had met.

It was odd, thought Gordon, how things sometimes turned out in life; as it seemed that his and Hamble's plan to save their planet now depended quite heavily on his recall of certain elements of that drearysome diatribe. His friend's address, for instance, which he remembered; partly because it had been only a few streets over from his own Shoreditch digs, but mostly due to the unforgettable sign that he had been briefed to expect, ranging across the shop front and taking up the entire expanse from left to right; if not a couple of stolen inches from the businesses to either side.

On reaching the building that bore the legend 'Netherwetter, Netherwetter & Netherwetter, Dentist & Blacksmith, no appointment necessary', Gordon had been surprised to find the street door to the rooms above, open and flanked by a pair of silent and unmoving, caped and helmeted bluebottles. A rather stout man with a beard that a hedge sparrow might easily mistake for a prime nesting site; bedecked in a blue and white striped, blood spattered apron that perfectly fitted Tiny's description of the family's most senior Netherwetter, was remonstrating on the pavement outside with a man whom Gordon took to be the officers' superior...

A sixth sense that Gordon had hitherto been unaware of his being in the possession of, suddenly alerted him to his target's proximity, and he turned, just as a large man with a silhouette that almost matched his friend's, rounded the corner of the street behind him. It was Tiny alright, but at a time in his life before he had had his head shrunk to a third of its original size.

"Tiny!" he said, in an emphatic whisper, reaching out an arm in an attempt to impede the big man's progress, "quickly, man; in here."

The giant paused; obviously perplexed, frowning and squinting down at Gordon, who was beckoning him into an alleyway, a hundred or so yards from his home.

"Quickly, man," Gordon insisted, "before they see you!"

"Afore 'oo sees me?" Tiny asked, tentatively following the stranger into the darkness of the shaft between two houses, "'Oo th'bluddy 'ell're you?"

This was always going to have been the tricky bit, Gordon knew: how exactly to explain a situation so unbelievably ludicrous as this, and to gain both the man's trust and his loyalty within the timeframe open to him?

"Toby Netherwetter, yes?" he began with a smile, as the man drew further from the eyeline of the detective, "'Tiny' to your friends?"

"'S'right."

"Recent graduate of the Royal College of Sherpas?"

"Delisted, bu' yeah: tha's me."

"Gordon Periwinkle," Gordon announced, holding out his right hand in greeting, "discoverer of the lost city of 'Periwinkle'."

"I've 'eard of ya', yeah."

"Well, I'd like to engage your services. Forthwith; as of this very moment! Union rates, plus an extra ten percent, if you promise to keep an open mind about everything that I am about to tell you…"

"Awright," said Tiny, delicately placing his tea cup back onto its saucer and staring down at Gordon, who was sat, disentangling crumbs from his moustache in the seat opposite, at a corner table of Mrs Lazenby's Teashop,

"Say I believes y'weird'n wundaf'll tale; why not: I've 'eard worse. Why w's there a pair a' peelers outside me ol' Pa's gaff?"

Holding the fingers of his left hand under his tache, Gordon forked the final piece of cake into his mouth, masticated thoughtfully; swallowed, and then replied: "I didn't hear the whole conversation, but it would appear that they were under the impression that you were harbouring a dangerous and wanted criminal in your room."

"Iggi?" Tiny blurted.

"Iggi?" Gordon repeated, equally as surprised to hear the name related as his friend had been to hear that his guest was a wanted criminal.

"You know Iggi?"

"We both did," Gordon confirmed, "in the other timeline."

"She w's 'urt," Tiny explained, "I w's 'elpin' 'er. Jus' nipped out f'sum shoppin'."

"Then it was she who was taken out on a stretcher just as I arrived."

Tiny's face dropped at this revelation.

"Well I 'ope they look after 'er. She w'sn't gettin' any better."

"Oh, I'm sure they will," Gordon assured him, "but don't worry. Stick with me and we'll be sure to see her again. Adventure forth?"

The wide, toothy grin that Gordon remembered of old, returned to his friend's face for the first time since their 're' meeting, though writ much larger, of course, as it was etched into a much larger head than he was used to seeing.

Forgetting himself, Tiny rose to his full height and punched the air, with a bellow of:

"ADVENTURE FORTH!" much to the consternation of the tearoom's other patrons...

* * * * *

Hamble withdrew the jewelled pin that held her hat to the bun at the back her head, with all the élan of a swordswoman unsheathing her foil in readiness for a duel. Placing the pin between her teeth, like a flamenco dancer might store a rose, she took off her hat and parked it on the corner of the desk in front of her. Slowly, but deliberately, she then began to remove her black, velvet gloves; finger by finger, laying them across her raised knee and smoothing them with the back of her hand, before finally taking the pin from her mouth and smiling demurely at the man whom she had come to see.

"My father sends his apologies that he is unable to attend you in person," she teased, "he is, regretfully, rather tied up at present."

Whilst the figure opposite her deliberated over his response, Hamble began to twiddle the needle-sharp hatpin around the fingers of her left hand, with the nimble dexterity of a card sharp or a close-quarters magician attempting to distract and discombobulate her victim. "He has, therefore," she added, when no reply appeared forthcoming, "sent me in his stead. Hamble Blaise; professor. Pleased to meet you, Admiral," and she held out her hand for him to kiss.

At least some of what she had just said had been true: her name, for instance, along with the fact that Harold Blaise was indeed tied up: tied up inside an old blanket; weighted down with bricks and an old chain and currently languishing on the bed of the Thames, just off Wapping pier!

She had petitioned for an audience with the Secretary; it was he, after all, who had first engaged her father to build a rocket capable of winning the space race for the Empire, but she had instead been offered an audience with Admiral Spatchcock: the commander-in-chief of the new 'Imperial Space Agency'.

"Shame," said the Admiral, eventually; leaning forward to endorse her knuckles with his fat, wrinkle-borne lips, then dropping back down into his chair, "would've quite liked to have picked his brains on a few points."

"I'm sure I can help you with anything you might need to know about the Victoria," she assured him with a slightly forced smile, "after all, I've been working beside him the whole ti—"

"Doubt it," the Admiral cut in, brashly, "bit above y'pay grade, I shouldn't wonder. Tea, m'dear?"

"No, thank you." she said tightly, biting down on her lip and digging the nib of the pin into her own leg. Sadly, time was of the essence and she could not afford the luxury of an argument.

"Why don't you try me?" she said instead, dragging the smile back onto her lips.

The Admiral tapped his pipe on the side of his desk, then languidly proceeded to refill it with a couple of pinches of fresh tobacco. He peered at her over the horn rim of his spectacles, as if weighing her suggestion, before deciding to humour her. "The return trip," he said, brashly; his brow beetling, "I've decided to pilot the bally thing meself, don't cha'know," he revealed, opening the file in front of him that Hamble had sent on ahead of their meeting, "and whilst I understand the principle of how we get it up there, I'll be damned if I can see where it says how the deuce we get it back down again."

"We don't," she said, with a wry pout; finally feeling as if she might have scored a point over the misogynistic old duffer. "It's a one-way trip into the annals of history," she said, "for posterity, don't cha'know. The ultimate sacrifice for Queen and Empire."

"Of course!" he blustered, his ruddy cheeks now scarlet, "never been afraid t'die f'me country, a'course, but given a little more time; say, a couple of extra weeks in the workshop: might old Harry not be able to knock up some kind of a 'reverse' gear? I mean, funding no obstacle; obviously!"

Hamble smiled, quite honestly this time.

"I wouldn't rightly know, sir; what with my being a girl and all, but the fact of the matter is, we don't have any more time. All the best intelligence is telling us that

Baron Von Greckle is only weeks away from completing his own Moon rocket, and where would be the point in going at all if we couldn't be the first?"

"Quite," he said, "quite." As she dug the pin further into her leg to prevent herself from laughing out loud.

"Now, the 'Victoria' is ready," she explained, "though I will have to get my father to make a few minor recalibrations to take into account the pilot's weight, so shall we say... a week on Thursday, for the launch? Gives you time to say your goodbyes. These are the plans for the trebuchet that needs to be erected in St James' Park."

Hamble passed him a second file, this one containing detailed plans that her 'future self' had remembered; paradoxically having worked out the rocket's delivery system two years from now and brought the idea back with her! It hurt her head just trying to think about it.

"See you at the launch, then," she said, collecting her hat and gloves together and exiting the office before she found herself unable to supress her laughter anymore...

* * * * *

Iggi could hear three distinct voices, all within close proximity: two of which she recognised, whilst the other was a stranger. It appeared that she was the focus of their attention, but what was worrying her slightly more than this was the fact that she could neither see them, nor move any single part of her body.

"She's alive," said the mystery voice, which she had to admit was a relief, as for a moment, just as she had started to regain her awareness, she had found herself wondering whether she had, in fact, passed over.

She remembered being knocked down in the street. She also had a hazy memory of being cared for by a man with a somewhat sarcastic pseudonym, but after that, nothing that she could hold on to.

"Your opinion, X," came the voice of her controller: the man whom they all referred to as the Secretary, from somewhere to her left, "I need to know whether she jumped or was pushed?"

Katie; or Agent X, as she was being referred to, was the nearest that Iggi had ever had to a friend. If what little she remembered of the last few days were true, then it was more than likely that it had been Katie who had been sent to retrieve her; Katie, who would have been expected to have executed her childhood companion if she had considered her compromised.

Iggi strained to hear the agent's reply, but found herself slipping into the realm of dreams once again, two innocuous words into Katie's report...

When next she tasted lucidity, it was to hear the voice of the one who seemed to be in control of the situation. He seemed to be some kind of a doctor: his diagnosis of her situation being that she was in a coma, brought about by an infection that she had contracted due to the lack of medical attention that she had received upon breaking her arm. The good news was that Katie's report must have exonerated her in the Secretary's eyes, as, rather than ordering her immediate cancellation, he had bade the doctor repair her damaged arm in expectation of her return to active service.

"Nurse? The bone saw, please."

She heard him ask, and immediately her mind raced.

"Should we not administer a sedative first?" the nurse quite sensibly queried.

"She's in a coma, nurse," the doctor replied, "how much more sedated would you suggest that she needs to be?"

"We know so little about comas," she heard the nurse answer, "some doctors believe that coma patients may still be awar—"

"Well, I'm not 'some doctors', nurse; I'm the bally Surgeon General, and *I* say she's out for the count! Bone saw; if you please, now! If I don't get this forearm off soon, she'll lose the whole th—"...

...a sound, like the sawing of wood that seemed to go on forever...

..."Nurse; if you would be so good to pass the soldering iron...

... "and finally, the Brass Fist..."

...a constant tap, tap, tap of metal on metal, like a hot shoe nail being driven into a horse's hoof...

When next she surfaced, it was to find herself in excruciating pain, and though whilst she would much rather not have been in such all-encompassing agony, she quickly realised that this meant that she was no longer comatose. She could sense light behind her closed eyelids, along with the odd flicker of movement in the world beyond. She could hear voices chittering in the distance and could smell... something bitter, though she could not quite place the scent. Tentatively, she attempted to ball her hands and felt the nails of her left hand digging into their corresponding palm, but of her right hand, all she could feel was searing pain.

Gingerly, she opened her eyes, which proved a much harder task than she might have anticipated, as her lids had become welded shut; presumably owing to their not having been opened for some considerable time. The light scorched as finally she prized them open, blinked a few times then attempted to focus on her surroundings. She was lying flat on her back, staring up at the ceiling; her head tilted slightly by the pillow beneath it. Above her she could make out an electric light bulb, though it was not burning, which, by the ambient light in the room told her that it was daytime.

Her eyes finally clear, she looked down at her body to see that she seemed to be wearing some kind of a brass gauntlet over her right hand, hence, she presumed, the fact that she had been unable to move her fingers. She slowly began to pull herself up into a sitting position; using her left hand to drag herself, as her right still refused to be moved. From this improved angle she could see that the gauntlet extended to a couple of inches shy of her elbow. She tried to remove it, but received a severe jolt of pain for her efforts. That was when she realised what the smell that she had recognised had been. Just beneath the rim of the gauntlet, she could see that the skin of her arm had been burnt; as if a wound had been cauterised and she suddenly recalled some of the noises that she had heard during her comatose moments.

"Ah!" she heard, instantly recognising the voice of the man who had amputated her arm whilst she had still been conscious, "you're awake! Allow me to introduce myself: I am Doctor Virgil Periwinkle and I have just saved your lif—"

What happened next, Iggi could not explain. Instinctively, she had recoiled; pulling herself away from the approaching figure. She had hefted her brass prosthesis with her, a moment before the doctor's chest had exploded, as it was hit at almost point-blank range by four high velocity bullets, that she was later to learn had been fired by a thought impulse from the knuckle mounted barrels of her brass fist...

* * * * *

"When were you going to tell me that my husband had passed away?" Methusela called up to her daughter, having brought her a fresh cup of tea.

Hamble's heart began to pound in her chest; almost, but not quite drowning out the puff and clatter of Tuppence, who was sewing space suits on the steam-driven sewing machine at the other end of the workshop.

"Pass me the quarter inch spanner, would you?" Hamble replied from the top of the ladder, "please."

She *had* hoped that her mother would just have accepted her earlier explanation for her father's unexpected absence; unlikely as that probably was, but when was anything in her life that simple?

"I thought I told you," Hamble replied, having given herself a moment to gather her thoughts, whilst tightening the last of the bolts that held the rocket's copper nose cone in position, "he won a large cash prize in an international inventing competition and he's taken himself off on the Orient Expre—"

"Yes, I know what you *said*," her mother answered, "but I just found his wheelchair and the breathing apparatus that you built for him under a tarpaulin out in the barn. Did the winning of such a windfall, by chance, also miraculously cure him of his infirmities?"

Hamble stopped pretending to tighten the other eight bolts; sighed heavily and came down the ladder. She could persevere with the lie, she thought; pepper it with a few extraneous details. That was certainly one option open to her, but she knew that tone in her mother's voice; she had heard it often enough when she had been growing up, and not just as a counter to her *own* childish 'fibs', but to the many and varied, outlandish *stinkers* that her father had tried to get past his wife, and she knew that, ultimately, she was on a hiding to nothing.

"Alright," she said, placing her quarter inch back in its wrap, between the eighth and the half inch, and wiping the sweat from her forehead on the sleeve of her shirt, "he passed away in his sleep a few—"

"Hamble Veracity Blaise!"

"*Alright!* …Alright," she agreed; finally defeated. She picked up her mug and perched her bottom against one of the wooden ladder's wider, lower rungs, "I killed him."

"You *killed* him?" her mother repeated, and Hamble became aware that on the other side of the workshop, the sewing machine had stopped clattering.

"Tell me that *you* were never tempted?" Hamble insisted, supping at her tea, "I was *there*, remember."

"Oh, Hamble: almost every day, my love," Methusela Blaise admitted, "the man was a nightmare, as a husband *and* a father. I never would have *done* it, though!"

"Perhaps you *should* have!" Hamble suggested. "If you *had* then he never could have sent you to Bedlam."

"True," her mother replied, "but a judge still would've done."

"Hold on," said Hamble, having paused and replayed the exact words that her mother had just used, "are you telling me that you *knew* that it was him who dobbed you in?"

"Of *course* I knew! Who else *could* it have been?"

Hamble was dumbfounded. Until very recently she had not known her*self*. If she *had* have done then she would have finished the old bastard off *years* before; she would not have been able to have stopped herself.

"And where would *that* have got you?" her mother asked, as if suddenly able to read her mind. "Now, let me tell you a little story," she said, settling herself down on an upturned barrel. "Before your father received his royal patronage, he had been a potless, potting shed inventor, selling his tin-pot contraptions from a stall in Spitalfields market every Sunday. We'd met whilst I'd still been working as a governess for old Octavian Periwinkle. I'd been on an outing to town with young Gordon and Aubrey, when we'd stopped at his stall. We married far too quickly, in retrospect; I think we both knew that, but we were young and he was exciting. Such dreams he'd had, back then; you'd probably have liked him if you'd known him then.

"I had to leave the Periwinkles when the old man noticed I was pregnant; as if it was my fault! Anyway, when you were just over a year old, I took on a new job at St Barrabus' Academy for Stray Girls; I had to: your father was bringing in so little at the time we could barely afford to feed you. I wouldn't have been able to work if they'd known I had a daughter of my own, so I lied to them. I had to leave it to your father to bring you up, and he schooled you at home as best he could, but, well: he only knew what he knew, so that's why you ended up following his path. As you'll recall, he wasn't what you'd call a natural father, nor was he a particularly *good* father or indeed a good husband, for that matter! His temper had always been too quick to ignite.

"After a couple of years at the school, I inadvertently discovered just what the girls of St Barrabus were being trained for and I didn't like it. I objected in quite the strongest of terms. When I got home that night, I told your father that I'd threatened to expose Father McNulty's little 'operation', but Harold was having none of it. We argued. I think he was worried that if I were to lose my job under such circumstances, then I'd be unlikely to find another and would therefore be under his feet all day long.

"So, he told Father McNulty about you. Well, they were so worried about what I might say about them that they had me committed on a trumped-up charge in the hope that no one would believe a word I ever said. I got him back, though," she revealed, as Hamble finished her tea.

"Wha' did y'do?" asked Tuppence, who Hamble had not noticed had been standing behind her the whole time.

"He was putting on a show as they dragged me off," Methusela said, "crocodile tears. He didn't think I knew, you see. Well, I bent over and I whispered in his ear; three little words: 'She's Not Yours'. That shut him up."

"So 'oose *is* she?" Tuppence pressed, "this farver McNutty's?"

"Good God, no!" said Methusela. "I was... *forced*," she admitted, "taken against my will. Coerced is probably the wrong word. It wasn't pleasant! So, I'm afraid to say, my dear: you're a Periwinkle."

CHAPTER THIRTEEN:

I DUB THEE

Of all the news to have reached his ears that morning, the unexpected death of Virgil Periwinkle had been the least to concern him. Although in the past he had gone to great lengths to both aid and abet the young Surgeon General's 'extracurricular studies', in order that the Empire's foremost medical practitioner might gain specialist knowledge that would see his standing elevated among the international scientific community, the Secretary had to conclude that the man himself had lately become something of a liability. The farrago caused by his eldest daughter's recent 'misjudgement' had left him open to criticism at the highest level, and so word of his untimely passing could be considered a blessing in disguise, as it had given his erstwhile patron one less thing to worry about.

Thankfully; along with his unique insights and indeed his various invaluable medical discoveries, Dr Periwinkle had kept a diligent record of each and every dealing that he had had with the members of the royal family, for whom he had acted as both personal physician and, when circumstance required, their surgeon, these past ten years. Whomsoever was chosen to fill the doctor's capacious shoes, he felt certain, would have no more problem disavowing any wild assertations that the press might be about to make regarding the health of Victoria's lineage, than the 'great' man himself would have done, and for that he would remain ever grateful.

What *was*, however, of concern to him, was the speed at which the German public had responded to the

Dutchman's newly proffered 'proof' that Princess Fedora was; in fact, a vampire of lore. The civil unrest that had begun overnight in Berlin had taken the Germans by surprise, with accusations flying with regard to the rest of Wilhelm's line, and calls for them all to be quarantined until further tests could be carried out. A small number of rabble-rousers had also begun calling for them to be 'staked', claiming to have evidence of exsanguinated cattle corpses found within the grounds of the royal estates.

The Secretary's first action of the day had therefore been to order that fresh blood samples be taken from the Queen, with senior members of the cabinet on hand to witness the process from needle to slide, in order to prove beyond doubt that she had no such disorder present in her system. Fortunately, the Victoria currently warming the British throne was *not* the Victoria whose granddaughter had given birth to the princess in question. She was an imposter, one put in place by himself and former Prime Minister, William Gladstone, when the original article had died back in '62. Other than Gladstone, himself, and of course, the woman whom they had chosen to replace the deceased monarch, no one else *alive* was aware of the truth of the matter.

Yet, even with proof such as this to hand, he felt sure that the public mood would not be assuaged forever, and that sooner or later the scenes currently playing out on the streets of Berlin would be copied in Trafalgar Square or outside the gates of Buckingham Palace. Confidence in the Crown would be tested, both at home and in the darker reaches of the Empire. There would doubtless be discord, followed by disorder and dissent, if not outright revolution or civil war. Something else had to be done, and done as quickly as possible, in order that public confidence in their leader be restored. The Moonshot, he knew, was his best hope for this: 'Operation: Giant Step'.

If handled correctly it might even be possible to create an advantage over their ailing imperialist neighbours that they might never recover from.

They would, however, have to move quickly. His agent in America seemed convinced that Uncle Jumbo's 'ENTERPRISE' was mere months from launch and, at least until the announcement of the recent German debacle, The Greckle's own rocket was *also* said to have been only a few last-minute adjustments from a launch of its own.

Gathering his papers, the Secretary rose from his desk and headed out of his office, pausing only to retrieve his hat from the stand by the door; his destination: Space Command, with the intention of chivvying the Admiral into an earlier launch, and to finally explaining to him the truth behind the lie that would form that 'Giant Step'…

* * * * *

"Damn and blast!" cursed Gordon, when his key failed to turn in the lock, "Tiny? If you'd be so good?"

Tiny; his 'newly acquired', yet trusty muscle, frowned indignantly, but stepped up to the plate none-the-less.

"I fought y'said as like this w's your gaff?" he queried, placing his shoulder against the door and giving the wooden jam a slight nudge.

"It is," Gordon began to explain, as the back door of number 142 Lombard Street creaked inward, "or at least it *was*."

The back door led into the pantry, where, in a shaft of light afforded them by the overspill of a nearby streetlamp, a large wooden crucifix was revealed, hanging on his wall in place of his crossed Zulu spears.

"However," he added; vexed in tone, "it would seem that, in my absence, my brother has once again taken vacant possession."

His gander compromised, Gordon took the stairs two at a time, marching straight into his bedroom; unafraid of what he might find therein.

"Pinky!" declared his brother, whom he discovered perched on the edge of the bed; naked, bar the Mitre atop his head, and with two young men, also noticeably naked, knelt before him as if in supplication. "We were praying for y'dear soul, old man, and look! We have been rewarded for our piety: the Almighty has spared you! They've set you *free*, Pinky!"

Ignoring the troubling tableaux before him, Gordon stepped past his brother and his friends; reached out, and pulled open the doors to his wardrobe. Behind him, the bishop pulled on his cassock, dismissing his two supplicants, who paused merely to collect up their clothes before dashing naked down the stairs and out into the alley beyond.

"I say, Pinky," said the bishop, who had risen behind him and was now circling Tiny like a camp circus ringmaster taunting a caged tiger, "what a marvellous specimen of manhood. Is he yours?"

"Catch!" ordered Gordon, lobbing a pistol, underarm, toward his batman, who was at that moment stood stock still as if in thrall to a rattlesnake. Tiny did as he had been bidden though, collecting and pocketing the weapon, whilst Gordon continued to root through his effects, calling back over his shoulder as he did so: "For the last time, Gerald: I am not on your bally 'team'! Neither am I 'going in to bat for the boys' nor 'sweeping the minister's back step'. Just because I own property in Shoreditch; prefer the teapot to the coffee grinder and am the owner of a rather magnificent moustache, does *not* make me a mighty mandrake! Tiny, here, is my Sherpa and we are currently engaged upon a rather important adventure. Tiny? Catch!" He shouted again, as a small box of shells sailed above Gerald's bald pate, to be caught in Tiny's ham fist. "Gerald, where the deuce is me pith?"

"Ah," said his brother, sheepishly, as Gordon took two more pistols from the closet, which he duly wedged into his belt, along with a catapult; a hunting knife, and a blow pipe that he had picked up on his travels.

"My pith, Gerald, my lucky pith! It has a bullet hole just above the left lens of me goggles and a spearhead protruding through the right... Gerald?"

"It's under the bed, Pinky, old thing."

"What's it doing under the *bed*, Gerald?"

"Got caught short in the night, I'm afraid; forgot to empty me pot; soz'n all."

"You pissed in my pith? Gerald, you are without a doubt the most odious example of a brother—"

"Oh, my Lord!" Gerald exclaimed, his hand moving to cover his mouth, "You just reminded me! You won't *know*, will you?"

"Know *what*, Gerald; what are you babbling about?" Gordon scolded, retrieving his helmet and emptying its liquid contents out of the window.

"Our brother, Virgil!"

"What *about* Virgil!" Gordon snapped, "Come on, man; spit it out! We're in a little bit of a hurry, here."

"He's *dead*, Pinky! Virgil's dead."

There followed a long pause as the news began to permeate Gordon's bullshit filter. "*Dead?*" he then repeated, "dead *how?*"

Gerald parked himself back down on the edge of the bed.

"Heart attack, old boy. Instantaneous, I was told; he wouldn't have known a damn thing about it."

"When was this?" Gordon asked, his anger dissipating in light of the sudden shock that his mind was attempting to assimilate.

When last he had seen his eldest brother, he had had him committed to Bedlam. And the time before that had been up on the Moonbase, where he had been attempting to *kill* him, though that had not yet happened in *this* time line and was now unlikely to do so, so he realised that he ought not hold that one against him.

"Yesterday," Gerald relayed, "whilst he was at work. Terrible business. Father is beside himself."

Gordon seriously doubted *that*...

To Gordon's face, father had always made it perfectly clear that Virgil had indeed been his favourite. In *his* eyes, Virgil had already achieved far more than anything that *he* could ever do. Virgil was the perfect son and always had been, but Gordon also knew that this was merely a parenting tactic of the old man's; one that he used in a similar fashion, for and against each one of them in their turn. To Aubrey it was *he* who could not be surpassed and to Gerald it was Aubrey. It was, as far as he was concerned, a way of keeping *all* of his boys on their toes.

Death, however, was another matter for father. Ever since their mother had died, the old man had considered it something of a cop out. Death, he had often explained to them, particularly *premature* death; whenever it chose to rear its ugly head, was the very pinnacle of decadence and slovenliness. Death, to Lord Octavian Periwinkle, was 'a man's ultimate weakness'...

"Who is looking after Beatrice?" Gordon asked, making the decision to down tools and go to her, before he had even finished asking the question.

"She's with Aubrey and Gertrude," came his reply, "as are Ethel and the children."

"And Tatiana?" Gordon asked. He had always had something of a soft spot for his eldest niece: the tearaway of the family.

"Still in Scotland with our uncle, I believe, but I understand she has been informed."

"Damnit!" Gordon swore, slapping his palm against the wardrobe door. Why had she gone to Aubrey's? "If she had been anywhere *else*!" he said, though more to himself than the other two. "Still, time is of the essence and we dare not dally a moment longer. Places to go; people to abduct. So long, Gerald. I expect you to be out of my home by the time I return."

Ushering Tiny ahead of him, the pair exited through the front door, and were comfortable inside a hansom in under than five minutes.

"'E's a rum'n an' *no* mistake," said Tiny, as the cab clattered on toward St James', "fancy wazzin' in yer own bruvver's 'at; I arsk ya'!"

"Hmm," Gordon erred, having forgotten all about that particular part of the reunion, removing the helmet in question from his head and placing it in his lap. "That he is, Tiny," he replied, "that he is, but it was certainly good to see him alive."

* * * * *

Her mother; it would appear, had a thing for men in uniform, judging by the way that she was watching the men from the Household Cavalry, anyway, as they attempted to hoist the 'Victoria' from the back of the Range Roller and up onto the trebuchet, using a combination of a crane-mounted winch and the combined brute force for which their regimented minds had been drilled. Hamble, however, had never found herself particularly disposed to the type of man who felt the need to be told what to wear; when to eat and how to cut his hair, unless; of course, it was her that was doing the *telling*, and it involved the use of lace basques; pan stick and jelly!

Not that her recent choices of 'consort' could be considered exemplary: Jack the bloody Ripper; an alien anarchist, and a very near tryst with her own damned brother, being but the most memorable! However, men in uniform, in her humble opinion, were not to be trusted and were generally to be avoided; with the curious exception of firemen, for which she did have something of a 'thing'. So, 'soldier' types, she revised: the kind of men entrusted to such delicate work as repositioning one's life's work; working upon the orders of yet *another* man in a uniform, rather than to any inherent initiative that they had long since had drummed out of them. *They* were the ones that she liked to avoid. Oh, and *peelers*; obviously. Never trust a man in a phallic helmet. Her mother had taught her that! There were currently *three* peelers sniffing around the Range Roller, trying, she imagined, to work out where the horses were. It had been ten days since the Bedlam breakout and there was only *one* such vehicle in London. It was surely obvious who owned it, so how had it taken them this long to track it down? 'God help them all,' she thought to herself, 'if someone were to kidnap the Queen!' She would likely end up on the *Moon* before these clowns had worked out that she was even gone! Still, 'let us not tempt fate,' she thought. She had important things yet to do today and she could not afford to waste any time helping the Met's finest with their enquiries.

Dragging her mother with her, she left the rocket to the soldiers and made her way towards the marquee that had been set up within the fenced perimeter for the entertainment of the Queen's guests…

Before heading over the river with her mother, Tuppence and the 'Victoria'; Hamble had made a brief stop off at the post office on Kensington High Street, from where, she sent a telegraph to Baron Otto Von

Greckle, courtesy of Castle Greckle, Germany. Out of necessity the message had been succinct, yet still she had managed to convey a large amount of 'carefully worded' information to the man who had supplied them with the wherewithal to travel to Mars and attempt to save the world. For a start, she had had to try to convince a man; who at this point in time would have had not the slightest of inklings as to who she was or to what she was referring, that they *were* in fact on the same side. She had then had to explain that she was embarked upon a mission that *he* had set in place, before telling him that it was now time to fulfil *his* part of that plan. To be fair to him, she had also told him what his part of the plan *was*. Whether he would believe anything that she had said, she had no way of knowing, until such time as his help was required, but it had worked with Tiny, so it was at least worth a try…

"Miss Blaise!" said a voice that Hamble knew, from a man in finer fettle than she would have expected to have found him, "I was rather expecting to have run into your father by now."

"Good evening, Admiral. Yes, he's—"

"He's checking the elevation," said Methusela, stepping forward.

"Splendid, splendid. And *you* are?"

"*Mrs* Harold Blaise. W*ife* of," Methusela answered.

"Ah!" said the Admiral. "Delighted to meet you. You must be terribly proud of your husband, Mrs Blaise, and *humbled* in the same moment to find y'self associated with his genius."

"Must I?" she asked, offhandedly, but was kicked in the shin, quite sharply by her daughter. "Yes, I must, mustn't I. Why of course I must. Why wouldn't I be? I just don't know where I'd be without him."

"Quite," agreed the Admiral, replacing his empty champagne flute on the tray of a passing waiter and availing himself of a full one. "Ladies?" he said, offering them the same.

"Don't mind if I do?" replied Methusela, helping herself to a pair and passing one to her daughter.

The Admiral frowned: the outward appearance of a suddenly occurring thought to a man unused to such things.

"I understood that you were under medical supervision, Mrs Blaise," he said, taking a slight step backwards.

"Day release," assured Hamble, "special circumstances. By the way, Admiral, should you not be getting yourself into your spacesuit by now? We're less than an hour to take off."

"Ah, well, *sadly* I've been stood down," he answered, "best man for the job and all; had m'heart quite set on the sacrifice, don't cha'know, but Her Majesty decided that I was too important t'lose. Needed me on the ground, y'see. In command. That's where me *real* talent lies."

'Bugger,' thought Hamble, that was *all* they needed at this late stage of the game.

"That could be tricky," Hamble told him, "all the calculations have been made taking your weight into consideration. You should have told m—"

"No time, m'dear. The switch was only made this morning."

"May I ask *who* will be flying my roc— my *father's* rocket instead, then?"

"Need t'know, I'm afraid, m'dear; need t'know, but I'll be sure to have a word with y'father when I see him. Tata f'now."

"Shit," said Hamble, as Admiral Spatchcock wandered away, presumably in search of another glass bearer.

"*Language*, Hamble, dear," her mother chided, but Hamble chose to ignore her.

"We're going to have to split up," she told her, "one of us needs to find Gordon and tell him that Spatchcock's not the pilot."

"But we don't know who it *is*!"

"Doesn't really matter who it is, does it? If you find him, just tell him to look out for someone in a space suit that's several sizes too big for him…"

* * * * *

"I said *hit* him, not *kill* him," Gordon chastised, standing over the prone body of Admiral Archibald Spatchcock, whom Tiny had just clobbered from above.

The old man had been taking a leak in the shadow of an oak tree, just behind the marquee, when the pair had seized their chance.

"Nah," said Tiny, kneeling at his victim's side, his head against the man's chest, "'E's not dead, boss; I c'n 'ear 'is 'art bangin'."

"Well, thank God for that! We're about to commit *treason*; the *last* thing we need is a charge of murder added to our crimes," snapped Gordon. "Now, take a leg and help me get him out of sight. Oh, and could you pop his… his…"

"His man'ood, boss?"

"Yes, *that*: his chap; his… *thing*. Could you pop it back in and button him back up? There's a chap. The man's an arse of the highest order; even tried to have me killed, once, but he's still a British gentleman and a gentleman has a right to his dignity."

Tiny stood, staring down at the Admiral's *in*dignity.

"Wiv respec', boss; th'Sherpa's code not wivstandin', you un'erstand, but you ent payin' me enough to wrangle wiv anuvva man's wanger. I'll *'it 'em* for ya', no problem

287

a'all; I'll even break'n enter for ya', but yer on yer own wiv *that*!"

"Well, *I* can't do it, *can* I! I'm a gentleman meself! And a gentleman, well… a gentleman does *not* go about touching other gentlemens'…"

"Man'oods, boss?"

"Yes, their *manhoods*; damnit! Not unless there's a dire medical requirement for him to do so."

An image of Sherpa Bellamy's calamitous injuries; sustained during their ill-fated Peruvian quest, flashed past Gordon's eyes and he felt himself shudder at the thought.

"'Ow's tha' work fer y'bruvva, then?" Tiny asked.

"Gerald is not a gentleman!" Gordon corrected, without missing a beat. "He's a *bishop*… And a pervert."

"Same fing where I comes from."

"Oh, f'fuck's sake," said Tuppence, who had been keeping watch for them at the back of the marquee, "get outa' me way, y'pair a' nancys; *I'll* do it! I's jus' a bit a' usel'ss excess skin. It won' *bite* yer!"

"'Ere, beggin' y'pardon, an'all," said Tiny, wincing in line with Gordon at the way Mrs Blaise's friend was manhandling the Admiral's… manhood, "but di'n't Miss Blaise say tha' we w's to knock 'im bandy, then get 'is space suit off 'im?"

"Cripes!" Gordon spat, dropping the Admiral's leg and stepping back, having just noticed something glaringly apparent that he really should have noticed before…

In retrospect; for their plan to have had a fair and proper chance of succeeding, it would probably have proved prudent for them to have had a man on the inside: an undercover contact, for instance, working for The Imperial Space Agency, whom they could have groomed and thus relied upon to have fed them security and itinerary details for the launch party. Sadly, they were *not* that well connected, nor had they had the time to become so; they were, therefore, working to what both Gordon and Hamble could remember of the arrangements made for the 'original' launch, some two years into the future and in a now defunct timeline.

Security for the launch was tight, as they had expected it to be. It was a wholly invited guest list, culled from the higher echelons of British society: Lords; Ladies; Barons and Baronets; Admirals; Generals; the Prime Minister; the odd high-ranking courtier, all with an array of friendly foreign ambassadors, thrown in, merely in order to humiliate them. The whole of St James' Park had been fenced off for the duration, with an entire shift's worth of bluebottles; all under the command of the Yard's infamous Inspector Abberline, on perimeter duty. 'God help those poor sods, for whom fate may have scheduled a mugging or a burgling for that night,' thought Gordon; duly imagining the night of rampant lawlessness on the streets of London town which was surely to follow. There were also likely to have been a number of Crown Agents at large; there to keep a close eye on the Queen and her retinue, and they were likely to be their biggest problem!

Infiltration options were always going to be few for an event such as this; one attended, that was, by the Queen Empress herself. They had considered disguising themselves as waiters or constables, even, but it was decided quite early on that neither Tiny nor Tuppence were likely to have passed muster in the garb of either, which had left them with but a single workable option. It was not a particularly audacious plan and should really have fallen at the first hurdle; Gordon had been convinced that it would have done and had said so, but then he had not been taking into account Hamble's natural abilities to blag and charm her way past the male members of any given sentient species.

The Greeks had thought of it first; leaving a huge wooden horse outside the gates of Troy, packed full of soldiers, all armed to the teeth and ready to do bloody murder just as soon as they had been taken inside. It should not really have worked even then, of course, but the ancients were not as bright and forward thinking as the people of the modern era and the subterfuge had gone down in history as a classic of its age.

Luckily for them, the average bluebottle was also not known to be the brightest of sparks, and, without the benefit of a classical education to warn them of such convenient plot devices, the Trojan horse scenario was once again employed to cunning advantage. It was to be a slightly different take on the old 'Greeks bearing gifts' idea, though. For a start, there were no horses involved; Hamble had simply hidden the team inside her copper and brass-plated rocket and then driven it into the compound herself. The principle, however, had been the same…

"Psst!… Oi, Gordie!"

"Nanny?" Gordon asked, without turning round; attempting to appear nonchalant with his champagne flute and his expression of mild indifference to the occasion; an attempt on his part to mingle, so that he might search for their new target without drawing any unwanted attention to himself.

"You're supposed to be with Hamble," he whispered, "not in here with the 'rabble'!"

"Slight change of plan," she said, from the other side of one of the tent's wooden support pillars, "they've switched pilots."

"Yes," he replied, "so I see. Could have done with that particular snippet a moment or two earlier, though, but thank you all the same. Who are we looking for, then; any idea?"

"Someone in a space suit with a fair degree of 'gather'."

"Got him!" said Gordon, as a slim, but athletic type, dressed in a ruched version of the appropriated deep-sea-diver's get up that he himself had worn on his *own* Moon mission, stepped across his eyeline. "Harvey?" he said. "They're intending to send poor Harvey Haversack out on a suicide mission? The poor sap has a wife and kids! Nanny, tell— oh, she's gone."

He had to find the others. The plan had been for Tiny to have donned the Admiral's space suit and to have him masquerade as the pilot in order to get close to the target, but that ploy was no longer viable, as everybody present would no doubt by now have *seen* Harvey, and would not just presume him to have put on a little weight between mingle and dubbing.

Gordon turned around and headed back to where he had left his companions; quite rightly presuming them to have stood out like gangrenous thumbs if allowed to wander within the main hospitality area.

It had not proved as difficult for him as he had imagined, to move from 'most famous face in the world', to relative nobody: a minor 'upper' whom people presumed to know, and so smiled, but could not quite place, and so moved on quickly. It was the position that he had played his whole life; until, that was, his vanity had decreed that he become the first man on the Moon. Being right back where he had begun, yet with the benefit of a little more than hindsight; to his mind, was something of a relief.

As he retraced his steps, another instantly recognisable figure floated into view, like a swan drifting by on the Serpentine.

"Gordon!" she squealed. "Oh, Gordon! I so hoped you'd come." And she suddenly broke down in his arms, sobbing like a child who had lost her balloon.

"Beatrice; my dear Bea! Shush, now; you're drawing attention and attention is something that we really do not need at this juncture!"

"I had hoped that you would have come to me, once the Blaise woman had rescued you. I so needed to talk to you, you see; to *be* with you, even. I wonder, where have you been for these past ten insufferable days?"

"Lying low," he explained, in a low whisper, taking her arm and wheeling her toward the tent's open flap. It was dark outside, but for a line of candle poles that had been staked into the turf in order to form a path of light from the gate to the bar. "I am an escaped lunatic, after all; according to the papers. Thank you; by the way, for felicitating my escape."

"It was my absolute pleasure, my dear, dear Pinky, and... Just so we're clear, I meant everything that I said to you at the hospital..."

"So sorry t'hear about Virgil," he said, thinking on his feet. He would have dearly loved to have taken her home at that point and to have shown her the extent of his own feelings toward her; feelings that had festered since first they had met, but now, sadly, was not the time. He had a world to save!

"Oh, Pinky, don't be! I know he was your brother, but... you didn't *know* him as *I* knew him! He was a cold, cruel man and I will not miss his touch nor the smell of death that constantly travelled with him. The world; I fear, will be a better place for his passing."

'She doesn't know the *half* of it!' thought Gordon.

"There is far worse afoot, though," she went on, and he noticed more than one hatted-head turn and acknowledge them as he tried desperately to calm his sister-in-law, who was quite obviously in need of a good lie down and a dose of smelling salts. He needed to get back to Tiny and Tuppence as their schedule was tightening, but how could he walk away from Bea when she needed his help?

* * * * *

In an ideal world Iggi would have liked to have had more time in which to acclimatise to her new hand; not to mention, to find herself an effective painkiller, before being thrown back out into the fray and expected to do the job that she had almost escaped from. The Secretary, however, had had other ideas.

To be fair, she thought, she was at least still alive; an eventuality that had been by no means a certainty only a few days ago. She was lucky: these were trying times, and her controller had needed all the agents that he could muster, and so she had found herself assigned to 'close guard' duty after only her second day of rest.

Her memory of the accident was now fully restored, as was her recall of the man who had 'saved' her, and those details were a matter of record; with a warrant having been issued for the capture of the giant known as 'Tiny'. She had not known him for long, but she would happily have bet her savings on the fact that he was a decent human being, rather than the enemy agent that they had painted him to be. She had liked him; trusted him, even: two accolades that she rarely pinned to anybody's chest, and she fervently hoped that she would not be the agent to find him, as she found herself unable to be convinced of the official take on his motives.

She had been partnered with Agent X: the same agent who had been sent to bring her in. It was likely, Iggi knew, that Katie had active orders to cancel her, should she show bad form at any point during the forthcoming mission. She had, therefore, to watch her *own* back, just as well as she would be expected to be watching the Queen's.

Iggi had never met the Queen before today, despite the fact that the Crown Agency was; to all intent and purpose, Her Majesty's personal bodyguard. Iggi was an assassin, not a babysitter, and totally unused to working with a partner, which meant that as well as her not feeling at her best, she was also working outside of her comfort zone, which was not a favourable combination.

Upon arrival at Buckingham Palace, they had been greeted by the Queen's *private* secretary; a man with the look about him of someone who had taken a bite more than he was able to chew. He had given them the usual spiel: "Do not attempt to make conversation with the Queen; only speak when spoken to; always refer to her as 'Majesty'; never look her directly in the eye. Never touch the Queen, unless to shield her from an imminent attack, and always make sure to stay a step behind her, except in an emergency situation where you may be required to use your own body in order to block an assassin's blow."Barely a moment later, the Majesty in question had appeared, flanked on either side by a pair of palace guards, who relinquished their responsibilities at the foot of the main stairs, snapped to attention, then disappeared into the bowels of the palace. This left herself and Katie to lead the monarch to her carriage… but without speaking to her or stepping ahead of her. Iggi could see that this was going to be an even harder assignment than she had expected!

The carriage ride to St James' Park had taken precisely four minutes. By the time the overdressed monarch had got both into and out of her seat again, they could all four of them have walked the short distance across the road and been merrily in situ with all the other 'knobs' that she was sworn to protect. It would probably have been safer too, as with four mounted members of the Household Cavalry covering the four corners of the golden state coach, they were; Iggi had noted, a much more obvious target for either a stray anarchist or a 'vampire hunter'; the bogeymen of the moment, than they might otherwise have been.

The Queen had said very little during the journey, other than to complain bitterly to Baron Stamfordham; riding with them, but looking as if he would rather have stayed behind to write his farewell note, about how cramped and uncomfortable the state coach was. She had still been complaining about her life of luxury and privilege when they had reached the marquee, her expression as dour and as doleful as it had been in all the pictures that Iggi had previously seen of her.

They were met by the Secretary, who ushered them through a flap in the back of the tent which led, via three short steps, onto a raised platform bedecked with flowers. What Iggi knew about horticulture could be written on the back of a penny black, but she knew a violet when she saw one, and the stage was awash with them. This, she was later to learn, was Victoria's 'rider', or at least a *part* of it! For the first time since she had 'met' her, she saw Victoria's face brighten, ever so slightly. Note to self, she thought: if ever she were to find herself in desperate need of a way to cheer the old girl up, stick her in a room full of her favourite flowers!

"Your Majesty," said the Secretary, with an obsequious bow, indicating that the monarch take the stage, where a lectern with a prepared speech upon it awaited her...

* * * * *

"How do I look?"

"Honestly?" asked Tuppence; her eyebrows raised, daring him to reply in the affirmative.

"This is *my* look, you know," snapped Gordon, indignantly. "I set the trend; everyone else is merely copying my style!"

"Tha's as maybe," Nanny's mouthy cellmate replied, "bu' y've go'a much bigga' arse th'n th'other bloke."

"Thank you, *Tuppence*, for your vote of confidence. I'm about to go in there and let the mad monarch put a sword to my neck. Anybody *else* feel the need t'pass comment on the plumpness of my posterior?"

"Nah, y'good t'go, boss," assured Tiny, "Wiv the 'elmet on, nobody'll suss a fing. Jus' don't turn round, tha's all!"

Both Tiny and Tuppence seemed to find that last retort hilarious, neither of them, to Gordon's mind, quite grasping the gravity of the situation.

Still smirking, Tuppence hefted his helmet into place and fastened the neck bolts. It was a modified version of Hamble's original design, being somewhat lighter, weight wise, and darker tinted, in the hope that their subterfuge would hold.

"There y'go," said Tiny, peeking his head around the tent flap, "I reckon that w's y'cue."

Gordon felt bad about having to bop poor Harvey like that; he was family, after all, but he knew his niece's husband well enough to suspect that, suicide mission or *not*, he would have felt duty bound to have stopped them from attempting to scupper the Queen's launch if they had not knocked him out; tied him up and stolen his space suit. At least when the bluebottles finally found him; stuffed inside a wicker laundry basket in a 'staff only' catering tent, they would be unlikely to accuse him of complicity! Gordon felt sure that Harvey would forgive him in the long run; he had, when all was said and done, saved both the man's life *and* his reputation…

"Where the bally hell is Spatchcock?" He heard the Secretary ask, from his position on the stage ahead of him; stage left of the Queen and sandwiched between a short, bald headed equerry type, with a face that showed him to be a martyr to piles, and, of *all* people: Iggi Shikiwana!

"Haven't seen him," Iggi whispered back, "want me to go and check?"

"No. Hold the line, agent."

Gordon had quite come to like Iggi. She had, after all, helped Tiny to save his life, though he had never entirely forgiven her for murdering his brother, Gerald, the first time around. However, he had to remind himself that *this* Iggi was not the *same* Iggi who he had left behind in Greckle's castle, way back at the start of this particular adventure. At this point in *her* timeline, the two of them had yet to meet. She was still a Crown assassin: one of their best, and the closest one *to* him, when it all kicked off. To *her*, he was nothing but a wanted lunatic who was about to go down in history in much the same way as Guy Fawkes had done, nearly three hundred years before him.

On the other side of the Queen stood a second agent; one whom, for a moment, he had almost failed to recognise. When last they had met it had been shortly before her demise and she had been in something of a sorry state: battered; bruised and bleeding from wounds all over her shattered body, but now she bore but a single scar: a deep, ugly welt that disfigured her otherwise quite comely countenance. It was Agent X.

He had not heard a word of the Queen's speech; having taught himself to block out her rather monotone nasal whine, years ago, but he noticed immediately when she *stopped* speaking, by the gentle ripple of applause that her words had incited among those gathered. He indulged another pang of guilt on the Harvey front, realising that his nephew-in-law had probably been quite looking forward to receiving his knighthood, however little time he was going to have to enjoy it, as a stuffed shirt in a white wig appeared from his right, bearing a gold fringed, red velvet cushion, upon which rested a ceremonial sword. On one knee before her; in a rather vulnerable and compromised position, he felt, Gordon shivered as he watched Victoria reach forward and lift the sword.

Placing the pointed end on his left shoulder, she announced: "I dub thee, SirHarvey Rupert Algernon Haversack—" the final word being Tiny's cue to fire a bullet into the air at the back of the marquee.

A collective scream rang out, courtesy of all the titled ladies present; several of whom fainted immediately, followed by a distant chorus of police whistles and a bellow of: "Bally anarchists!" from the Secretary.

Gordon moved with all the speed of a rocket being fired toward the Moon. He knew that he had but the one chance to act whilst everyone was distracted, so in a single, fluid movement, he withdrew his revolver, leapt to his feet, and dug the weapon's barrel beneath the monarch's chin. Iggi was the first to react, lifting her golden gauntlet to cover him. A beat later, Tuppence appeared on the opposite side of the tent and began firing her own pistol into the air. Presuming that they were being shot *at*, the good and the great began to panic, stampeding in all directions at once, like a flock of startled crows on a freshly sewn field. In the distraction, Gordon grabbed the Queen and pulled her to the right, whereupon a flap opened in the side of the tent to reveal Nanny; armed with a customised wheelchair, into which Gordon piled the Queen, as if she were a fairground Aunt Sally being put back into storage. As he did so, Nanny dragged a rope around their captive and tied it tight, holding her arms firmly to her side, just as they'd rehearsed back at The Old Fire Station.

A shot rang out, clipping the side of his helmet; missing the glass by less than an inch, on account of the shooter having been jostled at the crucial moment.

"GO!" shouted Gordon, as Nanny spun the chair, released the handbrake and jumped onto the back of the clockwork powered disability aid, which then rumbled its way across the field toward the rocket.

"Unhend me, commoner!" snorted the Queen, "You'll heng for this!" But any further protestations were drowned out by the wind and another shot hitting the turf beside him. A third shot caught him square in the shoulder, spinning him like a top and throwing him to the ground. The *same* damn shoulder that he had been shot in the last time.

The pain was exquisite, but the adrenalin that was pumping through his system at that point gave him the strength to push himself back up. He knew that he had to run, despite the fact that his natural cowardice was telling him that this might be the perfect time for him to lie down and have a little nap. Gordon had read about how; in the face of extreme life or death situations, the inherently wimpish were sometimes capable of pulling off great feats of super-human fortitude: lifting great weights in order to rescue those trapped beneath them; reaching incredible speeds in pursuit of a mugger who has made off with a lady's reticule, or simply wrestling with a crocodile (as had been the case with Sherpa Tennyson in Botswana) in order to secure themselves a few extra minutes of life, thus helping their masters to escape to safety. He felt as if he had been down for a week, but he knew that it was more likely only seconds, as he pulled himself back up and retrieved his pistol. Someone was running toward him. Dazed, he squinted into the dark and was sure that he saw a glint of metal caught in the candlelight... Iggi Shikiwana!

Gordon had no desire to shoot her. In another life they had been friends; in another timeline they had been a part of the same mission, but he had the advantage, he felt, *if* he took the shot now. He was still, but she was moving. He thumbed back the safety catch and took aim as another bullet impacted just shy of his left foot, spattering the glass of his helmet with dirt. He had only once fired a gun at a human being before; and that had been at Iggi's *fellow* agent, Agent X, who had been trying to shoot *him* at the time. He had thought that he had killed her; such close range would ordinarily have ensured as much, but it had taken a lot more than a bullet to the chest for *that*. Fish had been his only other targets, and he had managed to miss most of *them*, but it was do or die, he recognised, as the space between them shortened.

Gordon fired and one of the candles on the path went out, but Iggi kept coming. There were others behind her now, shouting and shooting in his direction: he was a sitting duck if he stayed where he was.

"RUN, BOSS!" he heard, above the melee. It was Tiny's voice, and not all that far away from him. It had a powerful note behind it, as if it were conveying far more than either the words that he had spoken or indeed the intent behind them. He was reminded of every one of his Sherpa's predecessors, in situations similar; sacrificing of their lives with one final 'run, boss' as they gave their lives to his cause: Passepartout; Tennyson; Ptolomy; Ceaser; Rasmus; Clive; Bampot; Chavez; Matsumi; Bellamy; Andho; Shadwrack; Tilly, and now Tiny. He had forgotten none of them; in fact, he had recently begun repeating this list of fallen heroes to himself, last thing at night and first thing every morning, in order to force himself to remember their great oblation. Letting instinct carry him, he turned and bolted after Nanny, for all that he was worth...

* * * * *

"If y'wanna shoot summ'en," Tiny said, forcing himself between her primed gauntlet and her rapidly retreating target, "then y'bes' make it me."

Iggi faltered; just for a gnat's nuts, but it was enough to lose her both her advantage over the runner *and* any chance of redemption in the eyes of the Secretary that she might have been hoping for.

Every instinct told her to fire: to kill this vile anarchist who was blocking her shot; to blow him to kingdom come and then drag his bloody remains back to her master, as a gun dog would a pheasant. But she could see his eyes now; less than a foot away from her own, and she knew that there was no way that she could do it.

"Get out of my way, Tiny! Don't you realise what's just happened?"

"Y'don' un'erstand," he pleaded, but it was more than a plea, she realised. This one really believed in what he was doing; in what he was saying, and not in the way that the many misguided malcontents whom she had already put down in the line of duty 'believed' in the righteousness of their respective causes. There was something *different* about Tiny: something… dependable; unequivocally honourable. This one really did believe that he was working for humanity's greater good.

"They're not gunnar' *'urt* 'er," he said, "they're tryin' t'save us all."

She grabbed him by the throat, though she knew that if he were to resist her then there would be no way that she could hold him. However, he let her do it, and he made no attempt to defy her as she frogmarched him into the treeline, away from prying eyes and the chaos surrounding them.

"Tiny, every anarchist I've ever *shot* has said much the same thing. Give me one good reason why I shouldn't kill *you*, here and now?"

She spat the words at him; though she was equally as angry with *herself* for taking her eye off the ball, as she was with *him* for having let her down.

"I carn' explain it 'ere," he said, "you'll 'ave t'trust me."

"Ha!" she scoffed, "is that how they sold it to *you*?"

She had let go of his throat by now and was pointing her loaded fist at his heart.

"They're fr'm th'future," he blurted, "'Amble and Gordon. An' i's an' 'orrible future, where th'world's bin invaded by Martians! They're tryin' to stop it fr'm 'appenin', but they need th'Queen t'elp 'em do it. I *know* it soun's daft an'all, an' I don't know 'ow it works, bu' I knows I believes 'em, an' I'm 'appy t'give me *life* t'make sure they succeeds."

Tiny closed his eyes; took off his hat and held it flat to his chest. He pulled himself up to his full height and took a deep breath. "Go on, then," he told her, "kill me, if y'must. I won't 'old it against ya'."

Her temper was boiling. She knew what she had to do, but something was stopping her. She was a cold, hard bitch working to uphold a system that she was not sure that she believed in. She killed people; it was what she did. It was what she was good at. She would even kill her best friend if given the order. But she had been forced into this life by a venal vicar with a vice for young girls, and an equally degenerate government mandarin. She had never been offered a choice. Tiny, however *had*, and something in that idea gave her hope. It seemed ridiculous; she barely knew him, but what she *did* know was that the kind of man who would give up the job that he had trained for so long for, in order to help a complete stranger in need, was the kind of man whom she could trust.

She was probably making a grave mistake, she knew, but then it was not as if she had never considered going AWOL before.

Iggi lowered her weapon, pouting up at the giant, who risked opening an eye to see why he had not yet been shot.

"What's the plan, then, big man?" she said, and Tiny's smile broke out again…

* * * * *

Iggi had dropped back, seemingly having let him go; for which he was truly grateful, as with a bally great hole in his shoulder and blood leaking from it like tea through a strainer, he did not have quite the stamina for his usual hot footed foxtrot through territories uncharted, whilst being pursued by machete-wielding natives; not that St James' Park was generally beset by anything more angry or heavily armed than a swan and some ornamental ducks.

As per his role as a Sherpa; as had been the case too many times before, Tiny's self-sacrifice had bought Gordon the time that he needed to gain some distance. He only hoped that it had been quick and not too painful for his old friend. The onus now fell upon Tuppence to fulfil their part of the plan, if indeed she had even managed to escape the agent's wrath!

Iggi, however, had been replaced, not only by a squad of Abberline's finest, who were even now racing toward him like a flock of screeching bats: their whistles screaming and their night capes flapping behind them, but also by a blurry wraithlike image, sprinting across the field from the direction of the marquee and gaining on him quickly, yet whom he recognised instantly by both her gait and by the battle cry that preceded her: a roar so wretched that it had chilled him to the bone the last time they had met. It could be none other than the woman that he had previously tried to kill; though purely in self-defence, he would argue: Iggi's associate, Agent X.

Gordon's heart was pounding as he reached the scaffold tower and began to climb, using the abandoned wheel chair as an initial leg-up. As soon as he was able, he kicked it away, then proceeded to pull himself up, one handed; his left arm still limp by his side; blood continuously draining from his wound and causing his head to swim and his vision to blur. Above him he could see the bottom half of the black-clad Queen, wedged in the open doorway and kicking like a tyrannical child, mid-rant, as Hamble and Nanny tried to pull her the rest of the way in. Meanwhile, below him, Agent X had reached the toppled chair, thrown it aside and leapt the first few feet up. She seemed more nimble than he recalled from their spat at the quarry, but in the electric floodlight that shone up from the base of the gantry; there specifically to illuminate the spectacle for those about to watch history in the making, he could see that this was because she was neither encumbered by the mechanical limb that had previously weighed her down, nor riddled with bullet holes and fighting her own mortality.

She was *also* pulling herself up one-handedly, though not in some noble desire to appear fair minded, but because she had in her other hand, a gun, and was shooting at him as she effortlessly closed the gap between them.

Gordon was not a violent man by nature, nor was he an anarchist, for that matter, and he certainly had never expected to find himself holding a pistol to the Queen's head, but of all the things that his decision to become the world's first astronaut had wrought upon him, these past few years, that which he had least expected to find himself doing was spanking the Queen's backside, and spanking it with such a ferocity that she would shoot through a door that was a good few inches too narrow to accommodate her girth, like a ball knocked to the boundary by WG Grace!

He had been so close; mere inches from safety. He had reached the lip of the door and had been groping for a handhold when he had felt himself suddenly slipping backwards; pulled by a hand that had taken a keen interest in his left foot. Simultaneously he kicked out in an attempt to dislodge his attacker, whilst digging his fingernails into the side wall of the rocket. He was going to fall the twelve foot or so that he had climbed: die senselessly, like Tiny and all the rest. But she had a weakness, this assassin, he knew because he had exploited it to his advantage the last time they had sparred. If only he could remember what it was…

…He felt his boot loosening as X yanked harder; attempting to dislodge him, while the last of his fingers lost its grip on the rocket…

…and then two more things happened, both suddenly and simultaneously: Hamble appeared in the backlit doorway above him; armed with what appeared to be a wicker picnic hamper, just as a hand snaked out at ground level, attached itself to his wrist and began pulling him upward. He heard a scream that was quite similar to X's war cry, as the hamper connected with her head, which in turn caused her to lose both her grip on his foot and her hold on the scaffold, and duly slip from his view…

CHAPTER FOURTEEN:

GOD SAVE THE QUEEN!

The Secretary stood in brooding silence looking down at the burnt, broken body of one of his best agents, who lay still and lifeless on the ground before him. He had watched her fall from the gantry against which the Moon rocket 'Victoria' had been berthed; seen her hit the ground, mere moments before its hijackers had ignited her engines. He had stared aghast as the rocket containing the kidnapped Queen Empress herself had been flung skyward by the primitive wooden trebuchet, and he stood there still; his hat in his hands, and considered his position...

It was the Martian agent 'Uncle', or Heptard Twizzlefyzt; as he had been known before he had come to Earth, who, as the original 'permanent secretary', had created the Crown Agency: a network of the finest spies; infiltration agents and assassins that the Empire had to offer; working in concert, charged with protecting their monarch and furthering his or her imperialistic ambitions around the globe. For just shy of sixty-four Earth years, the British establishment had relied upon the expertise and acuity of the individual agents assigned to that team, along with the two men to have borne the title 'Secretary'. Two men, who, in their turn, quietly and enigmatically; always one step removed from public perception, had been as much a driving force of England's imperial evolution as had any number of bigoted, egocentric politicians and moonstruck monarchs to have made their mark in that time.

The Crown Agency had been instrumental in sculpting the very realm over which Victoria had reigned for so long, thwarting numerous royal assassination attempts; their reputation ensuring that few had the audacity to contrive such crimes as had been committed here today. So what, he asked himself; as the last of the highborn guests were led away to their awaiting carriages, had gone so wrong that such a travesty could have been enacted before the eyes of the entire world? The agency had thrived for so long for one simple reason: its controller was in possession of certain facts; facts that none among the one and a half billion souls currently inhabiting this damp and oppressive world, were aware of. None of *human* origin, anyway...

He wondered now, as he stood watching Abberline's men attempting to escort the gentlemen of the popular press back behind the cordon, whether he may not have seriously underestimated his opponent. For he was not the *only* Martian present on this planet at this time; not the *only* one capable of seeing the bigger picture. There was one other: 'The Greckle', or 'Baron Otto von Greckle of Prussia'; to use the name that he had been adopting since his arrival here on Earth, just a few local years into his Cell's own, *official* mission.

As The Greckle, he had become their people's most notorious criminal: a wanted rebel; anarchist and agitator, infamous even *before* The Cell had been sent to Earth to prepare the humans for assimilation. Somehow he had managed to evade capture; to steal a rocket and pilot it to Earth.

The Cell had received a transmission from the Moonbase; the last communiqué between the infiltration team and their controllers. It had been a simple message: a coded signal, informing them that they had 'company'.

The Greckle's intentions had seemed obvious to Uncle. On Mars he had been a vociferous opponent of the Ruling Council's plan to absorb humanity into the Martian hegemony, and; unable to persuade them to think again, he had promised instead to a take a more direct approach. He had come here to sow unrest at ground level; much as he had been doing for decades back home. He would set human against human, wherever possible, in an attempt to foster a mood of resolute xenophobia among them; thus undermining The Cell's mission and making the planet unsuitable for colonisation.

The Greckle had been one of three Martian dissidents to have left Mars and come to Earth: an architect; a technician and a politician. Together they might have made formidable opponents, but their rocket had been intercepted by the Moonbase and had crashed on landing; killing two of the team. Only the politician had survived. Unperturbed, he had struck out alone, aiming still to be a nuisance; 'a fly in their ointment', as the humans themselves might say; doing whatever he could to irritate and to expose The Cell, but his influence had been limited and his resources few, and as time had gone by, Uncle had begun to deem him a lesser and lesser threat. Had this been a mistake, he wondered now?

They could simply have had him killed; he recalled having made that suggestion to Uncle at the time. It would have been an easy task, back then, but Uncle had vetoed the option. Murder of another Martian was the highest taboo, regardless of his or her crimes, and besides, was it not better to let him live? He was powerless to affect their plan, or so Uncle had thought at the time. Was it not more poetic, then, to let him live to see that plan to fruition…?

"Secretary," said the inspector, lifting his hat and then nodding politely, "I thought you might be interested to know that we have apprehended one of the miscreants."

The Secretary looked up, a frown on his brow; startled by the policeman's sudden intrusion. His mind had been elsewhere, mulling over reports of The Greckle's recent activities; a pan of panic simmering on the back burner as he began to put the pieces together in his head. He had learned only last month that his opponent had finally gained the favour of the Kaiser and had since begun in earnest; recruiting a team of scientists on the German monarch's behalf; experts in their fields, no less, who might work with him to develop a new generation of weapons. For the first time in some considerable years, The Greckle's movements and the circles in which he turned had become of real interest to the agency. Was it possible, he wondered, that his agents had missed something? The Greckle was well protected, these days; that much he knew, but the Crown had had an agent quite close to him for some time. Was it *possible* that his agent had been misled; duped or even compromised? The team, responsible for today's debacle, had to have got their information from somewhere; information known only to himself and his nemesis. He had checked Professor Blaise's calculations himself. Although he had had no intention of *sending* it there, the old man's rocket *was* capable of *reaching* the Moon. There was nowhere else that they could have intended to take it and no other reason that he could see for their abducting Victoria. Had the agency been infiltrated? Was that why Shikiwana had been taken out of play: had she been *turned*? After all these years, he pondered; aware that the inspector had again made his introduction; after all that he had done to further the council's plan, had The Greckle finally defeated them?

"Sir?" queried the inspector, again.

Two rather battered constables had arrived at Abberline's side, both men handcuffed to the miscreant in question. The one on the right sporting a blackened eye and an angry cut to his cheek; the other, a bloody nose and a split lip.

The Secretary's frown deepened as he stared at the pouting, still struggling prisoner, pinioned between them.

"I *know* you, girl, don't I? But where from, I wonder…?"

"Prisoner goes by the name of Tuppence Ha'penny, sir," the inspector continued, "late of Bedlam Asylum, from where she escaped a week ago last Sunday. She was apprehended in the process of releasing the launch lever on the trebuchet—"

"Oh, yes," said the Secretary, interrupting the inspector with a smile, "I remember *you*! You're the pervert who attempted to seduce a member of the royal line."

It was not the first time that the head of the Crown Agency had had to wipe a prisoner's phlegm from his eye and, if indeed he was able to wring some useful intelligence from this woman, then he doubted that it would be the last. He noticed that she too bore the scars of her recent altercation with what passed for the forces of law and order in this city.

"On your knees!" he spat, prompting the policeman on her right to kick her into compliance.

The Secretary then produced a long, slim, tribarrelled weapon of Martian construction, from a holster at his side that had previously been hidden by his frock coat. He cocked it, and with his arm fully extended, pointed it directly between the prisoner's wide and terrified eyes.

"Who were your accomplices and what is your connection to The Greckle…?"

* * * * *

"Now, correct me if I'm wrong, here," Gordon whispered excitedly from the seat directly behind her, as he struggled to remove the muselet from a bottle of vintage champagne with just the one hand available; a bottle that her mother had 'liberated' from the launch reception earlier, and which she had intended to keep intact until they had a positive result to celebrate, "but if I recall my royal protocols correctly from the *first* time I was knighted, then it's one Y'Majesty, followed by any number of 'Ma'ams', topped with a low bow and one final 'Majesty' before backing out of the room, am I right?"

"Quite frankly," Hamble answered, following his lead and keeping her voice low, though it was fairly pointless, she realised, in so small a cabin, "I doubt she'd give a damn *how* you address her, considering the way you've treated her *so* far today."

She swivelled her pilot's chair around to face him, continuing: "and I wouldn't try backing out of *that* door, if I were you; we're currently a long way up."

Hamble matched her comments with a cheeky smile, which she quickly withdrew, realising how easily it might have been misconstrued as 'provocative' in present company, and; therefore, entirely inappropriate in light of recent revelations. "Just pour her a glass and see how it goes," she suggested, "we're all in this together now."

"My God, woman!" he snapped, taking her quite by surprise with his overtly emotional outburst; his voice now peaking at the very edge of what might still be considered a whisper; on the verge, she felt, of some kind of hysterical meltdown, "I'm trying t'be *contrite*, here, y'know! Surely you don't think I gained any sense of *pride* from treating my Queen in this fashion? I'm a *royalist*, don't cha'know; through and bally well through! I have nothing but the utmost respect for my monarch! That which I did," he raved on, his volume rising all the while; his breathing so fast now, in the low air pressure of the cabin that he was in very real danger of hyperventilating, "I did," he insisted, placing his good hand against his chest and above his heart, "for my *country*—"

"Hend *hwhich* country hwould *thet* be?" interposed the Queen, who was sat at the back of the cramped, cylindrical cabin; her arms still roped to her sides, clearly having earwigged the entire exchange.

It was at this precise moment that the cork in Gordon's bottle chose to pop, ricocheting off the ceiling; the floor; both walls and finally Victoria's regal forehead itself, before coming to rest in her lap.

"England!" he snapped sharply, spinning to face her, then turning to each of them in turn as if daring any of them to suppose otherwise, "Bally England!"

"A laekely story," said the Queen, "did my grendson put you hup to this?"

Flummoxed that anyone should doubt his allegiance to the British Crown, as well as appearing at something of a loss as to how best to pour the drinks with his left arm in a sling, Gordon merely gibbered unintelligibly by way of a reply. He had lost a lot of blood and was looking decidedly peaky, Hamble felt. Her mother had patched him up as best she could from the rather basic first aid kit that the ex-governess had insisted upon bringing along, but it was obvious that; rather than champagne, what he really needed was a pot of Darjeeling followed by a few hours kip and a chance to order his thoughts.

Calming himself; on his former nanny's advice, with a couple of slow, deep breaths, Gordon wedged the bottle between his knees and passed everyone an empty glass, which he duly proceeded to fill for them. It was Hamble who noticed that the Queen; who she had noted had not refused a glass, was, however, unable to drink from it.

"Mother, untie Her Majesty, would you?" she asked, "it's not as if there's anywhere she can go now."

Free to move once more, the first thing that Victoria did was to slap Gordon hard across both cheeks…

There was only one thing worse; in Hamble's opinion, than discovering that you have been having regular, intimate relations with Jack The Ripper, and that was discovering that Jack The Ripper was also; in fact, your brother!

She had reached the melancholy stage of alcoholic consumption: the maudlin and self-pitying phase; a state heightened, she deduced, by the fact that their blood had no doubt thinned in the low air pressure of the rocket, causing the effects of their inebriation to become markedly exacerbated. She certainly could not recall ever having become quite this tipsy on just the two glasses of fizz before! Gordon had only managed the one glass before passing out where he sat and her mother had become a little too 'relaxed' in the company of the woman at whose pleasure she was supposed to have been serving a sentence! Even the Queen seemed to be having a little trouble coping with the effects of her hypoxia: her accent having slipped; for a start, the squiffier she had become.

Over those two glasses, the kidnappers had introduced themselves and offered their guest a slice of sponge cake to soak up the champagne; it had been all that they had had left to eat for their three-day journey to the Moon; Hamble having lost the hamper whilst attempting to save Gordon from Agent X. The Queen, however, had declined, which Hamble's mother had found hilarious, as she had baked it especially; convinced that it would be an icebreaker, as Her Majesty would not have been able to resist a cake named in her honour. Victoria had joined the laugh, as had Hamble. Gordon, however, had continued to snore, making the three women laugh even louder.

"Right," said Hamble, straightening up, with the express intension of bringing a little order to the situation. "Your Majesty," she began, "it's about time we told you what's actually going on."

In the seat beside her, her mother snorted and began to giggle.

"Mother, *please!*" Hamble berated, "this is important. The Queen has a right to know why we've abducted her—"

"Hif hits money hyou hwant," said the Queen, haughtily, her expression returning to the one on the stamps, "they hwon't pay it. They'll simply claim that A was an himposter and give the job to the next hin lane. Hit was halways the Secretary's beck up plen."

"It's not about *money*, Majest— Ma'am. We need your *help*," Hamble stressed.

"Hyou hwant me to h*open* something for hyou: ha fectory, perheps, hor ha new poorhouse? Hor his hit my petronage thet hyou require? For hyour cherity?"

"*Again*, no, Ma'am; it's something *far* more important than that— hold on," Hamble said, pausing to pick up on the Queen's previous intimation, "you mentioned a 'backup plan' of the Secretary's?"

"Hyes," Victoria affirmed, smiling sardonically, as if having just put the white king into 'mate'.

When it became obvious that Her Majesty was not intending to elucidate, Hamble prompted her with an "And?"

The Queen's smile broadened.

"Haim hafraid hyou've rather hwasted hyour tame, kidnepping me," she explained, "hyou see, haim not the real Queen Victoria. The Secretary hwill no doubt heve denounced me by now hend brought hin may replacement."

"Not the *real* Victoria?" asked her mother, "then who the hell *are* you?"

"Hay used to be known es Ena Crabtree," the woman in the black lace, 'widow's weaves' ensemble and the costume jewellery crown explained. "The horiginal Victoria dayed horv the flu, thirty hord years ago. Rather than pass the Crown hon to Bertie, who; quite frenkly, hwasn't ready for the responsibility, the Secretary hend the Prame Minister; hin their hwisdom, recruited *me* to teke her plece. Happerently, hay looked quate lake her. Hay hwasn't hoffered the choice; hay was simply told thet if hay *didn't* fulfil may duties, hay would be 'retired' hend replaced by someone who hwould. He'll have hanother hin the wings halready, hay shouldn't wonder; though he mey just plump for Bertie, this time; hif he thinks he'd be hable to *control* him. Hwone never knows with him these days; thet straenge menh is *hobssessed* with furthering the Empire; hwone hwould think he hed hen hulterior motive."

"Hmm," hummed Hamble, "how much do you *trust* the Secretary?"

"Hey, trust him to *kill* me, hif hay become ha liability," she said, "hend to hev my children sent to the hworkhouse."

"You have *children*?" Hamble asked. "Then let me tell *you* a story, *Ena*, about the Secretary; who would dearly love to turn every last *one* of us into something that we weren't born to be."

Checking the empty bottle for any last droplets, Hamble shifted into a more comfortable position in the cramped confines, "Then you can decide whether you want to help us to stop him from doing to everybody *else* on the planet, what he's done to *you*…"

* * * * *

"Evening, Honoria."

Moneypenny jumped, turning sharply at the sound of her own name being whispered at close quarters, and by a voice that she knew only too well. Instinctively, her hand went to her reticule; a purely automatic reaction for an Agent of The Crown, but she paused before drawing her weapon on a fellow agent.

Honoria Moneypenny had just left the bunker: the command centre of The Imperial Space Agency; secreted beneath Trafalgar Square, and her workplace for the duration of her current 'deep-cover' mission. There was a raised concrete plinth on the west side of the square; the only one, as yet, to remain unadorned by a bronze effigy of some such 'Hero of the Empire'. Housed discretely within its left flank was the secret entrance to the facility below, through which she had just stepped, to find her arrival duly anticipated.

"Iggi," she said, cautiously, "what are *you* doing here?"

"Waiting for you," Iggi answered, betraying nothing as she waited to see how her colleague might react to her presence. "Your shift finished an hour ago, Nora," she noted, "I knew you'd have to come up at some point, if only for air."

"The Secretary told us that you'd gone rogue," Honoria said, hurriedly, "he's issued your cancellation order—"

"Obviously. So, are you going to shoot me, then?"

Iggi watched her contemporary's eyes, rather than the hand gripping the pistol inside her bag, and she wondered for a moment what she really *would* do if put in a similar position...

Both women were graduates of St Barrabus, with Iggi three years Honoria's senior. Though their paths had crossed only the once during their time at the mercy of Father Seamus McNulty, it had been a turning point in the younger girl's fortunes. Katie, Iggi's closest friend in those days, had gone a little 'off the rails', following Iggi's unexpected mutilation of her face. She had not yet come to realise quite what a favour her friend had done her, and in the immediate aftermath had begun to take her anger out on some of the younger, prettier girls; one of whom had been Honoria Moneypenny. It had been Iggi who had saved her; extricating her from a particularly savage beating at Katie's hands, and Iggi who had made it clear that, from that moment forth, she was under her protection...

Iggi knew the rules well enough. The Crown Agency was the country's ultimate security service; there was no room for sentimentality within its ranks. If an agent were deemed compromised, then standing orders dictated that once discovered, they were to be put down on sight. Iggi knew this, of course, and until recently had not doubted her ability to enact such an edict herself, if the specific order be given; but lately, her way of thinking had begun to change. She had been having her doubts about her continued employment at the agency for some time, to the extent that she had been squirrelling away whatever money she could spare and making plans for her disappearance; but the accident, and the subsequent loss of her right hand, had convinced her that she could afford to prevaricate no longer. Her days of stalking and killing for Queen and country were over.

And then there had been Tiny. Tiny had saved her life, and in return she had chosen to spare his. She had 'chosen'; *that* had been the turning point. It had been the first time that she had made and acted upon an important decision of her own since she had taken a knife to Katie's cheek all those years ago, thus saving her friend from a life in the 'entertainment division'. Hers and Tiny's association should have ended there, and it probably would have done too, but her new 'friend' had explained to her how he been entrusted to fulfil an important mission; one that she had felt compelled to help him to complete. It concerned the man for whom she worked and *that* had been the deal maker. She would have been lying if she had said that she had ever really trusted the Secretary; he was, after all, something of an enigma: a man for whom there was suspiciously little background information on file, and whom even those supposedly his superior, seemed afraid of. She had followed his lead all these years because she had been trained to do so, but she was also aware of the consequences for noncompliance. All that had been about to change, however, when Tiny had shown her something that had made her rethink her position entirely...

"No," Honoria replied, removing her hand from her bag, but leaving the gun inside, "I'm not going to shoot you, but walk with me; it's not safe here."

The pair crossed St Martin's place and continued into Duncannon Street; arm in arm as they walked, in the hope that, at least to the casual observer, they might appear as merely two friends out for an evening stroll.

"Thank you for not killing me," Iggi said, once they were out of range of the closest of passing ears.

"I might yet," Honoria replied, without a hint of a smile. "It all depends on what you have to say."

"You owe me that much at least," said Iggi, reminding her colleague of their past association.

"You were part of the plot to kill the Queen—" the agent began, angrily, but Iggi cut her off. They had reached The Strand by now; turned right, and were heading down Craven Street toward the Embankment.

"Is *that* what he told you?" Iggi asked, smiling. "Ha!"

"It's not funny, Iggi!" Honoria chided, "Frankly, it'd be a lot better for you if I *did* kill you; I owe you *that* much! Have you any idea what *they'll* do to you if they find you first?"

"The Queen isn't *dead*, Honoria," Iggi said; deadpan, "despite what the news sheets say. She's perfectly safe. Tell me, how much do you trust our lord'n master?"

"The Secretary?" she confirmed, continuing: "About as much as any of us, I expect. But don't forget, Iggi: we none of us work for him because we *trust* him; we work for him because we trust what he'd do to us if we *didn't*."

Iggi was quiet for a moment, as they passed a pair of off-duty, but still uniformed soldiers, heading in the opposite direction. Both men winked and smiled at Honoria as they passed; with the intention, Iggi presumed, of eliciting some kind of a rise out of herself: taking her; as their types so often did, for a rather effete young man on the arm of a pretty young girl, some way above his station.

"Some information has come into my hands," Iggi eventually said, when they were once again alone, having chosen to ignore her baiting, "information that would suggest that he may not be quite who we all think he is."

Honoria said nothing to this, waiting for the denouement, and so Iggi continued. "Are you aware of a character by the name of 'Otto Von Greckle'?"

"Of *course* I am," Honoria replied curtly, "he's the Kaiser's armourer."

"But have you ever seen a photograph of him?"

They had stopped by now, having reached the carriageway, that, once crossed, led them on to the paved promontory beside the river. Once seated on one of several iron benches; each giving a perfect view of the waterway beyond, Iggi withdrew a picture of the German Baron from one of the capacious pockets of her duster and passed it to her fellow agent.

Honoria frowned as she stared at the photograph.

"They could be brothers!" she exclaimed, "they have exactly the same features! I always thought that he was rather an odd-looking chap and I'd never seen his like—"

"They *are* brothers!" Iggi told her, though she was aware that she did not have any proof to back up her assertion. It may have been true; she did not know, but it added credence to her tale. Tiny had given her the picture and it had been given to *him* by the leader of the group responsible for abducting the Queen. He had been quite insistent that they *had* proof; not only of the Secretary's duplicity, but also that he was not of this Earth, and that it was crucial to the security of the entire *world* that they find their quarry; secure him and take him to wherever it was that he called 'base camp', as quickly as possible; there to await further instruction. It was of course possible that her new friend was a fantasist: Iggi was not so stupid as to have dismissed this likelihood out of hand, but she had found herself drawn to the man; trusting him, even though, right at that moment, she would have been at a loss to have explained quite why. 'Sometimes,' she told herself, 'you just had to go with your gut,' but she was not about to tell *any* of this to Honoria! She needed her onside; *they* needed her onside, but there was likely to be both a limit to what she would believe and to what she would be prepared to do to help them.

"You know, I often wondered why we were never sent to kill him," she said, putting the picture back in her pocket. "*You* must read the dispatches," she went on, "he's dangerous! Our best intelligence suggests that he's using the scientists that have been going missing in Europe these past months to create a new weapon of some kind. You'd have thought he'd have been the obvious choice of a mark to take out of play, but no, not according to his nibs."

"You think the Secretary's a Hun agent, then?" Honoria asked.

"I *know* he is," she said, turning to face her; having finally felt that she might have won her trust. "And we've a duty to *stop* him," she added, for veracity's sake.

There followed a pause, during which Iggi wondered if she might have been a little premature to have presumed her friend's compliance, but after a few seconds, Honoria sighed; closed her eyes resignedly and asked: "What do you need me to do?"

* * * * *

"Perheps hay *will* heve thet slace hof cake hafterorl," said the Queen: wide eyed, but, to her credit, having listened to Hamble's fantastical tale in earnest and without interruption until the orator had come to a natural break.

To the best of her abilities, Hamble had spent the past hour condensing and relaying all of the salient points of their adventure thus far. She had told the Queen how; in *their* version of reality, the Moon mission had been *faked*, and how the Crown Agency had tried to have Gordon killed in order to keep the rest of the world from uncovering the truth. She had explained that this had been done in order to expand the British Empire's influence around the world and how this in its turn had been the groundwork necessary to facilitate a bloodless invasion of the Earth by Martians in the year 1898. She had told her about Von Greckle and how he had disagreed with his people's plans; instead, helping them to fight back, and of Professor Boff and her somewhat unlikely, yet none-the-less convenient 'Rewind' process. She had relayed how Gordon and she had travelled back along their own time streams; via a brief stop-over on the planet Mars, in order to prevent the events that would ultimately lead to the end of everything that they held dear. She had told the tale; as told to her by Von Greckle, of how the original Victoria's predecessors; along with their respective prime ministers, had been played by a Martian infiltration agent who had been sent to Earth as far back as the 1830s, in order to prepare the way for this future invasion. And finally, she had revealed the *name* of that agent; or at least, the name by which they all knew him: the Secretary.

She had not known quite what to expect by way of a reaction from the one-time magician's assistant from East Dulwich, whom they all knew as 'Victoria Regina'. It could have gone either way, Hamble had felt, but the Queen had neither laughed in her face, nor called 'bullshit' on her heartfelt story; she had merely accepted her cake and begun to ruminate.

"My pleasure," mother had mumbled, when no royal thanks had been offered.

It had probably been of use to Hamble that this had not been the first time that she had met the Queen. Back in their own time, she had become quite a favourite of the monarch's, following the Moon mission celebrations that the palace had held in their honour. Hamble had enjoyed many a pot of Darjeeling with the most powerful woman in the world, whilst regaling her with her plans for female emancipation, along with her expectation that women would one day enjoy as equal a role in society as their brothers, fathers and husbands, and of her *own mother's* intention of one day standing for parliament. This, she felt, had given her something of an insight into the kind of fanciful notions that their ruler would or would not take seriously, and had helped Hamble to temper her telling accordingly.

Having finished her cake, Victoria passed her empty plate back to Methusela; dabbed at her lips with a napkin;

gave *that* to Methusela too, then; ruffling her skirts, reached down and pulled a long, silver flask, moulded to the shape of her calf, from an ornate leather holster that she wore below her left knee. Unscrewing the cap, she passed the flask across to Hamble; to the indignance of Methusela beside her, who accepted it with a raised eyebrow.

"Hit's ha concoction hof may hown," she explained, "something hof hen hacquired teeste. Single malt whisky with a generous tot of cleret."

"Jesus *Christ*!" said Hamble; the cocktail having rebounded off her taste buds a nanosecond prior to its inventor's explanation.

Whilst still reeling, the 'Chelsea and Kensington Competitive Gin Quaffing' champion of 1896, passed the flask to her mother, who knocked back a generous slug; smiled, said: "I've had worse," and passed it on to Gordon, who was just beginning to stir. He sat up; rubbed his eyes; took a swig, then promptly returned to the state from whence he had just awoken.

"So," said Hamble, though trying not to let her tongue touch the sides of her mouth, "it's a ludicrous tale when I say it out loud, but it's the Gods' honest truth."

The Queen smiled and took a sip from her flask.

"Hit most certainly his," she agreed, "hintrepid; bold; hextraordinary, hend; hif hyou've gorn to such diabolical lengths to hensure mey complayence, then hay must suspect, completely true. I never laked that man, hyou know: so terribly cress."

"'Cress'?" queried Methusela.

"Yes, cress," said the Queen.

"She means 'crass'," Hamble translated.

"Hwhat you heven't hexplained, however," the Queen went on regardless, "his hwhy hwe har trevelling to the Moon, hend quate *hwhat* hwe hare hexpecting to find hwhen hwe get there…"

* * * * *

It seemed that no one had seen the Secretary since the launch debacle, two days ago. Iggi had this on the best authority, that being Honoria Moneypenny, who; in her undercover role acting as Admiral Spatchcock's own personal secretary, had spent the past two days attempting to track him down at the old man's behest. She had also admitted to fielding enquiries from both the Queen's private secretary and that of the Prime Minister; who had been particularly eager to find him, in order that he attend an urgent meeting with a visiting foreign dignitary; but, evidently, their target had gone to ground. Perhaps, she thought, he had put two and two together and come to the conclusion that his cover had been blown? Did he, she wondered, have a backup plan: a hidden rocket, maybe; a way off the planet, as Tiny had been suggesting? Who knew what was and was not possible, if he was, as they suspected: an *alien*?

But time was running out. According to Tiny, they only had a matter of hours left to find both him *and* his transmitting equipment before the rocket reached its destination. After that, it would be too late…

"Iggi,"

"Nora,"

The pair had met; as arranged, in the penultimate pew of St Martin-in-the-Fields, the church abutting Trafalgar Square's east side.

"Tell me you have something," said Iggi, as Honoria slid along the bench toward her.

"Possibly," the agent told her. "We've had Colonel Haversack raging all morning; I've never seen him like this before. Apparently, his sister-in-law was abducted from Kings Cross station yesterday evening, by a character fitting Abdul's description."

"Abdul?" asked Iggi. It was not a name that she had heard before.

"Agent A?" Honoria queried. "He's a deep-cover agent. Nasty piece of work."

"One of ours, though?"

"Definitely one of ours! Now, I did some digging," she continued, producing a folded sheet of paper from the pocket of her coat, which she held in front of Iggi, "*this* woman," she explained, indicating the photograph that she had clipped to the top corner of the file, "is the anarchist that the police arrested at the launch—"

"Tha's Tuppence!" exclaimed Tiny, from the row behind.

"Shhh!" shushed both agents at once.

Honoria continued to frown at the man whom she had been introduced to at the previous day's fruitless meeting.

"Inspector Abberline admitted to the Admiral that he had handed this Tuppence character over to an 'Agent A'—"

"This Abdul character, again," Iggi remarked.

"—The day before yesterday. Now," said Honoria, drawing Iggi's attention to the next page in the file, "it'd seem that there's a connection between these two women—"

"They 'ad a *fing*," said Tiny, miming an action with his fists to better elucidate his further: 'girl-on-girl!' description. "Wha'?" he went on, noting that both agents were now grimacing toward him, "I 'eard 'er tellin' th'professa'," he backpeddled, "tha's why she w's in Bedl'm, see, 'cause Tatty wotsit's a toff'nall."

"The file says simply that they had a 'liaison unbefitting a lady of Tatiana Periwinkle's station'. Colonel Haversack's sister-in-law was then exiled to Scotland at her family's insistence. She was on her way home for her father's funeral when Abdul extracted her. It's *my* assumption that the Secretary is intending to use *her* to get information from the other—"

"He's in the crypt!"

"That was my thought, yes."

"Th'crypt?" asked Tiny, "wha', as in righ'ere'? Unnerneaf us?"

"No," said Iggi, "but he's close. The crypt is where he takes his prisoners—"

"*Tortures* his prisoners," corrected Honoria.

"It's what they call the basement of the Houses of Parliament," she exclaimed. "Of course!" said whilst slapping her forehead with the flat of her hand, "I was thinking his *office* would be his base of operations. It is; after all, where he spends the bulk of his time, but no: we've both been in his office *dozens* of times; if he *does* have some alien transmitter in there, *I've* certainly never noticed it, have you?"

Honoria shook her head.

"Which means he's done our job *for* us, Tiny: he's right where we need him to be!"

Without warning, Honoria suddenly drew her pistol.

"It's too quiet," she whispered, "even for a church. Something's wrong."

She had barely uttered the words when a dark figure appeared in the knave ahead of them.

Iggi checked behind them and spotted a second, identically dressed 'agent' covering the building's main entrance.

"And it'd been going so well," said Iggi, spotting a second pair of black-clad clones, approaching from the west side. All four stooges were armed with Lugers, if Iggi's ability to clock a make and model of weapon from a distance of up to and including fifty yards had not deserted her. This would suggest that what they were looking at were a squad of Hun agents.

"Standard four-two?" whispered Honoria to Iggi, referencing the prescribed defence procedure that had been drilled into both of them for situations such as this.

"Ladiez; ladiez," announced a tall man with a thick German accent, similarly attired, though in a more expensive looking dark suit than those of his underlings. "Oh," he added, as he passed into the transept, leaning heavily on his cane, "und gentleman, I zee.Allow me to introduze myself—"

"No need," shot Iggi, standing and aiming her brass fist directly toward him, which elicited a similar response from the Luger-sporting quartet, "Baron Otto Von Greckle, I presume?"

"At your zervice…"

* * * * *

"I name this Moon," said Gordon, giving the flagpole two last, hearty thumps with his mallet for good measure, "'The Moon'. And I claim it," he went on, raising his right hand to his eyebrow in traditional military salute, "for the British Empire, in the name of Victoria Regi–"

"Don't be ridiculous, boy!" said his father, strutting across the luna surface toward him bedecked in the tallest of tall hats; puffing vigorously on a large Cuban cigar, and dragging a small boy along by the ear behind him. "'T'ain't yours t'claim, is it? Y'brother beat y'to it, didn't he; just like he always did. Y'just don't have it in y'; *do* you, Pinky, eh, what? Beatrice? Hamble? Ha! Y'were fourth for a *reason*, boy!"

…There was something wrong with this picture, thought Gordon, though he would be jiggered if he could put his finger on quite what it was…

"And that flag pole," his father continued; the index finger of his right hand rigid in its singular condemnation, as it so often had been on a Sunday morning, pre-church parade, "'Tisn't straight, boy, what!"

He watched as his father twisted the dangling child's ear, which; oddly, he felt, even through his space helmet, "and the flag's moving; it didn't ought t'be doing that, but y'know that, don't y'boy? Wouldn't be moving if *Virgil'd* planted it, oh, no!"

"Octo' Periwinkle, now you leave that boy alone!" said his mother, stepping out from the old man's shadow; her gentle Welsh lilt reminding Gordon of fresh linen; boiled eggs and dandelion and burdock: the tastes and the smells of his youth. He had not thought about his mother in years. He had been but seven when she had died; almost thirty-two years ago, and he had spent so little time with her, unlike Virgil, Gerald and Aubrey. He had been raised by Nanny, who had been fulfilling that role for him ever since.

"He can't help being weedy," his mother persevered in his defence, and he frowned, remembering her using those exact words before, "he's the fourth of four," she explained to her husband, "the fourth of four; the fourth of…"

Déjà vu. Gordon had been in exactly this position *thrice* before: crumpled in an undignified heap, bearing the scrapes and the scars of a rather indecorous; nerve jangling, not to mention death defying, landing. He vowed now, as Queen Victoria was his mortal witness, never to undertake a voyage by rocket again!

Picking himself up from where he had fallen, he found himself wondering aloud if it were even possible to land such a vehicle with*out* crashing the damned thing, and therefore *not* arriving at one's destination concussed and looking for all the world as if one had woken up on top of a Welsh slag heap with no reliable memory of the night before. He did, however, hesitate before blaming their pilot out of hand, as, against all the odds, they were at least still alive; though this was due, he felt, more to her skills as a designer than to her actual piloting prowess.

In his opinion, the Egyptian had made a slightly better fist of it the last time he had been here, though not by a truly significant margin, he would have to admit. His mind, therefore; being the mind of an upper-class, privately educated, male member of British society, began to lead him down a rather perilous path of partisan conjecture, that he already knew he would *not* be voicing in present company.

The thought in question was that the crash might have had something to do with the fact that the fairer sex were not ideally predisposed to the art of driving; what with there not being a side-saddle position at a rocket's helm. However, even as he had thought it, he felt himself cringe a little on the inside, as if such a notion; although a popular premise at the bar of The Adventurers', along, no doubt, with many other 'gentlemen only' establishments in the wider city, no longer tallied with that which he knew of those of the feminine gender, from recent practical experience. He had already received a rather meaty backhander from the Queen Empress herself, quite recently and he was aware that he was currently outnumbered by three to one, but quite besides his fear of suffragist reprimand; if he had learned nothing more over the past couple of years in the company of such feisty; untameable fillies as Hamble Blaise and Iggi Shikiwana; and to some extent, Nanny, then he had most certainly learned that their star was in the ascendant and that the male perspective was no longer to be taken as read. It had, for him, been a journey as bumpy and as injury prone as the average Moon landing, but he was beginning to see that; very much like a *man*, a woman could also be much more than the sum of her (far more aesthetically pleasing) parts...

"Is everybody alright?" Hamble asked, as the dust began to settle and the crew began to stir.

The Queen, who was sat directly on Gordon's left, suddenly began to gag; her last whisky cocktail obviously having gone down the wrong way.

"Your Majesty?" Hamble asked.

The Queen coughed once; regally, Gordon felt, then belched; rather *less* than regally.

"Hay hwunce rode horl the hwey to Saint Porl's Cathedral hin thet rediculous steet coach, hover horl those demnedeble cobbles," she explained, "hend horv the two journeys, this was bey *far* the more pleasent hexperience."

She looked to Gordon, as if daring him to disagree with her, but he decided against.

"If you'd like," Hamble offered, handing the monarch a canteen of water: the very last of their meagre rations, "I could have a little look at that for you when we get back home; see if I can't 'punk it up' a bit; perhaps replace the horses with a steam engine?"

"Hay rather layke the horses," the Queen replied flatly, leaving something of a pregnant pause, into which Nanny duly stepped:

"Well, I do hope there's someone home," she said, "now that we've come all this way." She picked herself up and, dusting herself down, added: "and they'd better have some food on the go, I'm famished! If I had to spend another hour cooped up in here with *you* lot, I might start to consider cannibalism."

It had been meant as a joke, Gordon felt sure: Nanny's attempt to make light of a grim situation and to fill the dead air, but neither Hamble nor Gordon, nor; for that matter, the Queen, so much as tittered in response. Gordon, because he was instantly transported back to the *last* time he had visited the Martian Moonbase, and the carnage that they had discovered within, courtesy of his own dear brother's inability to temper his carnivorous appetite; whilst Hamble, he presumed, would have been thinking along similar lines, though rather than from a sibling's point of view, Gordon imagined her to be rueing the fact that she had shared such a monster's bed. He would not have liked to have passed a guess at what was going on inside the Queen's head. For all *he* knew, cannibalism may well have been a *thing* in royal circles. It really would not have surprised him.

"Alright," said Hamble, retaking control of the situation, "helmets on; check each other's clips like I showed you, and let's get this over with. The fate of the world rests on the shoulders of the four of us. Gordon?" she asked, indicating the door, which was slightly higher up the wall than it would have been if she had managed to land the thing on its wheels, "would you do the honours?"

With the best will in the world; with his left arm in a sling, the unwinding of a wheel lock was always going to be an impossibility. However, Nanny came to his rescue, as ever she had done; smiling at him in that maternal way that he would liked to have remembered his *real* mother doing, but, sadly, could not. She would have been proud of him, though, he hoped, for what he was about to do: being the first man to step onto the Moon (chronologically speaking), as well as the man chosen to represent their species in the very first 'inter-being' conflab in the history of the world.

Retrieving the furled flag from the clip that held it to the rocket's side wall, he pushed open the door; took a deep, empowering breath, and thrust forward his weighted right foot—

"Er, Gordon?" enquired Hamble, placing a restraining arm against his own, "aren't you forgetting something?"

"I don't think so," he replied, checking his helmet clips and then looking to see that he still had his mallet attached to his belt.

"Never walk ahead of the Queen?"

"What? Oh," he said, his heart sinking, as it dawned on him that after all this, he was *still* going to be but the *second* person to walk on the Moon.

The Queen smiled as she sidled past him, then; with the aid of the reduced local gravity, pulled herself up to the opening. Behind her, both Hamble and Nanny braced her, then pushed until she slipped through the hatchway and disappeared from view. Hamble was the next to go; hauling herself up with all the ease of a gibbon, propelling itself from tree to tree. As she went she pulled her mother along with her, leaving Gordon to caress his battered ego: the fourth of four…

* * * * *

"I come in peace," the German commander entreated, holding up his hands in surrender.

The three plotters remained silent in their pews, uncertain of their situation as yet, but mindful that they were currently on the back foot. There had always been the chance, Iggi knew, that the security services, or indeed, members of their own agency, might have discovered them and scuttled their plans; hence their clandestine meetings at the back of the church, but they had certainly not anticipated this particular turn of events.

Removing his tailored longcoat and passing it backward to be received by one of his goons, the Baron sat himself down on the bench next to Tiny.

"I am not the enemy," he exhorted, having decided to dispense with his less than convincing German accent. He affected instead, the even more disconcerting inflection of an Oxbridge educated toff, though one for whom English was obviously not his first language: his pronunciation of the word 'the', being that which gave him away to Iggi, as any native English speaker would have known instinctively to have pronounced it 'thee' when using it before a word beginning with a vowel...

"We are," he insisted, "on the same side; though I do understand if you find it difficult to believe such a thing. I know the task which has been entrusted to you," he went on, "and I appreciate how much you must already have taken on trust; relying on your instincts as human beings rather than that which you have been taught to accept over your lifetimes."

"How; exactly?" Iggi asked, as much by way of declaring her indignance as her wish to claim some answers. "How do you know what we're trying to achieve? Who told you, and how did you even find us?"

Iggi had told no one bar Nora of their concerns regarding the Secretary, and neither, she trusted, had Tiny; which to her mind left only two outcomes. Either this Tuppence character had broken under torture or Nora had sold her out. If that were the case...

"It would seem," the Baron explained, smiling widely, "that we have a mutual friend, albeit one whom none of us really knows yet: a Professor Hamble Blaise?"

"An'ow'd'you know th'prufessa', Hun?" Tiny chipped in, angrily.

"Like I said," the Baron replied, "I don't, or at least I don't in this timeline. Please," he said, holding up his hands again, "no more questions for the moment. Time is short for us, as I'm sure you will attest. Let me explain; there is far more at stake here than the petty rivalries between our two Empires."

At the click of his fingers, his guards lowered their weapons; nodding curtly, then retreating from sight.

From what little information Tiny had been able to give her, Iggi had presumed the Baron to have been in league with their quarry. They were both alien to this world and she had seen no evidence to suggest that they were otherwise opposed. Was it plausible, she dared to wonder now, that he could actually be of help to them? From his insistent and overtly cordial tone, she considered it at least a possibility.

"This world is under threat from beings from another world," the Baron said, "I know this because I myself am of that world, as is your Secretary: the one who has been manipulating your society in order to prepare this world for the invasion that is to come. I came here many years ago with the express intention of derailing those plans; you see, not all of my kind believes in the methods by which our Ruling Council operates.

"Two days ago," he went on, "I received a telegraph from your Professor Blaise, someone whom I had previously only been aware of by reputation. In her communication, she made it clear to me that she had knowledge of both my origins and my intentions, even though I have never spoken of this to any of your kind. She claimed to have travelled backwards in time at my own insistence, and she told me of a plan that I would set in motion three years from now.I had already begun to plot such a plan; a plan that she would have had no other way of knowing about, unless... unless she was telling me the truth. In order to convince me of her voracity, she told me how to repair the rocket that I travelled to this world in many years ago; something that had eluded me until now, and of the name of an old friend of mine on Mars who is in possession of the wherewithal to transport a person backward in time. She also went on to tell me of Tiny here's involvement, and of her hope to recruit your good self, Miss Shikiwana, to our ultimately, mutually beneficial cause. Apparently, in the future, the three of us are acquainted and are working together on a secondary plan, in case this one were to fail.

"So," he said, turning from face to face in order to encompass them all, "it is my belief that we four can be of some help to each other; our goal is the same and both parties possess information that will be of use to the other. May I be so bold, then, as to presume an accord?"

* * * * *

If, over the course of the past nine months, someone had asked Alyce what she had least expected to see through her window on any given shift, she seriously doubted that she would have found herself describing this! How could she have done; it was not even supposed to have been possible! However, she was now one hundred percent certain that the scene playing out before her eyes was indeed the very last thing that she would have expected.

Alyce gagged on her muesli; soggy cereal and rehydrated milk catching in her throat, as the thing on the other side of the glass gouged itself a path across the flat, grey plain; finally coming to a halt, almost exactly opposite the base. She dropped the book that she had been reading and put down her bowl, sloshing milk onto the control panel beside her. There followed a spark and a flash and a thin wisp of grey smoke from behind the bulb that she had just shorted. The cabin lights dimmed momentarily as the system reset itself.

"Watch Officer Troll?" came the voice of the base commander over the intercom, "is everything alright up there?"

Alyce pressed the speak button on her control board.

"You might want to come up here and have a look at this, Commander," she reported, hastily wiping the milk residue from the panel with her sleeve and looking for somewhere to hide the book that she should not have been reading, "We've got… company."

*****

The pair had entered the Palace of Westminster without undue palaver. The lone porter on duty that evening had accepted their Crown warrants with only the most cursory of glances, waving them through on the presumption that their arrival was, indeed anticipated. Their plan, however, such as it was, relied quite heavily on this not being the case. Time was of the essence, with far too much of it having been wasted already, in their trying to decide whether or not to take the man in charge of developing their country's closest rival's arsenal, at face value.

Taking the stairs two at a time, Iggi and Nora reached the third floor in less than four minutes, quickly locating the Secretary's rooms at the farthest end of the corridor. Iggi then knocked at the door and received a terse 'come' from a voice on the inside.

Both agents were familiar with the Secretary's secretary, Miss Clementine; a rather brusque, eternally sedentary woman in her late thirties: austere; sober and prematurely greying, and who's renowned disapproval of her employers' various female agents' activities, those whom; despite the curse of the career path that had been imposed upon them, had yet managed to retain a sense of humour, and who often exploited her for their own amusement.

"Afternoon, Clemmy," said Iggi, irreverently, as they walked toward her desk on the other side of the room, "is he in?"

"The Permanent Secretary, Agent Z," Miss Clementine reported haughtily, "is not to be disturbed. If you would like to leave a mess–"

"So, he is in, then?" asked Nora.

"He is not—"

"To be disturbed," repeated Iggi, "Yes, we heard you. Tell you what, why don't you come with us and see for yourself why he doesn't wish to be disturbed?"

Reaching behind the desk, Iggi grabbed the secretary by the arm, dragging her with them as Nora put her shoulder to the interconnecting door; breaking its lock on her third attempt.

The Secretary's inner sanctum was; as they had expected, devoid of life, human or otherwise. On the back wall, behind the desk; in front of which they had both sat many times during the past years, was a packed, floor to ceiling bookcase. At its centre, an integral door stood slightly ajar, leading to a narrow, downward-spiralling stone staircase beyond.

"After you, Clemmy," Iggi insisted, pushing the humourless aide ahead of her and into the stairwell.

'Human shields' were not Iggi's idea of fair play, but needs must when the devil drives, she thought; besides which, they could not afford for Miss Clementine to alert the palace's own security detail; quite probably, at the cost of even more innocent lives.

Iggi was familiar with Augustine Clementine's file. She was a spinster and an orphan, just like all the other St Barrabus girls. She would be mourned by nobody. She reminded herself of this fact as she pushed her ahead of them, as the trio wound down the ancient stairs; her hand clamped firmly over the older woman's mouth.

Clementine had only a moment to take in the scene that greeted them as they rounded the final twist that led out into the basement beyond, made famous by Catesby and Fawkes, three hundred years earlier. One moment; the last that she would ever know, to recognise her 'honourable' employer, drenched in the blood of one sobbing victim; whom he had tied to a wooden crucifix in front of a second tortured woman. One last moment of life was all that she was to know; though time enough, Iggi presumed, to acknowledge the agent who raised his pistol and shot her dead...

"That's Abdul," said Nora.

Moving quickly, to a prescribed zigzag tactic, she described a half circuit of the cellar, pausing only once she came to the heavy wooden door at the back. Meanwhile, Iggi; still using Clementine's now lifeless corpse for cover, kept Abdul busy, blocking the stairwell. Reaching the door, which they knew led out on to a short wooden pier that ran alongside the river, Nora turned the key to allow the cavalry to enter for the pincer assault.

Caught in the middle, it took the Secretary a second to realise what was happening; a second that he did not have, as Tiny had entered the cavern ahead of the Baron, and in five giant's strides, had reached the alien infiltrator and clobbered him with one of his huge ham fists.

The Secretary went down, a look of sheer incredulity on his face, and Tiny immediately turned his attention to the prone Tuppence, lashed naked to the closest of the racks.

"Leave me," Iggi heard her tell him, "'elp Tyana down first. I c'n take care a'meslf."

Iggi did not hear Tiny's response, as a bullet from Abdul's weapon strafed her temple contemporaneously, knocking her backward and causing her to drop the bloodied rag doll in front of her. Dazed, her head felt as if it were being held beneath the water line, with both sound and vision blurring into one. She was therefore oblivious to her attacker's further advance; until, that was, he placed the cold steel phallus of his weapon between her lips. Iggi opened her eyes and strained to focus, eventually seeing Abdul looking down on her, like a cat playing with a mouse; making sure that the rodent knew just who had caught it. Looking back at him, along the polished tri-barrels of an improbably long hand gun, she noticed some of the finer details of his face for the first time. He was an ugly bastard; that much she had noted as soon as she had clapped eyes on him, but it was only from this angle that she was truly able to appreciate the extent of that ugliness. What wisps he still had adorning his oily pate were few, and had the texture of the fur generally found gracing the arse cracks of the average male. Riding his rather Neanderthal, ridged brow was an unbroken line of thick, black hair, grown as if it had been expecting to have adorned the face of a Cyclops. This was itself underscored by a second, shorter wodge of greasy bristles, wedged between his nostrils and his top lip. Scattered between his cracked and peeling lips; littered among the stubble and the loose flakes of dry skin, he kept a collection of pox scars; themselves punctuating the many and varied bulbous moles and scabs that he had obviously been nurturing for something to pick at when he was bored.

Iggi had spent her life around the very worse elements of the human species. She had been hoping to see at least one beautiful thing before she died. Sadly, that was not to be, as her world suddenly exploded and everything went black…

"Iggi? IGGI?"

It was Nora's voice, though as if from a great distance away. Realising that she had still to be connected to the mortal realm, Iggi struggled to move; automatically reaching up to wipe what would turn out to be a mixture of blood, bone and brain matter from her eyes, her nostrils and her mouth. Pushing Abdul's headless remains from her chest, she pulled herself back up and scanned the room to see what she had missed.

"Thank you," she said to Nora, who offered her hand to help her the last of the way up.

Tiny had freed the two girls; found them their clothes, and was now busy tending to their various wounds, while the Baron had secured the Secretary and was dragging him towards a brick alcove on the far side of the cellar, where an array of blinking technical gadgetry; the likes of which were totally alien to her, were flickering in the gloom like a mystical portal to another world.

Iggi flipped open her pocket watch and as she did so, saw that Tiny was doing likewise on the other side of the room. The pair exchanged a smile on realising that they had made it in time.

"Alright, your Baronship," she said, looking over and catching his eye and wondering quite what they would have done at this point if he had not have had his embassy track them down, "it's time to do your bit."

CHAPTER FIFTEEN:

THE PERIWINKLE PERSPECTIVE

The Union Jack stood proud at the edge of a large crater, its cloth stripes rigid and unflappable in front of the rather dented rocket 'VICTORIA'.

"For what it's worth," said Hamble, posing beside Gordon: one knee up and one knee down, in front of her illustrious Majesty: The Queen Empress Victoria, ranged behind them, one hand on the flagpole, affecting her most imperial of all assumptions, "I'm sorry.

"No, I am; really," she insisted. "I know you wanted to be the 'first man on the Moon'; what with Virgil having pipped you to it before, but… having a *woman's* feet taking that first giant step, well… Just *imagine* what a difference that will make to the new world we'll be creating if we get this right!"

Gordon sighed visibly, so much so that the glass in his helmet clouded over.

"I know," he replied, magnanimously, "and you're right; of course, you are. It's just—"

"Gordon!" bellowed Nanny, pulling her helmet-encased head from beneath the black, woollen shroud that covered the back of the camera, "Eyes front, dear; eyes front!"

He had not heard her words, but rather read her lips, as in the vacuum of space, no one could hear one's nanny bellow. He could only hear Hamble because their helmets were touching.

"I suppose I'm just an old colonial at heart," he finished, seeing Hamble smile through the glass of their two helmets.

"I have a sneaky suspicion," she said, as her mother manhandled the three of them into a new attitude, before stepping back behind her tripod, "that there's a little more *to* it than that. You had something of a bullysome father, did you not?"

Gordon chuckled and was reprimanded once more for fidgeting.

"I suppose *Virgil* told you that did he? Yes, he wasn't the *best* parent a fellow could've had; that honour must go to your *own* dear mother who's been like a... well, a *mother* to me. I haven't seen my father in years; except in my nightmares, but y'know, he's never far from my mind. Yes, I would've liked to have been the first," he added, dolefully, "simply to have proved the old goat wrong. I may have been the fourth Periwinkle of four, but sometimes the runt succeeds!"

"It wasn't Virgil who told me," Hamble corrected him, smiling at him in a way that he had never seen her do before.

"Ah!" said Gordon. "Yes, Nanny. She did rather suffer at the old man's hands *too*; as I understand it."

"You don't know the *half* of it!" Hamble told him sharply, then softening, offered: "Would it help your bruised ego at all to know that you *weren't* the fourth of four, but in fact the fourth of *five* Periwinkle offspring? And that the *fifth* was not only *female*, but illegitimate, t'boot? And that it was *this* runt who was actually the first *human* to set foot on the Moon?"

Gordon paused at length, as he digested her revelation.

"The *Queen* is my *half*-sister?"

"*NO! I* am, you great dolt! The Queen's feet were the *third* down. We pushed her too hard and she floated off. We'd only just caught her when you came out!"

"You're suggesting that *we* might be siblings?"

"There's no 'suggesting' about it, Gordon."

"But *how*?" he asked, incredulity in his voice.

"Would you like me to draw you a picture? Suffice to say, she wasn't a *willing* participant."

"Well," he said, after another lengthy pause, "what can I say? I always thought we had a connection; you and I."

Gordon held out his hand and Hamble reciprocated.

"Welcome to the family," he said, and it was this picture that would grace the front covers of newspapers around the world the following day...

Rasmus had gone first. He had at least spoken the lingo, so it had seemed prudent to send him in ahead, just in case there was a problem; this was, after all, a somewhat out-of-the-way, way station. They had shot him; once in the chest. Gordon had caught him as he had been thrown backwards by the blast...

The look on the faces of the Moonbase team as he, Hamble, Nanny and the Queen stepped into the control room, reminded him very much of that fateful day in Bujumbura and the glare that the assembled locals had given him as he had lain his former Sherpa down to the floor.

It was a look that Hamble recognised too: the same look that she had witnessed the day that she had taken her prototype 'Rebreather' to The Inventor's Guild, hoping to win herself a patron. She had reserved her slot in her 'father's' name, and upon his reputation, no less. She really ought to have anticipated the reception that she had received when the all-male council had realised that she had not, in fact, been one of *them*...

He *had* thought that someone might have met them at the door. They had knocked, purely out of politeness and a desire to kick things off on a diplomatic footing, regardless of the fact that the base was, technically speaking, on their property, but they had been ignored. They had, therefore, worked their way through the airlock and made their way to the command centre, uninvited, with Gordon at the helm because he knew the way.

"His thet Welsh?" the Queen had asked, indicting a sign on the wall with a red arrow beneath it, as they had been removing their helmets in the airlock anteroom.

"Martian," Gordon had replied, authoritatively.

"Hought hwe not then be more hwary hov the Welsh?" she had postulated.

"I'm sure it's just a coincidence, Ma'am," he had told her, but his Welsh heart had filed away the thought that she had set burning, for later perusal.

Despite their lack of a valet on hand to greet visitors at the threshold, it seemed that the base's entire staff had assembled in the form of... well, he *had* been considering the term: 'welcoming committee', but the look that they were receiving seemed less 'welcoming' and more 'territorial', which was odd, he thought, considering whose territory this actually was!

"We come in peace," Hamble ventured, stepping around Gordon, whom she felt was probably likely to balls it up at this point; as, it seemed, was his instinct. She held out her hand, but quickly realised that, although this was the automatically accepted form of greeting within the bounds of the Empire, it did not necessarily translate above and beyond that boundary.

Squeezing between the two of them, the Queen decided to throw in her *own* penny worth:

"Hayy claim thees bese for the British—"

"I *think*," your Majesty," Hamble suggested, taking the monarch's arm and guiding her to one side, "that we've hit something of a snag, vis-a-vie 'language'."

A movement among the assembled caught Gordon's eye, as a blue-haired, pale-skinned Martian began to worm her way through the throng, armed with what appeared to be a notebook and a pencil. A taller, older, more authoritarian looking female, wearing a much more fitted uniform and a peaked cap, followed her through the gap that she was creating for herself.

"Greetings!" said the younger, obviously more junior of the two, smiling broadly down on the four visitors as she arrived at the front of the assembled.

"ALYCE!" exclaimed Gordon, eliciting a frown from both Martians.

"I'm sorry," he recovered, realising that in their original timeline, he and Alyce would not meet for another three years, "yes, greetings; absolutely!"

Alyce stepped forward, consulting her notepad as she moved.

"I," she began, falteringly, to a series of stunned, yet obviously impressed expressions from her gathered comrades, "am... Watch Officer Troll... But, yes: you may call me Alyce."

Gordon stepped forward and bowed his head, before gently and cautiously reaching forward to take her hand, which he kissed lightly on the knuckles.

"Charmed," he said, "and very pleased to make your acquaintance."

This sent the Martian rifling back through her handwritten notes.

"Keep it simple," Hamble whispered. "Stick to the script."

"Quite," he clipped, continuing: "I am Captain Gordon Periwinkle and these are my comrades: my... *sister*, Professor Hamble Blaise-Periwinkle; our mother, Nan— *Methusela* Blaise and *this*; I am humbled to announce, is Victoria Regina, Queen Empress and *leader* of the planet below."

Alyce; who had been scribbling furiously throughout Gordon's introduction, smiled, then turned to her superior and began to translate.

"Blaise-Periwinkle?" Hamble whispered back to Gordon.

"You don't think it has a certain ring to it?" he responded.

"No," said Nanny, from beyond his left shoulder, "I don't."

"This," said Alyce, turning back toward them, and indicating the woman who was quite obviously in charge, "is Commander Parramour Basstock."

Commander Basstock stepped forward and nodded curtly. Hamble presumed this to be the equivalent of a handshake in Martianeese.

"For the sake of... *everything*, Ma'am," she whispered backwards toward the Queen, "I'd respectfully advise just going with the flow, protocol wise. They know as little of *ours* as we do th—"

"Commander Parramour," Victoria began, stepping forward; the stones in her crown glistening in the electrical illumination of the control room, "hit hwould happear thet hyou har trispassing hon may Moon."

"Shit," said Hamble, not quite under her breath.

"Hit hes come to hour hattention," the Queen continued, "thet you heve colonial hintentions toward may plenet; thet you heve*hinfiltreated* hour society with a spey; a spey thet we heve caught with his hends hin the till, hes hit were. Now," she announced, as she strolled along the front line of her audience, as if she were greeting a line of entertainers back stage at a theatre, "the question remains hes to quaite *what* we har going to do abite hit?"

"What happened to the diplomatic approach?" Gordon whispered across to his half-sister.

"It was *your* idea to bring her!" Hamble snapped back, with Gordon's response of:

"I thought her presence might lend a little authenticity to proceedings," following hot on its heels.

They were all suddenly distracted by a green light which had begun to blink to the beat of an alarm, on a bulb-festooned console to the left of the room.

The commander obviously recognised it for what it was; as, spinning on her heels, she began issuing commands in Martianeese to the underling closest to the panel. At a flick of a switch from the minion in question, a screen of about four-foot square lit up among a bank of what Gordon could now clearly see were several screens, ranked above that particular station. He frowned as the backlit 'projection' resolved from a grey, swirling miasma, into a series of zigzagging lines, followed by a collation of horizontal stripes, before finally metamorphosing into a human face. And not just *any* human face either, but the face of Iggi Shikiwana, whom he had last seen three days ago as she was attempting to kill him.

"Hello?" said a crackly, tinny voice from the ether. It was Iggi's voice, though her lips on the moving picture remained static for a couple of seconds before mouthing her 'hello'. "Can you hear me?" she continued, remaining slightly out of synch with her displayed image, "Professor Blaise?"

The base commander was becoming increasingly agitated, as Alyce translated Iggi's words for her.

"I can't see *you*," Iggi went on, "but I'm reliably informed by the Baron here, that you can see *me*. I can't pretend to understand *how*, but in for a penny, I say."

A few convenient seconds passed before Iggi spoke again, during which Alyce was able to translate her transcript for the commander and her crew, before Iggi's face was suddenly replaced with that of the Secretary's.

"Reefus Questergard!" said the commander.

"*This*," Iggi continued from out of shot, "is your Martian spy. As you can see, we haven't *killed* him: he is in safe custody, for now. Whilst I'd be *more* than happy to slit the alien shit's throat, in recompense for actions perpetrated against the interests of the citizens of this world, we would imagine that *you* would quite like him back intact. I'll leave it in the hands of our 'first contact team' to negotiate his release. This is Iggi Shikiwana—"

"And Tiny!" Tiny added.

"And Tiny," Iggi acknowledged, "signing off and awaiting instruction."

Hamble could not help but smile at the coming together of such an outrageous, audacious and; if she were being honest, *unlikely* plan, and she shared that smile with both her mother and her new brother.

Alyce stepped forward again; a somewhat cowed looking Parramour Basstock behind her, if Martian expressions could be decoded in a similar fashion to those of a human.

"The commander would like it known," Alyce began, "that on behalf of The Ruling Council Of Mars; as dictated by standing order '110446', she respectfully acquiesces to your demands with immediate effect, with just one condition."

"Hold on," said Gordon to Hamble, "but we haven't *made* any demands yet! I've still got 'em in me pocket somewhere—"

"And that is," Alyce continued, that you return both our agent and the anarchist to us, unharmed. Any attempt at retribution will be met with extreme prejudice—"

"If I may interrupt?" asked Hamble of Alyce, a little confused, "what IS 'standing order 110446'? Just so we're clear."

"It states," said Alyce, translating on the fly from a book that the commander had passed to her, "that if at any time during the period of 'world three's' preparation, the dominant species of the planet were to become aware of our operation, or is; at any point therein, able to develop the means by which to contact the observation team, then the operation shall be considered forfeit."

"Which explains *why*," Hamble pondered aloud, "the Secretary was so keen to make the space race appear 'won', so that no other nation would bother to try to build a rocket. If he had been able to've made us lose interest in interstellar travel and discovery, it would have given *him* more time to prepare us for colonisation!"

"We apologise," Alyce said, on behalf of her commander, "for any… inconvenience caused, but from our observations of your society, we had been entirely convinced of your primitive nature and therefore your suitability for our colonisation programme."

"Hapology haccepted," said the Queen, "mey hay meke hey small request, however? Hit would seem thet hour two species do heve rather a lot hin common. Hit would, therefore, meke sense for hus to forge diplometic ties hof some sort. Hwould hyou be so good hes to put my proposal to hyour Ruling Council; hobviously hon receipt hov the 'prisoner', hend hin the meantime, hay hwould like to commandeer hyour trenslator has hay temporary hembessedor to may hEarth. Hwould thet be hegreeable, do you think?"

"Go 'the Queen'!" said Methusela. "And there I was thinking she was just a puppet of the establishment: a rallying, patriot-inspiring figurehead on whose shoulders to hang a xenophobic, misogynistic, outmoded and oppressive ideal, designed to keep those born into wealth and power rich and powerful, to the detriment of everybody else!"

"Nanny!" said Gordon, "I never took you for an anarchist."

"Then Gordie, dear," she said with a twinkle in her eye, "you haven't been listening properly!"

EPILOGUE...

To suggest that the past couple of days had been anything other than a whirlwind of entirely unprecedented proportions, would be to intimate that Alyce Troll had an extremely limited capacity to appreciate the serendipity of her situation, and this would not only have been a grave insult to the newly installed 'Martian Ambassador To Earth', it would also have been very wrong indeed.

For it was true that she had attempted to take her sudden and undue elevation somewhat in her stride; to play down this unique and unanticipated opportunity that she had been gifted, in front of her commanding officer, her colleagues on the Moonbase and in her missives to her family back home; but the fact was that Alyce had not stopped beaming since her feet had first touched the ground.

She had taken the three-year observation posting on the Moonbase in order to help her to pay her way through university. It had been her dream to one day become a linguist, and this job had offered her an unparalleled opportunity to observe the many spoken languages of the planet below at first hand. Ultimately, she had been hoping to apply for a translator's position on one of their *own* moons, back home, but it was true what 'they' said; she acknowledged, that 'talent was one thing, but success in life was dependent entirely on one's being in the right place at the right time'...

She had sensed a strange amalgamation of feelings that she could not put a name to, a mixture of both jealousy and relief from her colleagues on the base, as she had bidden them all farewell. Jealousy, that she of all of them;

a lowly student 'watch', had been chosen to visit 'world three'; to live there among the humans until the Ruling Council could find a more experienced and better qualified, permanent replacement for her, and relief that it had not been *they* who had been chosen for such a daunting and potentially dangerous mission. She had, however, sensed nothing but kindness and acceptance from the Earth party, consisting of Gordon Periwinkle; Hamble Blaise; her mother, Methusela Blaise, and Queen Victoria, as they had travelled down to the planet in the base shuttle in the company of Commander Basstock and her security detail. She had continued to feel this warmth from her new friends; the latter in particular, who had shown her a huge respect, going so far as to billet her; for the duration, in her own, rather substantial home, where she had gone on to receive regular visits from humans said to be important to the running of the world.

Alyce would stay at the palace for the better part of the following year before being offered a London residence of her own; not all that far away, in a building that would henceforth become known as 'The Martian Embassy'. It would be here, at number forty-four Berkeley Square, in the summer of 1897; whilst preparing to attend the society wedding of the decade, that she would suffer a seizure: a spontaneous mental attack of some kind, that would see her body wracked with the most exquisite, unadulterated pain. Falling to the bed, her hands clasped firmly to either side of her head, she would fight to remain conscious and breathing whilst her mind was bombarded with images of events that she had no recall of ever having experienced. She would see the faces of those whom she has come to know and care for, but in situations that were as alien to her as she was to them when first she had arrived on their planet. Memories, yet not memories; dreams, yet not dreams: visions, then, she presumes; if that were possible, of things yet to pass?

Gordon Periwinkle lies trapped beneath the rubble of a fallen building; Tyana floats adrift in the blackness of space; Tiny and Boudicca are falling to Earth from a punctured balloon. There is a rocket buried in the sediment beneath a central London lake, and the Queen... the Queen is dead! She sees a woman: a Martian woman, whose face is both known as well as not known to her. The woman is instructing her; encouraging her to affix a pair of electrodes to her temples and to... rewind?

And then, almost as suddenly as it had arrived, the pain is gone, and Alyce knows exactly what she has to do next...

* * * * *

To be continued in 'The Periwinkle Perspective' (Volume Four): FOR ALL WE KNOW, to be published November 2023...

THANK YOU

Thank you as per to Darren Laws and the wonderful editorial team at Caffeine Nights. Thank you to Nikki Bloomer, Lynda Easton and Dean Turner for their continued support and allowing us to use their images for the cover, as well as to Johnathan Lambton and Craig Jenkins for photos taken throughout the series. Ongoing thanks goes to 'the doktar', Chris Cracknell, for superb model making. Thanks again to Nikki Bloomer, our fabulous Steampunk Queen Victoria, and all the staff at Waterstones Milton Keynes for always dressing up, getting into the spirit and being so supportive. Thank you to Terry Molloy for a fantastic job on the audio book, not an easy task but he did it beautifully! Thank you to Caz Tricks and Sean Calvert at Stony Radio for advanced reading and great promotional work. Thank you to Emma Sparre-Newman for scouring gravestones for some fantastic character names used throughout the series. And finally, to all the wonderful people that have read and followed the series so far and left such amazing reviews everywhere, we cannot thank you enough. Stay with us, good people, there is so much more to come, Adventure Forth!

Paul

About the Author

Paul lives in Aston Clinton, Bucks, with his wife, Donna, from where they run three telephone box libraries and a school library, whilst looking after cats; a goat; a sheep; various chickens and Samantha, the very, very naughty tortoise.

The Periwinkle Perspective Hexalogy

1. The Giant Step (2020)
2. Those Among Us (2022)
3. The Story Untold (2022)
4. For All We Know (2023)
5. The Brotherhood of Man (2024)
6. What We Leave Behind (2025)

all for Caffeine Nights Books.

Also by the same author

Books

'Down Among The Ordinaries' (United Press) 2004.
'The Kult Of The Kazoo' (RRRANTS Books) 2009.
'Quaking In Me Stackheels' (Desert Hearts) 2011.
'RRRantanory Little Stories' (Desert Hearts) 2013.
'The Edinburgh Fringe in A Nutshell' (Burning Eye Books) 2015.
'Does My Bass Look Big in This?' (Black Pear Press) 2018.
'Lyrical, Quibble & Quip' (Black Pear Press) 2023.

Facebook theperiwinkleperspectivevolumeone
Twitter PaulEccentric
Instagram pauleccentric
www.theantipoet.co.uk

Jonathan Lambton photos www.4freckles.com
Facebook Lynda.Easton70
Facebook vintagedapperchap
Facebook craig.jenkins.58323